EPSILON

To Collette,

Please enjoy. Keep up your writing. I'd like to see you on the bookshelves too one day.

EPSILON

JOHN J. RUST

Library of Congress Number:		00-193125
ISBN #:	Hardcover	0-7388-5167-1
	Softcover	0-7388-5166-3

This is a work of fiction. Names, characters, places and incidents either are the product of the author's imagination or are used fictitiously, and any resemblance to any actual persons, living or dead, events, or locales is entirely coincidental.

This book was printed in the United States of America.

To order additional copies of this book, contact:
Xlibris Corporation
1-888-7-XLIBRIS
www.Xlibris.com
Orders@Xlibris.com

CONTENTS

PART THREE THE CONFLICT

THIS NOVEL IS DEDICATED TO MY MOM AND DAD, WHOSE LOVE AND SUPPORT ALLOWED ME TO PURSUE ALL MY DREAMS.

ACKNOWLEDGMENTS

THIS BOOK WOULD not have been possible without the help of many great people. Thanks go out to Sgt. Ben Frazier for all his information on the Philadelphia Police, Darrell Smith of the Embry-Riddle Aeronautical University Physics Dept. for technical advice on how magnetometers work, my cousin Kathy for her advice in the fields of law and biology and my Uncle Joe for his medical advice. I can't say enough about the Prescott Critique Group. Tom, Geri, Michele, Lynn, Vern, Velma and Ed. Their insightful, and sometimes brutal, comments helped turn a rough draft into an awesome novel. Also thanks to Tom Wright for designing the cover, and to my long-time friend Greg Chiaramonti, who's initial computer sketch of Epsilon was the basis for the cover.

"Power tends to corrupt, and absolute power corrupts absolutely."—Lord Acton.

"There are a thousand hacking at the branches of evil to one who is striking at the roots."—Henry David Thoreau.

PART ONE

THE GATHERING

ONE

POWER. IT FLOODED every fiber of Yuri Drovinov's being whenever he gazed upon his creation. Years of work, of sacrifice, would soon culminate in this hot, barren wasteland.

What I do here today will change the world.

The Professor forced his eyes from the weapon and observed the multitude of Iraqis swarming about the hardened aircraft shelter. Once again he took out a handkerchief and wiped the sweat from his brow. *How do they deal with this damn heat?*

For someone who had grown up in Moscow, with its bitter winters, hot meant the mid seventies or eighties. Here it was closing in on a hundred and ten degrees.

The sound of rotorblades caught Drovinov's attention. He turned toward the open hangar doors and watched a small Alouette III lift off to begin its patrol. Four other helicopters—two Mi-8s and two Mi-2s—sat near the cratered runway. They and a scattering of Jeeps and trucks represented the only visible signs of life at the small airfield in central Iraq. Much of the base still bore the scars of the Gulf War.

Bombed out buildings, runways with more craters than the surface of the moon, even three burned out SU-7 fighter-bombers. No aircraft had flown in or out of here since 1991. It had always been considered a minor base, even during the war. That made it perfect for Drovinov's purposes.

He turned back to his creation. At over a hundred feet, it nearly filled the hangar. The long, clear barrel with its oblong base may have looked utilitarian to most. To Drovinov it was absolutely beautiful.

If only those who had forsaken him and his work years ago could see him now. Gawk in awe—no, in *fear*—at his triumph. The imbecilic politicians in Moscow who sold out the Soviet Union. His jealous peers. Even his wife and daughter. How long had it been since he last thought of them? Then again, why would he *want* to think about those two sows? They never understood how he felt after his rejection by the nation he so loyally served. He even tried to beat some understanding into them, if those broken bits of drunken memories were accurate.

"We have completed our final checks, Professor," said a bearded technician in decent Russian, bringing Drovinov back to the present. "All systems are functioning perfectly."

"Very good. Clear your men from the hangar. I'll be in the control room."

"Yes, Professor." The technician turned around and directed his men. Drovinov headed toward a nearby stairwell. He stopped at the bottom in front of a thick metal door similar to those on navy ships. He spun the handle a few times to unlock it and stepped into a dimly lit, concrete corridor. That led to another stairwell, two more corridors, then another metal door. An Iraqi soldier with an AK-47 slung over his shoulder stood in front of it. The red, triangular patch on his upper left sleeve identified him as part of the Republican Guard. Drovinov presented his identification. The guard snapped to attention and opened the door.

Drovinov stepped into a brightly lit room with three rows of instrument panels. Sixteen TV monitors divided into two rows dominated the front wall. Above them hung a picture of Iraq's president. The country's flag stood in the right front corner.

Most of the people occupying the consoles were Iraqi. Two were Russians who, like Drovinov, sold their services to the highest bidder. A French electrical engineer who fled his country after being investigated for shady dealings with Iraq and Libya manned another console.

Drovinov walked down the small flight of stairs to join the two men in front of the monitors. One was a thin, clean-shaven man with a mousy face, badly combed thin black hair, and a white lab coat. Beside him stood a roundish, unfriendly-looking fellow dressed in khaki with decorative shoulder boards and chest ribbons.

"The final checks have been completed," Drovinov announced. "The laser is ready for testing."

"I'm still waiting for our final security checks to be made, Professor," Al Mukhabaret Colonel Hassan Fahmil told him bluntly. "It should only be another few minutes."

Drovinov bit his lip in impatience. He wanted to get on with the test.

The Russian looked up at the monitors, trying to pass the time. Six were shots of the laser from various angles. Others displayed the air base. Four screens showed a Soviet built MAZ-543 eight-wheeled transport vehicle, which normally carried SCUD missiles, parked on a hill a mile-and-a-half from the hangar. Another camera was perched on the vehicle itself.

Drovinov caught his reflection in one of the monitors. Much as he hated the oven-like desert, it did improve his physique. His squared, smooth face sported a deep tan. A thick mane of silver hair covered his head. His loose fitting casual shirt and slacks covered a body that had dropped the fifteen pounds gained during his prolonged vodka indulgence. That had come soon after his abandonment.

Drovinov's mind wandered back to his previous life. He'd barely been handed his physics degree at Moscow State University when he became a research assistant on one of the Soviet Union's top secret anti-ballistic missile programs. In just a few years he moved up to Projects Director.

His experiments in laser weaponry were the most successful in the Soviet Union. While others envisioned a system of space-based laser satellites, he knew a land-based system would be more practical, less expensive and easier to maintain. He planned for a number of strategically placed lasers, along with a series of mirrors built on mountains or on orbiting satellites, that could protect his country not only from ICBMs, but low flying bombers and cruise missiles. No nation on Earth would dare challenge the *Rodina.*

However, "Drovinov's Shield," as he liked to call it, would never happen.

Glasnost and *Peristroika* swept the country. The frenzy of reform brought private business, the collapse of the Party and the death of the Soviet Union. Money for his project dried up. His complaints to Moscow about more funding fell on deaf ears. The fat, brain-dead politicians who thought they ran the country told him they barely had money to put food on the shelves of grocery stores. It got so bad that Drovinov's facility would shut down for weeks, even months, at a time to save money.

If anything good came from those forced vacations, it allowed him to pursue another long time interest.

Drovinov ventured to Tunguska in Siberia, site of the mysterious 1908 explosion that had fascinated him since his University days. The blast flattened trees for twenty miles and knocked people off their feet four hundred miles away. Explanations ranged from a meteor strike to anti-matter to a mini black hole.

His great discovery came less than a mile from ground zero. While examining local soil and mineral samples, he uncovered a small deposit of uranium. Tests showed their molecular structure to be unlike anything he had seen before. Could this be what caused the Tunguska blast? Or was this a result of it?

He bribed his way back into his research facility to further test this new uranium, labeled U-500. It proved more powerful than the U-235 isotope used in the manufacture of nuclear weapons. By his calculations, less than forty pounds of U-500 could generate enough electricity to power Murmansk. Such a discovery would put him in the company of pioneers like Bohr, Curie and Rutherford. He could lift the *Rodina* out of this new dark age.

Drovinov's superiors did not see it that way. His findings were dismissed by the President's addle-minded chief scientific advisor. A ploy to wrest more money away from Moscow. They unceremoniously dismissed Drovinov from government service.

After everything I gave them. Sacrificed for them.

They'll pay. They'll all pay.

Drovinov noticed a Republican Guard captain approach Colonel Fahmil. He quickly informed him the test area was secure.

"Finally. Let's get on with it."

The Russian took up position behind the first row of consoles, followed by Fahmil and the thin physicist, Dr. Mahmud Siana.

"Bring the reactor on line."

With the flick of a few switches, the small reactor, similar in design to those used in Russian deep space probes, came to life. Fueled by the U-500, it began pumping electricity through conduits and wires into the large free-electron laser.

"Reactor on line," announced one of the technicians. "Power transfer initiated."

Drovinov and Siana watched the readings on their console. The electron beam running through the electric field in the laser steadily increased its speed. When it achieved sufficient acceleration, the beam would pass through a magnetic field where every other magnet was of reversed polarity. The electrons passing through this field would begin to wiggle and change direction, emitting and absorbing energy. Once they became "excited," they would emit coherent radiation, the energy output of which formed a laser beam.

The biggest problem with the free-electron laser is it absorbs more power than it projects. Most scientists in Drovinov's field agreed that between twenty to twenty-five percent of the laser's energy would be converted into a beam. Thanks to the Uranium-500 and a few modifications of his own, Drovinov increased the conversion rate to thirty percent. While that may not sound like much, it was enough to unleash a pulse almost eleven million watts strong. More than enough to level the Kremlin with one shot.

"You realize, Professor," Fahmil interrupted his thoughts, "your weapon will make us the undisputed power in this region. America and its lackeys will be in for a surprise the next time they attack us."

"This is only the first of many tests, Colonel. And the laser will need a proper system of mirrors for it to be operational."

"Do you think your plan to put these mirrors on our helicopters will work?"

"It is possible. Since your country does not have the capability of launching satellites, it is the only alternative we have."

Drovinov went back to his readings. Military men were all the same. Narrow-minded. Impatient. None of them realized the work that went into something this advanced.

"Electrons have achieved sufficient velocity," Siana declared.

"Introduce electron beam into the electromagnetic field."

"Electron beam is passing through the electromagnetic field," announced a technician.

Drovinov looked up at the monitors, his breathing and heartrate increasing in anticipation. Any second now.

"Malfunction! Malfunction!"

Drovinov spun in the direction of the Russian technician who had cried out. "What the hell are you talking about!?!"

Colonel Fahmil and Dr. Siana also looked to the technician as he continued. "The electromagnetic field is absorbing *all* the energy from the electrons. And it's drawing more power from the reactor."

"Cut off the power!"

The technician played with switches and dials for several seconds. "Controls won't respond."

No! No! No! This can't be happening! "Shut off the damn reactor!"

The technician went through the procedure again. "Control rods won't respond. I can't take the reactor off line! The laser's absorbing more and more power."

"Power readings are off the scale!" Siana voice cracked from panic. "The laser's overloading!"

Drovinov's entire body went ice cold. *Could my calculations have been so wrong?*

"Professor? What does this mean?" Even the hardened Colonel Fahmil looked worried.

Fahmil's question snapped Drovinov out of his stupor. His brain immediately clicked into problem solving mode.

"I'll have to cut the power from the laser itself."

Drovinov bolted up the stairs and out the control room. Fahmil watched him go, then turned to Dr. Siana. "What will happen if he cannot shut off the power?"

Siana didn't seem to hear him. He stared obviously at his instrument panel. The Al Mukhabaret colonel grabbed Siana by the shoulders and spun him around. "What will happen if he cannot shut off the power? Answer me!"

Dr. Siana gasped, "It . . . it'll . . . explode."

The color drained from Fahmil's angry face. He prayed to Allah that the bunker would protect them from any explosion.

Drovinov ran faster than he ever remembered, struggling for every breath. But he had to push himself. He had to make it. It had taken him two years to build the laser. In seconds it could all go up in smoke . . . literally. He could not permit that. He could not fail on the brink of his greatest triumph.

Dammit! Move faster!

Drovinov burst into the hangar and rushed toward the laser. He ignored the deep hum that filled the entire structure. Instead he concentrated on the small panel to the laser's power source. Drovinov reached out. His fingers just brushed its surface when a brilliant white flash blotted out his vision.

The explosion, equivalent to a six megaton blast, vaporized the base instantly. Colonel Fahmil, Dr. Siana and everyone else in the control room perceived a blinding white light before they were erased from existence. The blast expanded across the desert nanosecond by nanosecond, consuming the Republican Guard patrols and the helicopter. An evil, orange-yellow mushroom cloud reached into the sky. Firestorms and hurricane force winds swept across the desert. The blastwave hit the small town of Qasr Amij forty-two miles away. Only the strongest of buildings, and there weren't many, survived. The ground shook as far west as Abues Siyar in central Jordan. A faint rumble was heard in Tel Aviv. Others, much farther away, also witnessed the blast.

Captain Lisa Ann Remmler had an hour to go to the end of

her shift when one of the enlisted men at her station exclaimed, "What the—? Captain! I've got a nuclear detonation. Central Iraq."

She swung her smooth, round, button-nosed face first to the enlisted man, then to one of the large screens on the wall of Strategic Command Headquarters at Offut Air Force Base, Nebraska. She blinked her sparkling green eyes. No, this wasn't a bad dream. A red dot flashed ominously in the middle of Iraq.

"Oh my God."

Lisa swung into action. "I want satellite confirmation now. Enlarge the area on screen and get me a map overlay. Find out what the Iraqis have in that area." She already had a red phone to her ear, connecting her with General Steven Alby, commander-in-chief of STRATCOM.

"General, this is Captain Remmler in the command center. We've got a nuclear detonation in central Iraq . . . Just now, sir . . . we're getting confirmation—standby, sir." Lisa looked over to Staff Sergeant Wendell Hobbs, who was waving for her attention. "Ma'am, DSP satellites confirm a nuclear explosion in central Iraq."

A lieutenant five consoles away hung up a white phone and turned to the captain. "NORAD also confirms the explosion."

Lisa relayed the information to General Alby, who told her he was on his way down and hung up. She replaced the receiver and looked up again at the blinking red dot.

Guess I can forget about sleep tonight.

The men and women who held the reins of power throughout the world spent the next several hours near panic. The President convened an emergency meeting of the National Security Council. Every American military unit went on alert. The carrier *USS Kitty Hawk* and its battle group were ordered from their station in the Arabian Sea to the Strait of Hormuz.

Another carrier group, led by the *USS Eisenhower*, cut short its brief stop at Diego Garcia and headed for the Gulf.

For other nations, the situation was even more tenuous. When Tehran learned of the explosion, four divisions of tanks and infantry hurried west to the border. Syrian soldiers guarding the border with Iraq reported a large mushroom cloud on the horizon. Their leaders in Damascus ordered all armed forces to full alert. Taking no chances, the nuclear weapons Israel denied having were removed from secret storage sites in the Negev Desert and placed on F-16s and intermediate range ballistic missiles. The armed forces of the Gulf states went on alert as well.

The news networks pounded the story. Everyone, from the anchors to the guest analysts to the man on the street, agreed that with Iraq possessing The Bomb, the world had become a more dangerous place.

No one really knew just how dangerous it had become.

TWO

HOW MUCH LONGER do we have to trek through this white hell?

Before today, Erich von Klest associated the word "desert" with sand and scorching heat. Now he knew desert could apply to cold areas as well. That described Baffin Island perfectly. A desert of snow, as far as the eye could see. Only the purple-blue mountains in the distance broke up the never-ending sea of white. But even they were speckled with snow.

Von Klest shivered, pulling his fur-lined parka closer to his lean, six-foot-two frame. Still the chill air assaulted his smooth face, even crept into the roots of his close-cropped blond hair. He wondered how the other two men with him fared. Though both had grown up in cold regions, one in Canada, the other in Norway, their bodies had grown accustomed, too accustomed, to the warmer climate of Uruguay.

This is crazy, Erich. Illogical! You're in the middle of nowhere based on a feeling.

But I have to be here. I'm not even completely sure why.

Until a few weeks ago, von Klest never even heard of Baffin Island, located about three hundred-eighty miles west of Greenland. Then the dreams started. So real, so vivid. Visions and feelings unlike any he'd ever experienced.

He told no one about them, not even Otto, his mentor and second father. Maybe they would go away.

They didn't.

BAFFIN ISLAND. Somehow, in his subconscious, Erich von Klest knew he had to go there.

I should go to a psychiatrist. I run a multi-national, multi-million dollar organization. I have responsibilities, plans, operations to oversee. How will this look to my-

He stopped cold in his tracks. It didn't even seem a conscious decision. Something just made him halt.

Von Klest stared across the vast expanse of snow. Some force pulled his mind from his body, stretching it over the tundra. His breathing increased. He caught a sense of something. Intangible at first. The words to describe it would not come. But the feeling swelled inside of him.

Power! His mind finally trumpeted the word. He closed his eyes, still visualizing the snowy wasteland in front of him.

Here. What I seek is here.

Von Klest's legs strode over the snow faster, almost acting on their own. He was oblivious to all else. The cold, his companions. Even the extra layers of clothing and equipment he carried disappeared. None of it mattered. What he needed was so close now. Von Klest let the force guide him, overwhelm him. No longer did it feel strange. He embraced it

Suddenly he stopped. The Canadian and Norwegian also halted, observing their leader in stunned silence.

Von Klest stood absolutely still for a full seven seconds. He then sank to his knees, as if his legs could no longer support the rest of his body.

The two men rushed to his side. "*Mein Herr!* Are you all right?"

He ignored them, staring at the snow.

"*Mein Herr,*" the Canadian continued. "What's wrong?"

"Edward, here," said the Norwegian, Nils. "Help me with him."

Both tried to raise von Klest to his feet. He waved them away. The German dropped on all fours. Frantically he swept aside piles of snow.

"Here. It's here. Right here." Von Klest looked back at his companions. "Start digging!"

Edward and Nils fell beside him. They broke out their shovels and ice picks and attacked the snow.

A half-hour later von Klest's shovel struck something neither ice or snow. The breath stuck in his throat. Every inch of his body tingled. It had nothing to do with the cold. "Here! It's right here! Dig around here!"

It took fifteen more minutes of digging before von Klest could remove the black object. A triumphant smile spread across his face.

Why does it seem so familiar to me? Where could I have-

Oh my God. The dreams. I . . . I know I've seen this in my dreams.

How is that possible?

"What is it?" Nils inquired.

"Looks like a big boomerang."

Edward spoke the truth. Naturally it was unlike any boomerang von Klest had ever seen. Black in color, made of some kind of metal. The blade itself sported a row of jagged teeth, with a reddish-green glass slit in the center. The back had three handles, one on the center, the remaining two on each end. Von Klest gripped it by the center handle and rose. The toothy smile expanded as he inspected his prize.

Edward and Nils rested on the snow covered ground, their muscles sore from digging. Von Klest seemed to ignore any pain associated with his recent labor.

"What is it, *Mein Herr?*" Nils asked.

Von Klest ignored him. All his attention was focused on the boomerang.

Desperate for an answer, he turned to his partner. "Do you have any idea what that thing is, Edward?"

The former Canadian Airborne Regiment sergeant shook his head. "*Nein*. I've never seen anything like that."

"Could it be something the Eskimos made?"

"I've never seen any Eskimo garbage that looked like that."

"It's power, you fools!" von Klest suddenly snapped, startling both Nils and Edward. "All the power I've ever wanted."

Edward noticed his leader's face. The Cheshire Cat smile, the glazed, unblinking eyes that focused like a laser on one thing and excluded all else.

Erich von Klest was quite mad.

Non-chalantly as possible, Edward moved his hand closer to that part of his waist where he stuffed his Heckler & Koch 9mm.

"God in Heaven!" Nils blurted in his native tongue and shot to his feet.

Edward looked at him, then at von Klest. At first he thought it was a trick of the sun. It only took a few seconds to convince him otherwise. The boomerang von Klest held was glowing! The brilliance intensified, crawling up von Klest's body.

Eyes wide, mouth agape, Edward slowly got up, watching the hazy, off-yellow glow envelop his leader's body.

"What the hell is going on?" his voice cracked. "*H-Herr . . . Herr von Klest?*"

Erich von Klest didn't hear him. Wearing a grin of sheer ecstasy, he lifted his head back and let the glow wash over him.

"What's going on!?!" the ex-Norwegian soldier backed away from his leader.

"How the fuck should I know!?" Edward too moved away from von Klest.

The glow absorbed the German's body. Suddenly it flared. Edward and Nils turned away, closing their eyes and throwing their hands over their faces. Several seconds passed before the flash subsided. The two blinked a few times, then faced forward.

The spot where Von Klest had stood was taken over by a humanoid figure in black armor.

"What the hell is that thing?" Edward wanted to say. The crushing fear prevented him.

The armor conformed nicely to the human body. The head, in some ways, resembled an ancient Egyptian jackal mask, with the protruding V-like "ears" and the narrow face. A small circular rim sloped down from the forehead over a rectangular reddish-green eyeslit. Two inches below it was a jagged, chevron-shaped "mouth." The squared off chest sported a dark red inverted chevron with jagged lines. The rest of the body; arms, fingers, legs, feet, were also squarish. Three rows of pyramid-shaped studs dotted the shoulders. In its right hand it held the large, black boomerang.

Edward and Nils gawked at the figure. Could this be real?

The thing gave itself a self-examination. Slowly moving its head from side-to-side, looking over its arms, its torso, the boomerang.

Satisfied with what it saw, it looked up at Edward and Nils. One step toward them was all the Canadian needed to go into action. He desperately pulled up the right side of his parka and fumbled for his 9mm.

"C'mon!" the panic-stricken Edward yelled at himself. None of his reactions seemed fast enough.

The armored figure was about ten meters away when Edward next looked up. Snapping off the safety, he chambered a round and leveled his 9mm with one hand. The thing stood still, regarding Edward, it seemed, with the same interest a person would show a squirrel in the park.

Emitting an animal-like cry, Edward pulled back the

trigger again and again and again. His index finger didn't stop working until the gun clicked empty. Out the corner of his eye, Edward noticed Nils facing him, eyes wide and breathing heavily. He glanced back in front of him.

It was still on its feet! Nine rounds and it still stood.

Edward continued to stare at the thing, as the pistol slipped from his grasp and fell to the snow.

The armored figure raised the boomerang horizontally. A glow came from its center. Edward jumped back as a green ray of light leapt from the boomerang and struck Nils just below the heart. The Norwegian crumpled to the snow, smoke rising from his chest.

Edward screamed in terror. He twisted around and fled. Because of the snow, his thick boots and multiple layers of clothing, he made little progress.

A *woosh* of air caught his attention. Edward looked over his shoulder. The armored figure soared *twelve feet* over his head. He followed it until it landed front of him.

"No, please!" Edward threw up his hands.

The thing's body whipped around. There was a flash of black metal. Edward felt something cold whip through his upper left arm, across his chest and out his right arm. He looked down. A streak of red ran across his chest. In horror, he watched blood gush out the wound, propelled by the last few pumps of a shattered heart. No scream came from his open mouth since. Both lungs were severed.

Ten seconds later, Edward crumpled to the ground and died.

Erich von Klest surveyed the ground where the two corpses lay. Blood congealed in the snow around Edward. He then ran his eyes over his black, boomerang-like blade, then up his form fitting armor.

Von Klest chuckled. Soon he threw his head back and roared with joyful laughter.

So this is the power I sought.

It took a minute for him to regain his composure. He studied the boomerang again. Von Klest found no blood on the blade.

Non-adhesive. Incredible.

Everything about this was incredible. A weapon that could fire laser beams, slice through a human body without effort and not have blood stick to it. The armor itself enabled him to jump nearly fifteen feet without a running start. Even absorb five 9mm Parabellum rounds without so much as a nick.

There were other powers von Klest knew he had. How he knew was a mystery. He just knew.

I'm invincible. Who in the world can oppose me?

Von Klest looked again at the corpses of Edward and Nils. Such a shame. Good, experienced men, both of them. But right now no one could know of the power he had discovered. At least not yet. Only one more loose end needed to be tied up.

Bieutok Ratoolmun spotted a cloud of red smoke in the distance, marking the position of Dr. Kessler's group. He turned the Sikorsky S-58's bulbous nose in that direction and landed two minutes later, kicking up a dense cloud of snow particles. Bieutok slowed the helicopter's rotors, keeping the engine warm. Once the snow settled, he looked for Kessler's group. Nothing.

The Inuit pilot shook his head. He'd choppered all kinds of people from one end of Baffin Island to the other for seven years. Most were amiable folks, especially the scientists who loved to talk about their work. But sometimes he had to deal with the militant environmentalists from America. They could be downright rude. Especially when they learned he once flew for an oil company in Resolute Bay before going into business for himself. Well, how else was he supposed to save enough money for a downpayment on his S-58?

Bieutok would have welcomed the rude environmentalists over the group he had today.

He unbuckled himself and headed into cargo bay. The Inuit slid open the door and stared out into the frozen wasteland.

"Hello! Dr. Kessler!" Bieutok got out of the helicopter and started walking.

Where the hell are they?

"Dr. Kessler! Hello! Anybody!"

He took a few more steps and gazed across the vast, white landscape. Some snow mounds to his right broke up the rather flat plain. Where could Kessler and his party be?

He thought back to when they took off from Pond Inlet Airport, his favorite place while growing up. Kessler and his friends were more than quiet. They practically went out of their way to ignore him. When they bothered to talk to him, it was in the most curt way. Amongst themselves, they would only whisper. They didn't strike him as typical environmentalists.

Maybe they're Nazis looking for lost gold, he thought jokingly.

Bieutok looked around the area. All the tracks seem concentrated in this one area. It didn't look like the Germans wandered off. If he could not find them in the next few minutes, he'd inform Pond Inlet. He didn't have the fuel for an aerial search. The Mounties would have to bring in every person and then some to search. They only had a small garrison on Baffin.

The Inuit turned back toward his chopper when he heard a deep *woosh* to his right. Bieutok looked. His eyes widened as he gasped in horror.

A figure in black armor, clutching a large boomerang, popped out of the snow mound.

Bieutok screamed, ran backward and tripped. The creature broke free of the snow mound and stalked toward him.

"No! No, please!" He held up his hands, begging. "WHAT ARE YOU!?!"

He never saw Erich von Klest, a.k.a Dr. Kessler, smile as

he glared at the terrified Inuit crawling backward through the snow. With one leap he was standing over Bieutok.

"Please! What do you want!? WHAT DO YOU WANT!?!"

The voice Bieutok heard was a hollow, mechanical one. "Your death."

Fear paralyzed Bieutok. His brain screamed run, but his body refused to cooperate.

The armored figure reared its right foot back and drove it into Bieutok's stomach. His ribs shattered like glass. Pieces of bone ricocheted all over his insides, tearing into vital organs. The breath shot out from his lungs. The crushing pain in his midsection quickly spread to the rest of his body.

Again the creature rammed a foot into Bieutok's gut. Without a sound, he rolled over, clutching his stomach. The pain blocked out the world around him, except for a hollow chuckle.

Once von Klest decided he'd had enough fun, he grasped the enlarged boomerang by one of the end handles and drove it through the mongrel's back. He split the heart in half. The Inuit spasmed, then went limp.

Von Klest withdrew the blade and watched as every drop of blood slid off the boomerang and onto the Eskimo. He secured the weapon to the small latch on the side of his right leg. Then he picked up the mongrel's body by the back of the neck with barely an effort. Von Klest dumped it in the Sikorsky's cargo bay, then dug up the bodies of Edward and Nils. Once the corpses were loaded in the helicopter, von Klest closed the side door and walked to the rear. He unlatched his boomerang and looked over the S-58 for a few seconds. Walking over to the middle of the helicopter, von Klest bent down and snaked his right arm and shoulder under where the tail and fuselage met.

Will I be able to do this? What will it feel like?

With the boomerang in his left hand and the helicopter in his right, von Klest straightened up. In utter amazement, the four-ton S-58 came off the ground. Suddenly, he felt his body become weightless. The German's heart threatened to burst out of his chest. His breathing quickened. Though common sense told him not to, he looked down. The white ground fell away from him. He was at least thirty feet in the air . . . and still rising.

"Oh my God!" he cried out in panic. His mind refused to accept this. Vertigo suddenly overwhelmed him. Von Klest nearly let go of the helicopter. He quickly shot his left hand under the Sikorsky's tail and steadied it.

Von Klest focused on the horizon. His breaths came at a steadier pace.

Fear gave way to wonderment. From his vantage point, he could see for miles and miles. The white, never-ending tundra, the purple mountains. Von Klest forgot his earlier complaints about Baffin Island. At one hundred-fifty feet, it really was beautiful.

He shook his head, forcing the frivolous thoughts from his mind. He had work to do.

With a single thought, he propelled himself, and the helicopter, forward. His speed steadily increased. Fifty kilometers per hour. Seventy. One hundred. One hundred-ten. He had no instrumentation to tell him how fast he was going. He just knew. A sort of mental speedometer, he mused. Moments later, he noticed other things. His ears weren't popping. He also felt quite warm. It had to be the armor.

Half-an-hour later, von Klest reached the shore. His arms felt a little stiff, but other than that, there was no evidence he had carried a four ton helicopter for thirty minutes. In fact, it felt no heavier than a copy of the Oxford English Dictionary.

He looked down at the Scott Inlet below, shaking off a momentary wave of vertigo. His arms uncoiled. The Sikorsky slid off his shoulder and plummeted toward the sea.

Von Klest followed the helicopter's progress into the cold

sea. Suddenly the sinking S-58, almost two hundred-fifty feet below him, grew before his eyes. Von Klest jerked his head in shock. He quickly accepted his newfound enhanced vision and watched the helicopter slide beneath the waves. Afterward, his vision returned to normal.

A search for the missing Eskimo and "Dr. Kessler's group" was inevitable. But the rescuers would concentrate between the Barnes Ice Cap and Pond Inlet. No one would find this helicopter for a long time. If ever!

"It appears I have chosen well."

Every hair on von Klest's body stood up. The voice was low, raspy, with an ice-chilling quality. Strangely, von Klest was not afraid.

He rotated his body in mid-air. A hunched, reddish-black creature floated ten feet away from him. Its flat snout, housing a slithering reptilian tongue and long, sharp, protruding teeth, extended about a foot-and-a-half. Two thin, curved horns sat atop its head. A pair of blood red eyes without pupils blazed a few inches beneath them. Spikes covered its back and dinosaur-like tail. At the end of its stubby arms were hands with eight-inch clawed fingers. A pair of squat legs supported its roundish body.

"There is much we need to discuss, human."

THREE

". . . The Phillies are off tonight, but they'll be playing a double-header tomorrow against Cincinnati. And don't forget, this coming Sunday . . . football season starts! The Eagles will be kicking it off right here in Philly against the Washington Redskins. And this year we're goin' all the way . . . hopefully. Lord knows it's about time."

Jack Remmler paused as the studio door of Keystone College's student radio station slowly opened. A black kid of medium build with a flat top entered and smiled at Remmler. The brown-haired, 19-year-old student with a round face smiled and waved. He returned to the microphone. "Well, gang, I'm done here. My man C.W. Whiz'll be taking over. Hope your first day back at school wasn't too bad. I'll be back next Monday. 'Til then, here's some Doors. Later."

Remmler clicked off the mike as the rumble of thunder and patter of rain that began "Riders on the Storm" filtered through the studio speakers.

"What's up, Whiz?" Remmler got up from his chair and high-fived his friend.

"Doin' fine, Remy," Chris Wilson responded, placing a CD carrying case on the control board's counter.

"Well, Mr. Wilson, you have the bridge."

"Thank you very much." Chris dropped a Puff Daddy CD into the player and programmed the desired song. "So how did your show go?"

"Pretty good. A few boners here and there. Hey, it's been over three months since I last did this. Gotta get the rust out. At least it wasn't as bad as my first show here."

"Even my first show wasn't as bad as yours."

"Fuck you," Remmler said with a smile.

The Doors song ended a minute later. Chris hit the cart with one of the station's IDs, then turned on the mike.

"All right, welcome back Keystone! C.W. Whiz here, takin' you through the rest of dinner time with the phatest sounds around! We're gonna kick it with the latest from Puff Daddy. Got some Dr. Dre and DMX on the way, right here on 890, WKCB."

Chris turned off the microphone and started the CD player.

"Ah well, here comes two hours of noise pollution," Remmler said, throwing down the gauntlet.

Chris didn't shy away from the challenge. Their friendly, running argument over whose music was better dated back to last year. "It's better than the yelping and same four guitar rifts you call music."

"Oh please. Every song you play has maybe ten words of English and a bad drum beat."

"And I suppose you can understand every single word Led Zeppelin sings?"

"At least everyone knows who Led Zeppelin is. Most of the guys you play are forgotten about in a year."

"But they're all now. You don't have to look through a history book to find out who they are."

Remmler snickered sarcastically. "I'll be back. I wanna check the wire."

He walked next door to the production studio. A printer connected to the Associated Press wire zipped away in the corner. Remmler ripped off the last printed page, reeled in the paper dragon and looked it over. He collected any sports related stories, along with a few news briefs. No surprise, the Iraqi Bomb dominated the headlines. Nearly every country in the Middle East had their armed forces on alert. The U.S. had two carrier battle groups in the region, with more forces on the way. Estimates put the blast between five and seven megatons. That would have taken more plutonium than the CIA thought Iraq possessed. The Agency was taking a lot of heat for its miscalculation.

I'm surprised the bastards tested it in the desert. I would've thought their first nuke test would be on Tel Aviv or Tehran.

Like many communications majors, Remmler was an information junkie. Also, as an avid reader of techno-thrillers, he felt he had a keener insight into world events than most.

Remmler stacked the sheets, discarding the unwanted stories. It took him half-a-minute to find a pen. He then circled the important stories and headed back to Chris in the studio.

"Here you go," Remmler placed the pile next to Wilson. "That should keep you entertained for the rest of your shift."

"Thanks, man."

"Well, I'm off to dinner. I'm starving. You eat?"

"Yeah. Turkey and mashed potatoes tonight. Actually it was pretty good."

"First dinner back always is. Then it goes downhill."

Chris chuckled. "You know it."

Remmler said good-bye and exited the studio. He strode down the hallway and bounded up a small flight of stairs. The aqua wall on his right bore a painting of a fat, hip looking brown bear with sunglasses and a blaring boombox on his shoulder. Beneath it was the station logo. Remmler emerged from the basement where WKCB operated onto the first floor of the Visual Arts Center. He made his way past classrooms, the TV studio and a lecture hall on his way to the exit. All the while, Remmler worked on a mental list of the things he had to do his first week back at school. Get his ID validated, pick up his Intro to Sociology book . . .

Then there were the meetings! Tomorrow he had one for the college's newspaper, *The Bear Facts*. The day after he had one for *Zenith*, the student-published conservative periodical. An hour after that came the semester's first meeting of the Keystone chapter of the Young Republicans. Remmler wondered if he'd have any time to sleep. He turned up his lips at the thought. So long as he didn't have another dream where he found himself surrounded by armored warriors from some Japanese Anime show, he wouldn't mind. Much as he liked the genre, after a whole week it had become annoying. Sometimes even disturbing, at least when he initially woke up.

Remmler shook it off. *Probably some subconscious bullshit thing. I got other things to do besides analyze my stupid dreams. I still have to-*

"Remy!"

Jack stopped near the glass doors leading outside. He turned and scanned the hallway for the sparkly, feminine voice he just heard. A familiar face appeared among the dozen or so students milling about the hallway.

She was five-foot-seven with a trim figure. Her white shorts showed off a pair of shapely legs tanned to perfection. Curly, sandy-blond hair crowned her attractive face.

Remmler's pulse quickened as she waved. "Remy! Over here."

"Cheryl!" He smiled and strode over to her.

Cheryl Terrepinn threw her arms around him and gave him a peck on the cheek. Remmler did likewise.

"Oh God, Jack. It's so good to see you again."

"You too," he replied as they released one another, much to Jack's momentary disappointment. "How are you?" He stepped back and quickly looked her over. "If I may, nice tan."

Cheryl flashed a smile. "Thanks. It took me half the summer to get it just right. Then I spent the other half keeping it up."

"Oh please. You live at The Shore. It's the law. You have to get a good tan." Images of Cheryl flashed through Remmler's mind. Of her in a bathing suit, lying under the sun in Toms River, lotion glistening on her bare skin. Blood flowed to the southern part of his body. *Thank God for loose-fitting shorts.*

"So'ja get dinner yet?" he asked after several minutes of small talk and catching up.

"No. I just got out of class. Mass Media." Cheryl rolled her eyes. "Ugh, it's gonna be boring. I've got Greendell."

"Oh boy, Mr. Excitement himself," Remmler said sarcastically. He had the journalism professor for a course last year. The man had the personality of a stack of bricks.

"Well, I'm headed over to the cafeteria. Care to join me?"

"Absolutely."

The two stepped out of the comfortable, air conditioned building into the stifling August humidity. They took their time, chatting about their summer vacations. Rows of trees along the side of the campus' main road shaded them from the blazing, late afternoon sun. Beds of colorful flowers dotted the grounds. No matter where they looked, it seemed every building, every parking lot, every bench, every lamppost fit in perfectly with the small section of Cobbs Creek Park reserved for the campus.

" . . .and then there was Sam," Cheryl said as they walked past the two-story, utilitarian-looking Rawley Hall.

Remmler raised an eyebrow. "Sam?"

"My boyfriend. Or, maybe I should say, my summer love."

"Oh," Remmler said flatly. A pang of jealousy swelled up

inside. He tried to convince himself it was stupid to feel this way, but he couldn't help it. Most men usually felt a flash of jealousy when a girl they wanted, but could not have, talked about other men. Jack Remmler was no different.

The memories flooded back. A year ago at freshmen orientation when he first met Cheryl. They hit it off immediately. The more time they spent together, the more he became attracted to her. After two rather platonic dates, Remmler asked her to the college's Fall Bash. They danced every slow dance together. Remmler knew this night would be special for them.

It all came crashing down when he walked Cheryl back to their dorm.

"Jack. I . . . I get the feeling you want a little more out of this," she had said.

Remmler felt something bad lay around the corner. With nothing to lose, he poured his heart out to her, told her exactly how he felt. Cheryl, on the verge of tears, said she didn't feel the same way about him. Then came the words every man dreads. "I think we should just be friends."

He and Cheryl barely spoke for the rest of the semester. When they came back from winter break, they agreed to put the incident behind them and remain friends.

"Yeah, I met him at the boardwalk. He worked a couple of booths down from me. He's a business major at Montclair State. It only lasted two months. Just didn't work out. Besides, I'm not one for long distance relationships."

"Oh," Remmler said again, feeling a twinge of happiness.

"So, any summer flings for you, Remy?"

He scoffed, then said half-seriously, "Please. You know my luck with women."

Cheryl didn't respond. *Oops. Dummy, why'd you say something like that?*

Better change the subject.

"So how's your brother?" Cheryl's older sibling, Alan, was a

6-RUST

radar operator aboard a Navy E-2 AWACS plane. Remmler met him last semester during one of the school's family functions.

Cheryl hung her head. "He's in the Gulf. Aboard the *Kitty Hawk*."

Remmler mentally kicked himself—twice. *Nice goin', moron. Maybe you should just shut up altogether.*

"I'm so worried about him. The whole Mid East is on the brink of war and he's right in the middle of it. God, I . . . I don't know."

He put a hand on Cheryl's shoulder. "I'm sure he'll be okay."

Cheryl looked at him. "Could I get that in writing?"

Remmler couldn't think of a response.

"I just feel so helpless."

Remmler's lip tightened. *Helpless.* He'd felt that way so many times. A news junkie since middle school, Remmler received a daily exposure to the world's miseries. His journalism teachers always lectured about being unbiased and detached from the stories you covered. But there were only so many murders, rapes, child molestations, wars and other assorted tragedies you could take before you had to feel about it.

If only I could do something about it.

Yeah, right. Like what the hell can a college student do about the world's problems?

Nothing, that's what.

He could wish all he wanted for the power to change the world, but it would never come.

Jack and Cheryl finally arrived at the Cafeteria Annex next to the Administration Building. Hopefully, surrounded by their fellow students, they could talk about happier subjects.

FOUR

I NEVER REALIZED *how barren this country was until now,* Erich von Klest thought as he flew over the vast fields of brown grass and leafless trees. Uruguay was even more barren this time of year. While most of the world sweltered in August, Uruguay neared the end of its winter.

In the few days since his return from the Arctic, Erich had nearly mastered the alien armor. It took a dozen flights to get over the vertigo he initially experienced. Now he could increase his speed and executed high speed maneuvers with no problems.

His attention turned from the rolling hills and prairies beneath him to the slightly overcast sky. The exhilaration was still there. To actually be one with the sky. Could this be how hangliders feel? Or astronauts on a spacewalk? Floating through the vastness of sky and space, the earth stretching below them, tempting them to scoop it up in their hands. This was the kind of power Erich von Klest had sought all his life. Up here, he was truly superior.

Von Klest's mind drifted back to the week before. He

had just disposed of that seal-fucking Inuit's helicopter when the devilish creature appeared. He still couldn't believe he hadn't been afraid of the repulsive thing. In fact, part of his subconscious felt that everything in his life had led him to this moment. His destiny. And destiny, no matter how hideous its face, should not be feared.

"Who . . . you!" Von Klest's voice held wonderment as he spoke to the creature. "My . . . the dreams I've had. I saw you in my dreams. How? How did you do that?"

The blackish-red creature emitted a gurgle von Klest took as laughter.

"Consider it a summons," it rasped. *"My way of bringing you to this place."*

Finally von Klest felt a little fear. *This thing got into my head! Into my thoughts! How the hell . . . ?* Von Klest suddenly knew what it felt like to be violated. He wanted to shout, "You bastard!" But instead looked down at his armor. Perhaps he could live with this "mental rape" if it meant keeping his newfound power.

"I have scoured this entire world for one human worthy enough to wield the tru'kat. *You, Erich von Klest, I have deemed most worthy."*

"Who . . . what are you? What is this?" He waved his hands over the armor.

"Your questions shall be answered, Erich von Klest. All who first embrace the power of the tru'kat *have a myriad of questions. Some I will answer. Others, you must find out yourself."*

"You are not . . . the Devil?" For the first time in his life, von Klest questioned his atheistic upbringing.

The entity's head straightened. Its voice boomed with an evil regalness. *"I am the Darkling! For eons uncounted, I have fostered the spread of evil throughout the cosmos. Of all those of your kind who oppose the followers of light, peace, good, or whatever term pleases you, I have deemed you best suited to carry out my will. To serve in my Dark Legion. To crush all who oppose what I embody."*

"Serve in your Legion!?!" von Klest's wonderment gave way to anger. "I have no time to waste with this Dark Legion of yours. My service is to the Aryan race. To the Reich!"

The Darkling's mouth opened wide with a deafening roar. Sun-yellow light exploded around its body and reached out to engulf von Klest. His body snapped ramrod straight. A million white hot needles pierced his skin, driving all the way to the bone. He tried to fight the pain. That lasted a split second. Every square inch of bone was crushed by a flaming, iron hand.

"STOP!!! ST-AAAARGH!!!"

"Insolent microbe! "My servants ruled half this galaxy while your insignificant species was learning how to walk upright! It is I *who bestowed this power upon you! And* I *can also take it away from you! Have I made myself understood, Erich von Klest?"*

"YES!!"

The light surrounding both the Darkling and von Klest subsided. Guided by his blade, the German flew over to the edge of the cliff and collapsed. The Darkling waited several minutes before von Klest could bring himself to his knees.

"What is it . . ." he said breathlessly, " . . .you want me to do?"

"Rule this world as you see fit. Crush all those who oppose our beliefs. Every time a follower of the light is defeated, my power grows."

"Ye . . . yes, sir."

"Very well. But be warned. There shall be another like you who will rise on this world. One who will champion and protect the cause of light. You must seek him out when the time comes. Destroy him. Claim his tru'kat *for me."*

"Who . . . who is this person? Where is he?"

"I shall show you all you need to know for now."

Von Klest still could not get over the Darkling's visual presentation of the history of the galaxy. His mind had been open to wonders he never imagined . . . and horrors he didn't want to think existed. All those other races out there. Different. Impure. Nowhere near human.

6-RUST

They all had to be destroyed. But first, Erich von Klest had to settle things on his planet.

He reduced his speed and came upright, landing near a clump of dead trees. Parked nearby was a battered, olive drab land rover. A tall, rugged-faced man with shock white hair and wearing bland, slate gray BDUs (Battle Dress Uniform) stood next to it. He looked down at his Swiss-made Traser Illuminator watch as von Klest's feet touched the ground.

"One hour, fifteen minutes!" Otto Kemp exclaimed, his eyes and mouth wide open.

Von Klest barely stopped his jaw from dropping. He couldn't believe he'd flown nearly 5,600 miles, from here to the northernmost tip of Columbia and back, in so short a time.

"*Mein Gott,* Erich. You had to be going over mach four!"

Von Klest held his *tru'kat*—his Warblade he liked to call it—in front of him. A yellowish glow blotted out his body and forced Kemp to shield his eyes. When the glow dissipated, von Klest's armor was gone, replaced by a dark olive sweater and khaki trousers. The Warblade had shrunk to an oblong rod the size of a Swiss Army knife.

"Mach four-point-five, *mein freund.*" von Klest pocketed the *tru'kat* and walked over to the long-time friend and advisor to him and his father.

"But how . . . ?"

"I keep telling you, Otto. I just know. Like I know fighting skills it would take two lifetimes to master. Like I know how to teleport or fire my Warblade's laser. I just do."

"*Phantastisch.* Imagine what *Der Fuhrer* could have done had he some of these suits."

"Then we wouldn't need to be here."

Both men hopped into the land rover, Otto taking the wheel. The old vehicle sputtered on the first try, then chugged to life on the second. Otto piloted the land rover onto a wide dirt and weed infested path that eventually led to Highway Three. That would take them back to von Klest's isolated estate near the Dayman River.

"I think my little exercises are done, Otto," von Klest stated as the vehicle hit a dip in the road. "I know what the suit can do. I know what *I* can do *with* the suit. It's time to move on to the next stage."

"Which is?"

Von Klest didn't answer immediately. Kemp glanced briefly at the younger man. He was about to ask again when von Klest finally replied. "I don't know. All these years, I've waited for the opportunity to do something . . . big. And I don't know what! I have a power that Hitler never had, that no one on Earth has. And I don't know where to begin."

"I'm sure Hitler didn't know where to begin when he formed the National Socialist Party. And, as you said, he did not have the kind of power you do."

Von Klest said nothing. He only stared out at the brown landscape.

Kemp pressed on. "So will you tell *die Eisen Garde* about this?" He referred to von Klest's handpicked squad of paramilitary bodyguards/commandos, his Iron Guards.

"*Nein!*" Von Klest snapped out of his daydreaming. "Not yet, anyway."

"But they're our most loyal men. If you-."

"Not now, Otto," von Klest abruptly cut him off, something he rarely did to the older man. "At least not until I've figured out what to do. Even then . . ."

Von Klest waited until the vehicle cleared a rather bumpy span of road before continuing. "You're the only other one who knows what happened to me. What I've become. The only one I can trust. The more who know about my power, even amongst my Iron Guards, the greater the chance for leaks. God forbid the Mossad, even the CIA, should ever find out about this. They'd swarm all over us."

"And they'd be powerless against you and that armor suit."

"True. But it would make rebuilding the Reich more difficult having to constantly fight off the *Juden* and their cowed followers."

The two men rode in silence until they reached Highway Three and turned west.

"I'll tell you what, though."

"Yes, Erich?"

"Whatever I do, it will be big. Historic. Not some petty 'statement' everyone forgets after they switch off the news. Mind-numbed teenagers shooting up a synagogue or firebombing Turkish apartments. Not this time. Maybe not ever, if everything works out."

"Anything specific in mind?"

Von Klest slowly shook his head. "Not yet. But I promise you this, *mein freund*. What I do will make Munich, Entebbe and Oklahoma City look like carnival sideshows in comparison."

He saw Kemp smile. For a moment, von Klest thought the older man would shed a tear of pride for the part he played in forming his passion and convictions.

Erich would make his father and grandfather proud. With his new power, he would restore the Reich to its rightful place in the world.

Paul Drake began to regret ever accepting the post of CIA station chief in Riyadh, Saudi Arabia. The tall ex-Army Ranger with close cropped, light brown hair and a chiseled physique could count on both hands the number of hours he had slept since the Iraqi Bomb detonated. Work consumed his waking hours. He ate lunch and dinner at his desk.

What I wouldn't give for just a half-hour at a bar with some good brews and a twenty-something waitress in short-shorts.

In a Muslim country, however, that was impossible.

Drake shuffled down the halls of the American Embassy. His usual ramrod straight posture long ago deteriorated.

Stubble sprouted across his face. The Ambassador, the most meticulously neat man he'd ever met, had given him a tongue-lashing about his disheveled appearance. Drake wondered if the balding, round-faced, four-eyed anal-retentive asshole cared that he'd been working non-stop for the last twenty hours.

He wandered past embassy staffers and Marine guards. The jarheads discarded their usual dress blues for desert camouflage BDUs, M-16s and sidearms. Drake eventually came to a brown oak door. The name plaque, stenciled in both English and Arabic, read: U.S NAVAL ATTACHÉ. CAPTAIN EVERETT LAWSON, USN.

He rapped on the door three times. "Come in," a voice on the other side responded.

The Agency man entered. Aside from the stacks of folders, papers and three-ring binders on the desk, the rest of the room was well maintained. Behind the desk, tapping away at the keyboard of an IBM computer, was a lean, bespectacled man with a thin face and receding black hair. He wore a white, short-sleeved Navy uniform.

"Jesus, Paul, you look like hell."

Drake muttered, "Yeah, I know." Had he not been so exhausted, he would have had a witty response for Lawson. Instead, he took a seat in front of the desk and skimmed through his files.

"Just got through briefing the Ambassador. Missed you."

"I've been working on my own brief. Have to give it to the Ambassador in an hour." Lawson turned away from his computer. "So how's 'Anal Al' holding up?" 'Anal Al' was the embassy staff's private nickname for Ambassador Algernon Waynecroft.

"What you'd expect. When things get thrown out of whack, he has trouble handling it. Why he got picked for a hot spot like here I'll never know. They should've stuck him someplace where stuff never happens. Like Iceland."

Lawson smiled briefly at the remark. Despite the inherent distrust between the military and the CIA, the two men had become good friends in their nine months together in Riyadh. Both had seen action in their time. Drake fought in Grenada and worked with the Mujahideen during the last few years of the Afghan War. Lawson served as executive officer on the guided-missile cruiser *Bunker Hill* during the Gulf War.

"Well, here's the stuff if you want to look at it." Drake handed his pile to Lawson.

"Thanks, Paul. Anything new?"

"Actually, yeah. Check out the photos. Our spy planes have been making passes over the area since the Bomb went off. There's a lot of activity going on around the crater."

Lawson studied the enhanced black-and-white photographs of the crater area. Several vehicles were parked near the edge, with dozens of people milling about.

"Lotsa trucks and people." Lawson looked closer. The people seemed to be covered in something shiny. "Radiation suits, of course."

"Unless they want instant cancer. We first spotted them two days after the explosion. The Iraqis probably waited for it to cool off before sending in their people."

Lawson looked at the photos again, marveling at the crater. "That is one *big damn* hole. How the hell could the Iraqis get their hands on this much uranium without anyone knowing?"

"I wish to God I knew. We always suspected any bomb Iraq built would be at least Hiroshima-sized, five times that at most. But that sucker was in the megaton range. One of their own villages got flattened by the blastwave. They must've either underestimated the yield of that bomb or just FUBARed the test." Drake used the acronym for Fucked Up Beyond All Recognition.

"Assuming it was a test."

Drake nodded. "Yeah. That thought crossed my mind too. If you're a third world country whose butt got trounced a few years ago and you got your hands on something like this, you don't test it in a desert. You test it on Tel Aviv. Or right here," he pointed to the floor, "in Riyadh.

"Hell, maybe it was an accident. Maybe they were transporting it somewhere, hit one too many bumps, and . . . Ka-boom!" Drake threw out his hands for effect.

"What about air samples? Any results?"

Drake shook his head. "None. Everytime I ask Langley for them, I get the same answer. 'The results are pending.' They've been pending for the last three days. That's a bunch of B.S. if I've ever heard it. They must have found something big to make them so tight-lipped."

"Whatever the air tests show, you can bet the cancer rates around here are going to skyrocket over the next century. Between this thing and Chernobyl, Europe and Asia are gonna be an oncologist's wet dream."

Captain Lawson looked through the rest of Drake's report, with the station chief providing commentary. The naval attaché then came across a list of twenty names, most of them Russian.

"The suspects?"

"Yeah. Who could have built The Bomb and who could have supplied the ingredients. We came up with half the names. The rest I got from every contact I have in the region. Even the Israelis. But God, don't let the Saudis hear that."

"Your secret's safe with me, Paul." The captain then noticed lines made in black pen drawn through two names. He showed it to Drake. "What are these for?"

"Eliminations. The German guy—Scheibler—Agency suspected him of trying to pawn uranium from the nuke plant he worked at to some 'dubious characters.' Iraq, of course. Libya. Hell, even the Syrians."

"So what's the deal with him?"

"Damn Israelis scooped us again. My Mossad friends told me they made Scheibler "disappear" two months ago. And the damn bean counters back at Langley didn't know jack about it."

"What about the guy at the bottom Ahh . . . Drovinov, is it?"

"Yeah," Drake nodded. "Some hotshot physics researcher. Once again we have Mossad to thank for his bio."

"They whack him too?"

"No. The info Mossad has on this Drovinov guy says he was high up in the Russians' Star Wars program. Then his project got canceled and he apparently fled the country. But I figure, if the guy's futzin' around with lasers, why would he mess with nukes? I crossed him out. Shorten our search a bit."

The rest of Drake's briefing took fifteen minutes. Afterward, he gathered his notes from Lawson, rose from his leather back chair and headed for the door.

"Oh, one more thing, Paul."

"Yeah?"

"Get some sleep."

"I will. Right after I check wi-"

Lawson cut him off, his voice rather stern. "You're not checking in with anyone, *Colonel* Drake. You've been on the go continuously for nearly a day. You look like hell, you're exhausted. Pretty soon you won't remember what two plus two equals. We need your mind sharp. Now I want you to go upstairs to the guest wing, find a room and crash for six hours. Otherwise, I'll have the embassy doctor sedate you."

Drake grinned and threw Lawson a salute. "Aye-aye, Captain." He was halfway out before Lawson hollered, "And Drake. I mean six hours. I see you walking around here, I'll order one of those brain dead walking muscles called Marines to knock you out and carry your ass back to bed. Clear?"

"Yeah," Drake nodded and closed the door behind him.

The guest room was rather large, decorated with ornately patterned wallpaper and wall-to-wall carpeting. A large photograph of the President hung over the red sheeted king-size bed. Drake didn't realize just how tired he was until he plopped down on the bed. He didn't even bother to remove his clothes or pull back the covers. As he drifted off to sleep, he prayed the world didn't go to hell in a handbasket before he awoke.

6-RUST

FIVE

"WELL, THIS SUCKER looks good."

Brian Doyle stepped back to examine the small beige pop up tent sitting in the middle of his dorm room. The stocky young man walked over his bed and jumped down in front of the tent. He got to his knees, stuck his head inside for a few seconds, then re-emerged.

"Lookin' good inside," Doyle's voice matched his round, lazy face. He got up and stared across the room at the tall, lean boy with moussed up blond hair. "C'mon. Let's take 'er down."

It took just a few minutes to break down the tent. Doyle tossed it in his closet with all the other camping gear. *Thank God there are places around here to do this. I'd go nuts if I couldn't get outdoors at least once in a while.*

"So that everything?" Eric Bouden asked as he leaned against the nearby dresser.

"Yup." Doyle ran a hand through his dark brown hair, which he kept a tad longer in the back than his police chief father would have liked. "Can't think of anything else we need."

"Well, just as long as we don't forget the toilet paper. No way in hell I'm wiping with leaves."

"Quit worrying." Doyle retucked his light blue Morgantown Police Department T-shirt. "This is gonna be great. 'Course, I've hiked tougher trails back in West Virginia."

Bouden faked awe. "Oh. Well forgive me for not being the experienced mountain man you are."

"Shut up, asshole," Doyle dismissed the comment with a wave of the hand.

"So how did you get *him* to come with us?" Bouden nodded to the other side of the room.

"I was on the phone with him a couple weeks ago. Mentioned we were gonna go on a little hiking trip to Springfield Trail the weekend we got back. I asked if he wanted to come along. Mainly I was just being polite. And he said yes. Shocked me. Hell, I tried to get him into the great outdoors last year. Always kept saying it wasn't his bag"

"So what changed his mind?"

"Beats me," Doyle shrugged. Then his soft voice grew serious. "Look, man. I want you to lay off Jack this weekend. Okay?"

"All right. I said I would."

"Well, I just want everyone to have a good time. Last thing I want is you two ragging each other every step of the way."

"Jesus, you made your point already. I'll lay off."

Doyle plopped down on the edge of his bed while Bouden remained standing. "You know, man. I never understood what you have against Jack. He's a cool guy. Just about everyone likes him. How come you guys can't get along?"

"'Cause he's annoying. He acts like a damn know-it-all. Always showing off what he knows about sports, politics, history, whatever."

"That's what makes him interesting."

"It makes him a pain in the ass." Bouden saw Doyle was

about to launch into another lecture. "But I'll leave him alone. Promise."

"I'm gonna hold you to that." Much as he liked Bouden, Doyle knew the guy's word could never be considered one hundred percent reliable.

I hope it is this time. Now that I finally got Jack to go on a hike, I really want him to have a good time.

Who knows? Maybe I'll turn him into another camping buddy.

Five minutes later, the door to the small room opened. In came Jack Remmler, with Chris "Whiz" Wilson in tow.

"Hey, Bubba. What's up?" he greeted his roommate before noticing Bouden. He just nodded to him. "Eric."

Bouden nodded back without a word. That suited Remmler fine. The less said between them the better.

"Want my advice?" He chucked his Phillies cap onto the top shelf of his closet. "Don't go near the cafeteria."

"Dinner sucked?" Doyle asked.

"Kinda. It was chicken hold the meat."

"Too bad we missed it. We went to Nuni Brothers earlier." Doyle referred to the pizza place up the street from Keystone College.

"Lucky." Remmler looked over to Chris. "We shoulda done that."

"Hey, I'm still waiting for that big ass check from my parents. 'Til then, I can't even afford a roll of Life Savers."

"Then we shoulda gone to Seven-Eleven if you're that poor. We coulda dined on mini Tootsie Rolls."

Chris laughed, then looked around the room. "I see you guys finally got your posters up. About time. This place was looking about as lifeless as a monk's bedroom."

"Hey, we had a lot to do this week," Doyle responded. "Takes time to get a room organized. Besides, we're lazy."

Remmler also checked out their room again, pleased with the job he and Brian did the night before. After four days neither one could stand looking at the antiseptic green walls and faded white ceiling anymore.

Remmler covered his side of the room with posters of Flyers star John LeClaire, Phillies great Mike Schmidt, New Jersey Devils goalie Martin Brodeur and Xena, Warrior Princess. An X-Men poster also hung above his plain metal desk.

"X-Men!?" Whiz took a step back in surprise. "Ain't you ever gonna grow up, Remy?"

He shot his friend a wiseass grin. "Hey. I can only act serious for so long."

Doyle's side caught his eye next. "Bubba" brought the obligatory hot girls in bikinis posters, along with posters of Pittsburgh Steelers quarterback Kordell Stewart and an artist's rendition of West Virginia University. He'd taped a photo of his family on the Gateway computer on his desk.

"So what's up?" Remmler perched himself on top of his desk. He made sure not to knock over the framed picture him, his mother, father and sister Lisa at his high school graduation.

"Nothin'. We were just checking out the gear. You jazzed for this, man?"

"Actually, yeah. I'm really looking forward to this trip."

"I still can't believe it," Whiz shook his head and sat on Remmler's bed.

"What?"

"You, that's what. The Suburban Kid going on a camping trip. Your only experience with the outdoors are those woods in back of your house."

Remmler had to grin. Like Chris could talk, growing up ninety miles away in Reading. "Well, now I wanna try something new. Besides, Bubba told me you ain't a real man until you've shit in the woods."

Eyes wide with amazement, Chris looked to Remmler, then to Doyle. "'Scuse me, but I think I'll find something else to do to become a real man."

"Just remember, Jack," Bouden said with a hint of smugness. "Out there you can't run back home if you need something."

Doyle turned to Bouden with raised eyebrows. His facial expression read, "Knock it off."

Remmler, however, was unfazed. "C'mon. This place is smack in the middle of a town for crying out loud. Shouldn't be that far from a Seven-Eleven."

Whiz laughed. Like Remmler, he also thought Bouden was a jackass.

"We're just warming you up, Remy," Doyle grinned. "Eventually we'll get you up to the Blue Mountains or one of the Susquehanna trails."

"Sorry, Bubba. Springfield's as far as I go into the wilderness."

"Yup. Can't take the suburbs out of this guy," Whiz joked.

Remmler snorted and gave him a dismissive wave. He caught a glance of his Pulsar Quartz watch. It read just a few minutes past 6:30. "You guys mind if I turn on the news?"

"Go ahead," Doyle replied. "It's half your room."

Remmler went over to the 19-inch color TV sitting atop a portable refrigerator and switched on the CBS Evening News. No surprise, the Mid East crisis led the newscast. He tuned in halfway through a soundbite from the President. Next came footage of the Secretary of State arriving in Kuwait City. A voice-over about his tour of the region followed. Then the Secretary stated how America's Arab allies would not tolerate a nuclear capable Iraq. The shot cut to the correspondent standing atop a hotel in Baghdad. He wrapped up by talking about "a tenseness among Iraqi officials, who feel the world is closing in around them, and could do something desperate if pushed too far."

"That sounds reassuring," Doyle commented.

"Either that or he's just saying it for dramatic effect," Whiz glanced at the West Virginian.

Bouden rolled his eyes. "Don't you guys ever stop watching the news?"

"Can't," Remmler didn't take his eyes off the TV as a segment began on the deployment of the 82nd Airborne to the region. "We're communications majors. It's in our blood."

"Hey, just do what I do. The news gets too bad, turn it off."

Now Remmler turned his attention to Bouden. The skin around his nose crinkled. He hated that head-in-the-sand attitude. His parents always told him that *never* solved any problem. "You can't turn off the world, dude."

"Whatever." He shot Remmler a sardonic grin.

A couple minutes later the first commercial break began. Remmler looked around the room, gesturing toward the TV with his thumb. "You believe this? Every other year this maniac has to crawl out of his hole in Baghdad and make noise. I'm tellin' ya, we shoulda whacked that walking pile of crap the first time around."

"I'll second that," Chris Wilson raised a hand.

Bouden then stood up and adjusted his bluejeans. "I think it's time for me to book. Later, Bubba."

He didn't even look at Remmler or "Whiz" Wilson as he left the room.

"Was it something we said?" Whiz asked.

Remmler shrugged his shoulders. "I hope so."

"C'mon, Remy. I already told Eric I don't want you two taking your usual potshots at one another this weekend."

"Hey, Bri. No prob. I'll be doing my damnedest to ignore him."

"Look, I know you and Eric don't get along. But he is a friend of mine. I couldn't not invite him."

"It's no problem, man. Look, I don't tell you who to be friends with. I can deal with Eric."

"I hope so."

"Hey. I'm sorry if he can't take my critique of every newscast I see. It's a force of habit. And right now I've had it with scumbags like that spreading nothing but misery in the world. And all we do is talk, talk, talk, while they kill more people."

Cheryl suddenly entered his thoughts. He remembered how worried she'd been about her brother the other day. How many other people across the country were in the same situation? All because of some slimebag who fancied himself the next Hitler.

"Good God. Why can't someone just wipe those s.o.bs off the planet?"

"Hey, I know where you're comin' from, Remy. My Dad's been a cop since I was born. He's been locking up criminals and watching slimy lawyers set 'em free, for years. Believe me when I say he has the same thoughts, too."

"Well, we're sure not gonna be able to do anything about it," Whiz noted. "All we can do is sit around here and complain."

"That's reassuring," Remmler grumbled. *Shit! Lance did something about people like that during Desert Storm. So did both my grandfathers in World War Two. Why can't I?*

What could I do?

"Uh-oh. Sounds like he's in one of those 'let me express my outrage at all the bad stuff in the world' moods." Whiz got up and walked over to Remmler's dresser, where he kept his video tapes.

"Let's see. What do we have to cheer him up? *South Park? Beavis and Butt-Head?* Oh yeah! *Ren and Stimpy?* I haven't seen the Happy Helmet episode in a long time."

Remmler couldn't help but smile. "All right. *Ren and Stimpy* it is." Better that than one of his Japanese Anime tapes. He still couldn't shake those damn dreams. Although after this latest news, maybe it wouldn't be so bad dreaming of himself in an episode of *Mobile Suit Gundam* or *The Guyver*. Imagine what they could do to those bastards in Iraq.

Whiz pulled out the appropriate tape and loaded it into the VCR. Doyle then opened the fridge and took out three cans of ginger ale. Remmler went to his closet and produced a bag of chips.

"Shall we make it a brain rot marathon?" Whiz suggested.

"Why not?" Remmler scooped out a handful of chips. "It'll be a typical Keystone College Thursday night."

The three settled back for a night of animated hilarity. Even as the cartoon began, Remmler couldn't keep the world's problems completely out of his mind.

Is this the only way I have of dealing with this crap? Watching a cat who looks like a dog and a dog who looks like a mouse do stupid things.

What other way do you have, Jack?

"You've been studying your goddamned data for days!" The President of the United States slammed a fist on his oak desk. "And every time you're in here, it's the same damn excuse. 'We don't know. We don't know.' I need to know, dammit! I want answers!"

Those gathered in the Oval Office froze in silence at the Chief Executive's outburst. He took some deep breaths to settle himself. It didn't work.

Dammit. I'm the leader of the free world. I should be able to keep my emotions in check. Not fly off the handle.

Then again, no one's had to deal with what I've been handed.

The President ran a hand over his face. The strain of the past week started to wear physically on the distinguished, graying man. Bags had formed under his bloodshot eyes and new wrinkles developed on his face.

He finally looked up at the stunned crowd. His hard gaze settled on the bespectacled female Army officer with a thicket of auburn hair.

"Um . . . begging your pardon, Mr. President. But we've just never encountered something like this before. Umm . . ."

Colonel Nancy Briggs cast her gaze to the floor, unable to look into the President's fiery eyes.

She was spared further grief by her companion from National Photographic Interpretation Center, or NPIC, who tried to save her from ruining her career further. "Mr. President, none of the data we've looked at is consistent with any type of nuclear explosion we've ever seen. We've used every sensor available on our meteorological and nuclear detection satellites to monitor ground zero of the Iraqi blast and the resulting fallout. Our Auroras and U-2s have taken over a dozen air samples. Nothing makes sense. The radiation levels from the fallout are unbelievably low. Maybe half the amount released during Three Mile Island. Now, the levels are higher in the blast area, but nowhere near what we'd expect from an explosion of this size."

"How high are we talking about? In non-scientific technospeak."

Navy Captain Peter Matson paused to do the mental calculations. The President guessed he was someone used to people around him understanding the numbers and figures he casually threw out. "It's not as bad as Chernobyl. We speculate you could stay in the area for two, three hours tops in a rad suit before it gets dangerous. If this was your 'normal' five megaton nuclear device, even an hour in that area, *with* a suit, would be pushing it."

"And this was not a 'normal' nuclear bomb?"

"No sir. As you can see here . . ." the dark-haired, angular-faced captain pointed to several computer enhanced images of the world spread out on the President's desk, "the pattern of the fallout is like nothing we've ever seen before. Usually, fallout goes in roughly a straight path, depending on which direction the prevailing wind pattern is blowing. But this . . . I don't know. It's spreading in all directions."

Matson traced his finger around a circular patch of red covering most of Europe, Asia and Africa on one of the satellite images. "Nothing—wind, weather patterns—has any effect on it. It's spreading across the globe exponentially. I don't know, it . . . it's like it has a mind of its own." Matson noticeably swallowed after that last statement.

The President gave him a curious stare, then looked back at the images.

"We've also picked up traces of unknown forms of energy in the fallout. We have no indication of what it is. We don't even know if its dangerous."

"Where will it end?" the President said in a whisper.

"Our latest projections show no sign of it dissipating," Colonel Briggs finally spoke, this time with a little more confidence in her voice. "It's continuing to move at the same rate it has been since we began tracking it."

The President sat in silence for several seconds, staring blankly at the pictures. "It'll cover the Earth?"

Matson nodded hesitantly. "At its present rate, it will cover the entire planet in five days."

The Chief Executive slowly turned to the lean, sour-faced CIA Director, Thomas Brock. "Does CIA concur?"

Brock looked to his own satellite imaging expert. The nervous, pot bellied, bespectacled man practically forced himself to nod. The Director of Central Intelligence turned back to his boss, the look on his face more sour than usual.

"Yes, Mr. President. CIA concurs."

"My God," stammered Edward Baronelli, the tan skinned National Security Advisor. "What will this mean? How can we stop it?"

The color drained from Matson's face. "Sir. I don't know if we can stop it."

Seconds later, the President shot to his feet. "I want answers. Get every and any expert you can get your hands on. NASA, Lawrence Livermore, Los Alamos, even the EPA. Anyone with any kind of theory on this thing."

"But sir?" Baronelli started. "What about security clearance . . ."

"I don't care about security clearances," the President angrily cut him off. "I'll sign the damn passes myself. I want to know what those bastards unleashed on the rest of the world."

He spun away toward the bulletproof windows behind the desk. His unfocused gaze swept over the White House grounds. *Dear God. Could this endanger the whole human race? Destroy it? No! That's not possible! Is it?*

He closed his eyes, wondering if any of his predecessors ever felt as helpless as he did now.

SIX

*I*T'S DARK. WHY *is it so dark?*

Are my eyes open? Are they closed? Why can I not tell? Is this death? Is there really a Hell?

Yuri Drovinov could see nothing, feel nothing. All he was aware of was the darkness.

Who am I? I don't know who I am. What's going on!?! What's happening!?!

Drovinov tried to move but couldn't. He couldn't even tell if he was breathing. Slowly, pieces of his life filtered back into his mind.

Yuri . . . Yuri . . . Yes. My name is Yuri Drovinov. Physics . . . Why . . .? Yes! I am a professor of physics . . . and . . . lasers!

It all flooded back into his brain. His free-electron laser. Something went wrong with the test. There was a flash.

Oh no. No. I am dead! This is the afterlife the religious people speak of. But how . . .?

Panic set in. Drovinov willed himself to move, but couldn't.

No. No! This cannot be happening. What's going on!? This cannot be death. It cannot be!—

No! NO!!! Drovinov couldn't tell if he was screaming or whether it came from inside his mind.

NOOOOO!!!!!!

A fissure of light suddenly appeared. Then another. And another. Soon dozens of them merged together. The spots of darkness were pushed away . . . or up? Light flooded Drovinov's brain. He tried to shut it out. It just kept burning through the darkness.

A brilliant, yellow tunnel lay before him. It seemed distant, but for some reason that didn't matter.

Isn't that what they say about people who have had near death experiences? They go down a tunnel of light?

Drovinov allowed himself to relax. *So there really is an afterlife. What is it like? Will I see long dead relatives?*

I must go to the light. I must.

Drovinov moved toward the light. Floating, disembodied, unable to sense one molecule of his body. For the first time in his life, he felt completely at peace with himself. Perhaps death was not so bad.

He finally reached the end of the tunnel. The light washed over him.

Yes. I can accept this now.

"What is it!?! What is it!?!"

Drovinov entire body jerked in surprise at the excited voice. His eyes opened. The feeling of tranquillity came crashing down.

The Russian found himself staring across the vast expanse of a crater at least a mile long. The blazing noonday sun beat down on the dark brown sand, fused into glass from the explosion. Four men in silver radiation suits stood thirty-five yards away from him. Two held AK-47s. Another clutched a box-like object Drovinov assumed to be a Geiger Counter. They talked quickly, in high-pitched voices. Drovinov had a hard time making out what they were saying. He noticed other silvery glints around the crater. More men. At least a dozen.

What's going on?

One of the men suddenly raised his assault rifle.

"NOO!!!" Drovinov brought his hands up in front of him as the end of the man's weapon flashed orange.

That's when it happened.

Uneven lines of black, crackling energy surrounded Drovinov's body. He blinked as sparks of flame burst in front of him. The second gunner joined in. The 7.62mm rounds from his weapon also exploded on contact with the mysterious energy field.

"Stop it!" Drovinov pleaded. He extended his open hand toward the silver suited men in a silent plea. The Russian almost went into shock as he saw a ray of black and gray energy leap from his palm.

"WHAT . . .!?!"

None of the four men had time to move. The dark energy knocked them all off their feet, disintegrating their containment suits and ripping the flesh from their bodies. The AK-47s exploded into a thousand pieces. When the beam dissipated, four charred, shattered skeletons lay on the ground.

How . . . How is this possible? What's happened to me?

The feel of the crunching ground beneath his feet finally brought Drovinov back to reality. It was, he suddenly realized, the first thing he had felt since his . . ."awakening." He looked down, barely able to choke off a scream.

His entire body was covered by this crackling, black-gray energy.

"What is it!?!" Drovinov tried to brush it off his arm. The attempt proved futile.

He looked up again. More silver-clad people rushed toward him. Another volley of AK-47 fire zipped his way. The energy screen appeared around the Drovinov again.

"Stay away from me!" He raised his hands. A surge of

energy leaped from his fingertips. Four more men became blackened skeletons. The survivors turned and fled, only to meet the same fate seconds later.

The threat dispatched, Drovinov looked up at the top of the crater. It looked at least a quarter-mile away.

Suddenly, Drovinov felt his feet leave the ground. He looked down. To his astonishment, he was actually rising into the air, climbing higher with each passing second.

Please don't fall. Please don't fall. What's happening to me!?!

Drovinov took his eyes off the fading ground. The crater wall rapidly fell away before him. Against his better judgment, he looked down. More than seven hundred feet of air was between him and the crater floor. The Russian's head began to spin. His body quaked. A rush of air whipped past his energy-laden body.

"NO!! STOP!!"

Drovinov fell over forty feet before he stopped and hovered again. He took a few deep breaths before looking down again. His heart beat like a jackhammer. Then he noticed a small hole in the bottom of the crater just underneath him.

My God. I was buried in there? For how long? How did I survive?

Drovinov raised his head and resumed his flight toward the top of the crater. He could see more silver suited men scrambling up the crater wall with rappelling gear. Drovinov easily picked them off, leaving a number of smoldering nylon ropes flailing in the air.

His breathing increased as he rose higher and higher. Fear gave way to exhilaration. *I can fly. I can actually fly.*

When Drovinov emerged from the crater, he heard the distinctive *thump-thump-thump* of a helicopter's rotorblades. He turned left and noticed a large Mi-8 "Hip" with Iraqi markings lifting off. Drovinov extended a fist and blasted the chopper into nothingness.

He hovered over the enormous crater and searched for any more signs of life. He found none.

Drovinov flew over the crater and onto the desert floor, where he sank to his knees.

"What have I become?" Drovinov whispered, staring down at the dark aura of energy surrounding his body. *I can fly. I can project energy. I am energy.*

"My life. My life is over. How can I live in the normal world like this? I can't! I'm a freak! I'm not even a human being anymore."

Drovinov threw his head back and screamed to the desert, "WHYYY!?! WHYYY MEEE!?!"

Tears welled up in his eyes. A sorrowful wail built up in his throat, begging for release.

That's when it struck him.

Why should I worry what others think? I have power now. Real power. I am power. I am perhaps the most powerful human being ever to walk the Earth.

Drovinov breathed deep, settling himself. A minute later he got to his feet. "Why should I fear anyone?" he said to himself, mainly just to hear another human voice. "They should fear *me!* I have the power to do *anything* I want."

He walked over to the edge of the crater. The scientist in Drovinov took over, trying to piece together what had happened.

"Obviously the laser exploded. My uranium must be responsible for this. But how? What is its secret?" A pause. "And why am I still alive? From the size of this crater, the explosion had to be four or five megatons. I was right at ground zero. Could that be it? Perhaps when the laser exploded, the energy released by the U-500 created a kind of energy pocket. Hmph! Maybe I will never know the answer."

Something down in the crater caught his eye.

"Hmm?" Drovinov squinted. "What is that?"

He thought he saw a yellowish shimmer. It looked as though the very air had wrinkled.

Then it was gone.

Drovinov shook his head. "Must be the sun. Damn desert."

He noticed his voice sounded different. Deeper, more echoic. Drovinov did a quick self-examination. He felt his lungs expand and contract. Then he wrapped his hand around his left wrist and squeezed. There was a pulse and he could feel his flesh. Rather warm, but still there.

"So I'm not pure energy. I'm still flesh and blood. I just resonate energy. Some form of energy.

"I must conduct more tests. Find out exactly what I have become."

Taking a deep breath, Drovinov left the ground and flew away. He felt more at ease now flying under his own power. Why not? This was a new kind of freedom Drovinov doubted few people on the planet could, or would, ever experience.

He took one final look at the enormous crater and smiled. One life for Yuri Drovinov had ended. Another was just beginning.

Jesus, this thing's heavy. Remmler adjusted the straps on his backpack. Try as he might, nothing could alleviate his discomfort. *Hope I don't fall over with all this crap on. I'll never get up.*

"You okay there, Remy?" Bubba Doyle asked as he closed the backdoor of his old, dark brown Chevy station wagon.

"Oh yeah, I'm fine," he lied nonchalantly, ignoring the bite of the straps into his skin.

Bubba locked the door and turned to his roommate with a grin. "Good job. Keep up the macho front."

He slapped Remmler on the shoulder and walked away.

"Is it that obvious?"

Doyle turned around. "Don't worry. You'll get used to the weight. Pretty soon, you won't even know it's there."

"If you say so." Remmler then muttered under his breath. "Pretty soon better be in the next couple of minutes."

He twisted his neck around as far as possible and glanced at his pack. Very little of what he carried actually belonged to him. The backpack itself, along with the sleeping bag, were loners from Bubba. His ex-Marine cousin, Lance, had given him the khaki webbing around his waist that held two tan canteens. Remmler figured to get a lot of use out of them, with the day being so muggy. Rounding out his load were extra clothes, including several pairs of socks and underwear, deodorant, some canned food, granola bars, two mini boxes of cereal, one of Bubba's fluorescent lanterns, a small first aid kit and a flashlight.

"You wanted to do this outdoors shit, jackass," Remmler muttered again. "Start liking it."

"Hey Remy!" called a tall, well-built young man with straight brown hair and chiseled features. "Let's go, man!"

"All right, all right," Remmler replied to Jim Elling, another one of Bubba's wrestling buddies. He was a personable young man who Remmler got along with fine. Unlike the remaining member of the group, Eric Bouden.

Adjusting his battered, red Philadelphia Phillies ballcap, Remmler headed over to his partners, praying the weight of the backpack wouldn't cause him to fall over.

"You all set?" Elling asked.

Remmler nodded. "You bet. Let's get started."

"Okay, troops," Doyle said, pointing to the woods just beyond the near empty parking lot. "Let's move it out."

He strode briskly toward the thicket of trees and bushes, followed by Eric Bouden and Jim Elling. Jack Remmler brought up the rear.

I guess this won't be too bad, Remmler thought as he glanced at the civilization around them. Nearby was busy PA 420. To his right, he could see several suburban houses and small businesses. Off in the distance was a park where children romped, young people played Frisbee or hackey sack and adults walked or picnicked. Remmler found it hard to believe a thickly wooded area lay in the center of all this.

I just hope there's a Seven-Eleven around here if we need it.

He stifled a yawn. Damn, if only he got more sleep last night. But those stupid dreams came back, thrown in with images of woods. These woods?

Nah, can't be.

Then why do I have this nagging feeling? The same one that kept me up half the night? I don't know. It's like I was supposed to have done something in that dream. What I don't have a clue.

Dammit, Jack. Enough! Gotta get your mind off it.

"'The woods are lovely, dark and deep . . .'" Remmler quoted Robert Frost as they entered the forest. "' . . .and I have miles to go before I sleep.'"

Elling turned around, grinning. "I didn't know you were a poet, Remy."

"Hey, it's one of the few things I remember from Dr. Haller's English Lit class. Just seemed appropriate here."

The group felt a little foolish for the first mile, decked out like professional campers with suburban Springfield just yards away. They drew curious stares from a few people as they trundled through Spring Valley Park.

It didn't take long before the signs of civilization disappeared, replaced by a thicket of trees and foliage. Occasionally they came across a child or two wading in the stream next to them, searching for crayfish, frogs and turtles. Remmler was grateful as they continued deeper into the woods. The trees blocked much of the hot summer sun and a cool breeze cut down the humidity.

He continued doing well when they reached the second mile of the hike. Remmler couldn't help being impressed with himself. It seemed he was in better shape than he realized.

Despite the fact his physical activity had decreased and he had gained two or three extra pounds since starting college.

This isn't so bad. I can handle this.

His attitude changed once they passed the remains of the old paper mill.

The trail began to rise and the woods were much denser than before. Remmler's breathing became more labored as the trail got steeper. His legs were incredibly tight and his shoulders and back felt ready to split in half. If not for the trees, the heat and humidity would have made this unbearable. Jack started to grab on to nearby trees and branches, wishing more than anything he could collapse right here and rest for two or three . . . days.

"Watch out here, guys," Bubba called out from the top of the trail. "It's really steep to the left."

Bubba, also using trees for support, moved past the incline, followed by Bouden and Elling.

How steep is this thing? Remmler wondered. When he reached the top, he looked left and swallowed.

The ground immediately angled off about thirty degrees. A few rocks and roots broke up the flatness of the ground. Beyond the edge was a forty foot drop to the stream below.

Remmler couldn't take his eyes off it. The summer heat couldn't stop a blanket of cold from wrapping itself around him. *God, it's like a natural sliding board.*

He was about to move on when a sharp tingling shot through his spine. It rooted him to the spot. He turned back slowly toward the slope, his wide eyes taking in every detail.

There's something down there. The thought didn't seem to be his own.

Jack didn't know what exactly was down there, but something inside told him he had to have it. A feeling . . . no. More like a craving. He didn't just have to have it. He *needed* it.

But if he went down that slope, chances were he would slip, slide off the edge into the water . . . and die!

6-RUST

Stop it, Jack. Just stop it.

He couldn't. The two thoughts battled for supremacy. Go down. Don't go down.

What's happening? Why am I thinking like this?

Stop it! I can't do it. I can't go down there.

It didn't matter. This feeling demanded he go down there and retrieve whatever it was that beckoned him.

Remmler lifted one foot off the trail . . .

"Yow, Remy!" Bubba called out from down the trail. "What's the hold up?"

Remmler snapped his foot back. His head whipped around, eyes still wide. A momentary wave of panic swept over him.

What the hell was that?

"You okay, Jack?"

Remmler's first attempt to respond died in his throat. He cleared it. "Yeah. I'm fine. I . . . I thought I saw something."

"Well come on," Bouden urged. "We ain't got all day."

"Yeah. I'm coming." He made his way down the trail and rejoined his companions. For the rest of the hike, Jack Remmler was uncharacteristically silent. He tried to put the weird experience out of his head.

He couldn't.

SEVEN

ERICH VON KLEST rubbed his thumb and index finger across his tired eyes. He looked back down at his 19th century mahogany rolltop desk, painfully trying to focus on the mess of papers, maps and books cluttering it.

How long have I been at this?

He turned away from the desk and looked over the large, elaborately decorated bedroom. A king-size bed with a wooden frame dominated the center of the room. Underneath it was a layer wall-to-wall carpeting. Two leather chairs were positioned at each end of the room and two large bookcases sat on either side of the bed. A painting of white stallions galloping across a meadow, stolen from a private collection in Warsaw during the Nazi occupation, hung over the bed. A large, French-style window made from bullet-resistant glass revealed the darkness outside. The personal bathroom opposite from it appeared in its reflection.

Von Klest was about to turn back to the desk when someone rapped on the large, oak door.

"*Wer ist es* (Who is it)?"

"It's me. Otto."

"*Eintreten* (Enter)."

The door slowly opened, and Otto Kemp entered. Standing in the hallway, dressed in slate gray BDUs, a headover and a swastika armband, was a young, hard-faced member of von Klest's Iron Guards. An stubby MP4 submachine gun hung across his chest.

Kemp shut the door before he spoke. "You've been holed up in here for hours, Erich."

"I know. What time is it?"

"Nearly two."

Two o' clock in the morning!? "Mein Gott! I didn't realize I'd been sitting here so long."

"Any progress?" Kemp eyed the cluttered desk.

Von Klest sighed, shaking his head. "All I've done is narrow the list of targets. All very tempting. I just can't make up my mind which one we should hit."

Erich handed his mentor a notepad. He looked it over. The United Nations building was at the top of the page. Other names followed. Jerusalem, Houses of Parliament—South Africa, the White House, the Kremlin, World Bank Headquarters and a dozen other places.

"These are very high profile targets."

"I intended them to be. Before I got the armor from the Darkling, we could have never even conceived of an operation this grand. But now . . ." a grin formed around von Klest's mouth. " . . . now there isn't a force on this planet that can stop me. Bullets, grenades, even anti-tank rockets. Nothing can damage my armor. Nothing!" Von Klest shot out of his chair and walked halfway across the room. "But which one to choose? All this power and I can't decide where to begin."

Kemp looked at the list again as von Klest listlessly paced the bedroom. "I would say Jerusalem should be our objective. The *Juden* are mankind's mortal enemies after all."

"Then maybe we should hit the World Bank instead. The damn Jews control all the world's money."

"True. But most people probably don't even know what the World Bank is. The more known the target, the more shock people will feel when we destroy it."

"Then what about the White House or the Kremlin?"

"The White House is a viable target. But the Americans are merely puppets of the Jewish Conspiracy. As for the Kremlin, those incompetent drunks, the Russians, would probably thank us if we wiped out their joke of a government. And attacking South Africa's Parliament might be a mistake. The Afrikaner Resistance Movement has many sympathizers *in* Parliament. We could seriously damage our relations with them with such an attack."

"Then, for you, it would be Jerusalem."

"Yes. It is the seat of Jewish power. In one blow, we could wipe out their Knesset, the cabinet and the Prime Minister."

Von Klest smiled and nodded. He clasped the older man by the shoulders. "As always, Otto, you make sense. Let me sleep on it. I'll make my decision in the morning."

"I understand. This is a major step for all of us . . . especially you, Erich. Whatever your decision, I will stand by you."

"Thank you, Otto."

They hugged briefly. "If only your father were alive to share in this," Kemp said afterward.

"I can think of no better way to honor his memory than by dealing a major blow to the vermin of humanity."

Kemp nodded with delight. "I shall let you turn in. You'll need all the rest you can in the coming days." He walked over to the desk to replace the notepad, when a piece of paper caught his eye. About a dozen or so words were written on it. All were crossed out. Except one: IMPERIUM.

"What is this?" he handed the paper to von Klest.

"I was brainstorming aliases to use when I'm in my armor. Our attack will make my powers public and I certainly can't broadcast my real name to the world. Every intelligence and law enforcement organization in existence would hunt us down. So I need an alter ego. A name people will associate with power, intimidation."

"'Imperium' certainly embodies those qualities."

"It sounds much better than "Carlos the Jackal." Besides, don't you think 'Imperium' has a certain Prussian ring to it?"

"Very."

When Kemp left, von Klest stripped to his underwear and fell into bed.

When the dawn came, Erich von Klest would take his first step down a path that would change the world forever.

Jack Remmler's eyes snapped open. He was suddenly awake, staring at the top of the tent. Sunlight reflected off the light green canvas. Outside a chorus of birds chirped.

Remmler sat up in his sleeping bag, surprised how alert he was. He had always been a terrible morning person, needing a lot of time once he woke up to get going. For some reason, that was not the case today.

He noticed Jim Elling still slept. As quietly as possible, he pulled himself out of his sleeping bag and put on fresh clothes.

What time is it? Remmler dug through one of the small pockets in his backpack until he found his watch. "Seven-Twenty," he whispered. "Still too damn early."

He still couldn't get over refreshed he felt. After the four of them set up camp the night before, sleep did not come easily to him. Remmler dreaded the prospect of crossing that slope again.

Why didn't I just go home for Labor Day? he had thought. *Why did I say yes to Bubba?*

He never pushed those thoughts from his mind. Still, by some miracle, he managed to fall asleep.

After strapping on his watch, Remmler crawled out of the

tent. He blinked several times until his eyes adjusted to the sunlight filtering through the tall, thick trees. Remmler got to his feet and looked around the campsite. Apparently Bubba and Bouden were still asleep in the other tent. Remmler wandered over to a tall oak and sat against it. His mind filled with nagging thoughts. Hazy bits and pieces of dreams from the previous night.

Try as he might, he could not come up with a clear picture. It seemed to be more Japanese Anime dreams. He wasn't sure. All he had were fragments with no form. Feelings of rage, anxiety and wonderment also slithered through his jumbled thoughts.

Remmler's hands enveloped his head. He shut his eyes, willing the images to go away.

"Stop it," he whispered forcefully. "Stop it." *What's happening to me?*

"Hey, Remy. Wake up over there."

Jack's head snapped up. The disturbing images vanished.

"You okay, man?" Brian Doyle asked as he got out of his tent. "Sleep okay?"

"Yeah. Yeah, I'm fine." Remmler got up and headed over to his roommate. "Just got up. Thought I'd veg out here for a while. It's . . . kinda nice out here."

Doyle nodded, drew a deep breath and looked around the woods. "You bet it is." He slapped Remmler on the shoulder. "See. You're already turning into an outdoorsman."

"Heh! Don't push your luck."

"Come on. Let's wake up Jim and Eric. We'll break down the tents, have breakfast and hit the trail."

Remmler snapped a salute. "*Jawohl,* O Fearless Leader."

Doyle flipped him off with a grin as they headed back to the tents. After packing up everything, the four wolfed down a breakfast of dry cereal and Granola Bars. When they finished, they strapped on their packs and moved out. Bubba took the point, followed by Jim and Eric. Jack brought up the rear. While the others jabbered away, all he could think about was the slope.

I don't want to go over it again. What if I zone out again? Why is this happening?

I'm not going insane, am I? No! It can't be that.

The ground gradually became steeper. Remmler knew the slope wasn't too far ahead. The anxiety closed around him like a giant fist, threatening to suffocate him. Sweat burst from every pore. His heart beat so hard he thought it would burst right out of his chest. Remmler wanted to shout to Bubba and the others. Ask them to turn around and go back. But what reason could he give? None that would sound rational.

I don't want to go over that slope. Please God, don't make me do it.

"Shit! Where's my canteen!?"

Remmler looked ahead to see Elling twisting around.

"What's the matter?" Bouden asked.

"I can't find my other canteen. Shit!"

"Aw jeez, Jim," Bubba moaned. "That was my brother Chris' canteen."

"Dude, I know. I don't know, maybe I left it back at the campsite."

"Why don't I go back and get it?" Remmler blurted without thinking.

"You sure, Remy?" Bubba asked "I don't . . ."

"No really. It's no problem."

"Look," Elling began, "I lost the damn thing. I'll get it." He looked at the sides of the narrow trail, cluttered with rocks and dense shrubs.

"Jim, it's a tight squeeze to get down here. You'll probably wind up knocking me and Eric into the bushes. I'm on the end. It's easier if I just go back and get it."

"I don't know, man? I mean, you don't have a lot of outdoors experience."

"Bubba, we ain't exactly in the middle of the Rocky Mountains. All I have to do is follow the damn trail. I'll be fine."

"What about up ahead?" Bubba nodded down the trail. "It is pretty steep."

Remmler bit his lip before replying, "Hey, I got by fine yesterday. It won't be a problem."

Doyle seemed reluctant to let him go off by himself. After a few moments, he finally relented.

"Okay, man. Tell you what. We'll hike up to the paper mill and wait for you there."

"Cool. I'll see you in a bit."

Remmler turned and headed back down the trail.

Elling looked back at Doyle. "You think he'll be okay?"

"Come on, Jim. Remy's not a blithering idiot. He'll be fine. Hell, civilization's just two miles in any direction. He's not gonna have any problems." *At least I hope not. Anything happens to Remy, his whole family'll probably drive down from Jersey and kill me.*

Aw, quit worrying, Brian. You're starting to sound like Mom.

"Okay, guys. Move out."

It didn't take long for Remmler to find Elling's canteen. Somehow it had gotten half-buried in a clump of dead leaves.

"How the fuck did you do that, Jim?" he wondered to himself. He picked up the canteen and stuck it in his webbing. After taking a swig of water from his own canteen, Remmler headed out.

The entire walk back turned into one prolonged anxiety attack. He tried everything to block out yesterday's experience. Humming to himself, reciting various stats from the career of baseball great Mike Schmidt, even coming up with various fantasies involving him and Cheryl Terrepinn. Nothing worked. Remmler knew he had only delayed the inevitable by offering to retrieve Jim's canteen. He would eventually have to cross the slope.

Nothing's gonna happen. Everything'll be all right. Yeah. It will.

It wasn't long before the trail started to rise. The dreaded slope soon came into view.

Remmler took three deep breaths, closed his eyes and prayed. *Please God, get me through this. Please.*

He opened his eyes and sucked in another deep breath. "Gotta do it some time, Remy. Might as well be now."

He put one foot in front of him. Nothing. No strange sensations. No anything.

"There. Nothing doing. Everything's gonna be fine."

Remmler continued up the trail, holding on to nearby trees for support. "Yeah, piece of cake," he said to himself. "See. Nothing's happening. I'm not crazy. I may be talking to myself, but I'm not crazy."

He reached out for another tree . . . and his foot slipped off the trail.

"OH SHIT!!" Remmler wrapped his arms around the tree as his legs gave way. Slowly, he pulled his legs back onto the trail. His breaths came in short, quick spurts. He lay on the ground for a full minute, trying to calm himself.

God, I want to be anywhere but here.

Jack finally pulled himself off the ground, only to discover his legs shook violently. He fell against a nearby tree, holding it for support. Jack rested his head against the bark, taking deep breaths to settle himself. He then looked down the trail. He was halfway across.

"Come on, Jack. You can make it. You can make it."

Once his legs stopped buckling, Remmler screwed up his courage and took a step down the trail. He grabbed a branch on the next tree and swung his other leg around-

The branch snapped!

Jack crashed on his side and slid down the slope.

"SHIIIT!!" He desperately clawed at the ground to stop his fall.

Oh God! I don't wanna die!

"HELP!" Remmler turned his head and saw the edge of the cliff getting nearer. Then he noticed something else. Something long and thin protruding from the ground. A branch? Whatever it was, it was close enough to reach.

He quickly turned on his right side, reached out with both hands and snagged it.

"UGH!!" The sudden stop ripped the air from Remmler's lungs.

"Just . . . don't . . . break," he begged the branch.

Remmler glanced at the edge. He was no more than fifteen feet from it. Fifteen feet from a plunge into the creek below that surely would have killed him.

God! I can't believe I came that close to buying it.

He looked up at the trail, wondering how the hell he could get out of here. The ground was too steep to walk up. He'd probably have to crawl back to the trail. That would be no easy task. Too bad Bubba didn't pack any mountain climbing equipment. But who could have foreseen this?

Remmler looked back down, trying to figure a way out of his dilemma. That's when he noticed it. The branch—or whatever it was he was holding—did not feel like wood. It felt cold, metallic. Jack ran his eyes over the object. It was covered by a thin crust of dirt. The end sported a spherical shape the size of a tennis ball.

"What the hell is this . . .?"

Remmler felt the stick begin to warm. His eyes quickly focused on his hands. The temperature rose gradually, but not hot enough to burn his hands. Remmler wanted to let go, but that would send him sliding over the cliff. If he could just find something else to hang onto . . .

The stick suddenly glowed.

Remmler's eyes widened. His body tensed as he watched the pulsating, off-yellow aura emanating from the stick.

What the fuck is going on!?! He wanted to say it. Stark terror choked him. All common sense fled Remmler's mind.

Let go! Remmler's mind screamed. *Let go! LET GO!!*

His hands remained tightly wrapped around the stick. The glow became more intense, and slowly crept up Remmler's arm.

C'MON JACK! LET GO FOR GOD'S SAKE!!

Jack's hands refused to obey.

HELP! SOMEBODY HELP!

Remmler was still unable to talk. Despite the humidity, a bitter cold swept his body.

"N . . . Nooo," he finally managed to squeeze out of his throat. The light grew so intense Remmler had to shut his eyes. Now his body warmed.

What's . . . happening . . . to . . . me?

Remmler sensed a brilliant flash. It subsided seconds later.

A terrified Remmler forced his eyes open. The sight caused his heart to leap into his throat.

All the dirt had fallen away from the stick, revealing its silvery, metallic surface. Remmler suddenly felt claustrophobic. He looked down.

"OH MY GOD!!!"

Remmler immediately shot to his feet, tearing the rest of the staff from the ground. He barely noticed the scalpel-like blade attached to the end as he looked over the red and white suit of armor that now encased him.

"What the hell is this!?!"

The legs, arms, and chest were bulked out. Below the knees, the legs squared off, turned red and ended at in what looked like oversized moonboots. A red line ran up the side of each leg, ending at the waist. The torso, with its protruding, barrel chest, sported a red triangle in the center, with two Isosceles triangles standing next to it, their tips pointing inward. The back of the hands were red, with a red line running up the side of each arm to the shoulders. It ended in a jagged circle around the neck. Just behind each hand was a red, jagged wristlet. He couldn't see the globular-shaped head that sprouted fan-like "ears." The forehead, which had a smaller version of the three triangle design, sloped into a hazy red duckbilled visor.

Remmler's jaw trembled. He began hyperventilating. Any attempt at speech proved futile.

God, what is this!?! How do I get out of this thing!?!

Jack managed a few ragged breaths as he tried to calm down. He could feel tears streaming down his cheeks. He had never been so scared in his entire life.

What's going to happen to me now?

EIGHT

"I HAVE DECIDED, Otto," Erich von Klest said as he swallowed the last of his danish. "We will strike Jerusalem."

Kemp nodded in agreement. The men sat at opposite ends of the table in von Klest's private dining room, finishing breakfast.

"Excellent, Erich," Kemp smiled, pushing aside his empty plate and reaching for his tea. "We've been waiting over fifty years for an opportunity like this. The destruction of the *Juden* government is sure to rally Aryans everywhere."

"It will." von Klest nearly lunged across the table with unbridled excitement. "With the power of Imperium we cannot fail! The damn Jews will be ground under our heels." *And I will be the* Fuhrer *of a new Reich!*

"We must act quickly, though. Each day that passes brings the Middle East closer to war. The Americans are building up their forces in the region. Even NATO seems prepared to commit large numbers of troops. The shooting could start any minute."

"Yes, you're right." Von Klest, now much calmer, returned to his seat. "If and when the shooting starts, Israel will not stay out of it like last time."

"It will be difficult. Their government facilities are undoubtedly under heavy guard."

"I can deal with any security the Israelis have. However, I will need my Iron Guards to back me up, make sure all of the Israeli cabinet and Knesset are dead. Getting them into the country will be difficult."

"Teleportation?"

Von Klest shook his head, "*Nein.* Too strenuous on my part. Each time I teleport, it leaves me temporarily weakened. The farther the jump, the weaker I am afterwards. I could be incapacitated for days doing something like that. And, I'd only be able to teleport one or two men at a time. It'd be easier to fly them over. We'll pass them off as journalists. Tourists or businessmen going over during such a crisis would arouse suspicion. Besides, the Jews will be watching out for Arabs, not Aryans."

"I'll alert our contacts in Israel to be ready to assist us. When will we start flying our people over?"

"As soon as our forgers prepare the appropriate documents. No later than the day after tomorrow. When we-."

Von Klest's jaw dropped. He slammed his back against his chair. A murky, black glow suddenly filled the room and quickly dissipated.

The Darkling floated at the other end of the room. For some reason, Otto seemed oblivious to its presence.

"*The time has come!*" the Darkling boomed, its voice carrying a sense of urgency. "*A Protector has risen on this world.*"

Von Klest sat speechless.

"What is it, Erich? What's wrong?" Kemp turned around. All he saw was a small cabinet with the elegantly patterned wallpaper behind it. He turned back to von Klest. "What's wrong? Is it . . . is it that Devil thing? Do you see him?"

"Hurry! There is no time to lose! A Protector is most vulnerable after initial contact with its tru'kat."

Von Klest nodded. "Otto," he didn't even look at his mentor. "You must leave now."

"Erich, what is-?"

"Go now!" von Klest shot out of his chair, knocking it over. "Please."

Kemp was taken aback. Rarely did von Klest raise his voice to him. Whatever was going on, it must be very important to Erich. Without a word, he got up from the table and left the room. After closing the door, Kemp stood next to it. He could hear von Klest talking. Only von Klest.

Otto closed his eyes. *Erich. What have you gotten yourself into?*

"How the hell did this happen?" Remmler wondered as he examined the strange armor encasing him. His eyes then focused on the ground, amazed he could still stand on this slope. Remmler rocked his legs back and forth. He didn't know how, but his "feet" gave him the necessary traction to stand up.

What do I do now? I can't go back to Bubba and the others like this. They'll freak out. What about my family? What'll they think? What'll the world think?

My God! I've become a freak!

Suddenly, the hair on the back of Jack's neck stood on end. A sharp buzzing grew steadily louder in his ears. He raised his head, feeling as though he was not in control of his body. A blue-gold flash appeared on the trail above him.

"What the hell . . . ?" Jack watched in awe as the flash dissipated. Prickly ice stabbed at his insides. He took a couple steps back.

"Wha . . ." his voice cracked. "What the fuck!?"

On the trail above stood a menacing figure in black armor, carrying a big boomerang. The . . . thing wavered on its feet for a moment, then regained its composure. It lowered its head, the reddish-green eyeslit locked on Remmler. He gulped. His hand tighten around the staff.

"Give me the staff," it demanded in a booming, hollow voice.

Remmler wanted to yell, "Here, take it!" and throw it to him. But something deep within his subconscious told him not to. The word *evil* flashed through his mind like Chinese firecrackers.

"I said give it to me. Now!"

Jack stood his ground. He just knew he couldn't give the staff to this thing.

"If I have to come down there, I swear you will die. Now give me the staff!"

He couldn't explain it, but something overrode his fear. Remmler saw this thing—this loud, bullying thing—as an amalgam of all the terrorists, despots, murderers and rapists he had seen in the news over the years. Always hurting and threatening innocent people. Thinking they were better than everyone else.

Anger boiled in the pit of Remmler's stomach. It raced up his throat and burst out of his mouth in an authoritative, "NO!!"

The dark figure seemed taken aback. "I have been more than patient with you." It brought that big boomerang to bear and started toward Remmler, amazingly able to keep its balance on the slope. "I'll have that staff even if I have to rip off your arm to get it!"

Suddenly Remmler's body whirled completely around. One foot came off the ground. His perfect roundhouse kick slammed into the thing's mid-section. The dark figure landed hard on its rearend. It slid toward Remmler, but dug its fingers into the ground to stop itself.

Remmler just stared in amazement. *Did I do that?*

Imperium angrily glared at the red and white armored figure. He could not remember a time he felt more embarrassed. *I'm going to kill that bastard!*

The dark figure raised its weapon. Remmler watched as a green glow formed in the center of the boomerang. An instant later a beam of energy slammed into his chest. The world spun. Sky and ground merged. All oxygen was pushed out of Remmler's lungs in one big grunt as he slammed into the ground and began rolling. He heard the thing say something, but couldn't make it out before the ground vanished beneath him.

"Oh my God!" he screamed. A rush of wind filled his ears. *I'm gonna die. I'm gonna die.*

Images of Jack Remmler's family flashed before his eyes as he hit the shallow water and its rock covered bottom. The jolt rippled down his body. Two seconds later, Remmler took a long draw of air. That's when he realized . . .

"I'M ALIVE!!!" He immediately sat up. He felt no more pain than a person who had fallen out of bed would experience.

I should be dead. Remmler stared up at the cliff. *That had to be a forty, fifty foot drop. This armor must-*

"Oh shit!" he blurted. The thing appeared at the precipice, staring down at him.

Remmler looked down at his hands. The staff was gone. A sudden flash of panic cut off his breathing.

Oh shit! Where—? He quickly turned his head from left to right. There! Lying in the stream, about six feet away.

Remmler reached out for it. Suddenly, unaided, the staff zipped out of the water. He nearly withdrew his hand in shock, but kept it out until he caught it.

How in the hell—?

That's when he heard a big splash. He turned back to find the dark figure standing over him.

"Who are you!?!" Remmler's gut grew cold. "What do you want with me!?!"

The dark figure stood fully erect, its voice booming regally. "I am . . . Imperium! I have come for your staff—your *tru'kat.*"

Common sense told Remmler to throw this Imperium wacko the staff and run. But there it was again. That *something* in his subconscious, telling him not to relinquish the staff. Not to this creature.

His hand tightened around the staff. "No. You can't have it."

Von Klest was aghast. He had chosen his words carefully, hoping to instill the appropriate level of fear. This cretin should be cowering before him now. So many men had withered before his commanding voice. How could this one remain so defiant?

"Whelp! I am the most powerful being on this planet! You will . . . you *must* obey me!"

With cat-like reflexes that amazed him, Remmler sprang to his feet, ready for action. What fear he had was kept in check by a primal anger. Anger at this jackbooted thug from space who demanded Jack lick his boots.

"I said you're not getting this staff! Now fuck off!"

Imperium paused for a moment. Remmler thought he heard teeth grinding. "You . . . *insolent* . . . dog! I'll see you choke to death on your own blood."

In one motion, Imperium bounded over to Remmler, swinging his boomerang over his head. It whipped down at Jack's skull. He swept his staff up and barely blocked the blow.

Remmler felt control of his body slip away. Something else took over. Some instinct that allowed him to counter Imperium's attacks.

Imperium followed with a swipe to the side. Remmler jumped away from it. With one arm he lashed out with his staff's blade. Imperium blocked it. The dark figure dodged three more swipes before taking another swing. Remmler brought up his staff and blocked it. The two closed. Imperium rammed his left knee into Remmler's side. He wavered. Imperium brought his fist down on the side of Remmler's head. He thought a Mack Truck crashed into his skull. His vision blurred. It took a few moments for Remmler to realize he had fallen face first into the stream. Amazingly, he still held onto the *tru'kat.*

Imperium stood over the fallen Protector, Warblade raised over his head.

"Weakling half-breed. Now you'll know the price for defying me."

He brought the blade down on the Protector's back. There was an unearthly *clang* of metal on metal. Imperium pulled back his blade and-

"What!?! No!"

Von Klest stared in bitter amazement. Only a small dent showed between the Protector's shoulderblades where the Warblade had struck.

Imperium heard a thrashing of water. He looked down as the Protector rolled onto his back, wrapped both legs around his right calf, then pulled him off his feet.

Remmler untangled himself from Imperium and quickly got to his feet. The dark figure rose from the water. Remmler swung his staff like a golf club. The balled tip caught Imperium across the cheek, snapping his head around. The armor prevented his neck from being broken.

Remmler shook his head and blinked, trying to clear the fuzziness from his head. That gave Imperium all the opportunity he needed. Fingers bent, he rammed the heel of his palm under Remmler's barrel chest. He sailed twenty feet through the air before landing with a huge splash.

God! My head's splitting apart. Remmler slowly rose out of the water. Imperium leveled his boomerang to fire another blast. Despite the pain, Jack quickly brought up his staff. A bolt of green energy leapt from the boomerang. At the same moment a similar ray shot out the balled tip of Remmler's staff. It stopped five feet in front of him and expanded into a shield to block Imperium's beam. He fired two more times. Both shots were deflected by Remmler's shield.

Imperium leaped through the air toward Remmler. He leveled his staff and extended the shield's beam. It slammed into Imperium. The dark figure spiraled into the water.

Remmler took a few wobbly steps toward his opponent. *Gotta . . . stay on him.* He wished he could sit down for a moment to catch his breath. But another part of his mind drove him to continue the fight.

Imperium quickly got to his feet. Remmler brought his staff up and fired. Imperium erected his own energy shield to block the blast. Before Remmler could get off a second shot, Imperium jumped into the air. Remmler looked up as Imperium aimed his boomerang and fired. He roared as bright green exploded in his eyes.

"Son of a bitch!" His free hand immediately covered his visor. He didn't even know he had fallen on his back.

"Oh God! I'm blind!" Remmler closed his eyes tight. His fingers desperately tried to claw through the visor.

That's when it happened.

Remmler's consciousness grew out of his body and enveloped the surrounding area. All his senses; sight, hearing, touch, taste, smell, merged into one ultrasense. He became aware of everything. He heard dozens of birds; the chirping of each one sounded like it was in his ear. He sensed the vibration in the water of three crayfish scurrying to safety. Beneath the ground, earthworms burrowed deeper into the dirt . . .

. . . and Imperium dove toward him.

"Shit!" Remmler jumped forward just as the beam slammed into the ground. The concussion from the blast propelled him a few more feet across the stream.

It's time I ended this. Imperium landed at the stream's bank and stomped through the water toward the Protector. The armored fool was on all fours. Imperium fired another beam. The Protector collapsed into the water.

No more lasers. Imperium wanted to end this personally, with his bare hands. To peel away the layers of metal around the upstart bastard, punch through his chest and crush his heart like a rotten egg.

Imperium's foot exploded against his opponent's globular head. He rolled on his back.

"I'm going to take my time with you now." His foot came down against the Protector's chest. He gasped for air that would not come.

The Warblade rang out against the Protector's skull. Again and again. Imperium saw a few dents around that three triangle design on the forehead. The next blow came from his fist. The Protector just rolled from side to side and groaned.

Von Klest drilled his eyes into his enemy's barrel chest. Gripping the end handle with both hands, he lifted the dark *tru'kat* over his head.

"DIEEEEEE!!!!!"

Something thumped against his chest. Again and again. Remmler assumed it was his heart, probably pumping out buckets of adrenaline.

Now the thumping drove deeper into his chest. Vibrating throughout his body.

He tried to concentrate, fight through the pain, focus this supersense he had. Find out the source of this thumping.

It didn't take long.

Oh shit.

Imperium hammered away at the Protector's chest. How many times had he hit it? Ten? Twenty? He'd caused several dents and gashes, but still couldn't break through.

I will. I must!

He raised the blade for another strike.

"No," the Protector suddenly groaned. He rolled away, but not before the blade grazed his left arm. Caught off guard for a moment, Imperium leaped over his prey as it struggled to get up.

"Oh no you don't."

Still on the ground, the Protector did his best to bring his staff to bear on Imperium.

Now's my chance!

He reached down and enclosed a fist around the *tru'kat.*

Something snapped in Remmler's mind. This thing, this dark, *evil* thing, was touching his staff!

NO!

Remmler would never know where the strength came from. He quickly wrapped both hands around the staff and shoved it forward. The balled tip caught Imperium in the jaw. He loosened his grip on the staff. Remmler yanked it away. He hobbled to his feet as Imperium regained his composure. Remmler took a swing and missed by a foot. Imperium lashed out with a high kick to the head. Remmler landed on his back again.

He sensed Imperium approaching as he struggled back up. How much longer could this go on? Imperium was kicking his ass. Kicking his ass, hell. That maniac wanted to kill him! The thought chilled Remmler. Somebody actually wanted him dead. Him! Average guy Jack Remmler.

This is insane!

But his subconscious refused to let him yield the staff to Imperium.

Only one way to make sure he doesn't get it.

Remmler haphazardly brought up his staff and loosed several shots at Imperium. Two struck the dark figure in the torso, stunning him. The rest went wide. Remmler groaned and lifted himself off the ground. He ran three steps to his right and jumped. The water zipped by. He expected to come down any second . . . any second.

What the—? Oh my God! Am I flying?

Even though he was barely four feet in the air, the thought still unsettled him. He quickly planted his feet back in the stream. When he turned around, Imperium stood about thirty feet away, glaring at him.

Remmler didn't know where it came from. It just popped into his mind. Like everything else with this armor. He grabbed the staff with both hands as Imperium leaped out of the water and flew toward him.

Come on. Come on!

Von Klest's heart nearly stopped when he saw a blue-gold flash blot out the Protector's body.

"No! No!" He halted in mid-air, aimed his Warblade and fired. Too late. The blast went straight through the flash just as it dissipated.

Imperium threw his head back. "Dammit!" He came back down in the stream. A growl percolated in his throat. Moments later he released it, slamming the tip of his Warblade into the stream bed.

"Dammit," Von Klest clenched his fist and shook his head. "I had him. I had him beat!" He looked around the woods in frustration. "Where did you go, coward?"

A tingle suddenly swept over von Klest's body. He tried to fight the fear, but couldn't. He cursed himself for that. But when dealing with something like this . . .?

He turned around. Hovering above him was the devilish form of the Darkling.

"Fool! You have failed me!"

NINE

"HE WAS BEATEN!" the just returned Erich von Klest shouted at the Darkling inside his bedroom. "How could anyone continue after that kind of punishment?"

"You are dealing with a Protector. Did I not tell you their powers are similar to yours? Your arrogance cost me another tru'kat. *Denied me more power."*

"I would have-"

"Enough of your excuses, ephemeral sub-creature!" Von Klest felt the Darkling's words tear through his body. The maddened entity continued. *"I told you to end the battle quickly. You gave the neophyte Protector the time needed to completely bond with his* tru'kat."

"Then tell me where he is so I can finish the job."

"The time for me to do that has passed."

Von Klest clenched both his metal fists. His body shook with rage. "What are you talking about!? Your power-"

The Darkling cut him off. *"Puny microbe. You cannot begin to fathom the power I possess. Or the limited amount of intervention a being such as myself is allowed. Or the reasons why.*

"It is now up to you to find the new Protector and claim his tru'kat. *I have given you all the assistance I am able to."*

Then what the hell good are you? von Klest thought bitterly.

"Do not fear . . . Imperium. You will have other opportunities to defeat this new Protector. Meantime, continue with your schemes. Help my power to grow."

"I will," von Klest said through clenched teeth.

"Excellent."

The Darkling melted away, leaving von Klest alone in the room. He finally flashed out of his black armor and just stood in place. His eyes refused to focus on anything as the fury within him grew. He should have beaten that Protector. That last second barrage took him by surprise. Allowed the coward to teleport to who knows where.

Von Klest had to admit he never expected the Protector to put up such a fight. He would not make that mistake next time.

Jack Remmler felt his eyelids flutter. Something fuzzy and brown filled his sight. Where was he?

He tried to lift himself up. Good God, his muscles felt like lead. The adrenaline that surged through his body during the fight was gone. He wanted to fall asleep right now.

No. Can't. Not yet. Where am I?

Remmler sucked down a breath and forced his arms to work. He pushed himself off the ground, glimpsing the trunks of trees and a patch of dirt in front of him. The staff remained clutched in his right hand.

What happened? How did-?

Remmler froze when he saw a small pond about ten feet away. He surprised himself when his head snapped up, taking in the trees, the ascending dirt path in front of him. That bush. The protruding branch on that tree to his left.

Oh my God. This can't be.

Remmler got to one knee and gazed at the familiar woods that lay in back of his house. The woods he played in as a child. He stared at the tree he and his friends always used to climb on. The one he fell out of and broke his arm when he was ten. Then he glanced over at the shallow pond. The pond he pushed his sister into when he was seven.

Oh yeah. I really want to remember that *beating right now.*

He looked around some more. *How did I get here of all places? I . . . oh man. Was it some kind of teleportation? Like on* Star Trek? *Somehow I knew I could do that. But why did I come here?*

Maybe it was a subconscious thing. All I wanted to do was get away from Imperium. Go somewhere safe. What could be safer than home?

Imperium? Why was he so intent on killing him? Remmler shook uncontrollably, realizing how close he came to buying the farm.

Why did this happen to me?

His eyelids grew heavy. His strength faded. Remmler sank to the ground and started to doze off. Just a little rest and he'd be fine.

Remmler's eyes snapped open. The air in the center of the dirt path shimmered, then glowed blue and white.

Oh God! How did he find me here?

Remmler closed his eyes, his brain screaming at the rest of his body to move. He finally dragged himself to his feet, aiming his staff at the glow. *Just blast him with everything you've got.* Remmler doubted he had the strength for another brawl.

The glow quickly took form. However, this figure looked less threatening than the last one.

Surrounded by a soft milky aura, the being was covered in long, heavy white robes. A snowy beard cascaded down to his stomach, while equally long white hair fell to his shoulders. His skin was pale, albino-like. Amazingly, his face showed no wrinkles.

The eyes intrigued Remmler the most. He could not tell

what color they were, but the energy, the intelligence, *the power* behind them was unmistakable.

The being reminded Remmler of pictures of Father Time, or the drawings of ancient wizards on the covers of *Dungeons and Dragons* books.

The floating old man raised his left hand in a non-threatening manner. Remmler flinched. "Do not fear me, Jack Remmler." His voice was soft and deep, like that of a kindly old gentleman.

For some strange reason, Remmler *knew* he could trust him. He raised the staff over his head, then slid it behind his back. Three clamps running diagonally along his back snapped over the staff, securing it. He walked toward the apparition, his fatigue forgotten.

"Who are you?"

"I am known as the Keeper. I am overseer of all Cosmic Protectors."

"Cosmic Protectors?"

"The human translation for the assemblage you now belong to. I am sure you have many questions you wish answered, Jack Remmler."

He shrugged his shoulders. "Heh. What should I ask first?"

"Many who initially acquire the power of the *tru'kat* have the same dilemma. They are beset by so many questions they cannot decide which one is paramount. I have found, in most instances, it helps to start at the very beginning."

"Okay." *This is a dream, isn't it?*

"Very well. Do not be afraid. What you are about to see will exist only in your mind."

Remmler gasped as the path, the trees, the pond, the entire area, melted away. In its place a spectacular, black-blue canvas sprinkled with countless dots of light formed. Brilliant nebulas and gas clouds of shining colors—blues, reds, oranges—swirled around him. Planets, their atmospheres a blend of colors, passed by at incredible speeds. Remmler could actually feel himself flying through the spectacular void of space. He was no longer afraid. Why should he be? This was quite simply awe-inspiring.

"Using your measurements of time, 300,000 years ago, much of this galaxy was ravaged by the followers of evil. Warriors, barbarians, criminals. All sought to increase their power. Worlds fell. Entire civilizations were eradicated. Atrocities were committed on scales unimaginable. There were those who tried to stand against this tide of evil. Some succeeded. Most failed."

Wide-eyed, Jack Remmler watched as the events the Keeper described unfolded before him like some great cosmic documentary. He watched armadas of strangely designed spaceships battle one another across the great void. Armies swept across planets in an orgy of violence. The beings participating in these conflicts looked nothing close to human.

The Keeper continued, "At one point, when it appeared evil would consume the entire galaxy, a number of what you would call wizards, mystics and religious leaders gathered on a desolate planet on the fringes of the galaxy. For days, they convened, conjured spells, prayed, all in an effort to find a way to halt this conflagration.

"Finally, at one enormous ceremony, all 10,302 beings merged their life essences into a single entity." The Keeper's eyes locked on Remmler's. "I, Jack Remmler, am that entity.

"Because of my new form, the actions I could take on the physical plane were limited. Therefore, I created the *tru'kats*—the staff you presently wield. I dispatched tens of thousands to every corner of the galaxy, to seek out beings of the most noble souls and righteous beliefs. The *tru'kats* gave their wielders incredible powers; a protective suit of armor, enhanced strength, flight, energy projection, protection from psychic attack, enhanced senses. Those who accepted this power were dubbed Cosmic Protectors."

"But how did I know?" Remmler inquired. "I mean, what this . . . *tru'kat* could do? How could I fight the way I just did?"

"The *tru'kat* contains the life experiences of all those who have wielded it previously. However, all the *tru'kat* shall pass on to you is knowledge of its use and the accumulated fighting skills of all those before you. Their memories lie dormant within the *tru'kat*, and can only be accessed during the most critical of times. Were that not so, your mind would be flooded with the life experiences of 6,876 beings. You would go mad and die in moments if that happened."

Remmler's jaw dropped. *6,876 people . . . things . . . aliens, used this thing before me!?!*

"Alone and in groups, the Cosmic Protectors fought evil throughout the galaxy, defeating foe after foe. So successful were they that for a two thousand year period, much of the galaxy experienced relative peace.

"Then the Darkling came."

"The Darkling?"

"A foul creature of ancient origin. The Darkling is an entity that feeds off the evil and chaos that exists throughout the cosmos. It recruited agents to steal the *tru'kats* from several Protectors. After having them converted by magic users to serve evil, the Darkling's followers—known as the Dark Legion—began a new reign of terror throughout the galaxy. The Cosmic Protectors have fought them and their allies ever since."

"And now that battle's come here? To Earth?"

"Correct, Jack Remmler. There is a delicate balance in the universe between good and evil. No one force can ever be allowed to dominate the other. The Darkling, however, seeks to destroy that balance in order to feed its own insatiable need for power. That must never happen, otherwise all creation would unravel into chaos. Therefore, on worlds where the Great Balance is threatened, a Protector shall rise to ensure that balance is maintained."

And I'm supposed to be this Protector? a stunned Remmler thought. "And this Imperium . . . thing, is responsible for upsetting this balance?"

"He is but one reason. There are others."

Others? Who else—? "Iraq. It's Iraq, isn't it?"

"You will learn the answers in time."

Thanks a lot. Now it seemed the Keeper was really getting into the role of the mysterious, all-powerful cosmic entity he thought only existed in *Dr. Strange* comics.

Remmler shook in frustration. "I don't get it. You're asking me to be this . . . Cosmic Protector? Why? Why me? I'm just a college kid. I'm not even old enough to drink . . . legally. And I'm supposed to protect the world from Imperium and other scumbags? Why me? Why not a Green Beret or Jackie Chan or something?"

"Destiny sensed something special in you. Your desire for justice, for doing what is right. That is more meaningful than mere fighting skills."

That answered his question . . . somewhat. The Keeper was right in one aspect. All his life Remmler wanted to help people, to see things done right. He tried to do it in his own small way. Doing volunteer work through school organizations, voting, writing a letter to his congressman every now and then. But it never seemed enough. He wasn't cut out to be a cop or a soldier. Didn't have the make up to be a doctor or an EMT.

But something like this? Yeah, I always thought it would be cool to be a superhero. And now's my chance.

But do I really know what I'm getting into? I say yes to this and I just know I'll have to face Imperium again. That wacko really wants to kill me! I never even did anything to him.

What if I don't accept and he takes over the world or something? Could I live with that on my conscious? Could I stand by and let him hurt or kill my family, my friends?

And what if things get too tough again and I turn rabbit? Or he kills me!?

Come on, Jack. Like you really had a chance back there. You had to run. Next time, you won't.

Remmler took a deep breath. Looking back up at the Keeper, he stood as straight as possible, his tone more formal than at any time he could remember. "Yes. I will accept your offer, Keeper. I will become a Cosmic Protector."

"You are willing to accept the responsibility that comes with wielding the *tru'kat?*"

A brief pause. "Yes. I will."

"You realize that the task ahead of you will be most difficult."

Remmler raised an eyebrow. "No one ever said life was easy." *At least that's what Mom and Dad always say.*

He couldn't tell for sure, but he thought he saw a smile on the Keeper's aged face before he spoke. "You have much wisdom for one so young among your species. Another reason Destiny chose you to become a Protector.

"Very well. Jack Remmler, from this day forth, you are a Cosmic Protector and the 6,877th being to wield this *tru'kat.*"

"I'll do the best I can."

"I am confident you will. Take great care, Jack Remmler. Your planet is entering a perilous moment in its history. So perilous, a Cosmic Protector is needed to maintain the Great Balance again."

What!?! "'Again'!?! What do you mean 'again'? There was another Cosmic Protector on Earth before me?"

"You shall learn the answer to that when the time is right.

"Good luck in your struggle, Jack Remmler. Remember, evil must never be allowed to gain the upper hand. Never."

Seconds later, the Keeper, along with the starry backdrop he created, vanished. Remmler found himself back in the woods.

"I don't believe it. There was another Cosmic Protector here before me? When?"

6-RUST

Remmler shook his head. The question would have to keep for now. But he was definitely going to look into it. Right now he had more immediate concerns.

He looked around at the woods. *Now how the hell am I . . . of course.*

He reached behind him and grabbed his *tru'kat.* The clamps securing it unsnapped by themselves. Holding the staff in front of him, Remmler took a breath and closed his eyes. He sensed the glow wash over his body, which suddenly felt lighter than air, almost non-existent. Then everything went black. His stomach shot into his throat.

Oh God. Don't puke.

His legs swerved from side to side. Then, just as suddenly, the feeling stopped. Remmler opened his eyes. He was back on the Springfield Trail, and happily, past the slope.

"Man. That was weird." *Then again, bodies probably don't take kindly to being broken down into millions of molecules and reassembled somewhere else.* Sensing no one else nearby, he gripped the staff with both hands and again held it in front of him. Like everything else he had done with the *tru'kat,* all he had to do was think it, and it happened.

Once again, an off-yellow glow engulfed his body. When it subsided, the armor had vanished, replaced by Remmler's backpack and clothes, including his beat-up Phillies cap. He patted his clothing to make sure it was real and breathed a sigh of relief.

I wonder where they went while I was wearing that armor?

Remmler then felt something metallic in his hand. He looked down to find an oblong rod the size of a Swiss Army knife in his palm.

His eyes widened in amazement. *So this is what happens to the* tru'kat *when I'm not using it. I wonder how.*

A sudden thought struck Remmler. "Oh shit!" Bubba and the others! They were probably wondering where the hell he was?

How long did all this take? Remmler looked down at his watch, but it didn't help. He had no idea how long he had been tied up with Imperium and the Keeper.

Better haul ass. Bubba may already be organizing a search party.

"What the hell's taking him so long?" Brian Doyle asked no one in particular. He looked at his watch again. Thirty-five minutes had passed since he, Eric and Jim arrived at the old paper mill. Still no sign of Jack. "He shoulda been here by now."

"C'mon, Bubba," said Elling, sitting against his backpack. "Dude, quit worrying. He'll be here soon."

Doyle shook his head. "I knew I shouldn't've let him go off by himself."

"Brian. This is an idiot's trail. You'd have to be a total retard to get lost here. Remy's fine."

"Shit, man. What if he took a spill down that slope? What if—?"

"Yow guys!" Eric Bouden called out. "You can all quit your worrying. There he is."

Doyle and Elling looked toward the distant woods where Bouden pointed. Emerging from the thicket was Jack Remmler.

It took a nearly exhausted Remmler about five minutes to reach them.

"Good to see ya, man," Elling slapped him on the arm.

"Where the hell have you been?" Bubba asked.

More than anything, Remmler wanted to tell them the truth. That he had become an honest-to-goodness superhero. Him, their friend. Jack Remmler. A nineteen-year-old communications major from Lawrence, New Jersey. He had been chosen to protect the entire planet. And if they didn't believe him, he could just whip out his *tru'kat* and change into his armor.

But he couldn't.

Remmler had thought long and hard during the walk back whether or not to tell anyone. Would his friends, even his family, be able to cope with it? Could *anyone* be trusted with his secret. He knew he would be making some serious enemies; drug lords, organized crime syndicates, terrorist groups, maybe even dictators of countries. Men who would do anything to stop him, including come after his loved ones.

No way Jack could take that risk. His choice to become a Cosmic Protector had to remain a secret.

"I took a break or two along the way. I told you I'd be fine."

"Bubba was all worried about you, Remy," Elling said as he got to his feet and slung on his pack. "He was about to call out a search party for you."

"Up yours, Jim."

Had he not had so much on his mind, Remmler would have come up with one of his patented smart ass remarks. Instead, he just said, "Hey, no reason to worry. I said it'd be no problem."

"Well, now that we're all together," Bouden declared, "how about we finish this hike?"

Bubba agreed and the four students set off down the trail. They had over two miles to cover before they reached the end. Remmler wondered if he'd make it. Thank God tomorrow was Labor Day and he had the day off from school. He'd probably need the whole day to recover. Too bad he couldn't change into his armor and fly to the parking lot.

Remmler suddenly flashed back to the previous day, as they were all motoring down Baltimore Avenue in Doyle's station wagon. Bubba had joked to him, "Once you get a taste of the great outdoors, you'll be a whole new man."

Brian Doyle had no idea how right he was.

6-RUST

PART TWO

THE PREPARATION

TEN

NO ONE KNEW why von Klest had called the meeting. The announcement was just for all Iron Guardsmen to report to the auditorium at 0700. Nothing more. Speculation ran rampant. *Herr* von Klest rarely called all his Iron Guards together. Could it be a major exercise? An actual operation?

The ninety-eight men filed into the spacious, well light auditorium in one of the mansion's sub levels. There should have been a hundred, but Edward and Nils were reported "lost" on Baffin Island, along with von Klest's pilot. None of them knew that after dealing with Edward, Nils and the Inuit pilot, von Klest teleported back to Pond Inlet, "zapped" out of his armor and told the pilot to return to Uruguay without him. Then, as Imperium, he followed the jet out over Hudson Strait and sliced off the tail section with his Warblade. The Learjet plunged into the cold water, solving another potential security leak. None of the Iron Guardsmen talked about the missing men. They knew better.

"*Achtung!*"

The Iron Guardsmen came to attention as Otto Kemp, walked in through the side entrance and onto the small stage in front of them.

Seconds later, Erich von Klest entered. Like all the others, he sported the group's "formal dress;" beige tunics, brown ties, beige slacks, light brown dress shoes and tan headovers. A swastika armband on the right arm completed the ensamble.

"*Sieg Heil!*" the men shouted in unison. Their right hands shot out in the typical Nazi salute.

Von Klest returned the gesture. "Be seated."

The Guardsmen quickly filed into the rows of folding chairs. Von Klest walked over to the lectern. On each side of the stage stood a flagpole bearing the Nazi flag. A painting of *Der Fuhrer* with a Nazi banner in the background hung on the front wall.

For a moment, he just gazed out at the men. His elite troops. Representatives from nearly ten countries. All with prior military experience. Many from units like the Green Berets, the *Fallschirmjager* (German Airborne) and Dutch Marines. Some even had combat experience.

These were Erich von Klest's most trusted men. But could they be trusted with this awesome secret?

What choice did he have? Powerful as he was, he was only one man. He needed help rebuilding the *Reich*. He needed his Iron Guards.

"Gentlemen," von Klest began. "Recently, an event took place that has given m . . . us, the power to do what we have dreamed of our whole lives. Carry on the legacy of our forefather, the great Adolph Hitler, and build a new *Reich* from the ashes of the old."

Some of the Guardsmen exchanged curious glances as he continued.

"The circumstances by which I came across this power are . . . rather extraordinary. But the important thing is that we have this power. And we shall use it to cleanse this planet of *Juden*, mongrels and other undesirables."

Von Klest paused again, staring out at the Guardsmen. The expressions on many of their faces contained a mixture of doubt and curiosity.

"I see many of you don't believe me. Understandable. I could stand here for the next hour explaining everything and you still wouldn't believe me . . . unless I show you."

He reached into his pants pocket and produced a small, black metal rod. A chorus of "Hmms?" and "*Vas ist das?*" rose from the audience.

"What you are about to witness is something not of this world. Do not be panicked by what you see. Remember, this power belongs to the Aryan race."

Von Klest wrapped his fingers around the rod and held it in front of him. For a second, nothing happened. Suddenly, an off-yellow glow surrounded his hand and crept up his body. The room filled with murmurs of amazement, disbelief and fear. Several Guardsmen jumped out of their seats.

"What is it!?!"

"What's happening!?!"

"What's going on!?!"

"Quiet!" Kemp snapped. "Be seated!"

The Iron Guards watched in astonishment as the glow engulfed their leader's body. They averted their eyes when it became too intense. When they looked back, von Klest was encased in black armor.

The spacious room filled with stunned and fearful voices.

"Is this a trick?" said one German.

"What the hell is that?" an American blurted.

"Silence!" Imperium boomed, raising his hand for effect.

The Iron Guards meekly obeyed, too stunned to believe what they were seeing.

"This is the power I speak of. In this armor, I am invincible. No force on Earth can stand against us. With you, my

Eisen Garde, behind me, we shall be the vanguard in the birth of a new *Reich!* One that *will* last a thousand years!"

In regal fashion, Imperium spread his arms above his head. Moments later he rose off the stage and floated down the aisle. Jaws dropped and eyes went wide.

Once he reached the end of the aisle, Imperium ordered two men to take their metal folding chairs and place them at the far end of the room. He sliced the first one in half with his Warblade. The second chair was blown to scrap by an energy bolt. He then went over to the wall, turned to the Iron Guards without a word, and drove his fist through one of the cinderblocks. He withdrew his hand from the hole, dragging fragments of masonry with it. The *Eisen Garde* just looked on in awe.

Imperium looked back at his men. "I can do the same to tanks, buildings . . . *and people*."

He held up his Warblade and continued. "When I am in this armor, you will address me as 'Imperium.' No one outside this room must know of my secret. Anyone who I even *suspect* of betraying my secret will be executed immediately."

More than one adam's apple bobbed up and down from a nervous gulp. *Good.*

"Now that we have this power, no more hiding! No more inaction! No more endless planning and pretending we're accomplishing something. Now we will act! We've spent decades building up this organization. Stockpiling weapons, raising money, recruiting contacts, soldiers and spies. It is time we put all those resources to good use.

"We shall strike at the heart of our greatest enemy. We shall go to Jerusalem and destroy the entire Jew government. The Knesset, the Prime Minister, the cabinet. Everyone!

"Who will stand with me?"

A dead silence hung over the room for several seconds. Finally, one of the Guardsmen cleared his throat, threw out his right arm and bellowed, "*Sieg Heil!*"

Others quickly followed. Soon, the entire room reverberated with shouts of "*Sieg Heil!*" Imperium nodded with satisfaction. First and foremost, he had chosen the Iron Guards for their unwavering loyalty to him. Despite all the unbelievable things they had just seen, that loyalty remained.

The Iron Guards continued their "*Sieg Heils,*" interspersed with shouts of "Death to the *Juden!*"

Von Klest smiled under his faceplate. The new Aryan Revolution was firmly underway.

Can't believe how quiet it is here.

Jack Remmler stopped along the banks of Cobbs Creek and gazed at the scenery. Several small Nannyberry trees ran along the water's edge. A few yards away was a white wooden bench facing the creek. Delaware County lay on the other side. Gray-white sprinkles, tombstones, broke up the lush green of Fernwood Cemetery. In front of it, cars darted back and forth along Briarcliff Road. To his left, a pair of Silver Maple trees obstructed the Alpha Xi Delta sorority's old, red brick house. The only thing missing from this scene were students. Almost everyone had gone home for Labor Day. That suited Jack fine. He needed time to himself, to think, to comprehend everything that had happened to him . . . and what *might* happen to him.

Remmler did not have time to seriously think about all this the day before. Tired to begin with, the moment he and the others got back to Keystone, they unpacked, showered and watched the Eagles-Redskins game. Jack barely stayed awake. After the game ended, with the Eagles victorious 33-6, Doyle went off with Jim and Eric, leaving him to get some rest. Remmler fell asleep minutes later, too tired to change out of his clothes. When he awoke and looked at his alarm clock, it read 10:16 a.m.

Brian was nowhere in sight. Jack didn't know if he ever came back to the room during the night.

After putting on fresh clothes and going to the bathroom, Remmler headed out of the red brick, white roofed Driscoll Hall, a co-ed dormitory built in the 1950s.

Okay. I got this power. Now what do I do with it?

Initially, he thought it would be no problem. Just 'zap' into the armor, fly around Philly and stomp on some bad guys. But the more he thought about it, the more problems seemed to crop up.

What exactly should he do with the criminals he caught? Tie them up and leave them for the police like in the comic books? Should he kill them? Even though he was pro-death penalty, Remmler wondered if he could actually take another life. Even that of some lowlife scumwad. *That's the difference between us and them. We actually think about what killing another person means. They couldn't care less.*

Jack decided to play it safe and kill only as a last resort. *I doubt the cops would appreciate someone leaving a pile of dead bodies all over the city, criminal or otherwise.*

And what about the police? They had never been known for their fondness of vigilantes. How would they react once he began his personal war on crime? Would they hunt him down? So what if they did? What could the police do to him? Arrest him? Unless they started packing howitzers, the cops had nothing that could harm him. But Remmler's beef wasn't with them. He had always been a big supporter of law enforcement. Hell, his Aunt Greta was a sergeant in the Mercer County Sheriff's Department and his cousin, Michael, was a cop in Cherry Hill. Jack couldn't imagine raising his fist to a police officer. But what if—?

Hell with it. I'll cross that bridge when I come to it. Besides, it wasn't the cops' fault crime had gotten out of hand in Philadelphia, along with the rest of the country. It was the damn legal system. Always handing down sentences way too lenient. Hardened criminals were constantly in and out of prison. The road to the lethal squirt was detoured by endless appeals and stays of execution. Then there were the politicians who would rather use money to fund useless, feel-good social programs than build more prisons or hire more cops. Even many parents were at fault. The ones who didn't punish their kids when they did something wrong, and the ones that just didn't give a shit about them.

First things first. I gotta test out these powers. Getting in better shape ain't such a bad idea either. While the armor enhanced his strength, it did little to improve his physical endurance. That had to change. He had to last longer in fights, especially if they were with Imperium.

Imperium. Just who the hell is he? Where does he come from?

Jack didn't know if it was funny or insane, but part of him wanted a rematch with that son of a bitch. Before, he would have gone out of his way to make sure he wasn't in the same time zone with someone like Imperium.

Maybe I should keep it that way. That maniac nearly killed me!

But the idea that the fight ended with him teleporting away didn't sit well with Remmler. Calling it "a strategic withdrawal" instead of "running scared" didn't help any. If he was supposed to be a Cosmic Protector, he couldn't run away from every fight that got too tough.

Remmler felt his stomach tighten. He realized he had not eaten since last evening. Well, a quick trip to the nearby 7-11 would remedy that. Then the real work would begin.

ELEVEN

General Faisal Nurabi wiped the condensation from the bathroom mirror and stared at a tired old face. The head of Al Mukhabaret suffered from too much work and too little sleep since that damn Russian's laser went up like a nuclear bomb. His puffy face drooped. Bags formed under his eyes. New gray appeared in his receding hair. He hoped a shower might rejuvenate him, but it didn't. Only sleep could do that, and Nurabi doubted he would get much until this crisis ended.

If I'm still around at the end.

Nurabi wiped the water from his mustache with his bare hand, then dried off his bulbous body. Slipping into his pajamas, the General waddled out of his private bathroom into the small bedroom. Like the rest of the little one-floor house nestled in the hills outside Baghdad, the bedroom was simple and barely decorated. No windows were present. They only provided potential assassins a good view. Not the trappings General Nurabi was used to, but this was only a safehouse. One of several he used in times of danger, which in Iraq seemed all the time. It was a lesson he learned from Saddam Hussein. Always spend the night in different places. Make it harder for your enemies to find you. Even if any of those "enemies" should find him, they would have to deal with his eight bodyguards, four outside the house and four inside. All superbly trained. And Nurabi himself wasn't defenseless. He kept a loaded 7.62mm Tokarev automatic pistol tucked under his pillow. In the closet was an AK-47.

Nurabi turned off the lights and settled into bed. He would allow himself four hours of sleep before returning to Al Mukhabaret headquarters.

As he closed his eyes, the General tried to think of his wife or one of his three mistresses. But the only thoughts that ruled his mind were of work.

All reports showed no let up in the build up of forces arrayed against Iraq. The *Kitty Hawk* battle group steamed off the coast of the United Arab Emirates, while the *Eisenhower* group sat outside the Gulf of Oman. Still a third carrier group had transited the Suez Canal into the Red Sea, this one centered around the *John F. Kennedy.* Behind them sailed a NATO task force made up of fifteen ships, led by the British carrier *Illustrious.*

On the ground, the American 24th Mechanized Division, using pre-positioned equipment, and a recently landed Marine Expeditionary Brigade had reinforced the armies of the Gulf nations. Protecting them was an umbrella of over six hundred ground-based combat aircraft.

But the Arabian Peninsula wasn't the only direction the Iraqis faced a threat. To the east, the Iranians had five army divisions along the border. To the west, Syria had close to 90,000 troops on its border with Iraq. Israel was more likely than ever to launch an air strike against Iraq, this time perhaps with nuclear weapons. To the north, the entire Turkish 2nd Army was on alert along the border. All the while the United Nations demanded Iraq turn over all materials from their nuclear weapons program to inspection teams—this time accompanied by armed U.N. escorts.

Iraq's forces were stretched beyond their limit. Allah knows the Kurds in the north and the Shi'ites in the south would probably take advantage of this.

All thanks to Drovinov and his damned laser.

Nurabi wondered what could have possessed the President to want such a device. The power expenditures were incredible, along with the price tag for the prototype alone. And how was Iraq supposed to come up with the intricate system of mirrors needed to direct the beams?

It had been a huge waste of time. All Iraq had to show for it was a big hole in the middle of the desert and a world that feared they were a nuclear power.

We never should have undertaken an operation to smuggle that fool and his damn U-500 out of Russia. All the resources, the money and risks it took to get him to Iraq. All wasted!

Nurabi's country had painted itself into a corner with no possible way out. They couldn't tell the truth about what caused the explosion. Then it would only be a matter of time before the world found out about Drovinov's special uranium that was undoubtedly responsible for the blast. What if they wanted to smuggle another load out to use in a much more responsible way? America and its lapdog allies would certainly take action to make sure such a thing could never happen. They couldn't lie their way out of it either. What could Baghdad say? That it *was* a nuclear bomb? That would be as bad as telling the truth.

We should have put all that effort into building real *nuclear bombs. At least then we'd have a chance against the Americans and their lackeys.*

Curse you to eternal hell, Yuri Drovinov! Your damn laser, your damn super uranium, will be the doom of my country.

The only good thing to come out of this was the fact Drovinov had been reduced to radioactive dust. The same with Colonel Fahmil and Dr. Siana. That made them convenient scapegoats, saving Nurabi's neck. For now.

On top of everything else, he still had no idea what happened to the survey team at the crater. Their bodies—what was left of them—were charred to the bone. The helicopter had been blown into a thousand pieces. Shell casings scattered throughout the area proved they had fought someone. But who, or what, was responsible?

Probably something to do with that U-500.

Minutes later the Al Mukhabaret chief fell asleep. His last thought before drifting off was that he would never get the chance to see Yuri Drovinov . . . and personally choke the life out of that miserable bastard.

Hasim Barhquem tightened his khaki jacket around him, trying to fend off the cold of the desert night. Like many Iraqi servicemen, Barhquem suffered from lack of sleep. He constantly stamped his feet and walked up and down the side of the house. Anything to stay awake.

Bored, Barhquem decided to scan the area with his Russian-made 7x30mm binoculars. He started his sweep to the west, in the direction of Baghdad. Normally he would have seen a myriad of lights that illuminated Iraq's capital. But with the threat of war, Baghdad was under blackout conditions. His country learned the hard way in 1991 how American bombers owned the night.

Barhquem looked eastward. The binoculars' low-light capability provided him a clear view of the hilly landscape around the safehouse. Convinced there was nothing around, he turned his glasses skyward, scanning for enemy aircraft. It also gave him the chance to do a little stargazing to relieve some of the boredom. Despite some overcast, there were a fair number of stars visible. In fact, Barhquem thought he could make out-

Suddenly a shadow flew across the sky in front of him. A

soft whistling sound accompanied it. Barhquem dropped his binoculars in surprise.

What was that? He frantically searched the night sky again. Nothing. His senses peaked, hoping to pick up the slightest smell, sound or sight that was out of place. At the same time, Barhquem unzipped his jacket. He reached for the small Czech-made Skorpion submachine gun in his shoulder rig.

"Watch Three, Watch Two. Come in."

The sudden burst from his walkie-talkie startled Barhquem.

"Watch Three, this is Watch Two. Do you read? Over."

Barhquem reached for the walkie-talkie attached to his belt. The last thing he heard was a loud crackling before the flesh exploded from his skeleton.

Hovering above Nurabi's safehouse, Yuri Drovinov easily disposed of the remaining three guards. They never even saw him. The black energy field surrounding his body provided the perfect camouflage against the night sky.

Drovinov hovered around the house until he found the front door. He landed six feet from it. Raising his arm, Drovinov blasted the door into splinters and walked through. Startled voices echoed throughout the house. Drovinov quickly scanned the interior. Two Al Mukhabaret guards jumped behind a couch for cover. Another ran out of the small kitchen into the living room. A fourth knelt in front of him in the hallway. He managed to get off three rounds before Drovinov unleashed his power.

General Nurabi suddenly woke out of a sound sleep and sat bolt upright in bed. He heard the chatter of small arms fire, screams and a strange crackling sound.

By Allah! Somebody's attacking!

Nurabi shook off his momentary panic. He knocked the other pillow off the bed, grabbed the Tokarev that lay beneath it and bolted to the door. He stood against the frame, put his hand on the doorknob and took two deep breaths. Nurabi threw the door open and dropped to one knee, gun extended. The hall light suddenly came on. The sudden change from dark to light momentarily disoriented Nurabi. He blinked quickly until his eyes adjusted. An acrid smell wafted into his nostrils. He looked down and recoiled in shock. The charred skeleton of one of his bodyguards lay scant feet away. Then he noticed the figure standing at the end of the hall. Nurabi's mouth and eyes widened as he focused on the . . . man?, whose body was enveloped by some dark glow.

"Allah have mercy," the General whispered.

The figure took a step toward Nurabi. The General screamed and pulled the trigger until his Tokarev clicked empty. He barely noticed the sparks flickering around the silhouette.

It kept coming.

"No," Nurabi whispered in disbelief. "No." The gun fell from his hand. He shot to his feet and pressed his back against the door frame. Fear prevented him from doing anything else.

"Who . . . what . . . who are you?" Nurabi couldn't keep his voice from trembling.

The pulsating figure stopped a few feet from him and leaned closer. "Yes. I doubt you would recognize me now."

Its voice was deep, like an echo. Nurabi looked closer, peering past the crackling black energy that surrounded its body. *Allah be merciful!*

"D-Drovinov?"

"Congratulations, General Nurabi. I can see the President made a wise choice putting you in charge of the Al Mukhabaret. You are so incredibly perceptive."

"But . . . but how? How did you survive?"

Drovinov pointed to the bedroom. "You'd better make yourself comfortable, General. We have much to talk about."

Nurabi sat on the edge of his bed and listened in amazement as Drovinov related his story about the explosion, his awakening and the massacre of the Iraqi unit investigating the crater. After that he had flown back to his house near Karbala to gather equipment and took refuge in the abandoned test site of Iraq's famed supergun. There he conducted experiments to learn about his new power.

"I can fly. At least up to Mach Two by my estimations. I have been able to reach an altitude of ninety miles without feeling the affects from cold or lack of oxygen. I can project energy blasts powerful enough to create a crater ten meters wide and six meters deep. And this aura protects me from all physical harm. If I concentrate hard enough, I can retract the field enough to allow myself to pick up items without having them atomized on contact.

"Also, it appears the energy field sustains my physical being. I need no food, water or sleep. And it would appear I need very little oxygen to survive. It is possible I do not need *any* oxygen at all."

Nurabi shook his head in disbelief. "It is all so . . . incredible. But how did you survive? The blast was over five megatons."

"I don't know!" Drovinov stomped to the other side of the room. "I was right *at* ground zero. By all physical laws, I should have ceased to exist. But I didn't and I have no explanation why. I can only theorize that it has something to do with my Uranium-500. There is still much I do not know about it. This did not happen to anyone else, did it?"

"As far as we know, no. If it had, I'm sure we would be aware of it by now."

"Mm, you're right. Most people would probably be anxious to use a power like this right away. We must assume, then, that I am the only one who survived the blast."

"But how?"

"Perhaps," Drovinov paused before continuing. "Perhaps

the fact I was in the center of the blast had something to do with it. Given the unusual nature of my U-500, it might have created some kind of energy pocket in the core of the blast that allowed me to survive, and absorb the energy.

"Still, all this is conjecture. It is quite possible I may never know what exactly happened to me." The Russian moved closer to Nurabi. "But the fact remains, I have this power.

"So, General. What shall we do about it?"

"Why ask me?"

Drovinov's voice had a decided edge, as if Nurabi should already know the answer. "Because you are head of Al Mukhabaret. You were responsible for getting me into Iraq in the first place. With Colonel Fahmil dead, you were the next logical person to make contact with."

A thought suddenly struck Nurabi. "But how did you find me? This is one of my most secluded safehouses."

Drovinov chuckled. "Oh please. With my ability to fly, and a pair of good binoculars, it was easy to monitor your headquarters until you showed up. It was even easier following you when you left. But enough spy stories. It is time we figure out how to take advantage of the opportunity we've been given."

"Opportunity?"

"Think, man! You hired me to build a laser weapon for your country. That effort is now circling the globe as so much radioactive fallout. But that failure has spawned an unimagined and perhaps fortunate result. The explosion has given me powers undreamed of by mankind. Powers that set me above all other men. Powers I am willing to offer the government of Iraq."

Nurabi stood up. "You are?"

"Why not? You contracted me to make your country a power to be reckoned with. I am merely keeping my part of the bargain, albeit in a different way. And given your current situation, I'd say you need my help."

"Then you know of our current crisis."

"I listened to the radio from time to time during my seclusion. If I correctly read between the lines of propaganda, I gather your situation is . . . desperate."

General Nurabi nodded and briefly spelled out the threats Iraq faced.

"In that case, I don't see how you cannot accept my offer."

"I will need to talk to the Revolutionary Command Council. I am sure they will accept your help. They have to if we are to have any chance against the Americans." Nurabi paused. His eyes narrowed and his posture straightened.

"Besides. You owe us."

Drovinov sounded shocked. "I . . . owe . . . you?"

Nurabi swallowed, trying to maintain his composure. "It was your invention that caused the explosion, that united the world against us. You are responsible for this problem. You rectify it."

Drovinov stood silent for several seconds. Nurabi tried unsuccessfully to determine his reaction. He feared his forceful tone angered the energized Russian, who could easily blast him to dust to satisfy that anger.

All Drovinov did was laugh. "My dear comrade, I will certainly rectify this situation. And in the process, I will make your country the undisputed power in this region. Perhaps even the world."

Nurabi's old, tired face brightened. Could Drovinov actually make good on his promise? How could he not? He had seen what the Russian's power could do. The Americans had *nothing* to counter it. With Drovinov's help, Iraq would redefine the term "superpower."

"I must call the Council and arrange a meeting immediately."

General Nurabi headed to his secure phone in the living room when Drovinov stopped him.

"Oh General."

Nurabi halted. "Yes?"

"Be sure to tell your Council I will require an increase in my fee. A . . . substantial . . . increase."

TWELVE

Oh God! I'm gonna die! I'm gonna die!

An invisible vice threatened to crush Jack Remmler's lungs. His legs were tight beyond belief. Perspiration drenched his sweatband, as well as his entire body. He'd have to jump in the shower before his Scriptwriting class. Luckily that wasn't for another hour. Plenty of time.

If he didn't collapse and die of a heart attack first.

Spotting a bench nearby, Remmler hobbled over to it and plopped down. He spent the next few minutes replenishing his lungs with oxygen.

"Now I know . . . why I never took up jogging," he mumbled. "This sucks! I bet . . . Superman . . . never has to do this shit."

This was the second day of Remmler's exercise program. He took things relatively easy the first, sticking to push-ups, sit-ups and Doyle's dumbbells. Today he decided to work on his endurance. Although not fond of jogging—he had yet to see a jogger smile—Remmler decided to give it a try. About thirty seconds after setting out from his dorm, he realized it had been a bad idea.

Just one circuit around the rolling lawn in the center of the campus known as Keystone Commons. That's all. Remmler made it three-quarters of the way. He wondered if he had the strength to make it back to Driscoll Hall.

Some superhero I'm turning out to be.

Remmler lazily rolled his head to the right. He noticed two other joggers—both female—in the distance. He leaned forward, squinting for a better look. Remmler thought he recognized one of the runners. Curled, puffy hair. A slender body...

Oh my God! Cheryl!

Forgetting his tiredness, Remmler sprang off the bench. *Can't let her see me like this.*

He began stretching, hoping to look more like a serious runner. It wasn't long before he heard Cheryl call out. Remmler stopped and waved to her.

"What, praytell, are you doing, Mr. Remmler?" Cheryl asked after she and her partner crossed the drive to join him.

"What does it look like? I'm jogging."

"You? Jog? I thought you always said jogging was for morons."

"Hey, guy's got a right to change his mind. Besides, that hiking trip I went on with Bubba, I found out just how out of shape I was."

"Well, it's good to see you're doing something about it."

Remmler nodded to the other girl. She was about an inch shorter than Cheryl, with short, close-cropped black hair, a small waist and a slender yet athletic figure. Not bad looking at all. "Who's your friend?"

"Oh God, I'm sorry. Jack, this is Audrie Davis. Audrie, Jack Remmler."

The two shook hands. Then Audrie said, "Don't you write sports for the paper?"

Remmler's face lit up. "Yeah. Yeah, I do. You've read my stuff?"

"Some. You did all those stories on the Women's Track team last year."

"Yeah," he nodded. "That was me."

"They were really good. Hell, most people around here don't even care about the track team."

"Thanks. But hey, you guys did good yourselves. You made it to the Division Two finals."

"You know, Jack also does a radio show."

"Really?"

"Yeah," he replied. "Mondays from four to six. I do a lot of classic rock. Some sports talk.

"So what brings you out jogging?"

"Just getting in shape for soccer." Cheryl grabbed hold of her right leg and stretched it behind her back. "Our first game is next week against Bryn Mawr. Say, you wanna join us?"

Yeah, and look like a wimp in front of you when I collapse from exhaustion. I don't think so. "Thanks, but I'm almost finished. Besides, I got class soon."

"Oh, okay. Maybe some other time."

"Yeah, sure." Remmler was already planning an excuse for that day.

After saying their good-byes, Remmler jogged off toward his dorm. He stopped running as soon as the girls were out of sight.

"Uhhhh." He bent over, resting his hands on his knees. As soon as he got back to the dorm he would head right for the showers. Hopefully that would rejuvenate him. Remmler needed to be up for tonight.

"Nice guy," Audrie commented as she and Cheryl stretched their legs on the bench.

"Jack? Yeah, he's great. Probably one of the last true boy scouts around."

"Cute butt, too."

Cheryl stopped her stretching and stared in surprise at her friend. "Audrie!"

She looked back at Cheryl with equal surprise. "What?"

"You already have a boyfriend."

"So? Doesn't mean I can't look. Oh come on, don't tell me you don't think he's cute."

Cheryl could feel herself blush. "Well . . . I . . . yeah. I mean, of course he's . . . Yeah, I think Remy's cute."

"So you two . . ." Audrie nodded off in Jack's direction, wiggling her eyebrows, "you know?"

Cheryl quickly shook her head. "Nooo, no, no, no. We're just good friends. That's all."

"But you must've thought about it?"

Cheryl stood silent for several seconds. *Jeez, can you drop it, please.*

Still she answered her "Well, sometimes I've wondered what it would be like. He was interested last year. But . . . but I think we're just comfortable being friends. Getting romantic will probably ruin it."

Audrie shrugged. "Oh well, there's plenty of other guys out there. C'mon. Let's get going."

The two set off to complete their run. Cheryl glanced back in the direction Jack had jogged off in. She shook her head.

No. We're just friends. Period.

Ben-Gurion International Airport, located halfway between Jerusalem and Tel Aviv, was not as crowded as one would expect. But given the fact war could break out at any moment, a war that could involve nuclear weapons, it seemed only natural that tourists stayed away. Still there were enough travelers to keep things busy: Religious pilgrims, returning and departing Israelis and tourists who figured they had stayed long enough.

A group of about three hundred were neither arriving or departing. They consisted of Israeli Defense Force soldiers assigned to keep Ben-Gurion safe from terrorist attacks.

It was hard not to notice the soldiers walking around the terminals in pairs. Decked out in their olive-drab uniforms with flak vests and webbing covering their torsos, each soldier carried enough hardware to take care of any threat that might pop up. Their main weapon was either a Galil Assault Rifle or the famous Uzi submachine gun, slung over their shoulders and dangling by their side for easy reach. Stuck in their webbing were eight grenades ranging from fragmentation to flash-bang to smoke. A combat knife also hung within easy reach.

More soldiers patrolled outside. Sandbag positions sat atop the terminals and control tower. Behind them crouched soldiers with machine guns and Stinger shoulder-launched antiaircraft missiles. Ramta RBY armored recon vehicles, similar to the U.S. Humvee, patrolled the airport perimeter. Each one sported a 7.62mm machine gun and a TOW missile launcher.

The Israelis looked ready to fend off some great siege. A fact not lost on the two new arrivals. While calm on the outside, inside they were a bundle of nerves. At every turn they saw a heavily armed Israeli soldier. Was he staring at them? Scrutinizing them? Questioning their presence? The two knew it was just paranoia, but in this business, a healthy dose of paranoia kept you alive.

The pair cleared the gate without incident. A search of their carry-on bags by airport security and a walk through the metal detector turned up nothing. They proceeded to baggage claim to retrieve their luggage, which security also searched.

Only one more obstacle remained.

"Passports please," the tanned, plain-faced customs official with her hair in a bun stated.

Both men handed over their documents. This part always made them nervous. Was the work good enough?

The customs woman scanned both passports for what seemed an eternity. The younger of the two looked down one end of the terminal to the other in the exaggerated fashion of an impatient tourist. Two soldiers chatted away near a lounge to his left. He looked back at the woman. If she-

The customs official looked up. "Anything to declare?"

Both men shook their heads and replied, "No."

"What is the purpose of your visit to Israel?"

"Business," the younger man replied in perfect English. "We're with the Associated Press, here to cover this . . . um, situation."

"Where will you be going in Israel?"

"Wherever my editor tells me to go," he replied, sounding a little flippant. The tone of his next response was more serious. "Most likely we will be shuttling between Jerusalem and Tel Aviv."

"And where will you be staying?"

"The Laromme in Jerusalem."

"Is this your first time in Israel?"

Both men answered "yes."

It took a few more questions before the customs official seemed satisfied. She stamped their passports and handed them back.

"Welcome to Israel," the woman said with the barest hint of a smile. "Enjoy your stay."

The two men thanked her and headed off. Ten minutes later they boarded a bus in front of Ben-Gurion Airport that would take them to Jerusalem.

Once seated, Erich von Klest and Otto Kemp exchanged smiles. They made it inside Israel without any problems. Now, if everything else could go as smoothly.

THIRTEEN

DESPITE THE CONTROLLED temperature of his armor, sweat covered Jack Remmler's forehead. His breaths came in quick, nervous gulps. Taking hold of his duckbilled visor, he slid it back over his head and slowly breathed in the warm night air. It didn't help his anxiety at all.

I never realized I was this hung up about heights.

Standing on the roof of Driscoll Hall against the square, red brick entrance topped by a white, sloped roof, Remmler stared up into the endless night. An irrational fear of being sucked up into that vast darkness swept over him. Remmler shivered and cast his gaze across the panoramic vista of the campus.

The view from Driscoll Hall's roof made it one of the more popular hang outs on campus. Turning around, Remmler could see the conglomeration of dorms around the student parking lot, their sides an uneven patchwork of lighted windows. To the left was the all-male Sieford Hall, where many upperclassmen and athletes lived. The gray, gothic-looking Becker Hall, the all-female dorm, stood directly across from it. On the other side of the parking lot sat Oakdale Hall, the rectangular, featureless co-ed dormitory.

Remmler looked the other way. The trees merged into one huge, dark puffy mass that threatened to swallow the other buildings on campus. Keystone Commons stuck out as a clear patch among the blackness. The half-moon's glow reflected off the water of the small pond in the center of the clearing. Beyond the campus he could see the lights and buildings along Cobbs Creek Parkway and Baltimore Avenue.

Most times people came up here for reasons other than the view. The roof was a notorious make-out spot. Of course though things usually went farther than that. Every so often, someone had to throw a "Roof Party." School officials tried to discourage it, citing the danger of someone falling off the roof. Remmler shook his head. A three-and-a-half foot rampart surrounded the flat part. Atop that was a connecting row of squat white marble columns. That made it tough for someone to take an accidental spill over the side. Still it had happened. The last time in 1991, when a sophomore boy fell to his death during a Roof Party. Remmler heard the idiot got absolutely trashed and did his own high wire act on the rampart when he fell. Because of that, school officials closed off the roof for two years.

Remmler shook the frivolous thoughts away. He had serious work to do . . . if he could get over this hitherto phobia of heights.

He stared back at the vast night sky. Until now he had just teleported to and from his training sites, usually deserted fields in the South Jersey Pines. Strangely enough, having his molecules rearranged and put back together somewhere else didn't bother him as much as flying. Aside from the momentary dizziness and disorientation, he felt no other ill effects.

But flying. Suspended high in the air. All alone. What if he fell? Sure, his armor saved him from that drop off the cliff along Springfield Trail. But that had only been a few dozen feet. Could it survive a fall of a few *thousand* feet?

Some superhero I'm turning out to be. Afraid of flying. I bet this never happens to the Human Torch.

Come on, Jack. Just close your eyes and go.

He pulled down his visor and shut his eyes. Immediately his "unisense" took over. Every detail of the surrounding landscape—from the smallest anthill to the tallest building—was laid out before him. He still couldn't get used to the feeling. The image seemed to be in his mind, yet outside it at the same time. His enhanced hearing picked up every conversation in the nearby dorms, any one of which could be singled out with a little concentration.

"I think I got the chapter on product distribution down."

That was Neil Kendall over in Sieford Hall.

"No way, man! Mets are takin' the East this year."

Freddie Sanchez in Oakdale Hall.

"Oh Pete . . . ooooh."

Whoops! Sounded like Janet Quinlinn in Becker Hall, "entertaining" her boyfriend.

Knock it off, Remy. The Keeper didn't give you these powers to become a super peeping tom.

After blessing himself, Remmler raised the *tru'kat* above his head. A invisible force grabbed him and yanked him into the night.

Please, God. Don't let me fall.

Jack climbed higher and higher. Fifty feet. Seventy feet. One hundred feet. He had no instrumentation to inform him how high he was going. He just knew. Remmler even knew his speed. Thirty-five miles per hour. Now forty . . . forty-five.

This ain't so bad. In fact, it's . . . it's . . .

Remmler couldn't find the right words. His fear quickly melted away. Up here he felt so . . . unrestricted. Free. The sky embraced Jack Remmler, and he returned that embrace. Did birds experience this kind of feeling? he wondered.

His body loosened. He brought his arms to his sides and corkscrewed. His altitude and speed increased.

"YEEE-HAW!!!"

Remmler leveled out at 18,300 feet exactly. He didn't care about the height. That didn't bother him. Nothing up here did anymore.

And to think, five minutes ago I was afraid of this.

Jack finally opened his eyes and looked down without fear. A huge smile broke out on his face. "This is beautiful."

He abandoned his unisense, even his night vision. Despite the clouds around him, Remmler had a spectacular view of the multitude of lights that blazed across the length and breath of Philadelphia. He noticed several blinking lights in the air far away from him. Had to be airplanes from Philly International. To his left, a dark, squiggly line broke up the sea of lights. The Delaware River. On the other side lay the city of Camden.

Remmler never realized he spent ten minutes taking in the grandeur of the two states. But he did notice he didn't suffer any side affects inherent in flying; ears popping, g-forces, loss of blood to the head. Another miracle of the armor.

"Okay, Remy. Time to see what this mother's got under the hood."

He closed his eyes, turned east and streaked off. Within minutes he had flown over Camden, Mt. Laurel and Medford on his way to the Atlantic Ocean. His speed rapidly increased. Two-hundred miles per hour. Three-hundred. Four-hundred. At no time did he feel uncomfortable traveling at such high speeds. Thanks to his unisense, he stayed out of the paths of other aircraft. He was also constantly aware of his location, as if he had an internal—what did the technothrillers call it? Oh yeah—Global Positioning System. By the time he reached Barnagat Bay, Remmler passed Mach One. He left behind a trail of sonic booms as he flew out over the Atlantic Ocean. His senses picked up hundreds of marine animals, from shrimp to bluefish to seals. There was a ship nearby too. Not very big. His unisense made out the "U.S. Coast Guard" emblazoned on the side.

Now let's see if this'll work.

Angling himself into a dive, Remmler hit the water with a resounding crash. He sensed schools of fish scurrying away as he cut through the water as easily as he did through the air.

"This is so unbelievable. God, I am so lucky. More than lucky."

Remmler arched his back, straightened out and headed for the surface. He broke the water, increased his speed and rocketed straight up into the night. He closed on Mach Two when his senses picked up a passenger airliner approaching. No problem. He angled his body a little and avoided the airplane by five miles.

Higher and higher he climbed. Remmler passed Mach Two. Then Mach Three. Mach Four.

This is faster than the damn SR-71. "ALL RIGHT!!! WOOO-WHOOO!!!"

He stopped around eighty miles up and opened his eyes. His unisense dissolved. Remmler could barely gasp at what he saw.

The world stretched below him. Even with the sweeping clouds over them he easily recognized the green-brown land masses of North America, Greenland and Europe. He had seen these kinds of views before, but only on TV from the space shuttle. To see them now with his own eyes was absolutely breathtaking. *Every person on Earth should be allowed this view at least once in their life.*

He felt compelled to reach out and grab one of the puffy white clouds that drifted over the land masses. To look east he saw the light of the sun on the horizon. Gazing north he marveled at the sparkling rainbow of the Aurora Borealis.

How easy it was, looking at the Earth from this height, to

forget about all the problems below. The crime, the famine, the diseases, the Middle East crisis . . . Imperium.

At that moment, Jack Remmler realized just how magnificent his Earth was. The passage in Genesis couldn't be more true; "God saw all that he had made, and he found it very good."

It was indeed very good.

He looked up to the heavens and gave a thumbs up. "Good job. And You can count on me to make sure no one messes up Your work."

Remmler gazed at the Earth for a few more minutes before deciding it was time to go.

Let's see if I can pull this off.

Tru'kat extended, Remmler dove back to Earth. In no time he passed the speed of sound. The Eastern Seaboard of the United States rushed up toward him. Remmler decreased his speed. He got down to subsonic as he neared the New Jersey coast.

In a few minutes, Remmler had flown across Jersey and arrived over its capital, Trenton.

All right. Right on target.

Remmler dropped under a thousand feet and slowly cruised over the Delaware River. He gazed out at the thousands of lights that brightened a city struggling to overcome decades of urban decay.

I can make sure Trenton doesn't get any worse. After all, this is where most of my family grew up. I should do it for their sakes.

Remmler glided over the numerous bridges that connected Trenton to Bucks County. He veered right and headed toward the dull gold dome of the capitol building. After buzzing around it twice, he proceeded northeast, increasing his speed slightly. Soon he was over the small township of Lawrence. He stopped over a knot of residential streets and opened his eyes. Unlike the hazy green of night vision lenses, he saw everything in its normal color. The armor made it look hard and a bit blurred around the edges, like in those NFL films from the 1960s. But it was a quantum leap better than any earthly night vision device.

Remmler focused on one house in particular. It instantly grew before his eyes. More of the suit's enhanced vision capability.

He ran his eyes over the medium-sized, two-story white wood house with blue roof and trim. Remmler shook his head in amazement. *In all the years I've lived here, I've never had this kind of view of my house.*

Wonder what Mom and Dad are doing.

His unisense picked up his father in his second floor office tapping away at his personal computer. *What a surprise.* It wasn't unusual for Robert Remmler, the co-owner of a real estate agency, to bring work home with him. Jack's mother, Mary, sat downstairs in the living room talking on the phone to his grandmother. On the back patio, Schmitty, Jack's Golden Retriever named after the great Philadelphia Phillies third baseman Mike Schmidt, was stretched out and resting comfortably.

It would be nice if he could drop in for a few minutes and visit, but he knew he couldn't.

"Oh well, take it easy Mom, Dad." Jack gave a little wave. "Time for me to get going."

He turned around and headed south.

FOURTEEN

It's great to be me, Charles Ringal thought with a smile. He kept the Piper PA-31 Navajo twin-prop plane straight and level as it droned over the Delaware River.

He had planned this day for two months. It was difficult, arranging the days off between the three other people and renting the plane for the day. But everything came off perfectly. They flew down to Baltimore in the morning and spent the afternoon touring the city's Inner Harbor. He even got the chance to get some night flying under his belt.

Charles Ringal did indeed have a great life. A successful lawyer with one of the biggest law firms in Philadelphia, he made a nice wad of money, had a terrific wife and a plush house in Mount Laurel. All by the age of thirty-three. His salary made it possible for him to pursue his other interest in life besides law . . . flying.

Charles Ringal first took the controls of an airplane at the age of fourteen. His uncle, who flew F-4 Phantoms in Vietnam, took him up in a Cessna one day. Ever since, flying had been in Ringal's blood. He seriously considered going into the Air Force before deciding he could make more money in law. Besides, he could always take private flying lessons.

"South Jersey Tower, Lima Two-Two-Four. Request descent."

"Lima Two-Two-Four," came the response from the controller at South Jersey Regional Airport. "Descend to three-thousand feet. Wind out of the sou-south-west at seven knots."

Even the wind is with me, Ringal thought. *Perfect day.* "Roger, South Jersey Tower. Lima Two-Two-Four leaving five for three. ETA fifteen minutes."

"Roger Two-Two-Four."

After a quick glance at the instruments, he turned with a smile to his wife, sitting in the co-pilot's seat.

Diana Torricello-Ringal was nine years Charles' elder, with a stunning figure, an attractive, tanned face with pearl white teeth and jet black, curly hair. Also a lawyer, she worked at a private practice in Philadelphia and taught law part-time at Temple University, where she first met Charles.

His mind drifted back to that day. He could sense Diana's nervousness as she stepped into the teacher's role for the first time. Luckily her casual demeanor and intelligence soon overcame that initial awkwardness. *Pretty hot for someone her age*, he remembered thinking.

Diana had a talent for going beyond the textbooks and into the realm of practical experience. That made Ringal seek her out after class for advice. A strong student-teacher relationship grew out of it. And his initial attraction for her grew stronger as well.

Aggressive as he was, Ringal never knew where he got the nerve to ask her to dinner. Her immediate "yes" totally stunned him. They went out just days after graduation. Neither one felt awkward, even when their conversations strayed away from law into more personal territory.

What started out as a passionate love affair soon turned

into a serious relationship. Two years later they walked down the aisle.

"Almost home, Di."

She flashed him that patented, gleaming smile that still turned him on. "You definitely planned this day perfectly, dear. I had a wonderful time."

"Well, there's still more to come."

"And just what do you mean by that?" She cocked an eyebrow.

"You'll see," an elfish grin crossed his boyish, blond face. He couldn't wait to see her reaction to the champagne and brand new white silk nightgown in their bedroom. Throw in some James Taylor in the CD player and she would completely melt.

The perfect ending to the perfect day.

Ringal turned back to his next door neighbors in the back. "We're going to be landing in fifteen minutes. You strapped in?"

"Yup. We're fine, Charles." David Farbed gave him a thumbs up. The plump, balding, bearded man then turned to his equally plump wife. "See, Lin. I told you flying would be no problem."

Linda, whose fingers still dug into the armrest, just nodded. "I'll just be happy when I'm back on the ground."

Charles smiled again. He knew how much Linda Farbed hated flying. But his powers of persuasion, which helped him in the courtroom numerous times, got her to come along on the trip.

"Don't worry. I'll get you on the ground in one piece. Trust me. I've been flying since high school. There's absolutely nothing to worry about."

This is just too cool! Remmler gleefully thought as he flew over the New Jersey Turnpike and Interstate 295, which ran parallel to it. Headlights moved up and down the highways like products on an assembly line. Forests surrounded the stream of lights. The lights of Cherry Hill and Camden lay in the distance. Remmler kept his head down the entire time, taking in the view. He had touched the edge of the heavens, seen whole continents laid out before his eyes. If only he could share it with somebody. Maybe even write some feel-good poem—even though he hated poetry—about it for *KeyNotes*, the school's literary magazine. It wouldn't be easy keeping all this to himself.

I can't believe there are people who are afraid to fly. If could only they see what I saw. They would . . .

A loud drone suddenly filled Remmler's ears. His head snapped up.

"Oh shit!"

The Piper PA-31 Navajo broke through the clouds and headed straight at him.

"Charles!" Diana screamed when she saw the . . . thing in front of them.

"Jesus!" Ringal's heart jumped into his throat. He jammed the controls hard to the right. The small plane groaned as it dove away from the . . . UFO?

Charles glimpsed the object as it darted away.

My God! Is that . . . a man?

At the same time, Linda Farbed screamed her head off in the back. "We're gonna die! We're gonna die!" David, being pressed into the side of his seat by the g-forces, grabbed his wife's arm and did his feeble best to reassure her.

Charles slowly brought the nose of the Navajo up and leveled out. He turned back to the Farbeds. "Is everyone all right?"

"Y-Yeah. I think so." David's voice, like the rest of his body, trembled. His wife was bawling like a newborn baby.

"My God, Charles," Diana squealed, clutching her husband's. "What was that?"

"I don't know!" Charles replied, fear making him sound irritable.

6-RUST

"I saw it!" David exclaimed over his wife's hyperventilating. "It was red and white. And . . . I swear it looked like a man."

Any other time and Ringal would have thought his next door neighbor was out of his mind.

Not now.

I know, he kept it to himself. *I saw it too. But it can't be. It's impossible.*

Suddenly the radio crackled. "Lima Two-Two-Four, this is South Jersey Tower. You have dropped two hundred-fifty feet and are out of your approach pattern. Do you have a problem? Over."

Charles stared blankly at the radio. His blood froze. *What do I tell them?*

"Lima Two-Two-Four, respond. Over." The controller's voice held a note of urgency.

Charles went to click on the radio and suddenly realized his wife was still holding his arm.

"Diana!" he snapped.

She let go, allowing Ringal to respond to the controller. "South Jersey Tower, this is Lima Two-Two-Four." Charles paused to take a breath. "We had . . . we had a near miss with a . . . an unidentified object."

Oh shit. I hope that doesn't get out. What kind of future is there for a lawyer who reports seeing a UFO?

"Oh my God! Oh my God!" Jack Remmler tried to calm the fearful pounding of his heart. He came to a hover and turned back in time to see the small plane straighten out.

"Oh thank God." *I could've killed them! I was daydreaming. I didn't see them. Oh my God, I almost killed them.*

Remmler watched the plane fly into the distance. A shudder went through his body, thinking about what might have been. He wanted to fly over and check on the people in the plane, see if they were all right. And apologize from the bottom of his heart.

Maybe I better not. I'd probably scare them even worse.

Remmler observed the plane a while longer, until he was convinced the pilot had everything under control. He then headed back to Philadelphia, keeping his speed at a reasonable two hundred miles per hour.

This time I ain't taking any chances.

His unisense guided him all the way back to Keystone College.

Chet Barker strode down the halls of the Moorestown State Police Barracks, heading for the conference room he normally used to write his stories. He hurried his step just a bit. It wasn't long until deadline and Barker wanted this one in *The Philadelphia Inquirer's* South Jersey section for tomorrow morning. A high speed chase along the Turnpike that started out as a minor traffic stop and ended with the suspect smashing his car into the side of the overpass at Exit Four. The guy was a mess of cuts, bruises and broken bones, but that didn't stop him from pulling a military Survival knife on the troopers when they approached his car. They managed to drop him with some pepper spray and send him off to Cooper Hospital University Medical Center in Camden. When he recovered, thirty-seven-year-old Thomas DiGerardo could look forward to a nice, long stay in one of New Jersey's lovely state prisons.

Nothing this cool ever happened in Hazleton, the lean, young black reporter reminisced. He'd worked for the paper in that small Pennsylvania town for three years before lucking into this gig with the *Inquirer*. At least here he had real news.

Barker passed by the radio room and noticed the young, lanky trooper with close cut, dark hair inside.

"Hey, Simon."

Trooper Simon Boswell looked at Chet and held up his hand.

"No, sir. We don't have any helicopters in the area," he

said into his headset. "No. No planes, either . . . Have you checked with McGuire?"

McGuire? Chet Barker's curiosity peaked at the mention of the Air Force base.

"What about Philadelphia International? . . . Okay, I'd suggest calling the smaller airports, sir . . . You're welcome. Goodbye."

Boswell turned to the reporter. "Sorry about that, Chet. What's up?"

"Nothing. What was that about?"

"Air traffic controller from South Jersey Regional Airport. Says one of their planes ran into a UFO during approach. Wanted to know if we had any choppers or planes in the area."

"Hmm. You said South Jersey Regional, right?"

Boswell nodded. "Uh-huh. What are you gonna do? Write a story about a Martian invasion?"

Barker laughed. "It might be worth checking out. Maybe good for a paragraph or two. Thanks, Simon."

"Anytime, Chet."

Barker headed for one of the payphones near the barracks entrance. If he got someone right away, and typed real, *real* fast, he could get both stories in before deadline. That would earn him some points with his editor.

He scanned the Yellow Pages until he found the listing for South Jersey Regional Airport. Five minutes later he was talking to the tower chief.

FIFTEEN

IT WAS A simple matter for Erich von Klest to sweep his hotel room for bugs. With his armor's ESP ability, it took seconds to determine no listening devices were planted in the room. He also scanned the entire Laromme Hotel and the area outside to make sure no Mossad agents spied on him.

Satisfied, von Klest "zapped" out of his armor, sending it to a small sub-dimension where it remained when not in use. Now he just had to wait for his guests to arrive. He occupied himself with a copy of the *International Herald Tribune* he picked up in the hotel lobby. It was the only non-*Juden* periodical he could find.

Fifteen minutes later he heard a knock on the door, a two second pause, then two quick knocks. Von Klest put down his paper and went over to open the door. Three muscular, well-built men wearing sunglasses and casual clothing stood in the hallway. Von Klest waved them in.

"The room is secure," he said after closing the door. "Were you followed?"

"*Nein*," replied the hard-faced Wilhelm Heinbrodder, a

former major in the German Airborne and current Iron Guards commander.

"Good. Let's get to work."

Von Klest removed the TV set and other extraneous items from the large dresser while Heinbrodder and his two partners pulled out several manila folders from their gym bags. They set them on the table and removed several black-and-white photographs and hand drawn sketches of the Prime Minister's residence and the Knesset building.

"Excellent shots, Major," von Klest complemented Heinbrodder as he looked at the pictures of the square, flat Knesset building and the Prime Minister's house in the city.

"*Danke, mein herr*. Our men took them right under the Jews' big noses. Just more news photographers, they thought. Idiots."

Von Klest allowed himself a smile. He had chosen their cover well. As journalists they could get as close as they wanted to their targets.

"They've turned the Knesset into quite a little fortress," he noted.

"We estimate a company-sized force guarding the building," Heinbrodder stated. "Sentries at all the entrances and outside the fence. There must be others inside. Four recon vehicles parked inside the compound. Machine gun and Stinger emplacements on the roof. There are also checkpoints on all the roads leading to the Knesset."

"And what about the Prime Minister's house?"

One of Heinbrodder's lieutenant's, a former East German army officer named Johann Leitz, answered that. "This is something that could be beneficial to us. The Prime Minister is spending very little time at his residence. He's making trips to other government facilities, touring military bases, meeting with mayors . . . and going to the Knesset at least once a day. Most of his cabinet have set up their offices there as well."

"This is better than we could have hoped for," von Klest looked at his men. "Now we can use all our men to assault the Knesset. I can't believe they're putting their entire leadership under one roof. Fools! They're just making our job easier."

"They probably think no one would be stupid enough to attack the Knesset with all the security around it," commented Heinbrodder's other lieutenant, an ex-U.S. Army Ranger named Norman Bennett.

"Then they'll only have themselves to blame when their leaders are lying in a pool of blood." Von Klest could feel the anticipation flowing through his body. *We're actually going to do this. Nothing can stop us.*

Suddenly, thoughts of the Cosmic Protector popped into his head. What if he showed up? Did he know *he* was Imperium? Did he know about his organization? His plan to destroy the Israeli government?

So what if he does? Let him try and stop me. Ride in at the last minute like the cavalry in those idiotic American films. Part of me hopes he does. I'll make sure he doesn't run away. Ever.

"Any problems you foresee?" von Klest asked Heinbrodder.

"The location for one. The Knesset is in a rather open area. If it were in the middle of the city it would be easier to infiltrate our men near it. Plus we'd have excellent vantage points for snipers.

"We can still sneak some, maybe most of our men, in before the shooting starts. There's always a big crowd of journalists and demonstrators outside the building. We can mix in with them."

"The crowd could also get in our way when the operation begins," Leitz pointed out. "Slow us down."

"A volley of grenades should take care of them," von Klest folded his arms. "Most of them will be dead or wounded, so we don't have to worry about dodging a panicked mob."

"Maybe we should keep some of the reporters alive," a smile slithered across Bennett's narrow face. "So they can record for posterity's sake when we blow away all the big wig kikes."

The others chuckled briefly, then got back to business.

"What about security at the checkpoints?"

"Pretty good," Leitz informed von Klest. "They search the vehicles and occupants quickly and thoroughly. Still, if we have to smuggle weapons in, there are some places we can hide them where we've noticed the Israelis don't look too hard. I think it also helps that we don't look Arabic. We haven't seen them harass Western reporters that much."

"They've also got a helicopter flying overhead," Bennett noted. "A Huey."

"I can take care of the helicopter." Von Klest then turned to Heinbrodder. "Do you have a list of the equipment we'll need?"

"Right here." He produced a white piece of paper from a manila envelope and handed it to his leader. Von Klest scanned the hand written list of weapons and other necessary equipment.

"Very well. Kemp and some of our embassy contacts are working to secure a weapons dealer. Meantime, start drawing up plans for the assault."

"Jawohl, Herr von Klest."

SIXTEEN

I STILL NEED a name, Jack Remmler thought as he flew over South Philly on his first official patrol. Veterans Stadium lay off to his right, dark and empty. The Phillies were off tonight. Cars streamed up and down Broad Street and the Walt Whitman Bridge Approach.

He brainstormed possible superhero names. All the while, his unisense guided him through the night. Remmler learned his lesson from the previous night well.

Something with red or scarlet in it? Scarlet Knight? Where did he come up with that? Maybe something space related? Star . . . Red Star? No. Too Communist. Star Raider? Uh-uh. Firewind? Maybe . . . perhaps . . . no.

I didn't think choosing a name would be so damn difficult.

Remmler shook his head. He'd think about it later.

Twenty minutes had passed since he left Keystone College. Luckily, Brian Doyle hadn't been around. He had a night class and would probably hit one of the local bars after with some friends. At least he didn't have to use one of his prethought up excuses to get out of the room; "I'm going to the library/take a walk/do laundry." Remmler decided not to use going to a friend's. It could make for an awkward situation if word got back he really didn't go see that particular friend.

So far his unisense picked up a few street pushers. Remmler would have nailed them if they hadn't been "working" in crowded places. He didn't think it wise to make his crimefighting debut in front of a crowd. Too much could go wrong. People could run in panic (he certainly would if some guy dressed like a tank carrying a bladed staff suddenly popped up). The punk could whip out a gun and fire indiscriminately. The cops could come. Remmler knew the day would come when he would have to face the public. He just wanted that day to come later than sooner.

The pushers, unknown to them, caught a break. For now. Jack Remmler would deal with them one day. Take that poison they sell and shove it down their fucking throats. For now, all he could do was shake his head and wonder who to blame for a society where scumbag drug dealers could do their "business" so openly.

If they only knew, Remmler thought as he headed north.

Maggie Stewart couldn't wait to get home. For the twenty-six-year-old nurse, it had been a day from hell at Metropolitan Hospital. Two minutes after she arrived at work, she helped with two ten-year-old boys struck by a car on their way to school. It took most of the morning to get the worst one stabilized and moved into ICU. Then came a heart attack victim. After lunch, which consisted of a salad and a diet cola, she assisted with a sixteen-year-old boy stabbed in a gang fight. The day ended with a middle-aged woman who lost control of her car and crashed into a divider on I-95.

After locking the door of her Subaru, Maggie sank back into the seat. *I could sleep right here.*

She rested for a minute before using the steering wheel to pull herself forward. Turning on the inside light, Maggie looked herself over in the rearview mirror. Her short blond hair was a mess. She spent almost a minute trying to fix it before muttering, "Screw it." She shut off the light, started the car and pulled onto 8th Street. Maggie decided to avoid her normal route home. Roadwork on Ridge Street made it a pain in the neck to get through.

Traffic was rather light this time of night. It shouldn't take more than twenty, twenty-five minutes to get to her Jenkintown apartment. Then she could microwave some dinner, take a shower and read a little of Jackie Collins' latest novel before turning in.

"Damn," Maggie swore as she caught a red light at an intersection half-a-mile from the hospital. She rolled to a stop and began tapping her fingers on the wheel waiting for the light to change. The radio station she had on was in a commercial break. She looked down and hit the button to search for another station.

Stevie Smith was hard up for cash—again. The rent for his fleabag apartment was overdue and his girlfriend needed an abortion (one kid was enough for *her* to deal with). Plus his friend, Rashid, kept bitching about the money he owed him for that used Ford he'd bought three months ago.

He'd been walking the streets for a good ten minutes, since leaving his brother's apartment after sharing a few beers. He would have used his car, but the engine kept giving him trouble. Maybe Rashid wouldn't get his fucking money for that POS.

His hand moved to the right side of his waist. Stevie caressed the small, metal object jammed into his pants. There was a grocery store not too far from here.

Stevie halted when he noticed the green Subaru stopped at the intersection. The light was red and the driver had her (at least it looked like a her) head down, fiddling with something.

Oh yeah. This'll do.

Lifting up his shirt, Stevie removed the snub-nosed .38 revolver from his waistband. Pulling down his black ballcap, he ran toward the car.

Maggie finally found something on the radio she liked when something crashed next to her ear. The young nurse screamed. Shards of glass cut into her face.

"Outta the car, bitch!" somebody shouted. A black hand reached in to turn off the ignition. She turned into the barrel of the biggest gun she had ever seen. Maggie leaned back in terror and whimpered.

"I said outta the car! Now! Move it!" The man pulled the door open and unbuckled Maggie's seatbelt. Keeping the gun trained on her, he grabbed her by the collar and dragged her out of the Subaru.

"Please don't kill me! Please don't kill me!" Tears streamed down Maggie's cheeks, burning when they made contact with one of her cuts.

The man slammed her against the side of the car. Waves of pain shot through Maggie's back. The gun suddenly came up under her chin. "Shut the fuck up, bitch! I swear I'll do you right here!"

Maggie's breaths came in short whimpers. Her eyes went wide with fear. She was too terrified to notice the man run his eyes up and down her petite body.

"You ain't bad for a white chick. Let's have a little fun."

Oh God! No!

He pulled Maggie away from the car and pushed her toward a nearby alley.

"No! Please! Please don't!"

The man threw Maggie into the alley. She landed hard on the pavement. Fire shot through her left forearm and left knee. She cried again. When Maggie rolled onto her back, the man crouched over her. His free hand clamped over her mouth. He pressed the barrel of the .38 hard against her forehead.

"You keep crying n' I'll blow your fucking head off! Now just sit back and enjoy the ride."

I thought this city was a mecca for crime, Remmler thought as he cruised across the sky. He was getting bored. It seemed so easy in the comic books. The hero went out on a nightly patrol, ran into a group of assorted scum, beat on them and left them for the cops.

One problem with that. This wasn't a comic book. This was real life.

Maybe I'll fly across the river to Camden. That place is a fucking war zone. I bet-

His unisense picked up a female scream, followed by whimpering. Then a tough, young voice. "You gonna get it good, bitch."

Remmler gasped for breath. *Oh my God.*

He hovered and let his unisense pinpoint the ruckus. Little over a mile away and six hundred feet down. He sensed the thug reach down and tug at the young girl's outfit. His fingers dug roughly into her breasts. The high-pitched ripping of clothes exploded in his ears.

"No! Please!" the victim begged. Her cries stabbed at Remmler's spine, paralyzing him.

This is for real. He's going to rape her. Oh my God!

More of the young girl's top was ripped open. She cried uncontrollably.

"How many times I gotta tell you to shut the fuck up?!"

The scum drew his right foot back and kicked the girl in the side. She wheezed and gasped in pain.

DO SOMETHING, JACK!!!

His blood boiled. He gripped his *tru'kat* tightly. His heart beat faster. Adrenaline surged through his body.

"You son of a bitch."

Remmler made a beeline toward them. *Gotta move. Gotta get there.*

The excess adrenaline made everything move in slow motion. Remmler kept increasing his speed. It was taking too long to get there. He had to move.

He angled his body to come in for a landing. Before he knew it, he flew over the street, over the attacker and his victim, then over the surrounding buildings.

"SHIT!!!!" He screamed loud enough for everyone on both sides of the Delaware to hear.

Remmler was nearly a mile away before he looped over, leveled out and headed back. This time he reduced his speed. He couldn't afford to make the same mistake again.

Please, God. Let me be in time.

He slowed as he approached the alley. Remmler straightened out and descended right between the two buildings. Once in the alley, he switched from unisense to night vision.

The scumbag had worked his way down to the woman's panties when Remmler boomed, "STOP!!!"

Stevie Smith looked up and jumped back. The warm September night couldn't stop the chill from penetrating his bones. His body trembled. The beer he drank earlier drained into his pants.

No way, man. This ain't happening.

The thing floated—*floated!*—to the ground. It wore some space age red and white get up. His eyes locked on the staff with a nasty looking blade on the end.

It landed in front of him and took one step.

"What the fuck are you, man!?!"

It took another step.

"NOO!!! Keep away from me, man!"

Stevie nearly tripped over his own feet as he bolted out of the alley.

Remmler ran after him, but skidded to a halt when he neared the woman. A nurse judging by the remnants of her outfit. She sat up against the wall, shaking. Her forehead rested on her knees. The tattered remains of her uniform were tightly clutched against her breasts.

Jack felt sick to his stomach. He almost felt like crying, watching this young woman whimper like a frightened child.

He leaned down, careful not to get too close.

"Ma'am? Are you okay?"

She gave no noticeable response.

"Ma'am?" Remmler reached out, then pulled his hand back. It probably wasn't a good idea to touch her now.

Slowly, the nurse lifted her trembling head. Her eyes, wide with fear and filled with tears, gazed up at a protruding red visor and globular head.

She shrieked in terror. Remmler took a step back as the nurse recoiled from him, trying to bury herself inside the wall.

"I won't hurt you," he said in a shaky voice.

How could someone do this to another human being?

Remmler didn't know this woman, but right now, more than anything, he wished he had the power to absorb the pain she was going through. Anything to make her feel better.

He clenched his teeth. For the first time in his life, Remmler felt true hatred. Hatred for the man—no! The sub-human slime—who did this.

"You're not getting away, scumwad," Remmler hissed, turning toward the street. He closed his eyes and let his unisense take over. The slime turned up a block away, still running.

Remmler turned back to the nurse. He didn't want to leave her, but he couldn't let that hairball get away. Next time he might actually finish the job on another woman. *It* had to answer for *its* crimes.

"Ma'am. I'll be right back. No one is going to hurt you anymore. I swear."

He ran out of the alley, tracking the would-be rapist with his unisense. *At least I can keep an "eye" on her too with it.*

He turned the corner and could "see" the scum dashing across the street toward a chest high chainlink fence that surrounded a weed and trash filled lot.

Why the hell am I running?

In mid stride, Remmler bolted off the ground and flew.

Any thoughts that made Stevie Smith a human being vanished. All that remained was the need to survive. To run. Run far away, as fast as he could. Run from the thing.

It flew! It fuckin' flew!

Stevie neared a chainlink fence. He could make it over easily. Then . . . then he'd just keep running. That was the only plan he had.

Almost there . . .

He skid to a halt, nearly falling on his rear. A rush of wind rose up. A red and white blur appeared in front of him. He focused his eyes.

The thing stood between him and the fence.

Stevie screamed in terror. The bulky armored figure showed no response to his shrieks.

Behind the visor, Remmler's eyes shot invisible lasers into the maggot. He had tortured that poor girl. Why? What possessed him to turn her into an emotional wreck?

Remmler had made a mental list of "tough guy" lines for times like these. Stuff Clint Eastwood or Bruce Willis uttered before they finished off the bad guys. But that didn't seem appropriate now. Not after what he'd seen.

"What the fuck are you!?" the maggot shook uncontrollably.

Remmler didn't answer. He took a step forward.

It all happened so fast. The slimeball's arm just snapped

up. He screamed something. Then came a series of flashes, followed by an equal number of pops.

Oh shit! Remmler flinched as the first of six .38 caliber rounds rocketed toward him. Two of the bullets missed. One ricocheted off his left arm and imbedded itself in a nearby lamppost. The other three were flattened when they impacted against his armor. The scumbag kept pulling the trigger long after the gun had emptied.

Remmler released a breath. He glanced down at his torso. No holes, no dents, nothing. *C'mon, man. If this armor can take a laser beam, what's a few piddly bullets?*

He glared at the dirtbag. He just stared at his revolver, then at Remmler, in shock. High pitched gasps of fear burst from his throat. The skell backed away, fumbling through his pocket for extra rounds.

"Keep away from me, man!"

He's scared. Good.

The transformation amazed Remmler. Slimeballs like this acted tough so long as they picked on someone who couldn't fight back. Now he was as terrified as the woman he tried to rape. Now he knew what it felt like to be the victim.

Stevie's hand came out of his pocket, along with several bullets that clattered on the asphalt. He managed to clutch one between his thumb and index finger. As he shoved it in the chamber, he heard, "You son of a bitch!"

He looked up. The armored figure stomped toward him. Stevie closed the cylinder and brought the gun up.

Remmler reached out and wrapped his right hand around the maggot's gunhand. He still managed to pull the trigger. The hammer came down on an empty chamber.

He squeezed lightly. Just enough to drive the scumbag to his knees. If a few bones got broken in the process, tough shit.

The maggot's hand caved in like tissue paper. Bones

snapped and popped, then exploded. There was a sickening "squish" as flesh compacted, followed by the rending of metal as the revolver transformed into a blob of steel. It mingled with flesh and bone.

The skell screamed in a way Remmler thought impossible for a human being. He quickly pulled back his arm. The blood and gore slid right off his gauntlet.

"Oh my God!" *What did I do!?!*

The maggot collapsed to the ground, clutching the lump that used to be his right hand. All the while he wailed like a banshee. Remmler looked down in stunned disbelief.

I did that. I crippled him. I . . . I didn't realize . . . Oh God forgive me. What did I do?

He watched in horror as the man rolled over on his stomach. The crying continued, like a five-year-old who'd fallen off a see-saw multiplied by ten. It quickly diminished into a howl, then a moan. Then nothing.

Oh God! Is he dead?

His unisense confirmed that the slimeball was still alive. *Musta blacked out from the pain.*

Remmler breathed a sigh of relief until his unisense picked up something else.

The nurse. Curled up in the alley. Crying.

He looked back to her, then to the unconscious thug.

I shouldn't feel this way. He deserved it, didn't he?

All of Remmler's focus shifted his right hand. The one he used to crush the man's hand. The blood and gore were gone. The armor's non-adhesive surface couldn't do anything to get rid of the memory.

I . . . I didn't know. I didn't know I used that much strength. Oh God, that scream.

The nurse's whimpering still filtered into Remmler's ears.

Come on, Jack. You gotta help her. Put it behind you.

Easier said than done.

Remmler took a few steps backward, then turned around.

Help the nurse. Help the nurse.

He hoped concentrating on the task at hand would block the image of the skell's mangled hand from his mind.

It didn't.

SEVENTEEN

"9-1-1 EMERGENCY." Dispatcher Shana Evans took the call.

"Yeah. There's a woman being raped." The street name followed.

Shana briefly noted the caller's voice sounded rather flat and deep, almost echoic. "Can you see her from where you're at?" she asked, at the same time typing the information on her computer screen and signaling another dispatcher to get a patrol car moving.

"Is she being attacked right now, sir?"

A pause. "Yeah. She is. Can you get someone out here?"

"The police are on their way."

"Good." *Click.*

"Sir? Sir!"

Shana got no response. She mentally cursed the caller. The impatient idiot didn't give her a description of the perpetrator. The officers would be going into this blind. That was always dangerous.

She wondered if the call was for real. Then two minutes

later another dispatcher received a call. Shots fired . . . in the same vicinity as the rape call.

Jack Remmler headed back to the alley after switching off his communicator. Yet another nice and convenient feature in his armor. He hated lying about the rape, but the Philadelphia Police were notorious for their long response time. Remmler didn't feel like hanging around longer than necessary.

He latched the *tru'kat* to his back before returning to the alley, hoping to appear less threatening. The nurse still sat scrunched up in a ball, whimpering. She didn't seem aware of his presence.

Remmler stood a few feet away, just watching her. He would not leave until the cops showed up. As distasteful as it was to admit, a part of him wanted to leave right now. He felt uncomfortable standing here, seeing this woman robbed of her dignity, weeping.

You think you're *uncomfortable, Jack? What about her?*

He wanted to help her, console her. But what could he do? He was no therapist. Saying "everything's going to be okay," sounded rather feeble.

Why the hell was I made a Cosmic Protector?

Remmler's enhanced hearing picked up the blare of a siren. He switched to unisense, and "saw" a police car barreling toward them, lights blazing.

"Time to go," he said as he unlatched his staff. Remmler took one last look at the woman and said softly. "It's okay. The police are here."

Maggie slowly lifted her head. This time she did not scream. She watched as the red and white armored figure flew out of the alley into the night sky. Shock numbed her mind. Her memory came in horrifying flashes. But something else was there. Something that settled her, if only a little. The realization punched through as she watched the figure fly away.

He . . . saved . . . me.

Eight-year veteran Dan Viterelli and five-year veteran Paula Norman were the first cops on the scene.

They spotted a green Subaru, its driver side door open and headlights on, stopped near the corner.

"This is the place," Viterelli said as he pulled in behind the car. Both officers got out of the white Crown Vic with blue and yellow trim, flashlight in one hand, and Glock Model 17 9mm automatic in the other. They heard whimpering coming from the alley and approached cautiously. When they shone their flashlights in the alley, they found a young woman huddled against the wall. Norman headed over to her, while her partner scanned the alley.

"No sign of the perp. Musta took off before we got here."

"Looks like she's in shock." Norman examined the woman's face with her flashlight. "I'll get her a blanket."

"Okay. Call for back-up and paramedics and stay with her. I'll check the area."

"Right. Watch your ass, Don."

"Always."

Officer Norman made the call as she headed for the squad car's trunk to retrieve the blanket. Viterelli headed round the corner. The streetlights provided a good deal of illumination, but there were still enough shadows, parked cars and porches a perp could hide behind.

Viterelli's heart beat furiously. He pressed his left hand against his shirt, feeling the P.A.C.A. bulletproof vest under it for reassurance. He then proceeded down the street, which seemed to stretch forever into the night.

Officer Viterelli kept to the sidewalk, checking under cars and in darkened corners of buildings for any sign of the perp.

He heard a siren in the distance. Back-up was coming. For him it couldn't arrive soon enough.

Moving further down the sidewalk, Viterelli saw a darkened form lying on the ground across the street. He sprinted to a nearby parked car for a better vantage point and shone his light on the lump. It was a man. Black. Wearing jeans, sneakers and a t-shirt. Most disturbing of all, he lay on his right hand. Viterelli shut off his flashlight and stuffed it in his belt. He rested his arms on the hood of the car and trained his Glock 17 on the man.

"Police!"

No response. Viterelli had no idea who the man was. He could be the perp, or a gang banger or some poor citizen who got hurt. Given the situation, he couldn't take any chances.

"Police! You on the ground! Don't move!"

He didn't move. In fact, he didn't do anything.

Viterelli moved around the car and slowly approached the man. He kept his gun trained on him the whole time. The man still didn't move. Sweat dripped into Viterelli's eyes, stinging them. He knew the humidity had little to do with his perspiring.

"Sir, can you hear me?"

No response.

Viterelli stood six feet from the body. He caught three glints on the ground and took a quick glance. Bullets. He then noticed a dark pool coming from underneath the body. Could he be a shooting victim?

The officer slowly bent down and turned the man over. He half expected to see a gun shoved in his face.

"Oh my God."

Within twenty minutes, the area was a flurry of activity. Over fifteen cops were on hand, including four detectives and a captain. Two ambulances had arrived, one for Maggie, the other for the guy whose hand looked like he shoved it in a trash compactor. Police labeled him the suspect, mainly because of the .38 revolver found on his person. Or more precisely, the mangled hunk of metal that had once been a .38 revolver. Even the most experienced cops scratched their heads on this one. The damn thing looked . . . well, like someone just crushed it. But that was impossible. No human being was that strong.

Not surprisingly the media soon arrived. This would be the lead story on the 11 o' clock news, especially after one uniformed officer mentioned the suspect's crushed hand and weapon. His superiors had not had time to spread the word to keep a lid on those facts.

The police fanned out across the neighborhood. They soon discovered one of Stevie Smith's bullets imbedded in the lamppost and marked it for Forensics. Residents were interviewed. Most didn't see anything, which didn't surprise the cops. They even came across the guy who called 9-1-1, who said he just heard the shots but didn't bother looking until several minutes later.

A detective going door to door in one of the nearby apartment buildings came upon the residence of an elderly widow who owned three cats and whose TV was constantly on whether she watched it or not. She informed the detective she had gone to her window after the last shot.

"It's gonna sound crazy, but I saw some knight in white armor knock down this man. Poor boy was screaming something fierce. About a minute later he stopped, and the knight fella just walked away."

Detective Sergeant Ed Caro, who succeeded in not laughing or rolling his eyes, politely thanked her and left. When he met up with his partner, Ralph Diaz, he told him about "the crazy old broad" and her knight in shining armor.

Across the street, a uniformed officer heard the same story from an eleven-year-old boy. Only he said the guy in armor looked more like Iron Man or a really fat Power Ranger. It even carried a staff!

The officer explained to the boy he had no time for comic book stories and asked him to tell the truth.

"But I'm telling the truth!" the boy jumped up and down to emphasis the point. "I swear!"

The mother leaned over him, hands on her hips. "You better stop lying . . . *or else.*"

The boy, in tears, pleaded with his mother that he was not making it up. She sent him off to his room, telling him he could forget about watching TV tomorrow. The mother apologized to the officer, who politely accepted.

Neither Caro or the uniformed officer mentioned the story to anyone else. They didn't have time for horseshit fantasies about knights and superheroes.

Three other people on the block also witnessed the armored figure incapacitate the suspect. None told their story to the police or the media. After all, who would believe them?

EIGHTEEN

"THIS IS INCREDIBLE," Yuri Drovinov declared. He gazed at the micrograph of his own cells, magnified between 20,000 and 40,000x by one of the most advanced electron microscopes in Iraq.

"Your cells have become vast storehouses of energy, Professor. Every sample we've examined contains levels of mitochondria are off the scale."

"Mitochondria?"

"Sorry. That is the compound in cells that produces energy. The amount of Mitochondria in your genetic make-up is unheard of in a human being."

"I never knew you were so versed in biology, Musti."

"I'm not. But I'm getting a crash course from some of my colleagues. You know my expertise is nuclear physics. Most of which you taught me."

Drovinov smiled at the praise from the stocky, mustached Musti Safim. He had met the Iraqi years before during an exchange to Russia. Drovinov considered him the brightest of the group from this backwards country, therefore worthy of his tutoring. Musti applied many of the skills he learned from Drovinov to Iraq's nuclear program, which he worked on in this very building. The Kassim Research Facility, in fact, was responsible for some of the biggest advances in this nation's nuclear weapons program. The West had no concrete proof of its true purpose. U.N. inspection teams had never gotten near the facility.

Now it was home to a team of the most brilliant minds in Iraq. Physicists, molecular biologists, biochemists. All with a singular purpose. The study Yuri• Drovinov.

"The cells in your body have mutated into miniature power plants. Their shape has changed, the nuclei have grown larger. The energy output is staggering. Just one cell sample from you was enough to power a small transistor radio. You yourself probably have enough power to provide electricity to all of Kuwait!"

Drovinov shook his head in amazement. "No human being could contain so much power."

"Correct. Though there are some organisms that produce their own energy. Fireflies, for example. But that's really a chemical reaction caused by a breakdown of adenosine triphosphate, which is used for short term energy storage in cells. The closest I can compare this to is an electric eel. Their cells produce electricity, as the name suggests. But their maximum output is about six hundred volts. They certainly can't generate a current over any distance."

"So you are saying I have the same cellular make up as an electric eel?"

"In a way, yes." Safim spread out the micrographs on a nearby lab table. "Now according to Dr. Mehburzaf, one of our pre-emanate biologists, eels and other marine creatures capable of producing their own electricity have what are called electric organs. They generate electricity the same way nerves do, only in larger quantities. These organs are very easy to distinguish. Large, disk-shaped and arranged in long rows. Now look at these micrographs and tell me what you see."

Drovinov studied the pictures. "I see the rows, just as you described. But the shape. More . . . more like a flower than a disc."

"And a thousand times larger than an eel's. Also pulsating. Since you do not need to eat, our only conclusion is this energy must sustain your physical body."

"But you still have no idea how I sustain this energy field? How it is able to recharge?"

Safim hung his head. "No, Professor Drovinov. We're not even close to figuring that out."

Drovinov nodded slightly, then continued. "There are other questions that still need to be answered. How did I survive the blast while everyone else died? Why was I transformed like this? And what kind of energy am I radiating?"

Safim stared at him, a look of defeat in his eyes. "Again, we cannot answer that. Right now we are accepting your theory of being inside an energy bubble during the explosion. Truthfully, none of us have a better one. We have no idea what kind of energy we're dealing with. Its power output is incredible, but the radiation level is minimal. We might be able to come up with an explanation if we had a sample of the U-500 used in your laser."

"Unfortunately, it was all destroyed, along with the laser. And getting more samples from Tunguska at this time is impossible."

"Which means most of our research will be guesswork. I must be blunt, Professor. We simply do not know what we're dealing with. This isn't a simple mutation we're studying. This is something never before encountered in human history. The accident literally transformed you into an entirely new lifeform. Something completely unique."

Drovinov's eyes widened at Safim's revelation. "Yes. I suppose I am."

"Safim seems to have more questions than answers about

Professor Drovinov," the President of Iraq stated. General Nurabi nodded as they watched Drovinov and Safim's exchange on one of the monitors in the facility's security room. They had learned to ignore the ever present static lines on the screen. The scientists told them it was the result of low-level electromagnetic interference given off by Drovinov's energy field. It affected all electronic equipment for about a quarter-mile. Most times it was more annoying than serious. Some of the scientists wondered if Drovinov could be used as a living electronic jammer.

"As Dr. Safim stated, Mr. President, this is a unique experience for all of us. We're learning as we go along. I imagine this was how the Americans felt when they were building their first nuclear reactor. We have discovered an entirely new field of biology with Professor Drovinov."

Nurabi, the Defense Minister and the President glanced at the stocky, bearded scientist with salt and pepper hair. After overseeing the country's nuclear weapons program for the last five years, Dr. Rosan Abbryquem now headed up the twenty other scientists who made up PROJECT: NEXUS.

"Biology doesn't concern me, Dr. Abbryquem," the President waved his hand in disinterest. "My concern is what Drovinov can do with his new power. He is the edge we've needed over the West for years. Better than any nuclear or chemical weapon. Drovinov is a living weapon America and its lackeys will have no defense against. He will be our spearhead into Saudi Arabia and Iran."

"Someone with that much power," Nurabi said, "will need a lot of money to stay under our control."

"Then he'll have it! Whatever amount he wants. I'll build him a palace and supply him with the finest whores in the country if that's what it takes to keep him loyal. This is our best chance to become the undisputed power in this region and bring the world to its knees. How many countries depend on Arab oil to keep their societies functioning? If all that oil was under our control, they'd pay whatever price we asked."

"But the embargo," Nurabi stammered.

"The embargo be damned. What is more important to a country like Sri Lanka or the Philippines? Standing in solidarity with the United Nations or keeping their economies from falling apart? They'll pay any price, no matter how high. Then we'll have more than enough money to keep Drovinov happy."

Nurabi looked over his shoulder to the Defense Minister. The two just stared at each other as their President spoke. They were used to such ramblings about how he would take over the Arabian Peninsula and force the Americans out. All they could do was listen politely and offer supporting opinions. To do otherwise meant death. But this time, with Yuri Drovinov, there could be more to the President's bombast than mere rhetoric. They may actually succeed. Erase the bitter defeat in Kuwait from their minds. How could they lose? The Americans—no one, in fact—had anything that could stand up to Drovinov. The question remained, could they control him?

What was it Lord Acton said? Power tends to corrupt. And absolute power corrupts absolutely."

Drovinov was as close to absolute power as any human being could get.

"Are you almost done with your experiments?"

Dr. Abbryquem had to concentrate hard to keep his jaw from dropping in shock. "M-Mr. President. We haven't even begun to scratch the surface of Professor Drovinov's powers. We have no idea what type of energy he radiates, the range he can project it. Even if he could deplete himself. We need time—"

"No! Time is one thing we do not have. We know most of Drovinov's capabilities. He demonstrated them on our troops. It's time we take him out of the laboratory and put him to use."

Abbryquem merely nodded. "Yes, Mr. President." What other response he could give?

A smile crept across the President's face, a face that a moment ago flared with anger. "Do not worry, Doctor. You may continue your experiments on Professor Drovinov. Until I call for him, of course."

"Of course. Thank you, Mr. President." Abbryquem tried his best to sound pleased.

The President dismissed the scientist, letting him return to work. Then he, Nurabi and the Defense Minister headed for the facility's parking lot. Four Republican Guard soldiers escorted them.

"Begin drawing up plans for the invasions of Saudi Arabia and Iran incorporating Drovinov once we get back," the President told the Defense Minister once they were in their limousine heading back to Baghdad.

"Yes, Mr. President."

"Our diplomatic corps will need to stall the United States and the U.N. while we plan," Nurabi said. "They won't attack as long as they're still negotiating."

"Our envoys will talk for as long as is necessary. Also, Nurabi, I need Al Mukhabaret to conduct thorough sweeps of all our agencies. Anyone you remotely suspect of being a spy, I want them *dealt with*. I do not want any security leaks on PROJECT: NEXUS."

"Understood, Mr. President."

"There is also something else we must do to maintain our security. And it concerns our foreign guests."

Jack Remmler could barely keep his eyes open as he trudged up the steps to the third floor of Driscoll Hall. He hardly got any sleep last night. Everytime he closed his eyes, images of the assault on that young nurse tormented him. The scumball ripping her clothes off. The woman curled up in a ball and crying. Him crushing the would-be rapist's hand.

Am I really cut out for this? The question plagued him throughout the night and into today.

The press jumped all over the attack. A couple of his buddies in Advanced Journalism this morning scanned a copy of the *Philadelphia Daily News.* The story made the front page.

Swell. No way I'll be able to get my mind off this now.

There was nothing in the story about a figure in bulky red and white armor with a staff. If anyone else had seen him, they probably didn't come forward for fear of ridicule. Speculation seemed to be the slimeball, not yet identified, fell on the street and a passing car or truck ran over his hand. *Yeah, right.*

The whole mess ruined his concentration at every class he attended today. How the hell was he supposed to be an ordinary student with all this on his mind? If only he could talk to somebody about it.

Screw it! All he wanted to do was sleep. Rest up for tonight's patrol.

After what happened last night? How the hell can I go back out there? Why the hell should I put myself through something like that again?

Dammit! Why do I have to care so much?

Remmler shook his head as he turned down the hallway. Maybe Eric Bouden had the right idea. If things got too bad on the news, just turn it off.

But that wasn't what his parents taught him. "You can't turn off the world, Jack." Mom said once. She and Dad encouraged him to know what was going on in the world. Maybe the fault lay in his ability to develop a bond with the stories he saw, especially the more tragic ones. He should have just remained an impartial observer like all his journalism professors preached. Not cared so much. Not vented his frustrations at the TV news. Not confronted his defense attorney uncle whenever he let another scumbag criminal back on the street.

He should just-

"Hi, Jack."

Remmler's head snapped up. His eyes were alert. All for a friend approaching from the opposite end of the hallway.

"Oh. Hey, Renee."

The short, cute Trinidadian girl with flowing jet black hair came up to him, a stack of pink papers in her hand.

"You okay, Remy?" Renee Canai took a closer look at him.

"Yeah, I'm fine. Just tired. Didn't get a lot of sleep last night."

Renee cocked an eyebrow and wagged a finger at him. "Jack, what did I tell you about too much partying? Honestly, what am I going to do with you?"

"I'm sure I can come up with a few suggestions."

Renee laughed. "Oh, I'm sure you could."

Remmler smiled. Thankfully, Renee wasn't bothered by such comments. Being rather flirtatious herself, she laughed right along with it, instead of making some ridiculous allegation of sexual harassment.

"Well, I hope you're not too tired to come out tonight." She handed him one of the flyers. He looked at the large, black lettering at the top. **Delta Phi Epsilon Presents...The Welcome Back Bash.**

Oh shit! That's tonight? Remmler had been so busy with his new powers he'd forgotten about the annual party welcoming back Keystone students. Maybe that's what he needed to forget about his problems.

"You are gonna be there, right, Jack?"

"Yeah, sure. I'll be there."

"Great. Save a dance for me," Renee nudged him playfully.

He smiled. "Count on it."

"Great. Well, I gotta pass out the rest of these flyers. See you tonight."

"Okay. Bye."

Renee sauntered down the hall while Remmler headed to his room. He stumbled inside, dropped his books on the floor and fell on his bed. No sign of Brian. Probably still in class.

Remmler looked again at the flyer still in his hand. He glanced over the entertainment advertised through narrow eyelids. Live DJ. Dancing. Food. Limbo contest. Door prizes.

His eyes came back to the top. **Delta Phi Epsilon Presents!** He focused on the first line, particularly one word. **Epsilon!**

Epsilon.

Something clicked inside his brain. His eyes closed and the flyer slipped from between his fingers.

Epsilon.

Heh. That would be a nice name. If I wanted to be a superhero

It was Jack Remmler's last thought before he fell asleep.

NINETEEN

PAUL DRAKE DIDN'T even bother knocking on Captain Lawson's door. He barged right in just as the naval attaché picked up the receiver of his phone.

"Big news, Cap."

Lawson put down the phone. No one with half a brain could have missed the sense of urgency in the station chief's voice.

"What happened?"

"The Iraqis are kicking everyone out."

"Who's everyone?"

"Everyone as in all foreigners," Drake replied as he stopped in front of the desk. "I mean *all* foreigners. We monitored it on Radio Baghdad. Tourists, embassy people, journalists, military advisors. They're making no exceptions."

"What about the U.N. observers?" Lawson asked. Iraq had added to an already tense situation by confining the United Nations nuclear inspectors at Baghdad's Al-Rashid Hotel, which had been made famous as CNN's vantage point for the opening hours of Operation: Desert Storm.

"Them too. Have a listen."

Minutes later both men entered the embassy's communications room. They heard the monotone announcer drone on about all foreign citizens having to vacate the country.

"They say they'll guarantee them safe passage out of the country," Drake translated the Arabic for the Navy captain. Ten months in-country and Lawson's understanding of the language just reached rudimentary. "Apparently, they're gonna get everyone together in Baghdad and either bus them or chopper them to the Iraq-Kuwait border for repatriation."

Lawson nodded with satisfaction. "Good. At least they'll be out of harm's way. I can't believe they're doing it again. Just letting all those potential hostages go. Stupidity strikes twice."

"Probably hoping it'll buy 'em some time, score some brownie points with the more sympathetic bureaucrats. Like back in '90."

"Didn't work then," Lawson noted. He then said, "What about the embassies? Who are they letting stay?"

"I don't think they're making any exceptions. I think they meant it when they said all must go."

"That'll make them damn unpopular with the few friends they have left. My God. What's gotten into them?"

"I don't know," Drake shrugged.

"'Anal Al' know about this?"

"Told him as soon as we picked up the broadcast. He's on the phone to Washington right now. I also informed the Saudis and Kuwaitis."

The two listened to Radio Baghdad, now broadcasting in English, for a few seconds before Lawson spoke. "They're going all out to isolate themselves, aren't they?"

"I gotta wonder."

"What?"

Drake turned to his friend. "If the reason they're doing this is because they've got something big going on. So big they don't want *anyone* to find out about it."

"Very good work," Erich von Klest held the stack of 500 dollar bills up to the ceiling light in his hotel room. "Getting those ex-Stasi forgers was one of the best things we ever did."

"Why waste such talent running a fruit stand in some dreg section of Leipzig?" Kemp stated as he finished putting the last few piles of counterfeit cash into the newly purchased brown suitcase.

Von Klest continued to study the top bill. His trained eye enabled him to pick out a slightly darker shade of ink. Any other deformities would not be noticed without a microscope. The Arab arms dealer they were doing business with tonight outside Ramallah would never know the difference.

Mongrel though he may be, the man had come up with all the weapons von Klest asked for; Forty AKS-74 assault rifles, three SVD sniper rifles, two ancient RPD light machine guns, nine RPG-18 anti-tank weapons, a hundred grenades and forty Makarov pistols. He even threw in a load of combat knives for free. The Arab knew his trade, which would make him a victim of his own success. A necessary security precaution.

Ach. *It's not like he's human.*

Von Klest placed the stack back in the suitcase, which rested on the bed. "Three million in fake American money."

"So what should we do with it after we make the exchange?" Kemp nodded to the suitcase after closing it.

"You've heard of the River Styx, haven't you?"

Kemp cocked an eyebrow. "*Ja*, Erich."

A thin smile crossed von Klest's lips as he looked at the suitcase. "Bury it with him. He can use it to pay Charon's fare. If he accepts counterfeit money."

The older man joined von Klest in a hearty laugh.

Detective Sergeant Ed Caro wondered if he'd ever permission to speak with Stevie Smith. Last he heard the maggot was dozing peacefully with the help of a nice sedative. Caro hadn't been able to get to him last night or this morning. Between the operation to amputate what remained of his right hand and the blood loss, he'd been pretty much out of it. When the would-be rapist finally woke, he immediately went into hysterics. He begged the nurses, orderlies and security guards trying to restrain him to "keep *it* away from me!" Whatever the hell that meant. After another dose of drugs, Smith hollered no more.

Caro's partner, Ralph Diaz, had tracked down a bunch of info on their perp. It didn't take long for the computer to find a match with the skell's fingerprints.

Stevie Smith. Typical street scum. Did eighteen months in county lock-up for agg assault and robbery. Suspected in other robberies, but nothing proven.

We got him dead to rights now. Just wish we knew what the hell happened to his hand.

With that in mind, the bald, thickly built, mustached detective went to the M.E.'s office. It turned out Francine Ballard had done the examination on Smith's crushed hand. After the usual small talk, the portly black woman in her mid-forties, who was a cousin of Caro's wife, led him to her small office.

"Ed," she began as she took a seat behind her cluttered desk, "I've been on this job for almost fifteen years. I . . . I've never seen anything like this. It's just not possible."

Caro raised an eyebrow. Francine was darn good at her job. Not like her to be stumped this bad.

"Okay, granted," he shifted in the old, scared wooden chair. The smell of formaldehyde hung in the air, even though the lab was way down the hall. Caro had been here so often it didn't bother him anymore. "Finding a punk with his hand crushed isn't an everyday occurrence, but there's no reason to treat it like it's out of a Stephen King novel. The maggot probably just fell on the street and a truck ran over his hand."

"No way. Even an eighteen-wheeler couldn't crush a hand like that. Oh yeah, it'll break all the bones, rip off skin, even snap off a finger or two. But nothing like this."

"What about heavy equipment? There is road construction on Ridge Street. Maybe one of their vehicles came down the street and rolled over his hand."

"And just kept going?" Francine leaned across her desk.

"Probably scared he'd get in trouble. Ever hear of hit and run?"

"Any evidence of that? Tracks? Trail of blood?"

Caro shook his head.

Francine took a breath before continuing. "A car or a truck cannot do this kind of damage to a human hand, much less a .38. A steamroller would have flattened it, expanded flesh and bone. Plus there'd be more damage above the wrist."

The medical examiner slumped back and turned away. She brought her fist up to her mouth and closed her eyes in thought.

"You okay, Francine?"

After a few moments, she stared back at him. "I don't know. I don't have any rational explanation for what happened to this Smith guy. Right now the only theory I have is that *something* wrapped itself around his hand and squeezed, crushing it and the gun."

Caro's brow furrowed. "You gotta be kidding. No human being could do that. Not even if he was jacked up on PCP."

"Look, I'll check the hand some more. Maybe I missed something. What I don't know."

"Do what you can, Fran-"

The cell phone in his jacket pocket rang. The Director of Security for Hahneman Hospital was on the other end. After a big nod of satisfaction from Caro, he ended the call and stuffed the Motorola phone back in his pocket.

"Good news?"

"Yup." Caro got to his feet. "Smith is awake and actually calm. I'm heading down to Hahneman to grill him."

"Good luck."

He thanked his cousin-in-law and exited her office. Caro hopped in his car and drove from the Medical Examiner's office on University Avenue to the hospital. Security guards and police officers assigned to watch Smith kept the press back as Caro headed for the intensive care wing. The would-be rapist with the crushed hand made big news all over the Delaware Valley. Caro counted at least thirty reporters, cameramen and photographers milling about the halls.

If it bleeds it leads. Caro knew that to be the credo of many local newsrooms. He wondered what they did if *it* was crushed.

Caro didn't say a word as he entered the room and pulled up a squarish, cushioned chair next to Smith's bed. He briefly glanced down at the bandaged stump on the skell's right arm.

"*No human being could do this,*" he remembered his earlier words.

"Stevie. I'm Detective Sergeant Ed Caro."

The groggy Smith made no attempt to respond. He just stared blankly at him.

"You hear me, man?" Caro added more force to his voice.

The perp nodded lazily.

"Good. Let me get right to the point. You're in shit deep trouble. We found you a block from where that nurse was attacked with your Johnson hanging in the wind and a mangled .38 that you apparently fired. Something tells me we run a check on that gun, it's gonna come back illegal. Am I right so far?"

Smith just looked at him with vacant eyes again. Was it the drugs or something else?

Caro stood up, his tone stern. "Look, we already have enough to charge you with aggravated sexual assault and illegal use of a firearm. We also know about that mugging you spent eighteen months in county lock-up for. Now, would I be right to assume that you've done a hell of a lot more than that?"

Again silence.

"We're checking into your past, Steve. If you've done anything else, we'll find it and add it to the attack on the nurse. You'll be looking at a thirty, forty year stay in Graterford or some other shithole state pen, with guys even badder than you."

The only sound from Stevie was heavy breathing.

Caro stared at the man, a little perplexed. By now Smith should be denying he had anything to do with trying to rape that nurse.

But he said nothing. No denials, no confessions. Nothing.

Caro tried another approach. "You're not helping me here, Steve. You start opening up, I could help get the investigation moving on the driver who ran over your hand. With the right lawyer—"

"Wasn't no car."

The detective's eyebrows went up a bit. *Well, well.* It *can actually talk.*

"What was that?"

The blank stare vanished from Smith's face. Caro watched the young man's muscles tighten. "Wasn't no car that did this." He nodded to his stump.

"Okay. The truck—"

"No truck, neither. Nothing ran over my hand." The skin around Stevie's eyes quivered. Was he about to cry? A second later a slight tremor ran down the length of his body.

What the hell could scare a street punk this bad?

"Look, man," Smith continued in a raspy voice. "I'll give up whatever you want. You just . . . just keep that thing away from me."

His voice broke. Tears slid down to his temples.

"What thing? Talk to me? Who did this—?"

"It wasn't a *who*, man!" Smith sobbed uncontrollably. His voice nearly gave out. Caro almost felt sorry for him. Almost.

He waited for Smith to stop crying. When tears no longer came the perp continued. "It was no person. It . . . it was like, dressed in armor or something. I put all my caps into it. Didn't flinch. Nothing. Point blank and he acted like it was nothing. I don't know what it was, man. A spaceman, a guy dressed up like a knight or something."

Caro maintained a stern look. Inside surprise belted him in the gut. *Oh my God.* A knight! Just like that "crazy old broad" he talked to had said.

Now this *was* turning into a Stephen King novel. Too bad he couldn't put it down on a nightstand.

Smith continued babbling about "The Knight" until Caro waved him silent. "Hold that thought."

The detective left for one of the visitor's lounges to use his cell phone. An hour later a police sketch artist arrived to take down Smith's description.

"Are you serious about this?" the artist asked Caro when they left the ICU room.

"Just bear with me on this."

The scrawny, bespectacled young man with unkempt black hair shook his head. "You ask me, this guy inhaled a whole friggin' crackhouse."

"No sign of drugs in his system. He did have some booze before the attack. Barely enough to get him buzzed."

Caro took the sketch from the artist and studied it. *Forget Stephen King. We're talking George Lucas here.*

"Guy's got a hell of an imagination."

The detective dismissed that with a snort. "Skells like that don't have any imagination. Certainly nothing like this."

"Whatever," the artist shrugged. "Tsk! I get paid for this either way. Good luck catching your Power Ranger."

"Mm," Caro grunted as the young man left. The detective then headed to Maggie Stewart's room two floors up. A nurse told him a psychologist was in there with her and couldn't be disturbed.

That's okay. I got a fallback plan.

He left the hospital and drove to the "crazy old broad's" apartment. She remembered Caro from the other night and invited him in. The TV was tuned to one of those ridiculous afternoon talk shows, something about girls who steal their mother's boyfriends. Caro politely declined tea and cake and asked the woman to tell him again what she saw last night. When she finished, he pulled out the sketch and showed it to her.

"That's him!" She nearly jumped out of her seat as she pointed furiously. "That's the knight!"

Caro just stared blankly at her for several seconds. *This cannot be.*

He headed back to the Medical Examiner's office, only to discover Francine had been summoned to the Police Administration Building on 8th and Race.

Oh great. Now the brass is putting their fingers in this.

Caro told the examiner on duty to have Francine call him as soon as she got in. He then went back to his station in the Sixth District.

Getting kinda late. Better give Margerie a call.

Margerie Caro wasn't surprised by his, "I'm gonna be home late" call. She'd dealt with far too many to count. At least she handled them better now than during their first few years of marriage.

After getting off the phone with his wife, Caro phoned ballistics. So far they determined that whatever Smith hit pancaked some of the rounds and fragments they had recovered.

Two minutes after he hung up with ballistics, his cell phone rang.

"Ed. Francine."

"Hey. Glad you called. I got some fresh info on the Smith case. Pretty way out stuff, too."

After detailing all he had, Francine put him on hold for a minute or two. When she came back she said, "Ed. I'm with Commissioner Simms right now. He wants you to come down to the Roundhouse and brief him."

Caro's eyes widened. *Brief the Commish? What did I do to deserve this?*

From all stories Caro had heard, Maynard Simms seemed a decent enough fellow. Still the detective preferred not to deal with anyone above the rank of captain. The higher you went after that, the deeper the bullshit got.

Why couldn't I get a normal *murder or rape case?*

In the end, he had no real choice.

"I'm on my way."

Ten minutes later Caro arrived at the white, figure-eight shaped Police Administration Building, a.k.a The Roundhouse. He was quickly escorted to Simms' office.

Just play it cool, Ed. Straight-forward. Stick to the facts and you'll be fine.

It went better than Caro expected. Commissioner Maynard Simms listened patiently to the presentation. In the end Philly's top cop decided neither the detective or the M.E. was laying down bullshit.

"Make out a preliminary report ASAP," the medium-built, black Commissioner with a round face and close cropped salt and pepper hair told them. "I'll send it to the FBI in Washington, along with the hand and the gun. Hopefully the Feds can find out how the hell this happened."

The next day all the physical evidence was onboard an FBI helicopter bound for Reagan National Airport. From there it went by van to FBI Headquarters. A short time later Caro's and Ballard's reports came in via fax.

It didn't take long for others outside the FBI to take an interest in the case.

TWENTY

"SO HOW LONG before they're all out?" the President addressed the question to CIA Director Brock.

"I talked to the Secretary of State in Geneva. He says the Iraqis can have all foreign nationals out in three days. Four at the max. Luckily, most of the foreigners in Iraq are centered in and around Baghdad, so that makes gathering them easy. Iraq isn't exactly a tourist hotspot. The authorities won't have to traipse all over the country picking up hikers and sightseers."

"They're repeating 1990," noted the stocky, balding Secretary of Defense. "They're giving up potential hostages."

"Let's not complain," the Vice President jumped in. "It'll be one less thing we have to worry about if this blows up into full-scale war."

"I'm not complaining. I just think it's a stupid move on their part. How willing would we and our allies be to attack Iraq if they decided to stick Western civilians at all their bases?"

"There's no sense in debating a moot point, people," the President said. "They're letting all foreigners in the country go. Let's just be thankful for that."

"I'd say now is the time to back off a little," offered a slender woman in her mid-forties with a plain yet attractive face and auburn hair. "Give the Iraqis some breathing room."

"That's the last thing we should do, Miss Preston," Admiral Richard Callingworth locked eyes with Lydia Preston, the President's Chief of Staff.

"Why's that?!" the former head of Princeton's political science department blurted. "They're letting all foreigners leave the country. They're not holding them hostage. It's the first positive sign we've seen from them. This could be the opening we need to get them to dismantle their nuclear weapons program."

"More likely it's a ploy to buy time. Maybe garner sympathy from other countries."

"You're being paranoid," Preston shot back.

"You're darn right I'm paranoid. They're the ones who exploded a five megaton nuclear device when we thought they didn't have enough material for *one* megaton."

"But they exploded it in the middle of their desert. Probably as a test."

"Next time they could explode one over Riyadh. Or Tel Aviv. Or maybe right here. I've read over a dozen scenario papers on how a foreign power could smuggle a nuke inside the United States. We're not dealing with the most rational people in the world. The regime over there has used mustard gas on their own people, invaded a country no bigger than New Jersey, raped and pillaged it like a horde of Fifth Century barbarians and destroyed every Kuwaiti oil well when they knew they were going to lose. These are the kind of people who would use nuclear weapons if given half the chance."

"All the more reason to back off now. Slow down on deploying troops to the Gulf. Give them a chance to breath easier."

"I have to take the Chairman's side on this, Miss Preston," Brock said. "Our chief of station in Riyadh faxed a report that he thinks the Iraqis are kicking out all foreigners because they may have something big going on."

"What?" Preston responded, daring the DCI.

"We don't know for sure. It could be they're building or deploying more nuclear devices. That would explain expelling journalists and embassy staff. The Iraqis can regulate the flow of information to the outside world all they want."

"All you're doing is guessing."

The outburst didn't surprise the President. He knew Lydia was often critical of the CIA. More than once she had said "those dimwits" probably get most of their information from "a ouija board."

But this time the head "dimwit" had evidence, not some theory plucked from midair. Brock pulled out several photos taken by a KH-11 satellite.

"This, Mr. President, is the Kassim Research Facility. It's about sixty miles north of Baghdad. After Desert Storm we got word the Iraqis were developing nuclear weapons there. Nothing confirmed, but our interest peaked when they wouldn't let the U.N. teams near the place." Brock spread the high-resolution photos across the President's desk. He pointed out the large number of vehicles parked around the facility, including a government limousine, increased sentry activity and a number of mobile SAMs strategically positioned in the hills and valleys leading to the research facility. Another set of blown-up photos featured three men in khakis and berets, surrounded by aides and bodyguards, walking across the parking lot.

"I think you recognize the guy in the center."

The President did. Even photographed from thousands of miles in space, the features of Iraq's leader were not hard to distinguish. The Chief Executive shook his head in amazement. He had seen satellite photos a hundred times before, but had never failed to be marveled by their incredible photographic capability.

"The one on the left is their Defense Minister," DCI Brock went on. "The one on the right, we've checked his shoulder boards. We're pretty sure he's their head of intelligence, General Faisal Nurabi. A trio like this doesn't go to a top secret research facility for a friendly visit. They're probably inspecting something important. That would account for the increased activity in and around the compound. Plus, just give me a minute . . ." Brock pulled out a sheaf of computer printouts. "Our ELINT—that's electronic intelligence—assets have picked up increased radio traffic to and from the facility. Most of what we've been able to translate are supply reports, which there have been plenty."

"What kinds of supplies?" National Security Advisor Baronelli asked.

"Computer equipment, food, personal care items. It all seems to point to the fact there are a lot of people at Kassim working on something important enough to warrant a visit from their leader and his chief thugs."

"Don't you have anything more concrete? You're still going on speculation."

"Speculation based on evidence, Miss Preston. Which right now is the best we can do. Unfortunately, we don't have much in the way of HUMINT in Iraq." The Director of Central Intelligence meant human intelligence, or layman's terms, old-fashioned spies. "We're working with the Israelis and Saudis to see if they have anything better."

The President leaned back in his leather chair and scanned the small group of department heads and advisors gathered in the Oval Office.

"Suggestions?"

"Keep the pressure on them," chimed Baronelli. "Continue with the build-up, call up more reserves. Let them know we will not tolerate a nuclear capable Iraq."

The Vice President nodded. "I'll go along with Ed's recommendation."

Chief of Staff Preston spoke next. "Press with negotiations. Especially after they've agreed to let all foreigners leave the country. Maybe in return we can relax our military build-up."

The President turned to the JCS Chairman and asked for his opinion.

"We have to assume the bomb that went off in their desert wasn't the only one Iraq had. I fear next time they'll use it for real. Lord knows there are enough juicy targets between Cairo and Tehran for them to turn to ash. I think it's time we considered air strikes against all Iraqi nuclear sites, known and suspected."

Lydia Preston nearly jumped out of her chair. "That's the last thing we should do now!"

"Miss Preston!" This time Callingworth didn't hide his annoyance at the Chief of Staff's cautionary approach. "We have a hostile country, with nuclear weapons and the will to use them, sitting in the middle of the world's most strategic land mass. We're dealing with a *global* threat here. Talking didn't accomplish anything in 1990. I doubt it'll do any good now."

"We need better intelligence before we do that," Brock told him. "We have to make sure we take out *all* their nukes on the first try. If we miss just one it could be disastrous."

"We've covered that," Callingworth stated. "We'll need to increase the number of U-2 and Aurora flights over Iraq. We also need to put some people on the ground. Special Operations Command has drawn up plans to insert U.S. and British reconnaissance teams into Iraq. It's similar to what we did prior to Desert Storm. We could make our first insertion forty-eight hours after you give the go-ahead."

"Mr. President," Defense shifted in his chair. "Currently

our forces are at DEFCON Four readiness. In light of Director Brock's estimates, I believe we have to up the ante and let Iraq know just how serious we are about having them end their nuclear weapons program."

"What's your suggestion?" the President bit his lip, fearing the worst.

The Secretary drew a breath and laid out his plan. Both the Vice President and Chief of Staff railed against it. Preston said the plan was inexcusable, that it could lead Iraq to use the foreigners as hostages instead of releasing them. The VP felt it would take them back to a Cold War mentality. The Chairman of the Joint Chiefs said it might be the only way to get Iraq to concede.

The President's staff bickered for ten minutes while he thought. He wondered if this was how Kennedy felt in October of 1962, or maybe more appropriately, Truman back in 1945. But this time the decision was his and his alone. He knew where such a path could take him if he acted . . . but if he didn't act, things could be even worse.

Amazing how the course of history can be determined by a handful of people in a small room.

The President made his decision. Now was not the time for air strikes, especially with all foreigners being evacuated from Iraq. Plus he doubted whether their allies would go along with it. He did authorize the increase of spy plane flights and the insertion of recon teams inside Iraq. As for the Secretary of Defense's proposal, the President ordered him to get the appropriate units into motion. He would hold off making the announcement until all foreigners were out of Iraq and America's allies consulted.

The meeting ended twenty minutes later. When everyone had left, the President placed a call to the Los Alamos Laboratory. He talked to the scientist in charge of the research team studying the energy field created by the Iraqi Bomb. The scientist, also the head of the Lab's Theoretical Physics division, said they had found nothing new. The energy field had encircled the planet, but no evidence could be found to suggest it was harmful to humans . . . or that it wasn't. The President prayed it would turn out to be nothing serious.

No such luck.

TWENTY-ONE

IT NEVER FAILS, Brigadier General Louis Clay pulled his non-descript Buick into his personal space at the Pentagon's parking lot. He was supposed to have the day all to himself. With his wife and daughter out shopping, he planned to take care of a few long neglected household improvements. Then it was off to his easy chair in the den to watch the Army-Baylor football game.

He just finished tightening the screws on the mailbox when the phone rang. The duty officer just said, "We have a hit."

In less than ten minutes, the stocky general with an egg-shaped head and thinning brown hair put on his olive dress uniform and pulled out of the driveway of his Hyattsville home. Traffic was a little heavy coming into Arlington. Tourists.

The five-sided building that housed the National Military Command Center was abuzz with activity. Clay walked by officers and noncoms from all four services as they rushed about the halls. He caught bits of conversations.

" . . . needs to know how many MiGs are there . . ."

" . . . get the screw replaced. We've got nearly forty M1A1s sitting on that ship gathering rust . . ."

" . . . good evidence there are chemical weapons there . . ."

" . . . more artillery along the Iran-Iraq border . . ."

But none of that concerned him.

Three floors below the building, the General walked up to a featureless black door with no knob. He took a plastic key card and slid it through the electronic lock on the side. The light panel on top changed from red to green and the door slid open. Twenty feet away lay another door. To the right was an enclosed counter with a serious looking MP sitting behind it. A layer of bulletproof lexan glass separated him from the rest of the world. When Clay appeared at the window, the MP looked over his credentials and flicked on the intercom.

"Clay, Louis H. Brigadier General. 546-44-1091."

The MP punched a few buttons on his keyboard, then checked his screen. A few seconds later, he said flatly, "Hand and retinal scan please."

Clay placed his right hand on the machine set up on a shelf protruding from the window. A green light flashed underneath his hand, rolling up and down like a copier machine. He then went over to the left side of the window, where another device scanned the retina of his left eye. The MP checked the scans on his computer.

"You're clear, General. Proceed."

The MP pressed a button. The six-inch steel door slowly swung open. Clay walked into another hallway, monitored by surveillance cameras, heat sensors and motion detectors. He rounded a corner and proceeded sixty feet to yet another door. This one had another MP sitting at a small desk off to the side. His shoulder rig, with the small MP4 machine pistol, was visible for the world to see.

"General," the MP nodded as Clay took the clipboard from the desk and signed in.

"Good day, Sergeant," Clay replied after the MP checked his signature and credentials. The General then opened the sliding door with his key card and stepped inside.

"The Inner Sanctum," as his group affectionately called it, was an oval-shaped room with six large screens dominating the front wall. Each one featured a variety of digital maps. Technicians filled three rows of computer consoles. A concourse separated each row. On the top level were offices separated by glass dividers, allowing its occupants a view of the entire room. Despite the lights and the glow from numerous display screens, the Inner Sanctum still had a rather shadowy look. Appropriate enough, since officially, this room and the men and women in it, did not exist.

Clay jogged up the stairs to his office. An Air Force major greeted him at the top.

"This better be a good one, Major Xantis."

The tall, lean, dark haired, olive skinned son of Greek immigrants replied, "I wouldn't bring you down here if it wasn't, sir. Let me show you."

Xantis followed Clay into his office and closed the door. The General seated himself at a desk with two phones and a computer terminal. A few filing cabinets sat on either side of the office, with three squat leather chairs in front of the desk. A small, wooden entertainment center stood in the left front corner of the room, a TV, VCR and stereo system contained within its doors. Next to it was a water cooler.

"Did you happen to catch the news about the punk in Philadelphia who got his hand crushed?" Xantis asked as he set his briefcase on the General's desk.

Clay paused a moment. "Oh yeah. There was a blurb about it in *The Post* the other day. Said a truck might have run over his hand. Cops say he tried to rape some girl. Serves him right if he did."

Xantis shook his head. "It was no truck. Some*one* crushed that punk's hand."

Clay cocked an eyebrow. "Some*one*?"

"Philadelphia Police faxed a report to the Bureau last night." Xantis handed the General a copy of said report. "We red flagged it when a copy was sent over to Justice."

The General looked over the report. The medical examiner concluded the suspect's hand, and weapon, were compacted, not flattened. Certainly, no human was capable of doing that. As for vehicles, maybe a bulldozer or an M1 tank could inflict that kind of damage. Not surprisingly there was no evidence of any such vehicles in that area.

Then came the interesting part. Two witnesses with no apparent connection claimed to have seen the possible UL, or Unknown Lifeform, squash the scumbag's hand. One was, of course, the scumbag himself. Hard not to notice some thing turning your hand into ground meat. The sketch astounded him. A little flashier than what he had previously encountered.

"What about the woman who was attacked? Did she see anything?"

"Don't know," Xantis replied. "Apparently she's repressing the whole incident. Only remembers bits and pieces."

"Did you go through the database? Find out if we have anything like this on file." Clay indicated to the sketch.

"We're doing that now, sir."

"Did you run the usual checks? Any UFO activity? Strange ground markings?"

"One report, sir. It's from Thursday's *Philadelphia Inquirer*: UFO sighting outside of Camden."

Clay quickly scanned the story. "Six feet long!?!"

"That fits the size of the UL. Of course it's still too early to tell if the two incidents are connected."

"Yeah. That's all we need. One that flies.

"Still, we've got enough to proceed. I'll alert the President, you get our assets moving. I want a team of agents sent to South Jersey Regional Airport with appropriate FAA covers. SOP; radar and radio logs, get hold of the people on the plane."

"Yes, sir."

"And have one of our field teams at Meade ready to deploy. Make it Echo Team. Bravo made the last bag."

"Yes, sir. General, I suggest we also use *Overlord* on this one."

General Clay nodded. "Approved. Get Ops to whip up some Justice Department credentials. I want the local cops and FBI kept away from this until we know what we're dealing with."

"Yes, sir." Xantis didn't even bother asking about the press. No one down here talked to them . . . ever!

Shortly after Xantis left, Clay got on the secure phone to the President at Camp David. Needless to say, the Chief Executive was not happy to hear the news. He already had enough on his mind.

"I trust your abilities and those of your people, General," the President told Clay. "Handle it."

It took over three hours for the appropriate IDs to be made up. Then they were placed in Major Xantis' briefcase. He and General Clay drove to Andrews Air Force Base, where they choppered to Fort Meade. There they briefed their men on the next mission to be carried out by Group Nine.

Jack Remmler tried to keep up as Brian Doyle again recounted their excursion to Bailey's Clubhouse. The roommates had gone out to the bar and grill with several of their friends last night. Neither had drank much. Doyle only had three beers. Remmler, as usual, stuck with soft drinks. They passed the hours bullshitting about sports and other "important" topics and laughing at their buddies as they got plastered.

It proved a nice distraction. The same with Friday's Welcome Back Bash. Unfortunately, once they were over, Remmler still faced the same problems as before.

He couldn't get that night out of his head. Watching the young woman break down into a quivering mass before him. The feel of meaty flesh and brittle bones as he crushed the scumbag's hand. The story was all over the local news. Even went national because of its sensational nature. What's worse, the lowlife now had a name. Steven "Stevie" Smith. The press had been able to dig up some of his tainted past. Served time for a mugging. Just eighteen months. Ran with some gangs in high school. Suspected of other crimes.

Why did I have to find out his name?

He tried to convince himself the slimebag deserved it. Then he'd remember the scream. A wounded animal couldn't even scream like that.

Remmler hadn't donned his armor since. He didn't want to deal with another situation like that. It made him wonder why he even bothered coming up with a name for his superhero alter ego.

Some hero, Remmler thought as he and Bubba Doyle entered Driscoll Hall. *I get my ass kicked by Imperium and run away like some nancy boy, then I cripple some guy and can't get it out of my mind. I'm surprised the Keeper hasn't shown up, taken away my* tru'kat, *and said, "Whoops. Sorry. My bad. This wasn't meant for you."*

I cannot be the best choice on this planet for a Cosmic Protector.

If only there were someone to talk to. But how would they react? He doubted his family or friends would understand, or be able to keep his secret. In desperation he went up to the roof this morning, pulled out his shrunken *tru'kat* and called to the Keeper. He never appeared.

I thought he was supposed to watch over all us Protectors, Remmler had thought disappointedly.

"Man, I still gotta get that list of terms done for my Greece and Rome class," Bubba said as he opened the door to their floor.

"Yeah. I still need to get through that one chapter in Sociology. Wanna finish that up before the Phillies game. That's not gonna bother you?"

"Nah. I'll be done long before then."

"Cool."

The two had just opened the door to their room when someone shouted from down the hall.

Remmler and Doyle turned. A lean young man with thick, slicked back dark hair and a slightly tanned complexion headed toward them.

"Ey! Vinny Goombah!" Remmler said joyfully.

Vincent Gambolinni, Mr. Stereotypical South Philly Italian kid, shot them an exaggerated wave.

"What's up, Vinny?" Doyle asked after the three exchanged high-fives.

"Yeah, what brings you by here on a weekend?" Remmler asked, waving Vinny into the room. Gambolinni was one of those commuter students who seemed to spend more time on campus than at home.

"I stayed at Jim and Alec's," Vinny told them as he sat on Jack's desk. "You guys get back from brunch?"

"Yeah," Doyle replied. "Thank God for cereal. At least they can't mess that up."

"So what's goin' on, man?"

Vinny reached into his pocket and pulled out four tickets. "Phils and Mets for today. Two-hundred Level, third base line. Primo seats."

"Dude, no way! Where'd you get those?" Remmler asked.

"Guy my dad works with. Couldn't use 'em. So he gave 'em to my dad, who gave 'em to me. It was supposed to be me, Geist, Alec and my brother, Donny, goin'. But Donny's girlfriend, her grandfather's havin' a birthday, so he's gettin' dragged to that.

"So which one'a you wants the ticket?"

The roommates looked at one another. "Wanna flip for it?" Remmler suggested.

"Nah. You go. Shit, I don't care about the Phillies. Besides, CBS has the Steelers and Patriots at four. I ain't missin' my Steelers to go see a couple of suckass teams."

"There's only one suckass team playing, and it ain't the Phillies."

"Okay, cool. You're in, Remy."

"Let me just put on the appropriate attire before we go." Remmler took off his T-shirt and rifled through his drawers for one of his five Phillies T-shirts.

"Aw, man. I wonder if this'll be like the last Phillies-Mets game I went to."

"What happened there?" Remmler asked as he pulled out his gray Phillies T-shirt with a drawing of Veterans Stadium.

Vinny hopped off the desk. "Oh, it was great! Some friggin' Mets fan two rows behind us got shitfaced, then took his beer and chucked it at this Phillies fan on the walkway. Guy came chargin' up the steps, yelling how he's gonna kick his ass. Security guards broke it up. It was fuckin' whacked."

"Oh great. Tell you what. Any Mets fan that wants to start a fight, I'll send him your way."

"Where's your sense of adventure?"

"Hey, I go to the Vet to watch baseball, not take part in Wrestlemania."

Vinny Goombah laughed. "Deal, man. Let's book."

Remmler grabbed his Phillies ballcap and turned to his roommate. "Have a good one, Bubba."

"You too, man. Hey! What about your homework?"

"This is college. Who does homework?"

Remmler and Vinny bid their final farewell and headed to the ballpark.

Running away from reality again, a voice in the back of Jack's head pestered him.

He ignored it.

TWENTY-TWO

"SO HOW MUCH does she remember?" Detective Sergeant Ralph Diaz asked his partner, Ed Caro.

"Little more than the previous few days," Caro replied as he got on the Vine Street Expressway heading toward Hahneman Hospital. "I talked to her shrink. She says she's starting to put all the bits and pieces together. Feels it might be time to get her to recall the whole thing."

"You think this coulda waited until Monday," Diaz straightened the short, black hair that rested above his round, tan, slightly pockmarked face. "I mean, the guy spilled his guts. We've got him on half-a-dozen charges. He's goin' away, man."

"I want a witness. That guy was scared out of his mind when he talked. Any snake oil salesman lawyer could make a good argument for coercion. I need that girl to point him out and say 'that's the one.' I don't want this son of a bitch back on the street. Ever." He then grumbled. "Like that'll really happen."

Diaz sighed. Ed Caro knew his partner had heard this

routine before. But so what? Eighteen years on the force only nourished his cynicism. How many times had he seen the courts release the scum he hauled in before even half their sentences were up? Even when he was successful, he never got the credit he deserved. Police, it seemed, only made headlines when charged with racism or brutality.

"So you really think there's something to this 'Knight' story?" Diaz asked as they got off the Expressway.

"Maybe. You got any other theories on what happened to that slimeball's hand?" When his partner didn't answer, Caro continued. "We need to see if that nurse saw the same thing."

"And if she saw it, you know what that means? Our three witnesses are a traumatized nurse, a convicted criminal and a shut-in. Who's gonna buy that story?"

"Then we'll just have to find this 'Knight' ourselves."

Caro pulled into the hospital's parking garage when the thought struck Diaz. "Did you think of checking out some costume stores?"

"They don't sell costumes that crush people's hands. Or .38s."

"Then . . . maybe some special effects companies. Like the guys George Lucas or Steven Spielberg use."

Caro laughed. "Oh great! Call Hollywood. Why not? Maybe they'll turn it into a movie."

"I'm bein' serious, Ed. Or, you know what? Maybe some robotics company. If anything out there can crush a man's hand *and* a .38, they must have it."

"You may be right, Ralph. We'll check into it when we're through with the girl."

Caro pulled his Toyota Camry into a space at the far end of the first level. The humidity hit both men as they got out of their air conditioned car and into the eighty-plus degree heat. They crossed at the light and headed into Hahneman. Several reporters still hung around the hospital, making Caro wonder if these people ever slept. The last news they had on

Stevie Smith was that he'd been moved out of ICU and into a private room, still under guard.

The two detectives approached the wing where Maggie Stewart's room was located. A hospital security guard stood vigil as expected. What wasn't expected was a tall, rather muscular man in his early forties with a stern, no-nonsense face topped by close cropped, curled red hair. He stood up as soon as the detectives appeared.

Who the hell's this stiff? Caro wondered.

Stoneface parked himself in front of Caro and Diaz. "You can't come in here." The man had all the emotion of a brick.

Caro tapped his badge with one finger. "Detective Ed Caro. Detective Ralph Diaz. Sixth District." He could see out the corner of his eye the guard staring nervously at his feet. Something was up.

Stoneface flashed his ID. "Justice Department. We're taking over this case."

Caro felt his blood boil. His forehead scrunched up and his eyes narrowed. *Who the fuck invited the Feds!?*

"Hey, no one told us anything about federal involvement," Diaz complained.

"You've been told now. This case is no longer a local matter."

"Bullshit!" Ed hollered, unable to contain his anger. "Since when do the Feds care about some punk who tries to rape a nurse?"

Stoneface remained impassive. "This case is now under federal jurisdiction. Leave."

"Not 'til I know why! Why the hell does this concern the Justice Department?"

"That's none of your concern. Leave now."

"It is my concern! This is our case. I need to talk to Ms. Stewart and that's exactly what I'm going to do. And until I get word from *my* bosses, telling me otherwise, you can sit in a corner with your thumb up your ass!"

Caro took one step forward. Stoneface moved in front of him. The fed casually reached under the bottom of his jacket and opened it just enough to give the detectives a peak inside.

Is he serious?

Caro gazed in surprise at the SIG-Sauer P220 stuffed into Stoneface's shoulder rig.

"I don't think I need to tell you the trouble you risk by interfering with a federal investigation, Detective. Your job. Your pension. Jail time."

Caro stared into the man's eyes. This guy was all business. He just knew this stiff would shoot him right here in the middle of the hallway without hesitation if they didn't vacate immediately.

What the fuck is going on here?

Diaz put his hand on Caro's shoulder. "Ed. Come on, man. We'll get this cleared up back at the station. Let's go."

Caro just nodded, too astonished and angry to speak. He backed away at first, then spun on his heel and followed Diaz down the hall.

Satisfied, Stoneface went back to his seat and resumed his post.

"Dammit!" Caro raged as he and Diaz turned the corner, startling several staffers and visitors. Their gazes fixed on the big, angry black man as he continued ranting.

"What the hell kind of bullshit is this!? When the hell did they show up!? This is our case! Our goddamn case!"

Diaz looked up and down the hall. Three nurses stopped in their tracks and watched Ed's tirade nervously. An overweight woman looked on with embarrassment. At her side was a cute, dark-haired girl no more than five-years-old. Diaz figured it was time to cool his partner off.

"Okay, buddy," he grabbed him by the shoulders. "Let's blow off steam somewhere else. I ain't exactly thrilled with this either."

Just then a stocky, middle-aged nurse with her graying brown hair in a bun approached them. "Is there a problem, gentlemen?"

"Yeah! The world sucks!"

"Sir, the disturbance you're causing is totally unacceptable," the nurse said in a soft yet stern tone. "We have visitors, children, people resting. They don't need to hear such language. Especially coming from a police officer." She wagged a finger at his face. "If you can't keep yourself under control, I'll have to ask you to leave . . . now."

Caro threw his hands up and slapped them down at his sides. He still wasn't done venting. "Sure. Why the hell not? All we're trying to do is our job." He then brushed past the nurse, muttering, "Be nice if people would let us do it for once."

Diaz flashed the nurse a smile. "Sorry. He's having a real bad day."

Ralph Diaz caught up to his partner, who remained silent until they were out of the hospital and in Caro's car. Had this been a cartoon, there'd definitely be smoke coming out of Caro's ears.

"Way to keep your cool, Ed," Diaz scolded him after closing the door.

"Don't start with me, Ralph."

"The hell I won't. *Madre,* Ed. You're a cop. What are people supposed to think if you're stomping down the hall yelling and cursing like that?"

"Ask me if I care."

Diaz rolled his eyes. He knew from past experience when Ed's temper boiled to this point, there was no reasoning with him. He decided to change the subject as Caro started the car.

"Okay, let's try to be constructive here. Why are the Feds so interested in this case?"

Caro waited until he backed out of the slot and proceeded

to the exit before answering. "I don't know—" he paused, tilting his head to the side in thought. "You don't think this has something to do with the Knight?"

"I can't think of another reason. Outside of that, and a punk with a crushed hand, this would be a regular sexual assault. Wouldn't interest the Feds."

"In other words, we stumbled on something big," Caro said as he drove onto North 15th St.

"Looks that way, doesn't it? Maybe this 'Knight' is some super secret government experiment gone haywire."

"We can speculate on that until the day after forever. Let's focus on what we have so far."

"Yeah. A guy dressed like a knight who crushed some pervert's hand and a fuckin' .38! Wanna talk some more about speculating?"

"What I wanna do is talk to Captain Feldman. Find out what all this federal bullshit is about."

"Just promise me you won't throw a shitfit if he gives you bad news. Okay?"

"It'll depend on how bad the news is."

Diaz rolled his eyes and prayed for strength.

"Let me tell you something, partner. Feds or not, I'm gonna find out the truth about this whole "Knight" business."

TWENTY-THREE

Jack Remmler had never been happier to be at a ballgame. A near sellout crowd filled Veterans Stadium, a good number of them Mets fans. The humidity was just tolerable. A steady supply of beer, soda and ice cream made the heat easier to deal with. Passing clouds kept the sun from beating down too much on the fans.

The game itself proved a see-saw battle until the Phillies pulled ahead in the late innings. The Mets rallied in the ninth, but came up short. Final score, Phillies 5, Mets 4.

Remmler forgot all his problems as a Cosmic Protector. For the first time in a week, he felt like a regular college kid.

"You guys better make sure you're hungry again in an hour," Vinny said as he, Remmler, Jim Giest and Alec Tanzone walked across the parking lot with thousands of other fans. "My mother's gonna cook you a meal you wouldn't believe."

"You sure she won't mind us there?" Remmler asked.

"My mom!? Nah. She loves to cook. Heh, what Italian mother doesn't? Nah, trust me, she doesn't mind. The more the merrier. Besides, I told her we'd stop by after the game."

"Cool," Tanzone said. "We won't have to eat that crap back at school."

The four piled into Vinny's small Honda Civic. Tanzone took the passenger's seat, while Remmler and Jim Giest sat in the back. It took nearly a half-hour to get out of the crowded parking lot and onto Pattison Ave. They passed the time listening to the Eagles post game report on the radio. Unfortunately, Philadelphia's football team didn't fair as well as its baseball team. The Eagles lost to the Minnesota Vikings 27-6.

"Well you're gonna have a lot to talk about on your show tomorrow," Geist told Remmler.

"Yeah. I'll tell you, I hope the Steelers bomb. If Shitsburgh wins and the Eagles lose, I'll never hear the end of it from Bubba."

"Hey, man," Tanzone said from up front. "Steelers look good. Could be their year."

"Honestly," Geist responded, "I think New England has a shot at goin' all the way in the AFC."

Remmler let out a guffaw. "Yeah right! Man, all that beer you drink's killed way too many brain cells. I can name five other teams in the AFC better than the Patriots."

"Hey, guys," Vinny said. "Wanna check something out?"

"What?" asked Remmler.

"Look over to your left."

The college students turned their heads as the car passed by a block of rundown rowhomes. Vinny nodded to a dilapidated brown one just ahead with a man and a girl standing in front of it.

"See where the black guy with the red beret is?"

"What about it?" Tanzone asked.

"That's our local crackhouse." The disgust in Vinny's voice was evident.

"You're kidding!" Jim Geist said incredulously. Remmler wondered if the only place his friend had ever seen a crackhouse was on TV.

"The hell I am. Fuckin' place is like six blocks from my house. Somethin', ain't it?"

Remmler stared dispassionately at the crackhouse as they drove by. The man in the beret topped off at about six feet, with a beard, a tie-dyed t-shirt and beat up jeans. But the girl stirred the most feelings in him. She couldn't have been more than thirteen. Dressed and groomed rather well. She could be a normal fixture at any junior high school in the country. What the hell was she doing at a crackhouse?

His gut turned to ice. The girl pulled out a wad of bills and handed them to the man. Remmler's jaw tightened in anger as he watched the man enthusiastically wave the young girl inside.

Son of a bitch! They'd actually let a little kid smoke that poison? Bastards!

"Whoa! They just did a drug deal in broad daylight!" Alec Tanzone sounded shocked.

"Welcome to the real world, Al. That shit goes on there everyday."

"What about the police?" Giest asked.

"You kiddin'!? Half the people here don't trust the cops and the other half just don't give a shit. Besides, there's a thousand other places just like that all over the city. Cops can't get 'em all."

Remmler silently stewed all the way to Vinny's house. The image of that little girl going into the crackhouse refused to leave his mind. Even the great dinner—Fettucini Alfredo with Mrs. Gambolinni's special sauce, garlic bread, pencil points and canolis—couldn't erase the memory.

Vinny had been right. The cops couldn't shut down this particular crackhouse.

But he could.

"This is our case, Captain!" Ed Caro shouted into the phone. "Our turf. We shouldn't be left out of this one."

"The Feds made it clear, Ed," a calm Captain Feldman replied from the other end. "Whatever's goin' on is real hush-hush. Shit, they didn't even tell me about it."

"That's all we need," Caro said as he paced in front of his desk. The telephone moved closer and closer to the edge with every sudden movement. "A bunch of spook shit. Are these guys really from the Justice Department?"

Captain Feldman paused. Caro thought he could hear him shift uncomfortably in a chair at his Eastwick home. "Honestly, I don't know. And it's not a good idea to talk about these kinds of things over the phone. But, let's just say it looks like there may be more to this 'Knight' story than we thought."

"Yeah. Why else-."

"Not over the phone, Ed," Feldman cut him off. "These are some big league guys they sent up. Don't get in their way."

"Yeah, but-."

"We'll talk later, Ed."

Caro's nostrils flared. "Yeah. Okay, Captain. Bye."

He hung up the phone and plopped into his chair. "I should fucking retire right now. I don't need this fucking shit."

"Not good news, I take it," asked Diaz, sitting at his desk across from Caro.

"No. Feldman said he was told this was a Federal matter. We're supposed to stay out of it."

Diaz dipped his head, his brown eyes widening. "You're kidding."

"Heh! I wish. If that joker at the hospital was from the Justice Department, I'm fucking George Jetson. Feldman sounded kinda nervous over the phone."

"Feldman! Nervous!?" Diaz looked astounded. They'd both heard dozens of stories from "Terrible" Tom Feldman's action days, including how the five-foot-eleven cop wrestled down a six-foot-five murder suspect. "That man would kick a grizzly bear in the nuts for fun."

"Well somebody got to him. This isn't the way the Justice

Department works. This has to do with that "Knight" character."

"But why?"

"That's what we gotta find out."

Diaz threw up his arms. "Whoa, whoa, whoa. The Captain told us to lay off."

"Actually, he told me not to get in their way. So we won't."

Diaz shook his head and wagged his finger at Caro. "You're playing with fire, Ed."

"Look, Ralph. We've got some . . . well, there's something out there that can apparently crush a man's hand *and* a gun. Yeah, this time it was just some piece of shit who tried to rape a nurse. Next time it might *be* the nurse. Or an old lady cashing her social security check. Or a cop. It's our job to make sure something like that doesn't happen again.

"Feds or not, I want to find out exactly what the hell is going on."

Warehouse 31C at the Philadelphia Naval Base hadn't been used in years. Just another casualty of Defense spending cuts championed throughout the 1990s by shortsighted politicians in Washington who thought with the Soviet Union dissolved and Iraq defeated in Desert Storm, America had no more enemies.

General Louis Clay might have thanked those politicians had the thought crossed his mind. The warehouse was perfect. Spacious, located in a rather remote part of the base. The perfect place for Group Nine's field headquarters.

It took just two hours to get everything set up. Generators, satellite link-ups, commo gear, computer terminals. The group even brought their own cots, plastic portable showers, field kitchen and port-a-pots. Mingling with the small base population was kept at a minimum. A row of TVs crowded one table, a set for each Philadelphia station. The communications personnel also kept tabs on the local radio stations, police bands, even 911. A squad of unseen sentries hovered nearby, with orders to use lethal force if necessary to keep unwanted guests away.

"Anything useful from the woman?" Clay asked his staff, sitting around a card table. Major Xantis was opposite from Clay. At the sides sat Major Brendan Chambers, ex-National Security Agency, ex-Defense Intelligence Agency, current Intelligence Officer for Group Nine and ex-Navy SEAL Captain Sam Elder, the Group's XO.

"She seemed to recognize the UL when we showed her the sketch," the brown haired, bespectacled, bookish Chambers answered. "Says she saw something like that standing over her. At least she thinks so. She's still traumatized by the whole event."

"And the assailant, um . . ." Clay looked through his files. "Steven Smith."

"Absolutely convinced he saw it. Still scared shitless over the whole thing."

"You made sure he wouldn't talk."

"I told him if he mentioned our meeting to anyone, he'd meet with an 'accident' when he got to prison," Chambers said flatly.

Clay nodded in approval. "Good. And the people in the plane?"

"Plumsted and Keller interviewed them," Xantis replied. "Everyone bought their FAA cover. The pilot and two passengers claimed to have seen the object. Their descriptions could fit our UL."

"Was any pressure needed?"

"None. The pilot and his wife are big-shot lawyers. They don't want this to get out. Afraid it'll hurt their reputation. Same with the other witness."

"Good. Makes our job easier," Clay turned to his staunch-faced executive officer. "Captain Elder. You have our deployment plans ready?"

"Yes sir. If you'll follow me over to the map."

Elder led the officers over to a city map pinned to a nearby bulletin board. "We've divided the city into ten grids, each one to be covered by two-man teams in civilian clothes and vehicles working dusk 'til dawn. We're in the process of acquiring the rest of the cars. We should be ready to go by tonight. In addition, we'll have three quick reaction teams deployed throughout the city for back up. They'll carry our heavy weapons; M249s, grenades, Armbursts."

"What about the two-man teams? How are they armed?"

"Sidearms and MP5 submachine guns. They've also got shotguns and sniper rifles in the trunk as back up."

Clay nodded. "Now what about *Overlord?*"

"I suggest using it at night. Both sightings took place between nine and eleven p.m. Plus we won't have to worry too much about being spotted by the public."

"Approved. I'd also like to send some people across the river into Camden. The first sighting took place near there. Also, integrate Camden into *Overlord's* search pattern."

"Yes, sir," Elder replied.

Clay looked again at the map. Philadelphia was a damn big city. Probably a million places to hide. He had barely a hundred men and women to cover it all

Why couldn't this have happened in the desert like the last one?

TWENTY-FOUR

For once, Jack Remmler couldn't wait to finish his Monday afternoon show on WKCB. From the time he woke up, the crackhouse he drove by yesterday remained constant in his mind. He made mental checklists in preparation for his assault. How many drug dealers would be in the building? What weapons did they have? What escape routes were there? Remmler tried to recall things from all the techno-thrillers he'd read and apply them here.

As soon as Chris Wilson relieved him, Remmler dashed out the door. He hurried across campus, past the copper, spiral-domed Marcus Fedder Gymnasium, past the athletic fields where the field hockey team was finishing up practice, and into a thickly wooded area of Cobbs Creek Park. There he reached into his pocket and pulled out his shrunken *tru'kat*. Holding it out at arms length, Remmler shut his eyes and concentrated. An off-yellow glow suddenly surrounded his body. When it dissipated, he was in his armor, the *tru'kat* at its regular size. Jack Remmler had become . . . Epsilon.

He flew off toward South Philadelphia, using his unisense

the whole way. He landed on the flat roof of a run down apartment building across the street from the crackhouse. Hiding behind the building's rampart, Epsilon observed the house with his unisense. The same guy he saw yesterday in front of the house was there again. Epsilon sensed a small automatic tucked into the sentry's waistband, covered by his t-shirt. His unisense swept inside. Two men chatted away in the living room. Their accent sounded Jamaican. Both carried weapons. Three flunkies so far.

He "looked" beyond them. A radio blasted reggae music. In the decrepit kitchen four people—two men and two women—sat on the floor smoking crackpipes. Some rats and cockroaches skittered by, not that the four jittery addicts noticed. Epsilon didn't expect trouble from them. They were probably so stoned they wouldn't care if a nuclear bomb went off. He shook his head. How could someone waste away their lives smoking that shit?

What if I'd been born here instead of in Lawrence? To the kind of loving parents I had? Could I have wound up in a place like this?

He left the question at that. This was no time to get abstract.

Epsilon continued his scan up the stairs. To the right was a room with two rickety wooden tables where three men busily cut, weighed and individually packaged crack and cocaine into vials. All three had handguns. Two Uzis and a shotgun rested against the rear wall. *So much for the assault weapons ban.*

Another room lay cross the hall, its door closed. A closer scan revealed-

"Holy shit!"

A man and a woman were lying on a beat-up mattress. The man had his lips wrapped around a crackpipe. The woman had her lips wrapped around something else. When she finished, her "boyfriend" let her have a toot on his other pipe. The slug didn't even bother pulling up his pants.

Epsilon kept his focus on them for a bit, his mouth agape. Outside of the one or two porn movies he'd seen since he got to college, he'd never witnessed an actual blowjob. He certainly never imagined one under these circumstances. Epsilon shook his head incredulously. He wondered if his Aunt Greta or cousin Michael ever encountered anything similar in their law enforcement careers.

I think this is enough. With one last glimpse at the couple, now lying stoned on the mattress, Epsilon turned his unisense elsewhere.

The final tally came to six bad guys and six addicts. He'd have to make sure the crackheads stayed out of harm's way. Even though they contributed to the decline of society as much as the drug dealers, they weren't the ones selling the shit. They were just being stupid, hurting themselves. The dealers knew what they were doing and hurt countless others. Like that little girl from yesterday.

He clenched a fist. *Time they got hurt instead.*

Epsilon scanned the crackhouse until the sun went down. A few people drove up and waited for the sentry to go inside to get their "merchandise." The couple upstairs left before sunset. Two hookers came by for some nose candy on their way to work. Another girl joined the four addicts in the kitchen.

Remmler's blood boiled with each passing minute. It sickened him that something like this was allowed to happen in the open. Well, it wouldn't if he had anything to say about it. Sure all the naysayers liked to point out if you shut down one crackhouse, another will take its place. If that was the case, then why bother? Why not just give up and let people snort themselves to death?

Because I give a damn!

Maybe another crackhouse would take the place of this one. But sooner or later, enough would be closed that it would make a difference.

You gotta start somewhere.

Shortly after eight, Epsilon decided he had waited long enough.

Let's do it.

He drew a deep breath and stood up. Placing one foot on the rampart, he angled his staff so the balled end pointed at the sentry. The man didn't notice him. All his attention was focused on the street.

Remmler took another deep breath as his unisense helped aim his *tru'kat.*

This is it.

A green energy beam leapt from the staff with an electric *snap*. A flash of fluorescent green exploded off the sentry's body, hurling him onto the brick steps. The blast overloaded his neural pathways, causing him to black out.

Epsilon looked down from his perch in satisfaction. *Well, that went easy.* The scumbag didn't even know what hit him. Of course, this was just the beginning. He hoped everything else went just as smoothly.

Making sure no one else was on the street, Epsilon flew down to the crackhouse. His gaze locked on the unconscious sentry for a moment. He'd wake up in an hour or so, probably with more aches and pains than a quarterback after a football game.

He checked over the house one last time. Most of the windows were boarded up. The two thugs downstairs crowded around the boom box smoking cigarettes. Jack wondered if they were filled with regular tobacco or something with a little more kick. Two small lamps lit the room, while the kitchen stayed in relative darkness. The crackheads in there probably didn't care much.

Epsilon stepped over the unconscious sentry and walked onto the porch. He scanned the door. Wood. Over an inch thick. Not a problem.

He stepped back, raising his *tru'kat* over his head. The blade went right through the hinges with ease. The door fell outward. Epsilon knocked it away with one arm, sending a shower of splinters into the air. What remained of the door cartwheeled to the other end of the porch.

"What was that?" One of the dealers cried as he reached for his gun.

"What-" his buddy began, only to stop when he saw the bulky, armored figure of Epsilon storm into the room.

The thug, a squat kid about seventeen, screamed and wet his pants. His buddy, a few years older with a Marine-style haircut, also yelped in terror. Still he managed to whip out his .32 caliber Llama ACP pistol.

Epsilon took a step toward them. The kid screamed and ran for the kitchen. His buddy fired his semi-automatic. Epsilon ignored the rounds as they smashed harmlessly against his armor. He aimed and fired at the fleeing teen, hitting him square in the back. The kid spread-eagled onto the floor just outside the kitchen. The other thug, down to his last round, spun around in surprise as he watched his buddy fall.

"Kenny!"

Four of the addicts in the kitchen lifted their heads like prairie dogs alert to danger. The fifth continued smoking his pipe, uninterested in the madness. They all shook for a few moments before one scurried to a dark corner on all fours. The others soon followed, making sure they brought their crackpipes with them.

The last dealer turned around . . . and screamed when he came face to face with Epsilon. In a flash, the staff swept up, catching the scumbag's gunhand with the balled tip. Epsilon's unisense amplified the pop and crack of breaking bones. The Jamaican's scream went up a few more decibels as he sank to his knees, clutching his hand in pain. The gun clattered across the room.

"Oh God! My hand!"

Any further screaming was silenced by Epsilon's heel

across the maggot's jaw. The Jamaican collapsed on his side, his jaw broken and teeth dribbling out of his mouth.

Three down. Three more to go.

"What the fuck was that!?" Jeffrey Upshaw exclaimed when he heard the shots from downstairs.

"Kenny and Robert! They're shootin,'" exclaimed the thug named Clarence. Like Upshaw and the other dealer—Colin—he had his handgun drawn.

"No shit, *mon!* Find out what's goin' on!" Upshaw violently waved him outside with a pudgy arm. After grabbing his Smith & Wesson 12-gauge, he tossed one Uzi to Clarence and the other to Colin. Clarence pocketed his handgun and raced into the hallway, his massive, shoulderblade length dreads bouncing up and down. He stopped at the top of the stairway . . . and screamed.

"What is it!?" Upshaw hollered, watching Clarence through the open door. His words were drowned out by the echo of the young man's Uzi.

Remmler wasn't sure how many rounds hit him. Didn't matter anyway. None got through his armor.

He lifted his left leg. The skinny dude with huge dreadlocks screamed and ran away from the landing. He never saw the Cosmic Protector put his foot through the wooden step as he tried running up the stairs.

"Shit!" Epsilon muttered as he withdrew his foot from the hole. "Smooth move, Jack."

He took the stairs again, this time more carefully.

Clarence dropped his Uzi and slammed the door behind him. He then shoved the old, rusted deadbolt into place.

"Yo, Clarence! What up?" Colin jumped around nervously, causing the paunch bursting through his undershirt to jiggle obscenely.

But Clarence didn't respond. He swung his head quickly from side to side, eyes wide with fear, almost hyperventilating.

"Da'fuck's wrong with you?"

Clarence ignored them. He rushed over to the table and, to his companions' surprise, overturned it. A white cloud of cocaine rose into the air as scales and razorblades clattered on the floor.

"What the fuck!?!" Colin blurted.

"Da'hell you doin', *mon!?!*" Upshaw screamed.

Clarence pushed the table toward the door. Upshaw ran in front of him, grabbing him by the shoulders. He ignored Clarence's fearful eyes, drenched with tears.

"Knock it off, *mon!*" Upshaw shook him with one meaty hand. The other clutched the shotgun. "What's wrong with you!?! Who's out there!? WHO!?!"

It took Clarence a few moments to catch his breath. His voice trembled when he spoke. "I don't know! It ain't human, *mon!* It ain't human!"

"Da'fuck's he talkin' 'bout?" Colin asked.

Suddenly the door exploded. Splinters big and small showered the room. The three men threw their arms over their faces. Upshaw felt wooden shards pinch his arms.

He put his arm down . . . and saw the bulky, red and white figure in armor standing in the doorway.

"What the fuck is it!?!" Colin cried as he backed up against the wall. Upshaw just stared at the thing, mouth agape, as he backed into a corner, shotgun haphazardly raised. Clarence dropped behind the table and curled up in a fetal position, whimpering like a puppy.

The armored figure stood motionless, as if pondering its next move. Colin decided that for him when he opened up with his Uzi. Upshaw fired his 12-gage once before dropping to his knees when two ricochets whizzed by him and smacked against the wall. He watched in amazement as it walked through the barrage unfazed.

"Die motherfucker!!" Colin screamed in panic as he held down the trigger until the magazine ran dry. The armored figure shrugged off every 9mm slug that hit it.

Colin screamed as the thing came face to face with him. It ripped the Uzi from the drug dealer's hands, crushing the barrel and casually discarding it.

"Please don't kill me. Please don't kill me," Colin begged, his pear-shaped body trembling.

"My God. Can't you be a man about it?" It said in a level tone.

Colin only wailed louder. He sank to his knees and clasped his hands together.

Epsilon just shook his head. This was embarrassing. A grown man bawling like a three-year-old that scraped his knee.

Only one way to end this.

He stepped back and leveled his staff.

"No! No please! NO!! NO!!"

The dealer fell backwards, unconscious when the stun beam nailed him in the chest.

Footsteps pounded behind him. Epsilon didn't have to turn. His unisense "watched" the pig the others called Jeffrey Upshaw bolt out of the room. He pegged him as the leader of this ring, considering all the orders he kept barking out during his surveillance.

Epsilon started to follow when he looked at the dealer in the corner, who looked even more pathetic than his buddy had been. He considered stunning the man, then decided *screw it!* The guy looked so out of his mind with fear he could lay there blubbering through the middle of next week.

Remmler was briefly amazed with himself. To think that he, an average college student, could instill such terror in a man who made his life threatening others. Of course, the armor and the staff probably had a lot to do with it.

Epsilon's unisense picked up the boss charging downstairs.

He turned to the wall facing the street. Time to take a short cut.

Upshaw's heart pounded furiously. He couldn't remember ever being this scared.

Gotta get away. Can't let it get me.

He flew down the stairs, not noticing the broken step until he put his foot through it. The floor suddenly rushed up toward him. The impact jarred his blubberous body. His chin burst open. His lip split.

Upshaw ignored the pain. The instinct to survive took precedence over all else. He pulled his foot out of the hole, catching part of his ankle on a protruding wooden shard. The handgun in his waistband, jarred loose by the fall, clattered to the floor as he got up. Upshaw left it. He had to get away.

He stumbled out the front entrance, unaware the door was no longer there. Upshaw ran down the steps . . . and tripped over the body of the unconscious sentry.

He screamed as he went airborne. Luckily his outstretched left arm cushioned his head when he landed.

A *snap* resonated from his elbow. Fire scorched his shoulder. Upshaw howled even louder. Despite the pain, his mind screamed *run run run!*

With just one arm and his knees, a sobbing Upshaw raised himself off the sidewalk. His left arm hung dead by his side.

Suddenly a guttural *boom* came from overhead. The drug dealer looked up. "NOOO!!!"

The armored figure burst through the wall of the second floor. A rain of wood, plaster and glass crashed onto the pavement in a jumble of noise. Several fragments caught Upshaw in his face and arms.

It came down right behind the debris, its feet crashing through the pavement. The thing quickly straightened up, pointing a threatening finger at him. "Hold it right there."

6-RUST

Upshaw went for his automatic, only to find it missing. He frantically scanned the area for something—anything—to use as a weapon. A glint caught his eye. He focused. An empty beer bottle lay by the house.

Upshaw rushed over to it. Picking the bottle up with his good hand, he turned back to the thing.

"Keep away from me, *mon!*" Upshaw cried in a high pitched voice, holding the bottle in a menacing fashion.

"You gotta be kiddin'." The thing took a step toward Upshaw.

"Stay away!"

It kept coming.

Upshaw reared back and brought the bottle down on the armored figure's head. He didn't even try to block it. The bottle shattered into a hundred pieces, several of which caught Upshaw in the face. He dropped what was left of the neck and covered his wounds.

Suddenly the world rushed by. It ended with him being slammed against the side of the house. More fire shot through his dislocated left shoulder and down his arm. He would have screamed had all the air not been knocked out of his lungs.

Epsilon briefly studied the man. He acted nothing like society's perception of a criminal; cocksure, menacing, tough as nails. This guy was just a fat, wailing pile of dogshit. About as tough as cookie dough.

He recalled the vision of that young girl going into the crackhouse—*this* scumbag's crackhouse. His anger boiled.

"You fucking maggot." He pulled Upshaw forward and threw him to the ground.

The drug dealer coughed and wheezed, trying to get oxygen back into his lungs. "Please don't kill me."

Epsilon shook his head. Take away their guns, their buddies, their power, and these slugs instantly turn into babies. He looked down at the blade of his *tru'kat.* It would be so easy. But Remmler doubted he had the gumption to actually go through with it, especially with the dealer lying on his side whimpering. That again raised the question. *Why me?*

Epsilon walked around the quivering Upshaw and shoved him onto his back with his foot. He had an idea, one that could take this slimewad off society's hands for a long time.

He moved the *tru'kat's* blade closer and closer to the hapless dealer until it hovered an inch from his neck. Fear suddenly choked off his sobs.

"You the guy in charge of this shithole?"

The wide-eyed dealer nodded, too terrified to speak.

"Good. Now listen up. You've just gone out of business. Sooner or later, the cops are gonna come by. When they do, *you will* tell them *everything* about your operation. You're gonna go down the list of every crime you've ever done, from dealing to jaywalking. You don't leave anything out. You with me so far?"

Upshaw nodded.

"Good. Now, when they haul your fat ass off to jail, you *will not* accept a plea bargain or any other kind of deal. You will confess and you will let the judge lock you up for a few decades. You fuck up any part of this, I catch you back out on the street selling drugs, I'll make sure no one *ever* finds your body. Understand?"

He nodded again.

"SAY IT!!!"

"YES!!! Yes! Yes! Oh God, please don't kill me!" The tears exploded from Upshaw's eyes.

"Better."

Before he could continue, Epsilon's enhanced hearing picked up something. A siren. Switching briefly to his unisense, he picked up a police car tearing down the street six blocks away. Some concerned citizen must have called 911, saving him the trouble.

Epsilon withdrew his staff and dropped to one knee. He

jabbed a finger into Upshaw's chest and hissed, "You're gonna pay for every ounce of dope you ever sold, you fat sack of shit."

The dealer just convulsed with sobs.

The police were getting closer. Epsilon stood up and took one last look at Upshaw. *Aw, what the hell.*

"Some advice, Shamu. When you get to the joint, make sure you always have a good grip on the soap."

Remmler snickered as he raised the *tru'kat* over his head and took off with a rush of wind. He was out of sight by the time the police cruiser arrived. Both officers had their Glocks drawn as soon as they got out of the car. Their jaws dropped when they got a look at the scene. One guy laying on the sidewalk crying, another guy sprawled out on the steps and a huge hole in the second floor.

"What the hell happened here?" one cop exclaimed as he and his partner rushed over to the dealers.

TWENTY-FIVE

I hope Margerie isn't too upset, Ed Caro thought as he drove down Moyamensing Avenue toward his home in suburban Eastwick. He'd called his wife and let her know to put dinner in the fridge so he could reheat it when he got home—again. Just another suckass part about being a cop. Strained, even broken marriages. They hadn't gotten to that point . . . at least not yet. It had also been hard on his ten-year-old son and six-year-old daughter. How many school projects, little league games and school plays did he miss while hauling in some skell, then taking the blame when he was back on the street hours later?

This job sucks. But what else is there for me to do?

Tonight was no different. Once Caro got off duty, he went to three of the largest costume stores in the city posing as a customer. He looked around, flipped through catalogs and asked the clerks if they had "astronaut" or "superhero" costumes in stock. He found nothing that matched the "Knight's" description. Caro expected it. Still it was the easiest lead to check out. Now it would get a lot harder.

Caro's thoughts were interrupted by the crackle of his police radio.

"Dispatch. Unit One-Twenty-One."

"One-Twenty-One go."

The officer gave his location, then continued. "We're gonna need paramedics and detectives down here. We got ourselves a crackhouse with eleven suspects. Looks like someone did a number on this place. Spent shell casings everywhere, plus one big hole in the side of the house."

It's him . . . it . . . whatever.

Oh well, Margerie's probably already pissed at me as it is.

Caro rolled down his window and mounted the red Teardrop Lite on the roof of his car. He pressed down on the accelerator and headed for the nearest exit.

He arrived at the scene ten minutes later. Three patrol cars and an ambulance were already there. Several residents had ventured out of their homes to watch.

One of the officers stopped Caro as he set foot on the sidewalk. He quickly whipped out his identification. "Sergeant Caro. Sixth District."

"Long way from home, aren't you, Sarge?" the cop, a well-built black man, asked.

"Yeah, well, I was in the neighborhood. Heard about this on the scanner. What's up?"

The officer, L. Page his nametag read, walked Caro over to the scene. "Got a Nine-One-One call about multiple gunshots in the area. This is what we found." Page pointed to the hole in the second floor, then over to the doorway with no door.

"Looks like someone was using some heavy artillery. That's all we need. Gangs with rocket launchers."

Caro looked down at the officer's belt. "Mind if I borrow your light?"

"Sure." Page handed his black Night Stalker III flashlight to Caro, who shone it around the hole.

"That must've been one hell of a bazooka."

"What'd you mean?"

"You see any burnmarks? Smoke?"

Page looked up. He saw no such thing.

"So what the hell did they use? A wrecking ball?"

Caro ignored the cop's remark and handed him back the flashlight.

"So what about the suspects?"

"We've got five crackheads. They're chillin' out in the kitchen. Fuckin' wasted."

Caro shook his head. "Probably won't get anything from them."

"Doubt it."

"Any dealers?"

"One we know about for sure." Page pointed to a fat Jamaican sitting with his knees tucked under his chin and blabbering away while a police officer and EMT examined him.

"Found him lying on the sidewalk when we got here." Page had to raise his voice as two more ambulances and a patrol car arrived with sirens wailing. "Name's Jeffrey Upshaw. Soon as we got over to him he started rambling on about who his suppliers were, who was selling him guns."

"Did you read him his rights?"

"Yeah. Said he didn't care. He had to tell us. I gotta tell you, Sarge. Something scared the crap out of this guy."

"What about him?" Caro pointed to the unconscious man on the steps being tended to by paramedics.

"We think he's a dealer. We found a Browning nine-mil in his pants. There's two more inside. One unconscious, the other with a broken jaw."

Before Caro could ask anything else, an officer emerged from the house. "Hey, Larry! I . . . who's that?"

"Sergeant Caro," Ed held up his badge. "Sixth District."

The lean-faced cop with a thin black mustache nodded.

"There's two more upstairs. One guy's unconscious, the other's curled up crying like a baby. Man, something scared him bad."

"Anything else?"

"Yeah. Wait 'til you hear this. You know that pervert from last week? The one whose hand got crushed?"

Caro held his breath and nodded.

"Well, apparently the same thing happened to an Uzi we found upstairs."

It was him!

Caro stalked over to Upshaw, surprising Officer Page.

"Excuse me," he said forcefully to the blond paramedic treating Upshaw's facial wounds.

The EMT looked at Caro in annoyance. "This man is injured. He-"

Caro abruptly cut him off. "Is there a chance this man could die in the next two minutes?"

"No, but-"

"Then move it. This is police business." Caro knelt down, crowding the EMT and forcing him to shuffle aside. He looked directly at the terrified Upshaw. Had he been white, his face would have been pale as a ghost. *Just like Smith.*

"Okay, buddy. Who did this to you?"

Upshaw looked at him, his eyes the size of dinner plates. "I . . . I've been selling drugs for the last seven years."

Caro grabbed him by the collar. "I didn't ask you that. I asked who did this to you. Who?"

Upshaw took three quick breaths. "It was . . . he . . . he had, like a spacesuit on. Like that. And he carried this big stick with a . . . a knife on the end." Upshaw started to break down. "We shot him! We kept shootin' him! Nothing stopped him! He wasn't human! He killed everybody, *mon!*"

"He's obviously delirious," the EMT stated.

"I'll say," commented the other officer.

Caro just looked at them. Outside of himself, his partner,

Captain Feldman, the Commissioner and Francine Ballard, no one else knew about the "Knight" story.

"What did he do to you? What did he say?"

Upshaw breathed heavily as he began his story. "We were . . . we were working . . . with the crack, you know. Puttin' it into vials n' stuff. Then . . . then Kenny and Robert started shooting. And-And Clarence, he—"

Upshaw's story was cut off by the screech of tires. Two plain sedans skidded to a halt in the middle of the street. A pair of suits got out of each car, waving Justice Department IDs.

"Shit. Party's over," Caro muttered.

"This area is now under federal jurisdiction," said the apparent leader, a blurry guy with a receding hairline. "I want everyone away from the house. No one is to talk to any of the suspects."

Caro didn't even argue this time. He just walked back to his car in silence. Some of the cops piss-moaned to the *Feds*, but eventually conceded and followed their orders to block off the street. The EMTs were the most vocal, insisting on treating the injured before they were moved. The Feds agreed, as long as one of them was on hand to watch. However, they could not be transported until more men arrived.

Caro sat in his car and decided to stick around for a while, see what happened. More suits arrived, along with more cops, who were directed to reinforce the police line around the crackhouse. A news van from Channel 10 showed up, its crew kept away. Then came another van. This one unmarked. Half-a-dozen suits got out of the back, lugging huge, bulky, silver briefcases.

"Sir, you're going to have to leave."

Caro looked up. One of the Feds was standing next to his car.

The detective smiled. "Sure. No problem." *Asshole.*

Caro started his car and drove off. He took one last look at the scene before turning the corner. The Feds were certainly taking this "Knight" thing seriously.

A thought struck him. First Smith, now the crackhouse. If he didn't know better, Caro would say there was something, or someone, out there doing this city a favor.

Just about every news organization in the city had reporters on the scene of the crackhouse assault. Even though the cops kept people from getting close, they could do nothing about the zoom lenses that focused on the gaping hole in the structure. Cameras also captured the dealers being loaded into ambulances, accompanied by *federal agents.* The addicts, accompanied by another agent, were put into a police van. Reporters shouted questions. The Feds ignored them and kept the cops and EMTs from talking to them. But they couldn't be everywhere at once. A reporter from Channel 3 caught two officers on tape discussing what happened.

"One of 'em says he got attacked by a spaceman," an officer said, then indicated his information was secondhand. At first the reporter shook it off. This had been a crackhouse after all. The perp probably had a snootful before they carted him away. It wasn't until he began interviewing neighbors that his mind changed. Two people—a young man and a middle-aged woman three doors down—reported seeing an armored figure carrying a staff, roughing up the man everyone on the block knew led the small Jamaican drug gang. Three more neighbors—not wanting to be the first to come forward for fear of ridicule—also claimed to see the same thing.

Calls were made to the police and local FBI field office. They were tight-lipped. The press learned the injured dealers had been taken to Mt. Sinai Hospital. However, the staff refused to give out any information.

The story led the 11 o' clock news and made headlines in the local papers the next morning.

Carlos Rande, a young nurse practitioner at Hahneman Hospital, read the account in the *Philadelphia Daily News* while riding the bus to work. Luck must have been with him this day. He got to the hospital fifteen minutes before his shift was scheduled to start. Time enough to find the number in the phone book for Channel 6, the local ABC affiliate. His favorite reporter on their evening news had been the one to cover the Stevie Smith story. Carlos thought she had a great body, even though she had to be pushing forty. He had managed to get her autograph, chatted with her in the halls and gave her some tidbits of information on Smith from time to time. Had she not been married with two kids, he might have gotten up the courage to ask her out.

The reporter just got into work when the receptionist told her Carlos was on the phone. She remembered him. The annoying orderly that latched onto her and volunteered his services as her man on the inside. The reporter was about to ask the receptionist to tell Carlos Rande she was busy but decided, *what the hell.*

Carlos told his favorite reporter Smith claimed he had been maimed by the same—thing—that allegedly attacked the crackhouse. She asked Carlos why he or no one else mentioned that before. The nurse practitioner answered that everyone who treated Smith thought he was, "off his rocker." It wasn't until he saw the paper that he realized Stevie Smith may have been telling the truth. After the interview, the reporter thanked him and promised to only identify him as "a hospital employee."

When Channel 6 aired its noon newscast, the lid blew off the "Knight" story.

TWENTY-SIX

"YES . . . YES, SIR . . . I understand . . . But since this is an urban environment . . ." General Clay almost pulled the receiver away from his head. The angry voice of his boss, the Director of the Defense Intelligence Agency, threatened to blow out his eardrums. "Yes, I realize that, sir . . . We will . . ."

A loud *click* on the other end of the secure line ended the conversation.

Clay breathed a worried sigh as he closed the lid of the fat, silver briefcase that carried his communications gear. He exited the small tent in the far corner of the warehouse that served as his private office.

"Trouble from the home office, General?" Major Xantis asked as he approached his sullen-faced boss.

Clay grunted. "General Meyer isn't happy this made the front page."

"Not everything did."

"Enough did to cause concern. The Justice Department's been flooded with calls from reporters. They're denying everything, but that just makes the damn press more curious. Now the cops are going to increase patrols. We try to interfere with that, we'll draw the kind of heat we don't need. We'll just tell Philly PD to call in if they spot this thing and take no action until we arrive. This whole operation is starting to go to hell. God help us all if our cover gets blown."

"Well, we do have some good news. Intelligence just finished their analysis of the incursion area."

"What did they find?"

Xantis led General Clay over to his desk, which was covered with photographs of the crackhouse. The Major picked up half-a-dozen black-and-white photos of the hole in the second story and handed them to Clay.

"This definitely wasn't an explosion."

"No, sir. No scorch marks, smoke. Nothing. Besides, an explosion that left a hole that big would have left nothing of the room. Probably would have burned out the whole second floor. Almost all of the debris from the wall was found on the street, which means *something* smashed its way *through* the wall and left these . . ." Xantis handed the General a photo of two indentations in the sidewalk that looked like rectangular footprints with a zigzag pattern.

"We estimate its height at about six feet," the Major continued while Clay stared at the photo. "Weight between four hundred to four hundred-fifty pounds."

General Clay shook his head. "My God. Its strength is unbelievable." He paused in thought for a few seconds. "You made plaster casts of these?"

"Yes sir. We also compared the pattern of the footprints with marks found on one of the victims' cheeks. They're identical."

"He kicked one of them!?"

"Yes, sir. Broke his jaw good. But I wouldn't be too upset. All the injured were drug dealers. Their boss spilled his guts about their operation to anyone who would listen. Whatever it was scared the shit out of him."

"What about those junkies?"

"Local police will handle them. They were stoned when we found them. Barely remembered what happened."

"Good. Even if they do say anything, who's going to believe a crack addict?"

"Something else, sir." Xantis handed General Clay a computer printout. He read it, then looked back at his operations officer. "They're sure?"

Xantis nodded. "Positive. Three of the druggies had low-level radiation readings in specific areas of their bodies. Two in the chest, one in the back."

"A directed energy beam?"

"Yes sir. But a kind we've never seen before. Apparently it only stunned the victims. We found bruises on what we believe are the points of impact."

Clay shook his head. "This has got to be extraterrestrial. We have nothing that can do these things."

"Or, it is possible it's ET technology somehow procured by a human. Mr. Upshaw—the leader of the gang—said it did communicate with him. In English no less."

Clay turned up his face. "Major, we have people at Area 51 who've been working on alien technology recovered *fifty years ago,* and still aren't anywhere close to figuring it out. I doubt some Joe Six-Pack is going to stumble across something like this and understand how it works like that." He snapped his fingers. "Hell, for all we know, it might have been monitoring our radio and TV transmissions to learn our language.

"Anyway, whatever this thing is, it's drawing a lot of attention. We don't need that. Hell, I wouldn't be surprised if the damn UFO kooks were already on their way here. We gotta get this thing contained and shipped off to Nevada where the eggheads can look it over before it makes another splash on the front page."

Clay put down the photos and printouts and headed over to the communications section.

"It is interesting, sir. Isn't it?"

The General stopped in his tracks and turned to Major Xantis. "What is?"

"That in both instances it only inflicted injury on criminals. Crushed the mugger's hand and attacked the drug dealers. He didn't even touch the nurse or those junkies."

Clay rolled his eyes. *That's all we need. A crimefighting E.T.* "Major, we cannot bank on that trend continuing. This thing has proven itself to be dangerous. Today it's rapists and drug dealers, tomorrow it could be some jogger in Fairmount Park. We do not have the luxury of trying to second guess its motives. If these incidents continue, we could have a panic on our hands. If that happens, Group Nine could be exposed. Our job is to bag this thing and turn it over to Area 51. Understood?"

"Yes, sir. I was just pointing it out as a fact. Nothing more."

Clay nodded. "Good. Carry on."

Xantis saluted and went off. General Clay headed over to the Group's communications section and told one of the signalmen, "Contact headquarters. Tell them to scramble Bravo Team immediately. Looks like we're gonna need some more help."

" . . . So me n' my brother, Donny, head on over there. Man, you shoulda been there." Vinny Gambolinni explained in exaggerated fashion to the small audience in Cheryl Terrepinn's room. She, Jack Remmler, Chris Wilson, his girlfriend Sheniese Thompson and Cheryl's roommate, Kelly Lin, were all waiting for Brian Doyle, to pick up a tape of the movie *Speed* from a friend.

"Cops had the whole friggin' street closed off. They had TV news vans there, the whole works. And these guys in suits kept going in and out of the place. Me and Donny said they had to be FBI. And the hole. Man, whatever it was did a good job on it."

"So what do you think it was?"

"Shit, Kell. If I knew I'd be selling the story to *The National Enquirer.*"

"It's probably some guy big time into special effects," Cheryl stated. "This whole 'Knight' thing is a load of crap. It's good for a comic book, but not in real life."

"Who knows? There might be something to it," Remmler smiled inwardly.

"Remy, I think you've ODed on *X-Files*."

He turned to the medium built black girl with puffed out hair. "Sheniese. You know there are a lot of unexplained things out there in the world. This could be one of them. Or, it could be like Cheryl said. One big hoax." Remmler had to restrain himself from laughing and saying, "joke's on you!"

"Hey," Chris Wilson spoke up. "Whoever it was shut down a crackhouse. I say good for him."

Remmler smiled to himself. *I am doing good. They all seem glad someone's out there doing something about crime. Maybe I am cut out to be a Cosmic Protector.*

He couldn't wait to hit the streets again, bust some more bad guys. See *them* afraid for a change. Looking back, that had been one of the most satisfying parts. Watching that fat, drug dealing scum act so tough at first, then turn into a whimpering pile of jelly. Wouldn't it be nice if he could do the same to Imperium?

Yeah right. Dream on. Remmler bit his lip at the thought of facing the dark armored maniac again. The crackhouse attack boosted his confidence. But was it enough for him to want to fight Imperium again?

Someone knocked on the door, followed by, "I got it."

"Get in here, Bubba," Cheryl called.

Doyle entered the room, holding up the video tape. "Okay. We are go."

"C'mon, Brian," Kelly smiled, pointing enthusiastically to the VCR. "I'm dying to see Keanu Reeves. God, he is so hot."

"Oh please," chided Remmler. "What does Keanu Reeves have that I don't?"

"Ooh, umpteen million dollars and the body of a god."

Remmler pretended to look dejected. "Gee, thanks. That makes me feel better."

"Aww." The short, slender Chinese-American girl with straight, shoulder-length black hair blew him a kiss. "You know I love you, Jack."

He flashed Kelly a smile as Doyle turned on the TV on top of a small, wooden, circular table in the front of the room. Everyone settled in. Chris and Sheniese snuggled together on one bed, Jack and Cheryl sat cross-legged on a beat up brown rug, and Vinny and Kelly sat on the other bed.

Doyle flipped to Channel 3 to set up the VCR.

"My fellow Americans . . ." was the first thing they heard from the set. Remmler immediately recognized the voice. The President of the United States.

"Hey. The Prez is on," Bubba explained.

"Who cares," replied Kelly. "Put on the movie."

"Hang on," Cheryl snapped. "I want to see this."

"Great," Sheniese muttered. "Probably gonna say we're at war."

Cheryl shushed her. If the President was on in prime time, Remmler figured it had to be something big. Something that could affect her brother in the Gulf.

" . . . at 8:30 a.m., Washington time," the President stared directly at the camera from behind his desk in the Oval Office, "the last foreign national in Iraq was escorted safely to a United Nations outpost along the Iraq-Kuwait border. We are pleased with the efforts of the Iraqi government to allow these men and women safe passage out of a potentially dangerous situation. Many in this country and around the world hoped to seize upon this gesture of good faith as a way to bring about a negotiated settlement to this crisis. This administration hoped that would be the case.

"Ever since Iraq's announcement four days ago to safely escort foreign citizens from its country, members of the State Department have tirelessly negotiated with Iraqi leaders, urging them to end their nuclear weapons program, allow inspections and halt the present military build-up in the Gulf region. We have been joined in this effort by the United Nations, the European Union, the Gulf Cooperation Council and the Arab League. We have offered Iraq further easing of the oil embargo and the opportunity for research into peaceful applications of nuclear energy under U.N. supervision. In all, the chance for the citizens of Iraq to experience the prosperity so many other countries in that region already know.

"Unfortunately, the Iraqi government does not see it that way.

"While the leaders in Baghdad have let all foreign nationals safely exit the country, the fact remains that those people were *forced* to leave. The fact remains, United Nations inspectors, in Iraq to supervise the destruction of ballistic missiles and other horrible weapons of mass destruction, were forcibly detained by Iraqi security troops. Iraq has refused to accept any of our offers of peace. In effect, they have closed themselves off from the rest of the world. Satellite photographs have shown increased numbers of tanks, infantry and artillery near the borders of Kuwait and Saudi Arabia. Activity around known and suspected nuclear, biological and chemical weapons sites have also increased. This proves that instead of working toward peace, the Iraqi leadership is preparing for war. A war that would pit this country and our allies, against a nuclear capable Iraq.

"With the end of the Cold War, we thought the specter of nuclear war had ended. That, apparently, is not the case. There are still those who would use fear and intimidation and force to get their way. Who would use a weapon capable of destroying an entire city, incinerating tens of thousands of innocent men, women and children in the blink of an eye.

"Well, I can assure you, my fellow Americans, we will not allow that to happen. We will not allow a renegade nation to bully our Arab friends with nuclear weapons, or threaten our vital national interests. Therefore, I have taken the following steps to insure we are fully prepared to meet this threat.

"I have authorized the call-up of 120,000 reservists to active duty. Some will remain stateside to help in various support roles. The rest will be deployed to the Persian Gulf. I have also ordered an additional carrier battle group, headed by the *USS Theodore Roosevelt*, to proceed immediately to the region. Our NATO allies have also agreed to contribute heavily to this operation. Plans are being finalized for a 150,000-member NATO force to be sent to the region, supported by over two hundred combat aircraft and fifty naval vessels.

"My next decision to ensure the Persian Gulf is protected from potential Iraqi aggression, however, did not come easily. There were days of debate, discussion and negotiations between members of this administration, Congressional leaders and our allies. In the end, we all reached the same conclusion."

The President took a deep breath before continuing. Something appeared to trouble him.

"This isn't easy to say," he diverted from the speech. Then his eyes peered ahead again, probably at the TelePrompTer mounted on the front of the camera that scrolled his speech, Jack thought. "The Iraqi government has demonstrated no interest in resolving this matter peacefully. Its armed forces stand poised near the borders of our Gulf allies. Its possession of nuclear weapons has forced us to respond in kind.

"Effective immediately, the armed forces of the United States of America will operate under the alert status known as Defense Condition Three, or DEFCON Three. Our strategic bombers and ballistic missile submarines will now be on standby for potential combat. Additionally, I am ordering one of our Ohio-class nuclear missile submarines to take up position within launching range of Iraq."

Every jaw in the room, probably every one in the world, Remmler imagined, dropped in shock.

"Oh my God," he muttered.

"Is he serious?" Sheniese blurted.

"The next step, should Iraq continue its threatening posture, would be DEFCON Two, which would mean the deployment of nuclear armed bombers and more ballistic missile submarines within striking range of Iraq. The next step after that, would be the unthinkable. Nuclear warfare. We absolutely do not want to cross that line. But if Iraq does not pull back from the brink, if Iraq uses its weapons of mass destruction against our troops and our allies, we will have no choice but to respond with our most powerful weapons."

Vinny shook his head. "Man, I don't fucking believe this."

"Let me repeat," the President continued. "That is an action of last resort. Iraq's leaders still have a chance to end this without a shot being fired. All they have to do is pull back their troops and allow U.N. inspectors into their country to oversee the dismantling of their nuclear weapons program. *We simply will not tolerate a nuclear capable Iraq.*

"In closing, I hope all of you will join me in sending our thoughts and prayers to all the brave men and women of our armed forces and those of our allies in the Persian Gulf standing against the forces of aggression. Please come home safely, all of you.

"Thank you and good night."

The picture faded to the CBS news desk for comments from the anchor and a panel of "distinguished experts."

"I don't believe this!" Kelly Lin exclaimed. "He's gonna launch nuclear missiles at Iraq? That's insane!"

"Kelly, he said that would only be as a last resort," Remmler responded.

"So what!? That idiot—" she pointed harshly at the TV, "—wants to start a nuclear war! Over what? Oil? It's not worth it."

"Yeah, well what do you think makes your car run?" Doyle pointed out. "And heats your home? And fuels ships and emergency vehicles and airplanes?"

"And what makes land uninhabitable for a hundred thousand years?" Sheniese chimed in.

"Hey," Remmler began. "Those nutbars in Baghdad started this whole thing. Maybe now they'll think seriously about ending this with a "boomer" parked off their shore." Remmler used the technothriller slang for a ballistic missile submarine.

"Yeah, Remy, but nuclear weapons? I mean—"

"Will everyone just shut up!" Cheryl suddenly hollered, cutting off Chris Wilson and startling the others. Everyone just looked as her head drooped. It was a full five seconds later before Cheryl looked up, her eyes glistening from the build up of tears.

"Oh God." Her voice was strained. "You guys . . . I'm sorry. I didn't mean to—"

"Don't worry about it, Cheryl," Bubba cut her off. "Look, we're sorry. It just slipped our minds about your brother."

Cheryl nodded before continuing. "It's just . . . it's just his ship is inside the Gulf. You know, the Persian Gulf isn't all that big. And now . . . now they're talking about maybe using nuclear weapons." Cheryl choked up. A tear ran down her cheek.

Kelly got off the bed and sat down next to her roommate, putting an arm around her shoulder. Remmler reached out and took hold of Cheryl's left hand. She squeezed his hand in response.

"Hey, come on, Cheryl," he tried to reassure her. "There's still a chance this whole thing will end without a fight. Besides, your brother's on an aircraft carrier. It's the best defended ship in the world. They'll be able to detect any attack Iraq may launch and stop it before it gets anywhere near the ship. Hell, your brother'll probably be the one to spot it in his Hawkeye. I'm sure he'll be fine."

Cheryl looked at Remmler. A slight smile formed across her lips. She wiped the tears away with her free hand. "Thanks, Jack. I hope you're right."

Cheryl gently squeezed his hand again. Remmler did likewise.

So do I, Cheryl. So do I.

TWENTY-SEVEN

THE BUNKER WAS one of several built across Iraq. This particular one lay only a few miles outside Baghdad. Thirty feet of steel and reinforced concrete protected its occupants from bombs. A layer of lead gave it added protection against any possible nuclear fallout.

The first floor of the bunker was devoted to security, with sleeping quarters for guards and the armory. The spacious, well lit second floor featured plush carpeting, elegant wooden and glass tables and comfortable chairs and couches. Furnishings one would find in the most expensive hotels.

The Iraqi leader rolled out of bed around five in the morning, the same time his counterpart's speech began in Washington D.C. He didn't even know about it until the captain in charge of the command center decided halfway through the speech that his leader should see this. He went to fetch the President, but by the time he got dressed and followed the captain back the speech had ended. The President angrily demanded to see the replay immediately. It took about thirty seconds to rewind the tape, during which time the Defense Minister came in, wearing only his pajamas and slippers.

The two sat down and watched the speech, which the communications officer had taped off a satellite dish. No translation was necessary. The President and Defense Minister spoke perfect English.

"That bastard!" the President ranted as he stood up, knocking over his chair. "That fucking bastard! He's lost any shred of sanity he's ever had." He turned to the shocked Defense Minister. "Don't just sit there with your mouth hanging open, you fool! The damned Americans have just threatened us with nuclear weapons! By Allah's name, they can't be serious, can they?"

The Defense Minister slowly got to his feet, coughing a few times before answering. "Mr. President. They do believe we possess nuclear weapons. This would be an appropriate counter. I'm surprised they didn't do this at the onset."

"The Americans will never launch a nuclear strike against us. They would become a pariah to the rest of the world. It's a bluff. That's all. They want us to back down and cower before them like feeble old women.

"I have *never* cowered before the Americans. I will not start now. They can send all their nuclear submarines against us." The President paused, then waved his hand in dismissal. "Bah! Let them. They'll never launch their missiles. They don't have the stomach. You see how they react when the Japanese remind them of Hiroshima and Nagasaki. They whimper and beg for forgiveness. The American President and the people who dictate his actions lack the will to use such weapons again."

"Perhaps, Mr. President," the Defense Minister nodded. "But . . . but we must accept the possibility—remote as it is—that the Americans could launch a pre-emptive strike against us. Just one of their ballistic missile submarines could cripple our country. They carry over twenty missiles with over two-hundred warheads combined. Enough to destroy every vital military and command installation we have."

"And there is nothing we can do to stop this?"

The Defense Minister shook his head. "The American submarine can launch its missiles from thousands of miles away, which they will undoubtedly do if they so choose. Our navy's anti-submarine capabilities are barely adequate, but that is a moot point since they can't get out of the Gulf. Even our radar network wouldn't be able to detect the missiles until they enter our air space. And we have no way of shooting them down."

The President clenched his teeth, turned and walked to the other end of the room. His blood boiled. He was angry, angry at feeling so helpless. Damn the Americans! Always flexing their muscles when they wanted him to jump through hoops for their "New World Order."

He would not be embarrassed by the them. He would not bow to them because they threatened him with nuclear weapons. No. This time he would bite back. He finally possessed the power to do so.

"You are wrong, my friend," the President turned and walked back to the Defense Minister. "We can stop the Americans."

"How?"

He President leaned closer and whispered, "PROJECT: NEXUS."

"Drovinov? But that could give the Americans the provocation to attack."

"No! It will make them think twice. What they will see is an Iraq capable of defending itself with the most powerful weapon in history. A weapon the Americans and their lackeys will have no defense against.

"Come. We must plan an appropriate demonstration. One that will make the Americans grovel in fear."

PART THREE

THE CONFLICT

TWENTY-EIGHT

NEITHER ED CARO or Ralph Diaz could remember a stranger start to their day. Caro arrived first at the station and headed right for his desk, opening the drawer that contained his chipped white coffee mug. Stenciled on the side was a pudgy, smiling policeman with a donut in one hand and coffee in the other. The caption read: GOT MY COFFEE, GOT MY DONUT, GOT MY GUN . . . NOW I CAN FIGHT CRIME.

Caro took one step toward the coffee maker when he noticed something yellow inside his mug. At first he thought it was a practical joke. Caro plucked out a yellow post-it note and read it:

Ed and Ralph
9AM Washington Sq.
Be sure to dry clean.
"Terrible Tom"

Diaz showed up ten minutes later. Caro handed him the note.

"What the hell's goin' on?" Diaz asked in a hushed voice.

"Guess we'll find out when we get there. Let's go."

Caro headed for his car, Diaz right behind him. All the while he wished for a normal job. An accountant or insurance salesman, perhaps. Being a cop had gotten too damn weird lately.

It took longer than normal to reach Washington Square with Caro "dry cleaning" to make sure they weren't being followed. The detectives took a circuitous route around the center of town, staying off expressways and using as many side streets as possible. Rush hour traffic had not let up. For once Ed Caro was glad. Lots of cars made it easier to get lost in the crowd. Diaz constantly checked the mirrors to make sure no one tailed them.

The detectives finally parked next to the Atwater Kent Museum. They walked across the parking lot to 6th Street, crossed over to the Liberty Bell Pavilion, walked through Independence Square, mixing in with the tourists, and came out on Walnut Street. They hiked another block before entering tree covered Washington Square. The two dodged a few joggers and roller bladers as they came to a small marble podium with a flame gushing up from the center. Caro and Diaz checked around the Tomb of the Unknown Soldier from the American Revolution. No sign of Captain Feldman. The pair turned left and walked further down the pavement until they saw a familiar figure standing behind a green wooden bench.

"You're late," Feldman said flatly. It was ten past nine.

"Sorry, Captain. You told us to dry clean. We did it in spades."

"Were you followed?"

"I checked," replied Diaz. "As far as I could tell, no."

Feldman nodded. "Lets walk, guys."

The three set off down the cement path. Feldman's eyes

constantly darted around the park, checking for any unwanted company.

"So what's up, Captain? Why all the James Bond stuff?"

Feldman waited a few seconds before answering. "You guys are investigating the 'Knight' affair, aren't you?"

Diaz stopped in his tracks, his face contorted in shock. Caro just looked at the ground, the muscles in his face tightening.

When neither detective would answer, Feldman continued. "Look, I know you were down at the crackhouse the other night, Ed. I got a call from Captain Turner at the First yesterday. Said one of my detectives happened to show up there and looked around. Wanted to know if you were working a case that might be connected with the crackhouse. One of the cops you talked to there remembered your name."

Now Caro stopped, hands on his hips and looking off to the side. He couldn't think of any excuses. *Busted!*

"Look, um, Captain . . ." Caro began softly.

Feldman held up a hand to stop him. "Save it, Ed. Any other time you guys disobeyed my orders, I'd chew each of you *two* new assholes, then suspend you. But this isn't any other time. Which is why we're meeting here."

He motioned them to continue walking. "Whoever's checking out the Smith case and the crackhouse sure as hell ain't with the Justice Department."

"We could've told you that," Caro responded.

"Just hear me out. The other day I call down to the FBI in Washington, see what they found out from the stuff we sent them on the Smith case. You know what they told me? All the material pertaining to that case was sent somewhere else."

"Where?" Diaz asked.

"I asked. They wouldn't tell me. I told them we were the ones who sent it all down there in the first place. Didn't matter. Just said it was classified.

"But here's where it *really* gets strange. I get to work yesterday, some suit's waiting for me. Identifies himself as an 'Agent Whitaker' from the Justice Department. Starts telling me to drop anything having to do with the 'Knight' or my ass is grass and Uncle Sam's the lawnmower. Then I finally get in my office, and find out the Commissioner's invited me to lunch. Turns out it wasn't out of the kindness of his heart. He told me he also got a visit from another 'Justice Department official.' Told him he can have all the extra men he wants on alert for this 'Knight' character. But that's it. We're just supposed to report it in to dispatch. *They'll* take care of it. Philly PD is not to get involved *at all.*

"Simms also told me he checked with some of his friends in Washington. FBI, DEA, ATF. None of them are investigating Smith or the crackhouse. Something real hush-hush is going on."

"So who's running this show? CIA? The Army?"

"Hell, Diaz, it could be some government agency we've never heard of. Or aren't supposed to hear of. Whoever they are, they wouldn't be making such a fuss if this 'Knight' story was a bunch of bullshit."

"So what do we do?" Caro asked. "Lay off?"

"Yes . . . officially. The Commissioner's just as upset about this as you guys are. Hell, might as well include me, too. If there really is some . . . *thing* running around this city making holes in buildings and crushing people's hands, we want to know about it."

"So you want us to play covert op, is that it?" Diaz said. "See what we can dig up?"

"You got it. This whole thing is strictly off the record. We're on our own if we get caught. You guys understand?"

Caro and Diaz both nodded.

"You sure now? These seem like some pretty serious assholes we're dealing with. We're talking a world of hurt coming down if we fuck up. Think carefully before you say yes."

"I'm in," Caro didn't hesitate. He then turned to his partner. Diaz seemed a bit more reluctant.

"Ralph? You in?"

Diaz paused for a few seconds, then shrugged his shoulders. "Shit, I'm probably in deep already. Yeah, I'm in."

Captain Feldman nodded. "Okay. You find out everything you can about this 'Knight' thing. Be real, real discreet about it. And watch your asses. Check to see if anyone's following you. And you might want to check for bugs or wiretaps."

Diaz's eyes widened. "You think they'd do that?"

"Frankly, I wouldn't put anything past these pricks, whoever the hell they are. Let's just be on the safe side."

"We better come up with a system," Caro suggested, "if we need to get together again to talk about this."

"Your right." Feldman thought for a few seconds. "Um . . . okay. If we need to meet, this is what I'll do. I'll take Ed's coffee mug and put it in the middle of his desk upside-down. That'll be our signal."

"Where should we meet next time?" Diaz asked.

"Let's make it the Zoo. In front of the polar bears."

Caro nodded. "Sounds good, Captain."

"Okay. You guys head on out. I'll leave ten minutes after you. Don't take the same route back."

"Will do."

Caro and Diaz started to leave when Feldman halted them. "By the way, guys. You got the Smith hearing tomorrow, right?"

"Yeah," Caro responded.

"How does it look?"

"I think the judge will hold him on bail. A pretty stiff one. Hell, I won't be surprised if he pleads out."

"Just play it by the book. I want that son of a bitch to rot away a good portion of his life in prison."

"You don't have to worry about that," Diaz grinned. "We'll give our usual stellar testimony."

"Sounds good. Now get back to work. And watch your backs."

The detectives waved good-bye and walked away, leaving the Captain standing to ponder a nearby bed of flowers. In the back of his mind, Caro wondered if they really knew what they were getting into.

When von Klest returned to his hotel room after another briefing with Heinbrodder, he found Otto Kemp sitting on the sofabed. The older man waited until von Klest closed the door before talking.

"We have a problem, Erich. Your friend has made the news."

Von Klest gave him a quizzical look. "What friend? Who are you talking about?"

Kemp got up and walked over to him. "Our contacts in America have been monitoring the news, as you instructed, for anything regarding this Cosmic Protector. He has surfaced in Philadelphia. He reportedly stopped the rape of a young woman, crippling the attacker. In addition, he has destroyed a crack house."

"Are they sure it is him?"

"The eyewitness descriptions match what you gave us."

Von Klest paused thoughtfully. "I hope the crackhouse wasn't one he could eventually link to us." Drugs were just another part of his endeavors to rid the world of "mongrel races." Through his organization's many legitimate and illegitimate businesses, von Klest shipped vast amounts of cocaine to the States, where his dealers deliberately targeted minority communities.

"*Nein*. It was apparently run by a Jamaican gang."

"*Gut*." Von Klest fought the urge to immediately change into his armor, teleport to Philadelphia and hunt down the Protector. He could taste it, how much he wanted to kill him. Prove his superiority.

But no. Not now. Not with everything planned out for

the attack on the Knesset. Besides, who knew if this Protector even used Philadelphia as his actual base of operations. He couldn't waste time traipsing all over that city. He had to commit to this operation.

When this is over, you're next, Protector.

"So long as he remains in America dealing with mongrel scum, he won't bother us. Still, alert our contacts there to step up their monitoring of Philadelphia. We are too far along in the operation now. I can't risk the Protector finding out about it."

"It shall be done, Erich."

"Even if he doesn't suspect our plans, the moment word gets out about our attack, he could teleport here. If he does, I will be ready for him. Then the Cosmic Protector can join the *Juden* pigs in Hell."

TWENTY-NINE

NOTHING ON THE high seas is more awesome than a United States Navy Carrier Battle Group. While a ballistic missile submarine can lay waste to whole countries, its job is to glide unseen through the ocean depths. A CBG is there for the whole world to see. Its centerpiece, a 77,000 ton floating airfield manned by over five thousand men and women, carried up to ninety aircraft. F-14 Tomcats that could shoot down hostile aircraft a hundred miles away; the dual-purpose F/A-18 Hornet, which could dogfight and bomb equally well; and the less notable S-3 Viking, used to hunt enemy submarines or refuel planes in mid-air. Supporting them were E-2 Hawkeyes, whose radar could track approaching aircraft, missiles and ships hundreds of miles away. EA-6B Prowlers jammed enemy electronics. SH-3 Sea King helicopters stood by to rescue any downed pilots. A protective ring of six cruisers, frigates and destroyers guarded the carrier. Their advanced radars could track over two hundred separate targets within a three hundred mile radius. Should any prove hostile, each ship had an array of missiles, torpedoes and guns to dispatch them. If anything got past this deadly gauntlet, the carrier had its own defenses. Three RIM-7 Sea Sparrow missile launchers and three Phalanx guns, which could spew out a hundred 20mm depleted uranium rounds a second, could take care of any errant aircraft or missile.

The carrier in this case was the *USS Kitty Hawk*, sailing ninety-five miles off the coast of the United Arab Emirates. Though built in 1961 and nearing the end of her operational life, she was still a capable ship.

Due to the confined space of the Persian Gulf, the carrier, more suited for the open ocean, needed more inner protection than normal. In addition to the Spruence-class destroyer *USS Deyo* acting as plane guard to pick up any downed pilots, the *USS Antrim*, an Oliver Hazard Perry-class frigate, covered the flattop's starboard side. One of Saudi Arabia's Sandown-class minesweepers patrolled two miles ahead of the group. The U.S. Navy would never forget that Iraqi mines caused the only damage to their ships during Desert Storm.

Armed speedboats were another concern. To counter this, two fast attack craft took up position on either side of the carrier: a Saudi Arabian As-Siddiq-class boat on the port side and an Omani Province-class boat on the starboard. Should they fail, the Americans had a number of .50 caliber machine guns set up along the sides of their ships.

An SH-60 Seahawk helicopter circled the CBG, its dipping sonar searching for any submarine activity. The Iranians had at least three Russian-built Kilo class subs in their arsenal.

More warships covered *Kitty Hawk's* front and rear dozens of miles away, with F-14s and Arab fighters overhead. Monitoring all this activity was a twin-turboprop E-2C Hawkeye one hundred miles north of the carrier.

"Those F-4s from Bandar Abbas are still coming up the coastline," Lieutenant Alan Terrepinn never took his eyes off his cluttered, green radar screen. As the E-2's air control officer, he directed all of *Kitty Hawk's* planes in the air and watched for potential threats.

"Call 'em out, Lieutenant," ordered Lt. Commander Frank Milinski, the combat information center officer.

"Contacts at coordinates zero-one-one-four. Speed four-eight-zero knots, angels fifteen. About one klick off the Iranian coast."

"Have the Qatari Hunters shadow them. No more than fifty miles away for the moment. If the Iranians cross their territorial waters, have the Hunters light 'em up with their radars. That oughta get their attention."

"Yes sir."

Terrepinn flipped to the proper frequency and relayed the orders to the Coalition fighters.

The young lieutenant rubbed his eyes for the third time in ten minutes. Three hours staring at his radar screen did nothing beneficial for his eyes. And he had one more hour to go before another E-2 from *Kitty Hawk* relieved them.

Terrepinn blinked a few times, then checked the screen again. Nothing out of the ordinary. The Qataris wouldn't be on station for a couple of minutes. Time to grab a soda from the cooler in the back.

Something popped up on his screen. A fluttering, electronic cloud.

Dammit. I just checked this thing this morning. What the hell's wrong?

Suddenly it vanished. Terrepinn watched the screen intently. Nothing. Were his burning eyes playing tricks on him?

It appeared again, this time as a faint glimmer.

Lt. Terrepinn ran a quick diagnostic. The GE AN/APS-125 search radar was working fine. But the fuzzy mass remained.

"Hey. Anyone have a contact at four-three-three-four? About ninety to a hundred miles northwest?"

Both Milinski and Ensign Adrienne Pennington, the radar officer, checked their scopes.

"No. Not a thing," the CIC officer replied.

"Same here. I—" Pennington stopped in mid-sentence. "Wait one. Something just popped up."

"I got it, too. Some kind dead spot in our coverage. Better check the hardware."

"I did, sir," Terrepinn swiveled his seat toward him. "The-125 and the main frame are working fine. It looks like we've got something out there."

"Can you be a little more specific, Lieutenant?"

"Negative. I can't get a bearing, altitude or speed on this . . . thing."

"Jammer aircraft?" Ensign Pennington offered.

"No. Then our whole screen would be affected. Besides, I doubt the Iraqis or the Iranians have any capable ECM aircraft.

"Ensign, increase radar power thirty percent. See if gives us better resolution. I'm going to raise Watchtower Four-One."

Watchtower Four-One was an E-3 Sentry, the bigger brother of the E-2C built on a Boeing 707 airframe, orbiting northeastern Saudi Arabia. After a brief conversation with their CIC officer, Milinski clicked off the mike and turned to the others. "The Sentry says they picked up something briefly. But it just dropped off their scope."

"Sir, radar power's increased thirty percent, but . . . I think it's just making it worse."

Milinski came over to Pennington's station and checked her scope. The cloud flickered violently.

"It's like . . . I don't know. Like it's warping the radar beam."

"Sir," Terrepinn called out. "This thing's definitely moving. I'd say maybe five, six miles since last contact. Estimate ninety miles west of our position. Moving due south."

"I'm gonna contact the carrier. Terrepinn. Vector Rodeo Flight to this . . . bogey."

"Roger." *Just great. In the middle of all this, we gotta tag a damn UFO.*

Taxpayers' money at work. Twenty-five million dollars and it picks now to crap out.

Lieutenant Commander Peter "Mickey" McOwen sent an invisible sneer in the direction of the E-2C he and the other F-14 were covering. All that high tech crap and they couldn't get a solid lock on this bogey.

"Rodeo Two-Five, this is Mistletoe," McOwen heard one of the operators in *Kitty Hawk's* CIC over his headphones. "Alert Five is airborne. ETA ten mikes."

"Roger, Mistletoe. We'll be waiting."

Ten minutes! So much for a quick response. The Alert Five F-14s, sitting on the deck fully fueled and armed, were supposed to be launched in under five minutes to respond to imminent threats. By the time those aircraft arrived, whatever was going to happen will have already happened.

"What the hell?" Lieutenant Randy "Suede" Dade blurted from the rear.

"What?"

"Some kind of electronic interference." The Radar Intercept Officer tried to adjust the fighter's powerful AGW-9 radar for a better reading. "Northwest of us."

"Must be what the E-2 picked up." McOwen got on his radio. "Rodeo Two-Seven, Rodeo Two-Five. You got that bogey on your scope?"

"We've got . . . something," replied Lieutenant Gerald "Yeller" Lopez in the other F-14. "Some kind of electronic fuzz. Can't . . . hey! It's gone! Scope's gotta be on the fritz."

"Negative, Yeller. Same on my scope. It's real."

"I'm getting electronic emissions," Lopez's RIO, Ensign Neil "Luggie" Trent, broke in. "Can't make sense of 'em. Never seen anything like it."

"Weapons hot," McOwen ordered. "Yeller, break left a

mile and drop two. I'll break right and climb two. We'll box in this thing."

"Roger."

Wings swept back, the two F-14s broke off and took up their assigned positions.

The RIOs swung their heads from side to side, hoping for a glimpse of the bogey. The sun was setting, turning the sky an orangish hue. Still visibility remained good. They should see something.

"Can you lock on to this thing?" McOwen asked his RIO.

"Negative. Nothing from the AMRAAMs. Sporadic readings from the Sidewinders."

"Mickey," Lopez's staticy voice called in. "My sc***oing. It's totally ***can't make out anyth*ng."

"Aff***tive here. Whate—"

"Emissions just spiked!" Dade interrupted. "It-"

"Jesus! What's that!?"

McOwen glimpsed a black flash the same time Trent cried out. The beam whizzed past Rodeo Two-Seven, missing it by thirty feet.

"We're-"

"Break! Break! Break!" McOwen cut off Lopez and shoved his Tomcat into a hard right bank. He then rolled left. Gravity's invisible hand threatened to squash the men in their seats. McOwen tightened his gut and grunted to fight off the g-forces. The fringes of his vision turned black.

He swung back toward his wingman. Suddenly there was another black flash. Then a fireball. McOwen craned his neck. His head felt like a bowling ball.

"No," his voice strained under the g-forces.

McOwen watched bits of metal that had been Yeller's F-14 spiral into the Persian Gulf.

"Get a lock!" McOwen ordered as he began jinking. Flying straight only made you a better target.

"No tone!"

"Get one!" McOwen flipped to the E-2C's frequency. "Northstar Zero-One! Rodeo Two-Five! We're . . . shit!"

"Mickey" banked hard right to avoid another black beam. He rolled the F-14 over when a second one shot overhead. A third ray appeared directly ahead of him.

"Oh-"

Beam and plane connected. Hundreds of pieces of metal, glass and flesh shot off in every direction.

"Search and Rescue en route to the area," Terrepinn announced minutes after Northstar Zero-One's last contact with Rodeo Flight

"Getting a lot of interference on the scope."

"We're at General Quarters!" Milinski hollered when he got off with *Kitty Hawk.*

"No other hostile air activity," Terrepinn scanned his screen. "The Qataris are asking for new orders."

"Tell 'em to stay with the Iranians. Current ROE. Any threatening moves, splash 'em."

"Roger."

Milinski went over to the radar operator's station. "Talk to me, Ensign."

"It looks like the bogey's moving, but . . . well. Commander, I've never seen anything like this."

Terrepinn also checked his screen. The blob was heading south. Toward them!

"Schumacher," Milinski contacted the E-2's pilot. "Evasive action. Possible bandit approaching from the north."

"Roger."

"There's gotta be something wrong with this radar," Milinski steamed as the plane banked right.

"I checked it myself, sir. It's fine."

"Same here," Terrepinn chimed in. "All our systems are working perfectly. Whatever the hell this thing is, it's real."

"Terrepinn. Vector the Alert Five toward the bogey."

Milinski started back to his station when Terrepinn heard over his headphones, "What the hell's that?"

It was Schumacher.

"What's go-"

Milinski never finished his sentence. He, Terrepinn and Pennington never saw the black beam that slammed into their E-2 and disintegrated it.

"Is the second Hawkeye away?" asked the muscular, barrel chested skipper of the *Kitty Hawk*, Captain Henry Van Hart.

"Yes, sir."

"Good," chimed in Rear Admiral Ted Brooks. The CBG commander stood behind Van Hart in carrier's eerily lit Combat Information Center. "Have it take up station eighty miles north of us and establish a data link with the Alert Five ASAP."

"Aye, sir."

"Alert Five is twenty miles south of Qatar," announced the Air Control Officer. "No report of hostiles."

"I want four more Tomcats to join 'em," ordered the plump, bespectacled admiral. "And put up six Hornets as well. Have them circle us five miles out."

"I suggest we also arm the Vikings for anti-surface and anti-sub duties, Admiral."

Brooks nodded. "Approved."

"Bogey moving toward us, sirs," a radar operator blurted. Both Brooks and Van Hart glanced up at the CIC's main display screen. It showed a computer generated image of the Persian Gulf and the positions of all known ships and aircraft. Coming down the middle was a fuzzy, wavy mass no one could positively identify.

"Still can't get a fix on it. Whenever it's on the screen, it seems to . . . warp our radar beam. I can't determine speed, altitude. Anything. Just that it's moving."

"Keep trying, sailor. I want to know what that thing is."

The Admiral tried to keep from sounding frustrated. He succeeded . . . to a degree.

Van Hart just shook his head. *What in the hell are we dealing with?* His only theory revolved around a new jammer system. He doubted Iran or Iraq could build one themselves. Maybe they had help from Russians ex-patriots or the Chinese.

"Lieutenant Carbra," he addressed the Filipino-American communications officer. "Any word from Rodeo Flight or Northstar Zero-One?"

"Negative, sir. SAR units have scrambled from Al Jubayl. The British minesweeper *Hurworth* and her escorts are en route to help."

"I want a fifty mile exclusion zone around this ship," Admiral Brooks swept his head the length of the CIC. "Any aircraft or vessel not squawking the proper code gets deep sixed."

A dozen or so voices replied, "Aye, sir."

"Admiral. CENTCOM on the line for you."

He took the receiver from a young petty officer. "Admiral Brooks . . . Yes sir . . . We have it on screen, but radar can't get a proper fix . . . Somehow it's warping the signal . . . I don't know, sir . . . It could be an EW aircraft . . ." Brooks used the acronym for Electronic Warfare.

"Captain!" the Air Control Officer hollered. "One of our Hornets has a visual."

Van Hart nodded. *Now we'll find out what shot down our planes.* "On speaker."

Every ear in CIC perked up. Admiral Brooks asked his CENTCOM superiors to standby for more information as he listened to the F/A-18 pilot.

"Dasher Two-Two. Tally on the bogey. Angels nine, bearing two-two-three-six. It's . . . it's black. Not a cloud. Going down for a closer look."

The Captain rolled his tongue inside his mouth. *Come on, Dasher. Give us something we can work with.*

"Gun camera rolling," Dasher Two-Two continued. "I don't***this is. It's some . . . Oh my God! It's-"

A dull thud rattled from the speaker. Then nothing.

"Dasher Two-Two's off the screen."

Dammit! "Launch SAR!" van Hart ordered.

"Do *Deyo* and *Antrim* have weapons lock?" Brooks asked.

The Tactical Action Officer checked his data link with the other ships. "Negative."

"Captain!" the communications officer called out, a growler phone in her hand. "Bridge for you."

The Captain took the receiver. "Van Hart."

"Commander Brodigan, sir. I think you better get up to the bridge. We've got a visual on the . . . bogey."

"On my way."

Kitty Hawk's CO rushed out of CIC. He tried not to think of the pilots he just lost. The time for mourning would come later. Right now he had to defend his carrier against . . .

What? Some dark cloud we can't get a proper lock on.

No exercise, no course at Annapolis ever prepared him for something like this.

Doesn't matter. Gotta deal with it.

Van Hart made it to the bridge in two minutes.

"There, skipper." His XO, Commander Neil Brodigan, handed him a pair of high powered binoculars and pointed. "Just off the port bow."

Van Hart brought the binoculars to his eyes. He increased magnification. There! Hanging in mid-air. A pulsating black blob.

"What the hell . . ."

"It's not an aircraft." Brodigan noted as an F/A-18 shot off the deck. "Not one I've ever seen."

For a moment, Van Hart remembered those stories about balls of light World War II pilots reported seeing from time to time. The mysterious "Foo Fighters."

That's as good a description as I can come up with right now.

"I want someone videotaping this now."

The Officer of the Deck picked up a growler phone and ordered all lookouts with camcorders to begin taping the object. Many already were.

"Captain, I've got the *Onizah* on line," a rail thin black radio operator announced. "They're closing with the bogey."

"On speaker."

The sailor flipped a switch and everyone on the bridge, as well as in CIC, listened to the Saudi communications officer's report.

" . . .it is like some kind of black cloud or bubble." The officer on the minesweeper managed to keep his accented voice steady. "It is descending."

Van Hart and Brodigan kept their gazes fixed on the bogey as they listened to the Saudi's play-by-play.

"Heavy radar interference. Unable to get weapons lock. We will-"

Captain Van Hart, Brodigan and the rest of the bridge crew watched in horror as a black ray shot down from the Foo Fighter. A geyser of flame and smoke shot up from the water.

"Holy—!" the XO stammered. "It took out the minesweeper. Just like that."

Van Hart lowered his binoculars. A chill shot up and down his spine. *What in the hell are we facing?*

"All contact with the *Onizah* lost," one of the CIC personnel announced.

Brooks turned to the TAO. "Do any of our ships have a lock on the bogey?"

"Negative."

"Tell 'em to use their guns."

"But without radar—"

"Do it manually! Tell 'em to use spotters if they have to. This thing isn't affecting their eyesight, is it?"

The TAO gulped. "I'll inform them, sir."

While the Tactical Action Officer contacted the other ships, Brooks went over to the Air Control Officer. "Show me what we have up."

The quiet-looking, red-headed Lieutenant Commander circled all the *Kitty Hawk's* aircraft on the main display screen. "One Hawkeye, one tanker, one Hornet, one Sea King, four Tomcats and *Deyo's* Seahawk."

"Pull back the helos three miles from our position. Tell the E-2 and the tanker to stay clear of us. Tell the Alert Five birds to return here ASAP and pull in the two F-14s covering our rear. See if the UAE can send up more fighters to take over."

"Aye, sir."

"Message from the bridge," someone blurted out. "The bogey's closing on us."

"Evasive maneuvers! Execute!"

The helmsman immediately spun the wheel right, beginning a series of zigzags. The escorts did likewise, as the battle group tried to make itself as hard a target as possible.

Van Hart glanced out the windows, checking on his escorts. The Saudi Al-Siddiq boat fired the first shot. *Al Sharqiyah*, the Omani attack craft, tried to maneuver into a better firing position.

The Al-Siddiq's shell missed by half-a-mile. The bogey—now a bandit actually, since it did attack—descended toward the group. Seconds later another shell screamed toward it . . . and also missed.

Al Sharqiyah swung around toward the rear of the carrier, its 76mm OTO-Melara gun tracking the target. The boat fired two quick shots. One round missed. The other blossomed into an orange-black fireball.

"Direct hit! Direct hit!" the Omani captain hollered to the rest of the battle group.

The celebration was short-lived. The bandit burst through the thick, smoky cloud left by the explosion.

"Impossible!" Brodigan blurted as he watched the object continue on as if nothing happened.

Van Hart held his breath. No aircraft on Earth could have survived a hit like that. *Is it even an aircraft? I don't know what to call this thing.*

Hostile! the duty part of his mind shouted.

"Target Goalkeepers on that thing."

"CIC can't get a lock," a sailor replied seconds later.

"Do it manually!"

The growler phone on the near wall rang. Van Hart picked it up. "Captain here."

"This is the Air Boss. Dasher Two-Six is ready for take-off. Can we send her?"

"Permission granted. We'll get into the wind on our next turn."

"Aye, Captain."

Just another problem he didn't need. He couldn't launch aircraft with the *Kitty Hawk* making sharp turns every minute or two. Van Hart would have to pick and choose his times to turn his planes loose.

The compact F/A-18 designated Dasher Two-Six shot off the deck from Catapult Number Two just as another F/A-18 appeared.

Dasher Two-Four, launched prior to the attack, swung back to engage the bandit. Staying out of Dasher Two-Six's flight path, the Hornet screamed toward its target, left wing tilted down and nose pointed at the object.

"Tally!" the pilot cried out. "No tone from Nine-Limas." He used the slang for the AIM-9L Sidewinder. "Going guns."

The pilot lined up the bandit in the gunsight of his electronically generated Heads-Up Display. Suddenly a black beam cut across the sky.

"God—!"

The beam burrowed through Dasher Two-Six's two GE F404-400 turbofan engines. Hundreds of flaming pieces of debris sputtered into the water below.

Dasher Two-Four's shaken pilot didn't even bother lining up his shot. Panic brought his thumb down on the fire button. The Vulcan rotary cannon in the jet's nose spewed out a stream of 20mm rounds. Every one missed.

The pilot growled at himself for jumping the gun. He quickly calmed down and settled the gunsight on the bandit.

"Got 'im! Takin' m-"

Another ray cleaved through the sky and took out the F/A-18.

The fast attack boats resumed firing, joined by the *Kitty Hawk's* CIWS guns. The yellow flashes indicating where rounds found their mark seemed to merge into one explosion. The bandit remained unaffected.

Now the .50 calibers opened up. Laser-like tracers zipped through the air. Joining them were puffs of smoke made by 76mm shells as their proximity fuses detonated. The black mass streaked through the curtain of lead that would have annihilated anything else.

It came within fifty feet of the Al-Siddiq and fired. The Saudi vessel exploded into nothingness.

On board *Al Sharqiyah*, three members of the bridge crew fled when the bandit came at them. The Captain screamed for them to return or he'd shoot them. His hollering was lost under the chatter of .50 caliber machine guns and the thumps of the forward deck gun.

The first sailor made his way around the aft mounted 40mm cannons, his eardrums shattered by their constant thundering. He stopped for a second. The immense pain forced him to cover his ears and caused his knees to buckle. The instinct to survive kicked back in. He grabbed hold of the top rung of the railing, leaped over . . .

. . . and the 420-ton attack vessel blew apart.

"Good God! Nothing's stopping it!"

"Get hold of yourself, XO!" Van Hart snapped, using all his control to keep his voice from cracking. He'd never been more afraid in his entire life. But he could not show it now. Not in front of his crew.

There has to be something I can do.

Nothing came to mind. *Kitty Hawk's* 20mm and .50 caliber guns had no effect on the black, pulsating bandit. It was impossible to get a missile lock on it. He doubted he could launch any more aircraft before it attacked them. Even if he could, it probably wouldn't do any good. The bandit already downed five fighters and an AWACS. He'd just be feeding it more targets.

Captain Van Hart shivered. This thing had rendered his billion dollar battle group impotent.

He noticed Commander Brodigan aim his binoculars at the bogey as it neared the *Kitty Hawk.* The XO squinted through the thin haze of smoke created by the gunfire.

"C-C-Captain. It's . . . it's a man!"

"What!? "

A few sailors looked their way as the XO jabbed a finger at the pulsating object. "Look for yourself, dammit! I'm not making it up. Look!"

Van Hart decided to relieve Brodigan after honoring his request. The man had gone to pieces.

He looked through his binoculars. *Oh my God!*

It was a man. Surrounded by a crackling field of dark energy. It—he—soon filled Van Hart's lenses. The Captain dropped the binoculars and stared at the thing in awe.

"What the hell's that?" one sailor shouted.

Everyone on the bridge turned to see. Several repeated

the sailor's inquiry. Three men just screamed in terror. Two broke down crying.

Captain Van Hart became oblivious to the noise. He just watched as the thing slowly crossed over the deck. *Kitty Hawk's* Goalkeepers and .50s ceased fire when it passed over them. Deck crewmen in brightly colored uniforms looked up and pointed. Some fled and sought shelter anywhere they could. The pilot of an F/A-18 idling on Catapult Number One popped his canopy and jumped out.

"This can't be possible!" Brodigan babbled. "How is this possible?"

Van Hart thought the same thing.

The "man" stopped five feet from the bridge and hovered. Brodigan backed away. "What is that thing!?! Can anyone tell me what that thing is!?!"

Van Hart remained rooted to the spot, eyes transfixed on the being. Terror completely shut down his mind. The . . . Energy Man raised his arms. Van Hart took a step back. A field of black swept over his eyes. Something rumbled in his ears.

Less than a mile away, Seaman Walter Norwell caught the fiery destruction of *Kitty Hawk's* bridge on his Navy-issue, waterproof camcorder.

"Jesus! What the hell is that!?" blurted *Deyo's*_sunken faced Fire Control Officer as the destroyer charged through the water toward the carrier.

The thin-faced, nineteen-year-old lowered his camcorder and turned to the officer next to him on one of the forward lookout nests. "I don't know, sir."

"Get that camera back up, sailor!" Lieutenant Coreland shouted. "The brass is gonna want pictures of this."

"Yes sir." The sailor instantly obeyed, zooming in on the *Kitty Hawk* as a second explosion ripped through her island.

Flames licked their way up and down the carrier's superstructure. Men and women on the deck ran in every direction. Pilots abandoned their planes. A squat yellow fire truck raced across the deck toward the island. Yuri Drovinov—Nexus—unleashed a black beam. The explosion obliterated the truck. Shards of metal ripped through the bodies of three crewmen. More shrapnel peppered a nearby S-3 Viking. Its fuel tank exploded. The fireball reached out to the six one thousand pound Laser Guided Bombs and four Harpoon anti-ship missiles the aircraft carried. It sounded like a hundred cars crashing simultaneously. Flames swept across the deck, absorbing everything in its path.

The fire enveloped another S-3 whose refueling hose was still connected. It blew up and set off a trolley of LGBs twenty feet away. More aircraft went up in the blaze. Flames cascaded over the railing, smothering the Landing Signals Officer's platform.

Nexus sent another blast through the inferno. It tore through the elevator platform and into the hangar. Crewmembers raced out of the fire and smoke filled area. Firefighters in their silver asbestos suits soon arrived, hoses in hand.

Another blast from Nexus knocked the firefighters down. Two trolleys of AGM-88 Shrike anti-radar missiles ignited. The explosion touched off a trolley of Sidewinder air-to-air missiles, then a main fuel line.

Nexus felt the shockwave through his protective energy bubble. The rear of the carrier erupted like a volcano. Aircraft, people and debris were tossed into the air like toys. The flaming wreckage of an EA-6B crashed down and skidded across the deck into a fully armed F/A-18. The resulting fireball consumed both.

"GLORIOUS!!!" Drovinov bellowed with laughter as he backed away from the flaming carrier. "I AM DOING THIS!!! ME!!! YURI DROVINOV!!! NEXUS!!!"

He hurled blast after blast into the stricken carrier. The flight deck became submerged in a sea of fire. Half the *Kitty*

Hawk's burning superstructure keeled over and crashed through the deck.

Another volcanic explosion shoved Nexus back about thirty feet. His body quivered from the shock. *What could have . . .*

He looked down. A billowing cloud of fire and smoke rose to the heavens. Beneath it lay the shattered remains of the *Kitty Hawk*. The fire, Drovinov surmised, must have found the main magazine.

"I DID IT!!!" Drovinov drowned in the enormity of his power. "I AM NEXUS!!! I AM POWER INCARNATE!!!"

A sharp whistling interrupted his triumphant laughter.

"What!?!"

He turned to see the *Deyo* charging toward him, firing her forward 5-inch gun.

"Fools! You will pay! ALL OF YOU WILL PAY!!!"

"Oh my God! Sir! It's coming right at us!" Norwell shouted to Lieutenant Coreland in a shaky voice. The Fire Control Officer ignored him as he continued directing the gun.

"Left two degrees! Elevation sixty-seven! Fire!"

The gun barked again.

Norwell's hand shook as the thing neared them. His mind shouted *run*, but fear paralyzed his body.

Two more rounds from *Deyo's* 5-incher went off in rapid succession. Then a forward mounted .50 caliber chattered. Tracers arced toward the UFO. Norwell's finger unconsciously pressed down on the zoom button. The camcorder automatically focused, and . . .

"Oh my God. Lieutenant Coreland! It's a—!"

The beam struck the forward deck. The gun was torn from its moorings as its ammunition cooked off. The explosions set off a nearby box-shaped ASROC anti-submarine missile launcher. It blew apart *Deyo's* bow.

Norwell and Coreland were blown off their nest and into

the water. The young seaman held onto his camcorder until he slammed into the water.

Nexus flew over the *Deyo*, peppering it with energy blasts. He looped back around and fired until the destroyer was engulfed in flames.

He sucked down a couple deep breaths. The strength briefly dripped from his muscles. Drovinov pulled it back in.

How can . . . No. It's nothing. I am fine.

He headed over to the last ship, the *Antrim*. Two shots blew the frigate in half.

"Dead. All dead!" Nexus announced as he flew out of the smoke. "BY MY HAND!!"

He halted in mid-air when he noticed two helicopters approaching the carnage. Probably hoping to pick up any survivors. Nexus easily downed both of them. He then turned east and flew off as the distant rumble of jet engines made their way over the horizon.

"Oh my God," the pilot of the lead Tomcat stammered as he got closer to the smoke. Moments later he soared over the smoldering wrecks of what had been his mighty Carrier Battle Group.

"They're gone. *Kitty Hawk*. The tin cans. They're . . . all . . . gone."

THIRTY

"... STILL NO LOCK ... firing blind ... better-" *THUD!*

"We're hit, we're ... Try to-" *BOOM!*

Thus ended the transmission from *Antrim's* Combat Information Center.

The President shook his head solemnly. It was the third time he and the National Security Council heard the recording, fed via satellite from CENTCOM-Riyadh an hour ago.

"Nothing." The frustrated Chief Executive stared at everyone in the cramped White House Situation Room. "It still tells us nothing. What the hell sunk our carrier?"

"None of the transmissions contained anything very descriptive. They referred to it as a 'bogey'—an unidentified object—then a bandit, or hostile aircraft. A few times it was just called 'the object.'"

The President glared at National Security Advisor Baronelli. "So what the hell is this 'object'? My God, aren't those people trained to recognize different aircraft?"

"Yes they are, Mr. President," JCS Chairman Callingworth quickly came to his service's defense. "Along with a variety of ships and missiles. All of which would have shown up on radar before they got anywhere near *Kitty Hawk*."

"But all the reports we've gotten show only sporadic radar contact with . . . something," noted the Vice President.

"Correct, sir. But remember, we only have bits and pieces of what happened. If we can get hold of the black boxes on some of the aircraft that went down, we might have a better idea what destroyed the *Kitty Hawk* group."

"Could it be a stealth fighter?" Chief of Staff Preston leaned forward, elbows propped on the long, rectangular table. "Maybe the Iraqis built one?"

"Impossible," DCI Brock shot her a hard stare. "Iraq doesn't have the technical experts or the facilities to build anything like a stealth aircraft."

"You didn't know Iraq was building a damn five megaton nuclear bomb. How do you know they're not building stealth planes?"

"That's different, Miss Preston. We had evidence that Iraq was building a nuclear arsenal long before they set off that bomb. There is nothing to even remotely suggest they're working on a stealth warplane."

"Look," the Vice President raised a hand, halting Preston and Brock's argument. "We don't even know if Iraq was responsible for this."

"Oh please," blurted the Secretary of Defense. "Who else could have sunk that battle group?"

"What about Iran?"

Callingworth leaned forward. "Unlikely. What would Iran have to gain by attacking us? They know we have enough firepower in the Gulf to lay waste to their whole country."

"Maybe they attacked *Kitty Hawk* to make us think the Iraqis did it, to draw us into a war. We'd decimate Iraq, and while it's weak, the Iranians move in and set up a fundamentalist government. Heck, that's what they've wanted to do for decades."

The SecDef stifled a laugh, then turned to Preston. "No way I can buy that. A plot like that is good for Tom Clancy, but not for the real world. Besides, the Iranians know we'd blast 'em back to Tehran if they set one foot over the border with Iraq."

"Veep's right," the President rested his balled fists on the table as he stood. "We really don't know who or what sunk *Kitty Hawk*." He turned to Callingworth. "Admiral. What would it take for the Iraqis *or* the Iranians to destroy *Kitty Hawk* and her escorts?"

Callingworth paused to think. "For both countries, it would have taken the bulk of their air and naval forces, which we would have picked up on radar and intercepted. Maybe a few attackers would've gotten through, but not enough to sink all six ships."

"What about mines?" asked the VP.

Callingworth shook his head. "It'd have to have been a pretty big and very cluttered minefield. That Sandown minesweeper would've spotted it easily."

"Maybe submarines?"

"The Iranians do have a few Russian-built Kilo-class diesel attack boats. Very quiet. They might be able to slip inside the carrier group. But they'd give themselves away the moment they fired. Even if they got all the ships, the ASW copters would've picked them off.

"Besides, that still doesn't explain what happened to our aircraft. They can't have all suffered mechanical problems at the same time."

"So what does that mean?" Preston turned up her hands in an exasperated fashion. "We're dealing with some kind of new, secret weapon?"

Dead silence for five seconds. Then DCI Brock responded, "I'll get my people working on it."

"You do that, Brock," the President sneered. He too was fed up with one surprise after another popping up and the

CIA standing there, shrugging its shoulders, saying "I don't know."

The President took a deep breath to settle himself. "Now, how's the rescue operation going?"

"We're pulling in every available helicopter and ship we can to help," said the Defense Secretary. "All military and civilian hospitals on the Arabian Peninsula are standing by to receive casualties."

"How many are we talking about?"

"No numbers yet, Mr. President," Callingworth flipped through his notes. "But from what I've heard, I think it's going to be pretty bad. The *Kitty Hawk* carried a complement of roughly forty-nine hundred. *Deyo* had a crew of nearly three hundred, same as *Antrim*, and about one-seventy combined on the minesweeper and the fast attack boats."

The VP quickly added up the numbers. "My God. That's over fifty-six hundred people."

"Holy Father," the President muttered under his breath.

"The American people will never accept casualties like that," Preston declared. "Not in this day and age. The congressmen and senators opposed to our presence in the Gulf, this'll just give them more ammunition to get us to fold up our tent and come home."

"The people on Capitol Hill who oppose this are just a small, vocal minority," the Secretary of Defense pointed out. "They're not as big as they were during Desert Shield."

"There are quite a few straddling the fence. When the first pictures of our ships sinking show up on the evening news, when the first casualty numbers are printed, when the first opinion polls come out, they may change their minds. We could wind up trying to settle this crisis with a divided Congress."

"Or it may galvanize them," offered the Vice President. "They could ban together and demand retribution."

"Like when Pearl Harbor was bombed?" Preston shook

her head. "Sorry, sir. Different generation. And Japan didn't have The Bomb. Iraq does."

"We can't afford to be intimidated," the President said sternly. "Not when a nuclear armed Iraq is threatening almost half the world's oil supply. And not when thousands of American sailors are lying at the bottom of the Persian Gulf. We'd lose all influence as a superpower if we back down now."

"We need to rush more reinforcements," SecDef stated. "Especially with the *Kitty Hawk* gone."

"Don't we already have reinforcements on the way?"

"Yes, Miss Preston. But many of them have heavy equipment that can only be transported by sea, such as tanks and armored personnel carriers. It could be well into next month before they're all in position. We need more forces there as soon as possible in case Iraq or Iran suddenly decide to launch a major attack."

"What do you suggest?" the President asked.

The Defense Secretary deferred to Callingworth. "Send in the 401st Tactical Fighter Wing's F-16s from Torrejon, Spain. Also, F/A-18s from the Marine squadrons in California. That should make up for *Kitty Hawk's* lost air wing. They should all be in position by next week. As a stop gap measure, the Egyptians have two F-16 squadrons based near Cairo that could be in-country tomorrow morning our time. They can hold the fort until our planes get there."

"Very well," the President nodded. "I'll talk to the Egyptian President once we're done."

"Meanwhile," Callingworth went on, "I'd like to move the carrier *Kennedy* out of the Red Sea and into the Gulf of Oman with *Eisenhower*. That means only the Brits' little carrier, *Illustrious*, and her dozen or so Harriers will be in the Red Sea until *Nimitz* and *Enterprise* arrive from the Pacific. We could ask the French to commit their new CVN, the *Charles De Gaulle*, to the Red Sea. It's not as big as our carriers. Holds about forty aircraft, including a dozen of their new Rafales. Best fighters the French have.

"Also, we have two Los Angeles-class attack subs in the Pacific—*Baton Rouge* and *Harrisburg*. I'd like to reroute them to Diego Garcia, load them with additional Tomahawks, and station them off Oman."

The President gave his approval.

"What about additional ground forces?"

"Most of our Rapid Deployment Forces are already in the Gulf. But our airlift assets are already stretched thin. We couldn't deploy our remaining RDF units there any sooner than a week to ten days."

"I'll get in touch with some of our Pacific allies," SecDef said. "Australia, the Philippines, South Korea. See if they're willing to commit any ground forces. They depend on Mid East oil too."

"Let's pursue that avenue as well." The President paused to take a breath. "Top priority, I want to know who attacked our carrier. We're sure to have a bunch of hawks inside and outside Washington crying bloody murder for retaliation. But dammit, before I send our men and women to die I want to make sure we're hitting the right people."

"Oh, if only you had a camera to record it all, Drovinov," Iraq's President gleefully bounded across the carpet of his plush private office in the bunker under the Presidential Palace. "Or would you prefer your new codename . . . Nexus? It has a ring of power to it, don't you think?"

The President laughed as he walked over to General Nurabi and the Defense Minister, standing near the mahogany desk. He excitedly grabbed their forearms, then turned to the 21-inch TV at the front of the room showing CNN. It was from them he first heard word of the *Kitty Hawk's* demise. Drovinov gave him a more detailed report when he returned to Baghdad. Curious how it seemed to take a while for him to get up to full speed during his flight back.

Bah! It means nothing. I am fine.

"I hope they're going to show pictures. I'd like to see what's left of such a proud fleet." The President's sarcastic air flooded the room.

"During the last war, the Americans tried to prevent their press from showing too many casualties," Nurabi said. "That may be the case now as well."

"Nonsense," the President waved a hand at him. "The Americans love their freedom of the press too much. Soon we shall see debris scattered all about the Arabian Gulf on the television. This is indeed the proudest day in Iraq's history. And we have you, Drovinov my friend, to thank for it."

Drovinov, standing near the front door, barely paid attention to the jovial leader. His mind was thousands of miles away. He had gone through another transformation out there, just as profound as the one in the desert that gave him these powers.

Yuri Igorovich Drovinov, son of a Moscow factory worker, at one time *the* top physicist in the Soviet Union, had single-handedly taken on the might of the American Navy . . . and prevailed. One of their mighty aircraft carriers was at the bottom of the Persian Gulf, along with five other ships and seven aircraft. He wondered how many people went down with them. Like it mattered. What were *human* lives to him anyway?

For all their vaunted missiles and radar and airplanes, the Americans were powerless against him. They could have thrown stones at him for all the good it would have done. What he did to the carrier group he could easily do to an entire navy, or a city. A whole country! What could stop him?

Nexus looked at the gloating President and his two lapdogs. Did he even need the Iraqis anymore?

"The Americans don't even know it was us who sank their

carrier," The President plopped down in a red satin covered, high backed chair. "Some of them think Iran did it. Which is good. While they are confused, we can prepare our forces for the invasion of Saudi Arabia."

The Iraqi leader turned to the Defense Minister and told him to present his plan. He removed a sizable map from his briefcase and pinned it to the wall.

"Operation: Driving Wind is based on Soviet shock tactics of massing armor for a swift and deep drive into enemy territory. The Republican Guard 4th Motorized Division would lead the 4th Tank Corps in a flanking maneuver in the west, with Rahfa as their objective. The Republican Guard 2nd Armored and 3rd Mechanized Divisions would spearhead the 5th Corps in a frontal assault across the Iraq-Saudi border toward Hafar al Batin. The Republican Guard 1st Armored and 7th Motorized Divisions would lead the 3rd Tank Corps through Kuwait into Saudi Arabia. Then all three forces shall link up and drive deeper into enemy territory, with infantry following on. Preceding the thrust would be a massive air, artillery and SCUD assault, employing chemical weapons on several fronts."

"And what of Nexus' role?" the President asked impatiently.

"Nexus would be used to strike strategic targets deep inside Saudi Arabia. I propose he first take out the Coalition's command and control in Riyadh, then hit, in order, Dharan Air Base, Al Jubayl Naval Base, King Khalid Military City, where they keep the American Stealth Fighters, and the ports in Muscat, Oman."

"How long before our forces are in place?"

"Many of our shock forces are at or near their demarcation points, Mr. President. It'll take another week for all our first wave units to be in position. Two or three weeks to get all our infantry units in place. It has to be done in a way to let the Coalition think we're reinforcing our forward positions, not preparing for an offensive."

"Too long. Carry out the operation when our shock forces are in place."

"But, Mr. President. Our infantry—"

"We do not need the infantry. We have Nexus. Any enemy forces we miss, he will destroy. Within days, the Coalition will be on their knees begging to surrender."

"But the Americans' missile submarine . . . ?" Nurabi reminded his leader.

"They will not dare use it when they see the destruction Nexus is capable of. The Arabian Peninsula will be ours by month's end. Then we can turn our attention to Iran, and once they're ground under our heel, Syria. Then we shall make good on our promise to reduce Israel to ash. By year's end, we shall control this entire region. Iraq will be a superpower in its own right."

The fool. Drovinov just stared as the President continued his maniacal rantings. Iraq's leader only had eyes for one small region of the world.

Drovinov had eyes for the world itself.

THIRTY-ONE

"ONE MORE, BUDDY. Just one more."

Jack Remmler's face contorted. He gritted his teeth and moaned. His arms and back felt like lead. But he had to do this one . . . last . . . rep!

He managed to lift the bar and locked it into place with Jim Elling's help. Remmler dropped his arms to his sides and breathed deep.

"Good job, dude," Elling removed the two ten-pound weights from each side. "You keep this up, you'll make the wrestling team this winter."

"Sorry, Jim," Remmler slithered off the bench. "Unless it involves wild costumes, drop kicks off the top rope and metal chairs, I ain't interested."

Truth be known he could probably make the team. The combat skills the *tru'kat* endowed him with remained even when he wasn't wearing the armor. However, he'd have to get into better shape before he could take on a wrestler—or any other big, tough badass—without his armor.

"You're watching too much TV for your own good. But

seriously, man, it's good to see you getting into better shape. Right now, for a guy like you, I'd say stay away from the weights. Go with exercise bikes, rowing machines, stairmaster. That'll tone up your leg, arm and shoulder muscles. If you want to use weights, use Bubba's dumbbells."

"What about running?" Remmler wiped his brow with a sweat towel.

"Well, I'm no big fan of running. Puts too much stress on the ankles and knees if you ask me. Probably better if you just walk. At least you won't get tired as quickly."

Remmler smiled. "I can handle that."

"Cool. C'mon, let's hit the showers."

Remmler followed his friend out of the weight room and into the large, carpeted area for the stationary bikes, treadmills and rowing machines. At eleven in the morning the gym was not crowded. He showered and changed and left with Elling out the east exit of the Marcus Fedder Gymnasium.

"So where ya off to now?" Jim asked.

"Eh, probably just hang out in my room for a while. Then grab some lunch."

Elling nodded. "Oh, by the way, pass this along to Bubba. Saturday night, big party at Phi Sigma Alpha. You can come too if you want."

"Me? C'mon, Jim. You know frat parties aren't my gig. Besides, most of the guys over there are dillholes anyway."

"No, some of 'em are pretty cool. Least the ones on the wrestling team are."

"So what makes you think they'd want me there? I'm no athlete or campus stud."

"Actually, a lot of them read your articles in *The Bear Facts*. Plus they're big fans of your radio show."

"Get the hell outta here."

"It's true, Remy. You're like a celebrity around here, man."

Remmler laughed it off. "If I'm such a celebrity, then

where are all the admiring babes that are supposed to be around me?"

"They'll come, they'll come."

"Heh. I thought at least one would come around last year. Well, you know how that turned out."

Elling was quiet as they neared the Student Center.

"What the hell's that?" he asked.

About three dozen students were gathered in front of the building. Some carried banners and signs.

"NO BLOOD FOR OIL" screamed one posterboard in red letters.

"THIS IS THE PRICE FOR OIL" declared another. Underneath the slogan was a crude drawing of an exploding ship with several stick figures falling into the sea.

"Aw shit," Remmler groaned. "It's the fuckin' campus radicals."

"Great. Why can't we send 'em back to the '60s?"

"I'll bet you twenty bucks I know what they're saying," Remmler said. "'How should we respond to Iraq sinking our ships? Run away.'"

"Yeah. God forbid we should ever kick ass on a country that kills a couple thousand Americans."

Remmler could make out what some of the protesters were shouting as they got closer.

"How many more deaths will it take to convince you!?"

"Do you want to see this planet covered by radioactive fallout!?"

"Impeach the Washington warmongers!"

"Make the military feed homeless children instead of killing them!"

The last comment stung Remmler. Both his grandfathers fought in World War Two. His cousin Lance drove an APC into Kuwait in 1991. Even right now his sister Lisa made sure no one lobbed any nukes at the U.S.

How dare they . . . ?

Remmler's eyes and forehead scrunched up in anger. He picked out the person who made the comment, some long-haired maggot with several earrings and an old Earth Day t-shirt. His fists balled up.

"Peabrained little cocksucker. I'm gonna give that fuckin' neo-hippie a piece of my mind."

He took two steps toward the protesters before a powerful hand come down on the back of his collar and steered him away.

"Just ignore 'em, Remy," Elling said. "Let 'em shoot off their mouths. Just remember, we're right and they're assholes."

Remmler released a loud breath through his nostrils. He looked at the protesters, then back to Jim. "Yeah, I guess you're right."

Elling smiled and took his hand off Remmler's neck as they moved on. They parted ways at the student parking lot. Elling headed for Sieford Hall, Remmler for Driscoll Hall. He replayed the protest over in his mind. People like that just pissed him off. Always thinking they could appeal to anyone's good senses. They just couldn't accept the fact that some people didn't want to see the light. That they were so corrupt they were beyond salvation. *The kind of people the Cosmic Protectors were created to fight.*

Remmler watched and read everything he could about the *Kitty Hawk* attack since it first hit the news. No one knew what or even who was responsible. According to the news reports, any air attack would have been detected by radar. Submarines could have done it, but sonar would have detected them when the first torpedo was launched. Mines could be a possibility, but the Coalition had a fleet of minesweepers patrolling the Persian Gulf. And that still didn't explain all the downed aircraft.

Could Imperium be behind it? Lord knew he had the power to run undetected through the carrier's defenses and send it to the bottom. That would make sense, given the Keeper's words.

"Your planet is entering a perilous moment in its history. So perilous, a Cosmic Protector is needed to maintain the balance again."

Remmler considered teleporting to the Gulf and searching for Imperium. But he would be long gone by now. Part of him was thankful. Visions of the fight on Springfield Trail still haunted him. Getting his ass kicked was bad enough, but running away like he did bothered him the most.

"Run away and live to fight another day." It's still running away.

At least it kept you alive.

And how many times do you think you can get away with it before you have *to face him?*

He pushed the thoughts aside. The only thing he could do for now was follow the news closely for any more "unexplained attacks" in the Middle East. Hopefully he could teleport over in time to catch whoever's responsible.

Maybe I'll luck out and it won't be Imperium.

Remmler entered his dormitory and took the stairs to his floor. He planned to head upstairs to check on Cheryl once he dumped his gym bag in his room. She had been a wreck since the news broke about *Kitty Hawk.* Reports listed an E-2 Hawkeye, the same plane her brother flew on, among the missing aircraft. Another E-2 had been airborne when the carrier sank and later landed at Dharan. Cheryl had no idea which plane her brother had been on, or if he had been on the carrier when it went down. A death toll of twenty-one hundred and climbing didn't help either. They could only pray that-

Remmler turned the corner and noticed a girl with shoulder length dark hair standing at his door. It wasn't until he got closer that he recognized her.

"Kelly? Hey, what's up?"

Kelly Lin looked up and came over to him. "Oh, Jack . . ."

He saw tear stains on her tan cheeks, heard the trembling in her voice.

Jack's insides collapsed. He knew.

Cheryl had not stopped crying since getting off the phone with her mother and step-father ten minutes ago. Her brother, Alan Matthew Terrepinn, Lieutenant, USN, had been listed by the Department of Defense as KIA—Killed In Action. Pieces of his plane had been found strewn across the Gulf. No chutes, no rafts, no life vests. Nothing to indicate survivors.

Remmler froze for a second when he entered the room after Kelly. He swallowed hard, the gulp sticking halfway down his throat.

Cheryl sat on the edge of her bed, her face buried in her hands. Her body shook with each violent sob. Two girls from the room next door sat on either side of her.

Remmler wanted to cry himself. He flashed back to that night in the alley with the nurse. The anguish she experienced after almost being raped.

Now it was someone Jack knew. Someone he cared about.

Kelly went over to her roommate and squatted on the floor in front of her. "Cheryl. Jack's here."

Cheryl lifted her head. Remmler gritted his teeth and choked back the tidal wave of emotion.

Cheryl's lovely face was flushed and damp from tears. Excess moisture blurred her eyes.

"Oh Jack," she whimpered, getting off the bed and walking over to him. She practically collapsed in his arms and cried.

"Alan's dead. He was on the E-2 that went down. Nobody got out. Oh God, Jack. Why? Why?"

She cried into his shoulder. Remmler wrapped his arms tighter around Cheryl, irrationally hoping it would take away some of the pain. His cheek pressed against her soft, curly hair.

He wanted to say, "It'll be all right," but stopped himself. Why the hell did people say that at times like this?

All the powers I have as Epsilon, and not one of them can ease Cheryl's grief.

God I feel useless.

They left Cheryl alone for a while. Kelly went off with their next door neighbors while Remmler stomped downstairs to his room. His sorrow for Cheryl's loss quickly turned to anger. Anger at the people responsible. People whose sole purpose in life was to spread death and misery. And they always seemed to get away with it. Remmler pictured them celebrating their achievements amid comfortable dwellings while people like Cheryl had to cope with the loss of a loved one—killed by their filthy hands!

Jack Remmler was sick and tired of it.

Fucking Iraqis! They had to be the ones who sank Kitty Hawk. *We shoulda finished 'em all off when we had the chance. They're nothing but troublemakers. And now they've slaughtered over two thousand people. Including Cheryl's brother!*

Maybe it's time someone slaughtered them.

Remmler slammed the door to his room. He reached into his pocket and pulled out his *tru'kat.* Looking up to the ceiling, he cried, "You want me to stop evil, Keeper? Well, watch me turn Iraq into a fucking cinder."

He gripped the rod with both hands. "Let's see how tough you bastards are when *I* come tearing through your country."

Remmler started to close his eyes. He paused.

Was this the right thing to do?

Of course it is! They have to pay!

But Iraq was a big country. Where would he begin? Would he just go up and down Iraq, destroying everything in his path? Even civilians? Many of whom probably hated the regime in Baghdad as much as he did. He couldn't do that. It would make him no better than the thugs ruling Iraq.

Fine! He'd go after military targets. But Remmler had no idea where Iraq's military bases were. And what if his attack provoked a war? Thousands, hundreds of thousands, maybe millions, might die. Especially if nuclear weapons were used. No way he could live with that on his conscience.

And what if Iraq didn't do it? What if it was really Iran? Or some third party? Imperium perhaps?

Remmler lowered his arms to his sides. His grip around the *tru'kat* tightened. Fingernails dug into his flesh, threatening to tear it open. His fist shook.

"DAMMIT!!" He flung the *tru'kat* hard as he could at the wall. It hit his John LeClaire poster, ricocheted off the wall and landed on the floor.

"Dammit!" Jack scooped up the *tru'kat* and stuffed it back in his pocket. He plopped down on his bed.

"Sometimes, Remy, you're too damn noble for your own good."

He sat and stewed for a while before clicking on the TV to try and take his mind off everything.

Some Cosmic Protector I am. World's going to hell and I watch TV. How pathetic am I?

Remmler turned to the local CBS affiliate, which showed a live press briefing from Riyadh. Vice Admiral George Mullen, commander of CENTCOM naval forces, gave an update on the *Kitty Hawk* attack. He estimated the death toll at fifty-five hundred, clearly the worst single tragedy in U.S. Navy history. The Saudi minesweeper and both fast attack craft were officially listed as lost with all hands. Only twenty of *Kitty Hawk's* crew had been found alive, most in bad shape. Eleven members of *Deyo's* crew turned up, only four from *Antrim*. The Navy had given up hope of finding any more survivors. Both Iraq and Iran denied responsibility for the attack.

Remmler sank further into depression as the press conference continued. He had been handed every kid's dream—to be a superhero—on a silver platter. And look what he was doing with it. What a joke he'd become. He thought it would be so great, fighting crime and battling the forces of evil and all that bullshit. He should have told the Keeper to find someone else. The Middle East was on the verge of war and he couldn't do a thing about it. Cheryl's brother was dead and he couldn't do a thing about that either. He couldn't even do anything about Imperium kicking his ass!

What the hell good am I?

Ralph Diaz stared at his stewing partner as they left the Criminal Justice Center in silence. He couldn't believe the man's self-control up to this point. No way it would last much longer.

Diaz opened his car door and settled into his seat as Caro got in.

Here it comes, Diaz thought after closing the door.

"Son of a bitch!" Caro roared as he slammed his fist into the sedan's plastic dashboard, cracking it. "Someone oughta put every goddamn lawyer on a fucking boat and sink it!"

"I ain't too happy about it either, Ed. Uhh . . . look, you want me to drive, since . . . well . . ."

Caro tossed him the keys. Right now he looked mad enough to run over the first person he saw that even looked like a lawyer.

The two cops got out and switched seats. Once they pulled onto Broad, Caro continued his rant.

"'Not in a rational state of mind.' Can you believe that fucking dickhead judge bought that bullshit defense!?"

"Just when you think you heard them all," Diaz replied. He spoke in a deep, throaty tone, mimicking the lawyer that got Stevie Smith off. "'Due to my client's serious injury and the fact he was obviously hallucinating, along with the disorientation of surgery and waking up in a strange place, he could not have been in a rational state of mind when giving his confession to Detective Caro.' I'm surprised he didn't throw in that his daddy womped on him when he was a kid and mommy never gave him a chocolate cake for his birthday."

"And that ratfuck bucket of slime says I tried to coerce him? I used his fear to get the confession I wanted? Bullshit! We knew he did it. Everyone in that courtroom knew he did it. And now Smith walks on some bullshit technicality? Just walks. We couldn't even get him on a weapons charge."

"Well, considering the gun got crushed into a blob of metal . . . Hell, between that and all the blood and gore, no way we coulda got a good print off it."

Caro shook his head. "Nothing. All that work and we get nothing. Now that nurse will have to live in fear for the rest of her life knowing that animal is still out there. Man, I'd love to drag that slimebag lawyer and that bleeding heart judge over to Maggie Stewart's room and make them apologize to her."

After a minute of silence, Caro continued. "You know, Ralph. Sometimes I wonder if we make any kind of difference at all. Lawyers and these damn touchy-feely judges keep letting these scumbags back on the street. They don't even seem to care about it. Just keep saying how we have to respect their rights.

"Why the hell did I ever become a cop?"

"Because you would've been bored out of your mind if you worked for the Water Department. Look, Ed, we win some, we lose some . . ."

"Jesus, Ralph! We're the police. Not the fuckin' Eagles."

"Ed, I know. And I hate this too. But times like these, you just gotta remember the victories."

"This should've been a victory."

"Yeah. I know."

Caro gazed out the window. "You know. Maybe that 'Knight' character didn't do such a bad thing."

"What do you mean?" Diaz asked as he whipped into the

left lane to get around an old lady going ten miles under the speed limit.

"Think about it. Smith'll be walkin' around for the rest of his life with a reminder of what he did. He's gonna think about it every time he looks down and doesn't see his right hand. At least the Knight did what the courts couldn't. He punished him. Gave him exactly what he deserved."

"Shit, Ed. You sound like you're condoning this."

"I don't know. Maybe I am. Can you honestly say you feel bad because he'll go through the rest of his life with the nickname Lefty?"

Diaz mulled over his response as he slowed for a red light. "Well, no. But Ed, we're cops. I mean, we can't be going around talking up this vigilante stuff."

"Well shit, Ralph. If the courts can't put these bastards away, I mean, maybe in some cases, people have to do something to protect themselves."

"C'mon. This ain't the Old West. That kind of talk is just asking for trouble."

The two drove in silence until they reached the station.

Most criminals would be glad to avoid a stay in jail. Not Stevie Smith. In fact, he was downright scared to be back on the street.

It was out there. Probably waiting for him. He heard it demolished a crackhouse in South Philly and beat the crap out of the dudes running it. Those guys had a ton of firepower. Not that they had any better luck against *It* than Smith. You probably needed a bazooka or some shit to take that thing out.

The moment he stepped out of the Criminal Justice Center, Stevie reared his head back and did a complete 360. He drew curious glances from passersby along East Penn Square. His eyes darted across the rooftops of the tall buildings surrounding the ornate City Hall. He continued on, checking the edges of the PSFS marquee atop the nearby bank building. Nothing there. Also nothing around the Hecht's store on his right.

But that didn't matter. Stevie knew *It* was out there, watching him. He looked down at his stump and trembled.

I gotta get outta here.

Smith took the bus and got off near his brother's place. Fred Smith gave him what money he could, then added if he needed more they could knock over a convenience store or something. Fred even offered to rob the place himself while Stevie drove the getaway car. Stevie freaked out, saying *It* would get him.

He took the money and said good-bye to his brother. Stevie took a SEPTA bus to Market Street, got off and walked to the Greyhound Bus Terminal on Filbert Street. He had enough money to get to Wilmington, Delaware, where his uncle lived. He hadn't talked to the man in five years and wondered if he'd take him in at all. But he had to chance it. He couldn't stay in Philadelphia any longer.

Smith sat in the back of the bus as it pulled out of the station. He didn't even bother giving the city one last look. He wouldn't be coming back here again. Not as long as *It* was still around. He'd change his name, disappear into the shadows of another city, in another state.

From now on, it's the straight and narrow for me.

THIRTY-TWO

"An experimental environmental suit," Captain Elder said to the Group Nine command staff, sitting around a folding table at their warehouse headquarters. "Designed for survival in nuclear, biological and chemical environments."

"We can say it was stolen from . . . let's just say a top secret research facility," added Major Xantis. "Then we can avoid having our "real" R-and-D installations deal with any awkward questions."

General Clay nodded. "Sounds good. We should be able to sell it to the Philadelphia Police."

"And the press as well," responded Major Chambers. "This is going to leak."

Clay turned to him. "Won't matter if it does. This cover story is just something to keep the cops happy. Make them feel they're part of the loop. The press isn't too much of a factor right now. It looks like most people are treating this "Knight" as an urban myth."

"That could change with a few more incidents like at the

crackhouse. We'd better have one of our FBI "liaisons" ready with a press release just in case." Chambers referred to the moles the group had planted in various law enforcement, government and military organizations to collect any potential UFO data they came across and send it to the black agency.

"Approved. Now, what's the word on Mr. Upshaw and his gang?"

"They'll be arraigned tomorrow," Major Xantis answered. "After that, the DEA will have them for a while. They're all anxious to confess to the police. That UL must have scared them good. In fact, one of them . . ." Xantis flipped through his notes. " . . .a Clarence Detmore, suffered severe psychological trauma as a result of the incident. To put it bluntly, he lost his marbles. He's being held at Philadelphia Psychiatric. Some of the shrinks think that's where he's going to spend the rest of his life."

"No mention of the UL in their confessions to police?"

"No, sir. We told them it was a gang dressed in Halloween costumes. They know better than to say otherwise."

Satisfied, Clay went on. "Anything new on the UL?"

Elder shook his head. "Nothing. Our teams have looked in abandoned buildings, sewers, parks. No sign of it. We still haven't covered half the possible hidey-holes in this city."

Xantis spoke next. "*Overlord* has picked up some peculiar electromagnetic readings. Could be related. Trouble is a city of over a million people with phones, computers and other gadgets can generate a lot of EM output. We're doing our best to sort through it."

"Stay on it. That may be our only way to locate this thing."

"He sure isn't making this easy for us, sir," Elder commented.

"Hmph. Do they ever?"

Captain Everett Lawson was dead tired by the time he

got back to the American Embassy in Riyadh. The naval attaché spent most of the day, and night, at the hospital at Abu Dhabi air base with the survivors of the *Kitty Hawk* attack. Interviewing them had been a painstaking task. A few kept fading in and out of consciousness, and didn't make much sense when they spoke. Others had to fight through intense pain just to sound coherent. Try as he might, Lawson couldn't keep his eyes from wandering from time to time over to the skin grafts covering the burn victims.

Thirty-five, Lawson thought solemnly during his few breaks. *Thirty-five out of over fifty-six hundred. And some of those might never leave here alive they're burned so bad.*

My God, what could have done this?

Lawson endured a long helicopter ride back to the air base near Al Kharj. Sleep was impossible with the loud, thumping rotorblades.

The helicopter touched down shortly after ten. A chauffeured staff car waited for Lawson. He slept the entire drive back to Riyadh. The driver woke him when they reached the embassy. Lawson headed for the wing that housed the CIA personnel. Not surprisingly, Paul Drake was still at his desk.

"Begging your pardon, Captain, but you look like hell," Drake must have noticed his sagging face.

"Thanks. Right now I consider that a compliment. 'Course you don't look any better."

"Yeah, well, aside from trying to get any *real* work done, I had the Director whining in my ear half the day."

"Tom Brock himself!? What did you do to deserve such an honor?"

"It's what we're *not* doing. He wants answers to everything. How many nukes Iraq has, who attacked *Kitty Hawk* and with what? I keep telling him we're working on it, but he just keeps pestering me. I'm about ready to make up answers just to get him off my back. I think he's getting pressure from the White House."

"And in turn, we get pressure from him."

Drake nodded. "You turn up anything in Abu Dhabi?"

"Talked to the survivors. Most of them are in pretty bad shape. I got a lot of varying accounts as to what destroyed *Kitty Hawk* and her escorts. Pulsating balls of light, streaks of light, a spherical object. Some people didn't see anything. They were below decks when their ship blew. Barely got out." Lawson sighed. "I don't know what to make of it. Hell, most of them were in such pain or so full of drugs they had no idea what they're talking about."

"Great," Drake snorted. "Just what we need. UFOs. Why can't our lives be simple?"

"You should've retired and gone into banking then."

Drake smiled half-heartedly. "We'll just have to dig deeper. Whatever destroyed that battle group, it wasn't anything as ridiculous as a bunch of flashing lights."

"The Knesset and Cabinet will next meet together Monday," Heinbrodder looked at the people gathered around the kitchen table of the small, sparsely furnished apartment overlooking Jerusalem's Hinnon Valley.

"Will we be ready in time?" von Klest asked.

"Yes, *mein Herr*. Unit Bravo is nearly finished concealing their weapons. Unit Delta can have their equipment prepositioned Sunday night."

Von Klest nodded. "Very well. Now, let's go over the plan again."

The briefing ended half-an-hour later. Von Klest left first, the others to follow every ten minutes or so. He took a bus back to the Laromme.

The city was incredibly crowded. An endless parade of people filtered up and down the sidewalks. Street peddlers, many of them Arab, were on almost every corner. The narrow stone roads caused one traffic jam after another.

Erich von Klest loosened his tie and flicked on an overhead switch. A jet of cool air washed over the left side of his face. It didn't seem to help. He still perspired, and felt slightly claustrophobic.

Jerusalem was just too crowded. Too crowded with Jews and Arabs, the filth of the world. How could any *pure* man live in such a place? He should just change into his armor and cleanse the entire city of its mongrel population. What could stop him?

Stick to the plan, Erich.

Von Klest started breathing easier. The assault would work. The plan was good, his men some of the best in the world, and as Imperium, nothing could stop him from destroying the entire Jew government.

THIRTY-THREE

KASIR AL-IBRIZZA WATCHED with disappointment as the crane hoisted the sagging net over the fishing trawler's deck. Barely one-fourth their usual haul, he guessed, examining the mass of albacore. Many of the fish squirmed as they slowly suffocated to death.

The small catch was nothing new to Kasir. Fishing companies all over the Gulf were suffering. Hundreds of vessels now roamed the Arabian Gulf (it was not the Persian Gulf to anyone on the Saudi peninsula) and jet aircraft, their engines booming like thunder, blasted over the water constantly. Coupled with the pollution of recent years, the marine population had dwindled.

A fisherman for nearly twenty-two years, Kasir had worked through many turbulent times; The Iran-Iraq war, the 1987 tanker war, Desert Storm. The hauls always dropped off during wars. Money had been tight on more than one occasion. Once or twice his very job was on the line.

Somehow, he survived. Allah must have smiled on him,

saw him through those hardships. He would see him through this one as well.

The tall, well-developed trawler captain with thick gray-black hair and a beard looked starboard. Off in the distance he spotted the sleek form of the destroyer *Babur*, Pakistan's contribution to the crisis.

It couldn't be over soon enough for Kasir. The military traffic kept them from sailing further out into the Gulf.

They should have taken care of that lunatic in Baghdad when they had the chance.

Kasir turned back as the fish spilled onto the steel deck's no-skid tiles. Young deckhands scurried around the pile, separating the good-looking albacore from the less appealing ones. Many scrunched up their faces and turned away, overcome by the powerful odor.

They are still young. They will get used to the smell in time, as did I.

Something whistled overhead. Kasir and his crew looked up as two dots passed high overhead. The captain felt he would be fishing in the middle of wars and crises for the rest of his days. But what choice did he have? Families across the United Arab Emirates—including his—had to eat.

His thoughts turned to his nineteen-year-old nephew, a gunner on an AMX-30 tank along the Kuwait-Iraq border. He silently prayed to Allah that the devils in Iraq would be defeated without losing his nephew—or having his country turned into radioactive ash.

"Captain! Captain! Look what I found!" one of the deckhands held up something black and squarish.

Kasir came down from the bridge wing and walked across the deck to the young man.

"It's a video camera." He wiped off the seaweed and other gunk that clung to it. "A nice one. Used to be anyway."

"What is it doing out here?" asked another deckhand.

"Some clumsy sailor probably dropped it. Maybe from

the destroyer over there." Kasir pointed to *Babur* as he took the camcorder from the deckhand—Mahmud.

"I guess he won't be sending any videos home to his family, huh?" joked the other deckhand—Yassiff.

Kasir examined the battered camera. The lens was shattered. There were nicks all over it. He wondered if there could be a tape inside.

The button to open the camcorder didn't work. Kasir had Mahmud fetch a screwdriver and together they pried it open and got the tape. Remarkably there was no water inside.

Mahmud noticed thick, chalky white letters stamped across the tape. "Look. It's got writing. What does it say?"

Kasir's eyes widened. The UAE fisherman knew enough English to make out the words U.S. NAVY.

Kasir took the tape and the camcorder to his boss after he docked in Abu Dhabi. Figuring it came from the recently sunk carrier, the two considered handing it over to the American Embassy. But Kasir's boss declared, "I have a better idea. Maybe we can get a little money out of it."

He remembered the British news crew that came by the other week to do a story on how fishing had suffered since this latest crisis began. He found one of their business cards stashed in his rolodex and called them.

The BBC crew gaped in awe as they viewed the tape in their Abu Dhabi bureau. They blew up certain sections and had an engineer run them through a computer. "It's a fake," many of the staffers asserted. But the video engineer found no evidence of edits or computer animation, things he doubted two fishermen had the ability to do.

Unless someone used a technique he wasn't familiar with, which the engineer didn't think possible, the tape was genuine.

After paying Kasir and his boss a suitable reward, they transmitted the footage back to England. Millions of viewers watched in awe as a pulsating, gray-black object destroyed the

Kitty Hawk. Calls flooded BBC headquarters in London, asking if this was for real. The operators answered in the affirmative.

Before long, other news agencies around the world picked up on the incredible story.

Jack Remmler walked out of Keystone College's chapel angrier than when he went in. The short memorial service only filled him with visions of Cheryl crying in his arms the other day. If only he knew who killed her brother, and everyone else on the *Kitty Hawk*. Someone to strike out at. To punish.

Iraq? Iran? Imperium? Who could it be? There has to be a way to find out.

At least a good number of students, faculty and staff showed up for the memorial service. That made Remmler happy. As it turned out, Cheryl hadn't been the only Keystone student to lose a relative in the *Kitty Hawk* attack. Another girl lost her uncle, a chief petty officer aboard the *Antrim*.

Two of the school's chaplains presided over the service; a rabbi for Cheryl and a Protestant minister for the other girl. Remmler caught very few of their words. His thoughts kept turning to Cheryl. He prayed she was holding up well, or as well as can be expected. They didn't even have a body to bury. Would they just put up a photograph of Alan Terrepinn?

I forget. Do Jews have viewings and stuff like Catholics do?

"So has anyone talked to Cheryl yet?" Sheniese Thompson finally broke the silence as they headed back to Driscoll Hall.

Kelly Lin shook her head. "No. She's got enough to deal with without us bugging her. Before her step-father picked her up, she told me she'd probably be back here this weekend."

"Why?" A quizzical look creased Brian Doyle's face. "Why not stay with her folks a while longer?"

Kelly shrugged. "Don't ask me. I certainly didn't ask her."

"Maybe she just wants to get back to a normal life as

soon as possible," Chris Wilson offered. "You know, try to get her mind off it. That's what my Uncle Dave did when his sister died a couple years ago. Hell, a week after the funeral he was back in his garage working on his old cars again."

Remmler looked down at the pavement as the group passed by the beige, squarish Freshman Hall. They shouldn't be having this conversation. Cheryl's brother shouldn't be dead.

Dammit! Why did this have to happen? Cheryl never hurt anyone in her life. What gave the bastards responsible for this the right to put her through an emotional ringer?

I'll get them, Cheryl. I'll get whoever did this. I . . . yeah . . . I give you my word as a Cosmic Protector.

If only I could tell you so.

When they got back to Driscoll Hall, Kelly went to her room, while Remmler and Brian returned to theirs with Chris and Sheniese.

"You guys mind if I turn on the tube?" Doyle asked. "Maybe it'll get our minds off this."

"No. Go ahead," Wilson replied.

Brian clicked on the TV. The four watched a CENTCOM spokesman, an Army colonel, get barraged by questions from reporters.

"Oh great. More Gulf shit," Doyle started channel surfing. All the stations were doing some kind of special report.

He stopped when the scene cut back to the ABC studios after the officer walked away from his dais.

"Colonel Robert Lendenhouse, the Public Affairs Officer for U.S. Central Command, Riyadh," stated the anchor. "It would appear from the Colonel's answers that the American military and its Coalition partners have not had time to sufficiently examine the incredible footage of the *Kitty Hawk's* destruction.

"With us now, hopefully to give us some insight into this extraordinary event, is Dr. Vinay Jahnoukta." The screen filled with the head of a deeply tanned Indian man in his mid-fifties with receding black hair and a salt and pepper mustache. "Dr. Jahnoukta is a molecular biologist at Duke University and a former member of SETI. He joins us live from Durham, North Carolina. Thank you for being with us, Doctor."

"SETI?" a perplexed Sheniese inquired. "What's that?"

"The Search for Extraterrestrial Intelligence," Remmler replied in a hushed voice.

"What does that have to do with anything?"

He ignored her, staring intently at the TV. The hairs on the back of his neck suddenly stood on end. *Oh man. What now?*

"Before we begin, Doctor, we'd like to run that footage provided to us by the BBC again for the benefit of our viewers and yourself."

The four students watched incredulously as the gray-black object blew *Kitty Hawk* apart, then turned on the ship shooting the footage. Several blown up stills followed, clearly showing the outline of a man inside the dark energy mass.

Dr. Jahnoukta admitted he knew of nothing on Earth that could give a human being such power. He speculated it could be possible experimentation conducted by extraterrestrials that caused the mutation. When asked if the Iraqi Bomb could have been responsible, Jahnoukta dismissed the notion.

"Only in movies."

Most of what Dr. Jahnoukta said was lost on the students. They remained awestruck by the incredible video tape.

"That can't be real. It just can't be."

"Can't argue with the video tape, hon," an astounded Chris Wilson replied to his girlfriend.

"This is just too unbelievable," Doyle shook his head. "I mean, a guy with . . . super powers? Like something out of the *X-Men*? It's . . . shit like that just doesn't happen."

"Do you think there's a way to stop it?" Sheniese's voice rose several octaves. "I mean, there's gotta be."

Remmler sat in silence. He stared wide-eyed at the TV, his mind replaying the attack over and over again.

I'm supposed to fight that!?!

It wasn't Imperium, that was certain. Could it be the threat to the Great Balance the Keeper warned him about? Who was it working for? The Iraqis? The Iranians? Some mystery organization? Itself?

Whatever this thing was, it had annihilated a carrier battle group all by itself. Flown through anti-aircraft fire without a scratch. Fired energy blasts that tore through steel like it was paper.

Are my powers enough to beat that thing? Jack wondered as he came face to face with his own mortality.

My God, I'm only nineteen. I'm not even close to finishing college. I have a broadcasting career to look forward to. I haven't even had sex yet! I'm too young to die. I don't want to die!

But . . . who else on Earth has the power to face that thing?

The answer was obvious. An Arctic chill swept over Remmler's body and cut into his bones. He slowly cast his eyes down.

His right hand shook uncontrollably.

THIRTY-FOUR

"OKAY, GUYS," FELDMAN rubbed his eyes. "We've looked over everything we could about this Knight character. It's Friday. Both of you go home and get some rest."

"Thanks, Captain," Diaz responded.

Caro clenched his jaw, wanting to continue. There had to be something they missed. Something they hadn't thought of. What it could be he didn't have the slightest clue.

Maybe the Captain's right. Caro tried to blink away the heaviness behind his eyes. *Maybe I do need some rest. Come at this fresh tomorrow.*

"By the way," Feldman got up as the two detectives removed their newspapers and notes from the desk. "I've got something tomorrow if you're interested in making some overtime."

"Lay it on us, Captain," Diaz replied.

"Henshaw and Craig are taking down a drug dealer along Vine. Ricks and Hillard were supposed to be their back-up, but Ricks' father took a turn for the worst. Looks like he'll be spending most of the weekend shuttling back and forth between University Hospital. And Hillard's kid came down with chicken pox. If you want, you can back up Henshaw and Craig."

Caro looked to his partner with a raised eyebrow. He'd rather work on the Knight case. *'Course maybe taking down a druggie'll make up for Smith being let loose . . . somewhat. Besides, I can always use the extra cash.* "Sounds good to me."

"Hey. I'm game," Diaz said.

"Great," Feldman nodded in satisfaction. "Be here tomorrow at four for the briefing."

Musti Safim got up well before dawn, quickly showered and put on fresh clothes. He had a full day's worth of experiments to perform on Yuri Drovinov—or Nexus as the government officials now called him. He knew the Professor would be up by now. The man didn't need sleep as *normal* humans do. Just another aspect of Drovinov's transformation he wanted to study.

That is, if Drovinov would let him.

Ever since the attack on the American carrier, Safim noticed his mentor had become more and more withdrawn. He didn't look forward to the experiments like he once did. Now he would walk out in the middle of them or miss them completely. It just didn't seem to matter to him anymore.

Safim left his quarters and strode down the corridor. He turned the corner to his lab. When he looked up he stopped in his tracks.

Yuri Drovinov appeared halfway down the corridor, escorted by the President, General Nurabi and a half-dozen bodyguards.

"Mr. President," Safim gulped. "General. I-I did not know you'd be here today. This early."

"Nor was there any reason you should," the President replied. "We have come to collect Nexus. The project here is canceled."

"But-but, Mr. President," Safim pleaded, standing in front of the entourage. "We still have many more tests to conduct. We don't know if-"

"You have experimented long enough. Professor Drovinov's services are needed elsewhere."

"But surely there-"

Drovinov cut the physicist off. "There is nothing more that needs to be done. I know all I need to about my power. Everything else is irrelevant. Now get out of my way."

"But, Professor Drovinov. You must un-"

Drovinov's arm snapped up. Safim didn't even have time to scream as the blast tore the flesh from his body. The scientist's charred skeleton collapsed to the floor.

"You've wasted enough of my time."

The group walked around Safim's remains without a second glance. Only Nurabi stared at the smoking, blackened pile of bones until they rounded the corridor. The head of Al Mukhabaret felt his entire body tremble. They were rapidly losing control over Drovinov. The man—was he even that anymore?—had just killed one of Iraq's top physicists as casually as one would swat a fly. It didn't seem to concern the President. He was completely enamored with Drovinov and his power. He jokingly referred to the Russian as his own smart weapon. But this smart weapon could think for itself. Nurabi wondered how long it would be before the weapon turned on its masters.

The President, Nurabi and two bodyguards got into the presidential limousine and removed their bulky lead vests. Drovinov and two other bodyguards boarded a Zil truck specially modified with a lead-lined canvas. The remaining two guards got into the second limo, the chase car. The three vehicles pulled out of the underground garage and took the desert road back to Baghdad.

Their departure did not go unnoticed.

"The big cheese is headin' out," First Lieutenant Carl Henderson, U.S. Army Rangers, whispered as he observed the small convoy through his starlight scope. He and five other Rangers had been nestled in the small trenches they dug into a sand dune two miles from the Kassim Research Facility since infiltrating Iraq nearly two weeks ago. "They got a Zil truck with 'em. Two guys in the cab."

"Any idea what's in the truck?" asked Staff Sergeant Walter Stowe, the team's radioman.

Henderson shook his head. "Your guess is as good as mine. More guards . . . nukes . . . hookers?"

"Want me to send it to MacDill?" Stowe referred to MacDill Air Force Base in Florida, home of U.S. Special Operations Command.

Henderson thought it over for a few seconds. "Our next check-in time is, what? 'Bout an hour? I can't see anything pressing about one truck. We'll put it in our regular report."

An hour and four minutes later, Stowe relayed the team's regular four hour report off a satellite to SOC in Florida. The analysts there checked off yet another visit by the Iraqi President to the Kassim Research Facility and the duration of his stay. The addition of the truck in the entourage was duly noted and filed away.

The analysts moved on to more pressing business.

The sun was just coming up when the motorcade arrived at the bunker outside Baghdad. The President and General Nurabi led Nexus to a conference room on the second sub-level, where they were joined by the Defense Minister. The President and Nurabi sat at the end of the table, while Nexus stood off to the side impassively. The Defense Minister stood by an easel supporting a map of northern Saudi Arabia, Kuwait and southern Iraq.

"We have decided another strike against the American Coalition is necessary."

Nexus just stared at the President and nodded.

"The discovery of the tape showing you destroying the American carrier has turned out to be a blessing. I have been monitoring the West's news broadcasts. The Coalition shows signs of breaking. There are protests in America and Europe calling for the withdrawal Western forces from the Gulf. Many nations are backing out of their commitment to send troops to Saudi Arabia. All over the peninsula people are fleeing the larger cities like frightened women.

"They are afraid of you. They do not know who you are, what you are. No one knows that you are working for us. Another attack will shatter the American Coalition and allow us to roll across the border unopposed when we commence Operation: Driving Wind."

The Iraqis waited for Nexus to respond. But he just stood silently. Several seconds passed before the Defense Minister cleared his throat and directed everyone's attention to the map.

"We have decided your next target will be here," he tapped his pointer on an area of Saudi Arabia near the Gulf coast. "Al Ghawar. The largest oil field in the world. Your primary objective will be the destruction of the pipelines in the Ain Dar subsection. Seven different lines connect there, including the Petroline. Another line connects to the Trans-Arabian Pipeline farther north. Cutting them would disrupt the entire country's oil flow. Saudi Arabia would be crippled, as will the military forces who depend on their oil."

"Opposition should be no problem for you," Nurabi flipped through his folder. "Our intelligence indicates a brigade-sized force of Saudi National Guard troops and Special Security police guarding Al Ghawar. They are reinforced by a contingent of soldiers from Bahrain and Morocco. Size undetermined. They also possess an undetermined number of helicopters and armored vehicles. Again, no problem for you. Plus the security forces are sure to be stretched thin. Al Ghawar is over two hundred-fifty kilometers long and thirty-five kilometers wide. All approaches to the oil field are covered by batteries of Patriot and Hawk surface-to-air missiles. Of course, the American fleet's SAMs were ineffective against you. This time should be no different.

"I have several photographs and maps of the area. You can use the pipelines as visual references to guide you to Al Ghawar."

Drovinov barely listened as the Defense Minister continued with his briefing. These hit and run raids were a waste of his powers. The Iraqis may think Al Ghawar was a big target. But Drovinov was thinking beyond one oil field. Beyond one country.

He had played along with the Iraqis long enough. They were just bloated old men who never outgrew playing soldier. Only he—Yuri Drovinov . . . Nexus!—had the real power and intelligence to lead.

Drovinov decided to carry out the Iraqis' raid. When it was over, things would be radically different.

The restaurant at the Laromme was half-full by the time Erich von Klest and Otto Kemp arrived. The two casually strolled across the room until they spotted a narrow-faced man with close cropped, dark hair wearing a brown suit sitting at a corner table. They joined him, quickly looked over their menus and called for their waiter. They ordered rolls, danishes and tea. They had carefully avoided any "*Juden* food" during their mission.

As soon as the waiter collected their menus and left, they began conversing.

"The Knesset and the Cabinet will hold an emergency meeting tomorrow. Apparently they'll be discussing what steps to take in light of that . . . thing that sunk the *Kitty Hawk*."

Von Klest raised an eyebrow at James Crawford, a former

U.S. Army infantryman and current Iron Guardsman. "Where did you get this information?"

"A Jew political reporter. Jacob Diman. Works for the Israeli Broadcasting Authority." Crawford had been posing as a UPI correspondent covering the Knesset. "He has a lot of sources inside the Knesset. That's how he got the information. I was able to confirm it with our contact in the German Embassy. It looks like a pretty big deal. The Knesset doesn't normally meet on Sundays. Respect for Christians and all that crap."

"What time will they all be there?" asked Kemp.

"Early-" Crawford stopped when the waiter approached with their tea. He continued after the *Juden* placed the cups on the table and departed. "Early afternoon. I couldn't get anything more specific."

"Everything is almost ready," Kemp stated. "It's just a matter of moving up the timetable."

"Very well. We'll carry it out tomorrow." Von Klest took a sip of his tea. It was rather good. He couldn't believe the Jews didn't screw it up. "We'll meet with the section leaders later this morning, then gather everyone at the abandoned warehouse we found near Bar Ilan *Strasse* for a final meeting."

"I think we should also talk seriously about what the Knesset and Cabinet are meeting about. First it was that Cosmic Protector, now it is a man with superhuman powers that can destroy warships. *Gott in Himmel*, what is happening to the world? Ever since . . . ever since you found that object..."

"Calm yourself, old friend," von Klest put a hand on Kemp's shoulder. "The Protector is one thing. But this thing in the Gulf . . . I don't know how that is possible.

"Contact our people in Uruguay. Tell them to look into this *ubermensch* in the Persian Gulf. We may have more things to deal with once we are done here."

THIRTY-FIVE

JACK JUST GOT off the phone with his parents, wondering if it would be the last time he talked to them. He tried to keep the conversation routine at first, talking about school, how the rest of the family was doing, et cetera. Eventually he brought up Cheryl. He had to get some of it off his chest. Mary and Robert Remmler were naturally upset to hear about the loss of her brother. They had met Cheryl on a few of their visits to Keystone and liked her very much.

For a moment, Jack wondered if he should tell them about being Epsilon.

They do have a right to know. They are my parents for God's sake.

And just how do I tell them? "Oh, by the way. Mom. Dad. I'm really Epsilon. You know, the armored guy who crippled the rapist and trashed the crackhouse. And now I'm gonna track down the thing that destroyed the Kitty Hawk *and I may not come back."*

Yeah. That'd work.

Jack Remmler sighed and swung his legs off the desk. He rubbed his hands over his face and sat silently for a minute.

Come on, Jack. You're not done yet.

Another minute passed before he picked up the phone and dialed again. There were three rings, then a click.

"This is Captain Lisa Remmler . . ."

"Dammit, Lis." Remmler closed his eyes in disappointment.

" . . .I'm unavailable right now. Please leave your name, number and a message after the beep."

Remmler paused for a full second after the nasally *beep* subsided. "Um, Lisa. It's me, Jack." *I can't do this on a machine.* "Um, give me a call when you get in, okay? Bye."

He slammed down the phone. "Dammit!" *God I hope she calls back.*

Remmler massaged his head with his thumb and index finger, taking some deep breaths to calm himself. *This is probably the first time I really wished I hadn't been a bratty little brother to Lisa when we were growing up.* If he had a nickel for every fight they'd gotten into, along with all the punishments their parents handed down as a result. If only he'd known then . . .

But what could he have done? He and Lisa were ten years apart. What the hell would an eight-year-old have had in common with an eighteen-year-old?

At least he made up for it when he got older. It wasn't long after Lisa left for the Air Force Academy that Jack's opinion of her changed. She was no longer the evil sister he once asked his parents to send away to an orphanage. He discovered he really did love his sister and missed her greatly.

When he entered his teenage years, Jack actually looked forward to his sister coming home on leave. The two were nearly inseparable during those times.

He had to talk to her one last time, before he went off to face . . . whatever it was out there.

She'll call back, Jack. Stop dwelling on it. You've got other things to take care of.

Remmler reached into the middle drawer of his desk and

pulled out a handful of loose-leaf paper. Brian was off working out with Jim Elling and Eric Bouden. Probably wouldn't be back for a while. He should be done before then.

It proved a frustrating process. Remmler considered himself a good writer—a necessity for any communications major. Still it took one hour and ten pieces of paper before he had what he wanted. Even then he wasn't all that happy with it. Of course, it wasn't something meant to be happy.

Remmler picked up the paper with his left hand. His right hand twirled the pen between his fingers, a nervous habit he developed over the years.

He read over the letter:

> Dear Mom, Dad and Lisa
> If you are reading this, then I am probably dead . . .

A little melodramatic. Sounds like something out of a bad movie. He continued.

> . . . And you probably know the reason why. In case you don't, the reason is because I am Epsilon, the armored guy in the news that attacked the crackhouse. Yes, that really was me.
>
> I'm sitting here wondering if I should tell you how it happened, but I doubt you'd believe me. In fact, I don't believe it myself. Sometimes I don't even know why I accepted this responsibility. Maybe I thought it would be great to help people, to be an actual superhero. The truth is very different. And now I'm looking at the possibility this power I have could get me killed.
>
> This may not be a manly thing to say, but I can't help it. I'm scared. I don't want to die. But I'm the only one in the world with a chance of stopping the

thing that destroyed the Kitty Hawk. I can't sit by and let millions of people be killed by this thing.

Please take comfort knowing it was because of you I used my powers to help others. You raised me to know the difference between right and wrong, to look for the good in everything, to treat everyone as equals and to help people whenever possible. I cannot thank you enough for the job you did raising me. I couldn't have asked for better parents, or a better sister.

In closing, all of my possessions I leave to you, to do with whatever you please.

I may not have said it often enough, but I love you all. Mom, Dad, Lisa, I love you and I hope I have made you all proud of me.

Good-bye.

Love,
Jack R. Remmler

Why can't I say this to them? Why am I writing this down? What is so damn hard about telling your parents you love them?

Remmler took a deep breath, folded the letter and stuffed it in an envelope. On the back he wrote: TO THE REMMLER FAMILY. He opened the middle drawer of his desk and taped the envelope underneath the top drawer.

That oughta do it. Remmler closed the drawer.

He headed for the door, then stopped. His attention was drawn to the pictures taped to his wall. He leaned closer, focusing on one in particular.

It was of him and Cheryl, taken at some party last year. Jack wore his teal blue Florida Marlins cap backwards, grinning like a Cheshire Cat with his arm around Cheryl. She also smiled with her arm around him. Both had a can of beer raised to the air.

Remmler reached out and stroked Cheryl's image with

his finger. He shook his head. "God, you think I'd be over it by now. That I'd just think of you as a friend. Maybe I do, but . . . sometimes . . ."

He withdrew his hand. "Dammit, Cheryl. I'm still in love with you. Maybe it's wrong, maybe I'm too damn stupid. But I am." *And I can't tell you. Not with your brother dead. You might think I'm trying to take advantage of your grief.*

But what if I . . .

No. There's no way I could make her understand.

Remmler sighed. "I wish it could have worked out between us."

He took one last look at the room, wondering if it would really be his last, and left. Father Donald, the college's Catholic chaplain, kept office hours Saturday afternoons before doing the evening Mass at one of the local churches. He'd go to him for confession before teleporting to the Persian Gulf.

The pounding of the rotorblades startled Muztafkiz Ahrammasbar awake. He quickly got to his feet and looked around. There! He howled in fear as he saw two helicopters flying low over rocky terrain. Panicked, Muztafkiz fled into the outcropping.

Tears exploded from his eyes. He knew it was unmanly to cry, but right now he couldn't help it. Not after everything that had happened to him today.

Even before his change, Muztafkiz's life had been anything but pleasant. With his father and two brothers killed in the internal strife ripping apart his native Afghanistan, he, his mother and three sisters crossed the border into Pakistan. They wound up packed into a shanty town with thousands of other refugees. Food was not plentiful, plumbing did not exist and diseases like cholera and dysentery ruled with deadly iron fists.

Muztafkiz thought he might have had one of those diseases. His body burned for days. Pain, like white hot knives, cut into every inch of his body. One of his sisters went to fetch a French doctor from the nearby International Red Cross station.

Muztafkiz remembered the look of surprise on the doctor's face when it happened.

Mud! Mud burst from every pore in his body. His mother and sisters screamed in terror as he got up and ran out of their shack . . .

. . . and kept running! He couldn't think of anything else to do. Even the Pakistani soldiers manning the camp didn't slow him down. In a panic, they shot at him a dozen times. Many bullets hit Muztafkiz. They had no effect.

Then, and he still couldn't believe this, mud *shot* from his hand and smothered one of the soldiers. Muztafkiz didn't even stop to check on him. He just continued running into the desert until he could run no more. He sat up against a rock outcropping to rest. Slowly, the mud retreated back into his body. Muztafkiz was human again. The nineteen-year-old Afghan prayed to Allah that he would continue to be before exhaustion conquered him and he fell asleep.

Now the Pakistanis were coming. He doubted they would let him explain his situation. More likely, they would shoot him on sight.

If only he could-

That's when he felt it. A shuddering sensation swept over his body. The pain dropped Muztafkiz to his knees. He looked down.

Mud covered his left arm.

"I have him!" Captain Zamis Delah heard the helicopter pilot's excited voice over his headset. "He's in the rocks up ahead."

"Set us down!" the Pakistani Army officer hollered over the wind and rotorblades rushing through the SA 330 Puma's open door. Still kneeling, he craned his head closer to the

56-RUST

door, looking around the harnessed soldier manning the helicopter's 7.62mm machine gun. "Tell Kilo Victor One-Two to land on the other side of the outcropping. We will try to box him . . . it in."

"Affirmative."

Delah turned to his troops behind him, urging them with hand gestures to prepare for deployment. He looked back out the door, watching the creature scurry through the rocks. It didn't even look human anymore. Just a big lump of grayish-black mud with arms and legs. To think an hour ago he nearly laughed off the order to go out and find it. How ridiculous was it? Some stupid Afghan turns into a "Mud Man," smothers a soldier to death and flees into the desert.

But Captain Zamis Delah was a soldier. Insane though the order sounded, he loaded up a rifle platoon in two Pumas and took off from their base near the Afghanistan-Pakistan border.

The Puma's wheels barely kissed the ground when the captain and his squad spilled out the door and rushed toward the rocks. Several Pakistanis let loose with their G3 rifles as the creature climbed over the rocks. Using hand signals, Delah directed his men to approach from the flanks. The deafening rotorwash of the helicopter made talking impossible.

The soldiers advanced, keeping the monster in sight the whole time. Many took up position behind the rocks, using them to balance their rifles, and fired. Delah knew with absolute certainty some of the rounds hit the creature. Still it scrambled between the rocks.

The soldier lugging the field radio on his back handed the receiver to Captain Delah, telling him it was a message from the helicopter.

"Red Team Leader. Go."

"This is Kilo Victor One-One. We have a clear shot at the . . . target. Permission to fire?"

"My men are clear. Permission granted."

The 7.62mm machine gun was barely audible over the rotorwash. Splinters of rock and dust shot up around the creature. Geysers of mud sprouted up from it. Delah's eyes widened with astonishment. At least fifty rounds struck that creature and it still stood.

The gunner let loose with another burst. The rounds just traveled right through the creature.

The monster raised its arm defensively and a stream of mud shot out. It passed twenty feet under the chopper and splashed on the ground, staining a few soldiers.

The monster unleashed another blast, this time following the Puma as it backed off. Mud splattered over the cockpit windows, blinding the pilot and co-pilot. More got sucked into the intakes. The rotors suddenly ground to a halt, pieces of it snapping off and flying in every direction. The Puma slid backwards, while the shattered blades skidded across the ground, spraying lethal fragments of rock and metal. Delah saw two of his soldiers decapitated, while two more were killed by flying debris. The Puma erupted in a ball of fire when it hit the ground, taking out five more soldiers.

Captain Delah and the radioman picked themselves off the ground and surveyed the carnage. Over half the squad was either dead or wounded. Delah grabbed the receiver.

"Red Team Leader to Gold Team Leader. Are you on the ground? Over."

The reply came back a few seconds later from his lieutenant. "Red Team Leader, Gold Team just touched down."

"Gold Team Leader. Proceed with caution. This thing just took out our helicopter. I have heavy casualties here."

"Acknowledged. We see him and are advancing."

Muztafkiz leaned up against a rock to catch his breath. Suddenly the mud disappeared from his body, much more quickly than last time.

"NOOO!!" He jumped out into the open in shock.

Muztafkiz closed his eyes and concentrated. His mud body was the only thing keeping him alive.

"Sir! It changed!" the Puma's doorgunner shouted to the pilot over the ICS. "It's human again!"

"Shoot, dammit!"

The gunner didn't hesitate. He swept the area around the now human Mud Man with machine gun fire. Two rounds blew off the left side of the young Afghan's head. Five more stitched him across the back as he collapsed to the ground.

The doorgunner ceased fire as the soldiers approached the body. The first three that came across the corpse pumped round after round from their G3s into it. By the time Captain Delah arrived and ordered them to stop, the Afghan's body had been torn open by over forty bullets. Monster or not, it was definitely dead.

"Red Team Leader to all units. Target neutralized. Repeat, target neutralized. Mission accomplished."

The Pakistanis didn't know this was only the beginning.

THIRTY-SIX

EPSILON REMATERIALIZED ATOP City Hall. He looked out over the sea of lights illuminating the city and shook his head in disgust.

"Four hours," he muttered angrily as he leaned against the statue of William Penn, the English Quaker who founded Pennsylvania. "I spent over four fucking hours flying up and down the damn Gulf. And what do I get for it? Nothing. Nadda. Zilch. What a waste of time."

Epsilon was sure his unisense would have picked something up during his recon. He had flown the length of the Persian Gulf, covering Southern Iraq, Kuwait, Saudi Arabia, Oman, Iran, even parts of Afghanistan. At one point he even searched underwater. But Epsilon could find nothing out of the ordinary. By the time he came back to Southern Iraq for a second pass, the sun began to rise. He did not want to risk being spotted. Things were tense enough, and the sight of a flying armored man could be the catalyst for a full blown war.

Frustrated, Epsilon looked up at the dark gray statue. "You'd think I could catch one friggin' break, huh, Will? I bet if I was Spiderman or Batman I would've found this thing by now. 'Course, I probably would've had a big clue, like a note saying 'this way to secret lair.'"

William Penn just stared silently over the sprawling city.

Remmler rolled his eyes. "Oh great. Now I'm talking to statues. I must be losin' it."

He stepped off the ledge, extended his staff and flew away.

I'll do a short patrol before heading back to Keystone. Maybe I'll come across a mugging or a robbery I can stop. Feel like I'm actually doing something useful.

Ralph Diaz jiggled the half-empty box of Milk Duds in front of Caro. The detective declined.

"That's just more time in the gym for you, buddy."

"Can't help it. I love these things." Diaz popped a handful into his mouth. Milk Duds were his favorite snack during stake out duty. He'd already gone through two boxes tonight.

The detectives were parked near the corner. Down the next street, to their right, a dark figure loitered around an old Chevrolet, while another sat behind the wheel.

"What time is it?" Caro asked.

Diaz looked at his Timex. "Ten minutes later than the last time you asked. This guy's late."

Caro grunted. "Wonder how long it'll be before this one walks?"

"Aw shit, Ed. Not Smith again. That's all you've been talkin' about since we got here. If it's not him, then it's the Knight."

"It doesn't piss you off, Ralph? This guy nearly rapes some woman, leaves her almost catatonic and walks outta court 'cause he was too scared when he confessed."

"Of course it pisses me off. Look, a scumbag like Smith, he's bound to fuck up sooner or later. At least when we hear about a perp described as a black male, early twenties, with only one hand, we'll know who to look for."

"Most likely after he's raped or killed someone," Caro muttered.

"I don't like the thought much either, Ed. And let's hope that doesn't happen. But we gotta play the cards we were dealt.

"Look, let's change the subject. Um . . . how about the Eagles' game tomorrow?"

"What's there to talk about? Giants'll probably beat 'em."

"Phillies?"

"They're gonna lose to Atlanta."

Diaz just rolled his eyes. "This is fun. God, for the sake of my patience, I hope this guy shows up soon."

Ten minutes later, a black Camaro with a single driver roared down the street in front of Caro and Diaz and parked nose-to-nose with Detectives Marvin Henshaw and Joe Craig's car. A lanky twenty-year-old with the back of his head shaved flung open the door and bounded out. He wore hundred dollar sneakers, baggy shorts, a Chicago Bulls jersey and at least five tons of gold around his neck. Three gold studs sparkled from one ear. Craig got out of the car carrying a duffel bag, while Henshaw went over to greet the kid.

"Got the money, man?" Scott Davis asked anxiously, stopping a few feet from the black, bearded Henshaw.

"'Course we got it, man. You think we fools?"

At the same time, the stocky Craig held up the duffelbag and shook it. The piles of bills could be heard rustling around inside.

"Good, good." Davis said, breathing heavily. He reached around and scratched the back of his neck in an exaggerated fashion.

Henshaw tensed a bit. This kid was jumpy for some reason.

"Okay. We got the money. You got the stuff?"

"Yeahyeahyeah. Thirty kees. In the trunk." He nodded toward the Camaro, still scratching his neck.

"Well, come on. Let's see it."

"Yeah . . . sure."

Henshaw took a step forward. Davis stopped scratching. In a split second, the detective knew what was about to go down.

The gun came out of Davis' shorts in a flash and turned on Craig. The first round from the compact M39 semi-automatic pistol struck the cop in the right side of the stomach. The second 9mm round whizzed by Craig as he crashed to the ground.

Oh shit! Henshaw didn't have time to draw his gun. He leaped at Davis and grabbed the punk's gunhand. The cop twisted Davis toward the car. The dealer resisted. Henshaw groaned, summoning all his strength to his upper body. *C'mon! C'mon!*

He pushed Davis against the Camaro's door. Henshaw tried to force the gun from Davis' hand when the drug dealer rammed a knee into his groin. The detective cried in pain and released his grip.

Davis pushed him away. "Motherfucker!" He swept the butt of his M39 across Henshaw's head. The cop fell to his knees.

"Shit!" Caro started the car and floored it around the corner. "It's a goddamn rip off!"

"All units standby!" Diaz screamed into the radio. By the time he gave their location, the car screeched to a halt, pitching him forward. "Assist officer! Officer shot! Officer shot!"

Caro flew out the door, .357 Magnum in hand. Diaz grabbed the Ithaca 12-gauge shotgun and followed.

"Police! Freeze!" Caro hollered as Diaz propped his arms on the hood, aiming the shotgun at Davis.

The drug dealer quickly yanked the dazed Henshaw to his feet and jammed the pistol against his head.

Oh damn! Now they had a hostage situation, with one of their own as the hostage.

"Back the fuck off, pigs!" Davis dragged Henshaw back with him. "I'll do 'im! I swear I'll fuckin' do 'im!"

"Don't make this worse for yourself, kid," Caro stated firmly.

Davis pressed his back against the white, cinderblock wall of a small electronics store. His left arm was wrapped around Henshaw's neck, the detective's body completely shielding Davis.

"What the hell?" Epsilon's unisense picked up the gunshots. It didn't take long to pinpoint them. The cops were already on the scene—two of them at least. Maybe he should let them handle it. They probably have more experience at this. Remmler had seen enough episodes of *Cops* and *World's Wildest Police Videos* to know how tense and unpredictable hostage situations could be.

Then he sensed the gunman's increased breathing and heart rate. The guy was nervous, which probably made him more likely to pull the trigger.

Epsilon shook his head. No way he could stand by and hope for the best.

I just hope I don't fuck up and get the hostage killed.

"That's a cop you got there, buddy!" Caro felt the sweat start to form on his brow. "Pull that trigger and you're looking at the squirt!" He referred to a lethal injection.

"I-I-I . . . I want a million dollars. And . . . and a helicopter."

The kid's terrified, Caro thought. *Has no idea what he's talking about.*

"No deal, pal. Give it up and no one gets hurt."

"N-No." Davis' voice wavered. "I'll-I'll waste him. I will, man! Gimmie what I want!"

Sweat rolled down Remmler's forehead.

Oh man, this guy's gone. What can I do? If I stun him, he could still pull the trigger. Even if I just show my face, he could blow the guy away out of fear. His back's to the wall. No chance to get him from behind . . .

That's it!

Epsilon scanned the building and teleported inside.

The store was dark, not that it mattered to his unisense. Metal shutters and bars covered the plateglass storefront windows. Epsilon could sense the cops outside negotiating with the gunman, who continued to ramble and threaten the hostage.

Gotta do this perfectly.

Remmler felt his expanded consciousness condense itself to the immediate area. He let himself slip into a trance-like state as his unisense took over. He no longer felt in control of his actions, but at the same time he was.

He felt his legs pumping. It took Remmler a few moments to realize he was running. His right arm shot forward, hand slightly angled. His left hand also snapped up. Suddenly his feet left the floor.

The two cops by the car jumped in surprise as Epsilon crashed through the wall. His right hand brushed against the hostage's head and knocked the dirtbag's gunhand away. With his left hand, he gave both men a push, propelling them away from the debris. The gun went off. The round struck the Chevy. The cop's left cheek hit the pavement hard. He was buried under his former captor, who in turn was buried under Epsilon. The crushing weight forced the air out of both their lungs. The slimeball dropped his gun. Chunks of cinderblock and plastic from the shattered stereos littered the sidewalk.

Epsilon quickly sprang to his feet, grabbed the punk by the collar and yanked him off the cop.

"It's him!" Diaz exclaimed. "Jesus, Ed! It's the Knight!"

Caro didn't even realize he had lowered his Magnum as

he watched in amazement while the Knight manhandled the drug dealer.

My God. It is real. What is it?

Davis' feet came off the ground. The guy had to weigh one-sixty, one-seventy at least. The Knight picked him up like an empty garbage bag and flung him through the air. Davis crashed against the metal shutter covering the store window. He fell spread-eagled to the ground.

"Holy shit," he heard Diaz mutter. The Puerto Rican cop quickly shook off his disbelief. "Police! Hold it right there!" That didn't come out with Diaz's usual forcefulness.

The Knight turned to them as Caro brought up his .357. *Like this'll do any good.*

"Oh boy," he heard the thing say in a hollow, almost computerized voice. Then it dashed through the hole in the building.

"Stop!" Caro started to run, then turned to Diaz. "Ralph. Look after these guys. I'll get him."

"Take this." Diaz tossed him the shotgun. "And be careful."

Caro nodded and took off. He holstered his .357 as he squeezed through the hole, the Ithaca 12-gauge extended. Diaz, meanwhile, tended to Craig, pressing a handkerchief against his gunshot wound.

The blazing red and white armor stood out in the darkened store. The Knight was nearly at the back door, fumbling with the bladed staff attached to his back.

How the hell do I arrest something like that? Hell, should I? He hasn't hurt any innocent people.

Caro stopped about twenty-five feet from the Knight and leveled the shotgun. "Freeze!"

The thing stopped, holding the staff in front of it. Caro swallowed as it slowly turned to him. More sweat drenched his forehead.

So is he gonna kill me? Bullets can't stop him. What if he decides to rip of my head?

No. He won't. He's only hurt perps. Nothing to indicate he'll do the same to others.

The Knight continued to stare at him.

How do I know he'll stay that way?

But he is doing something about crime in this city. Should I even try *to stop him?*

What the hell are you hanging around for, dumbass? Remmler asked himself. *Leave!*

But he continued to stare at the cop. All he had to do was teleport or run out the back and fly away. Then that would be that. Did he feel the need to explain himself to someone?

Shoulda just ran down the sidewalk instead of coming in here. Then this would've been over. Stupid!

Well, maybe I can make the most of this.

Epsilon slowly raised his hands in front of him. "I'm not going to hurt you."

The cop said nothing.

Remmler took a deep breath. He could hear sirens in the distance. "Look, officer." He kept his voice as mellow as possible. "That shotgun won't do anything to my armor. Just back off, okay. I am not going to fight the police."

The officer moved a few steps forward, then slid behind a shelf in the aisle, blocking anyone's view from the outside. To Epsilon's amazement, he lowered the shotgun. *What the hell?* He didn't think police gave in that easily.

"What are you?" the cop asked breathlessly.

Epsilon didn't know if the cop would believe the truth, or even if he should tell him. "Just . . . consider me a protector."

The cop paused for a few moments. "Why are you doing this?"

Epsilon started to put his hands down. "Because somebody has to.

"Well, are you gonna *try* to arrest me or what?"

The cop took a few more steps toward Epsilon. The sirens grew louder. "I . . . I wanna help." His voice trembled a bit.

Remmler's eyes widened. His head came forward. "You what!?! Um . . . won't that get you in trouble?"

"Yeah. If I get caught." He shook his head. "I must be outta my mind. I don't even know what you are and I'm offering to help. But I've been a cop in this city for eighteen years and I haven't seen things get any better. The courts let these animals walk while they tie our hands with stupid rules. We get no respect from the press or the public.

"I've been following your case. The assault on the nurse, the crackhouse."

Epsilon nodded.

"Point is, you don't worry about rules or excessive force or anything like that. You just do what it takes to stop the bad guys."

"You're putting an awful lot of trust in me."

"I know you left those junkies alone in the crackhouse and only went after the dealers. I know you could've killed them easily. Me too, even. But you didn't. You've got some kind of moral base.

"Look, you want to make a real difference? Let me help you. I can give you names of drug dealers, mob big shots, street gangs. We could really have an affect on crime in this town."

The cop put the shotgun in his other hand. "What'd you say?" He extended his right hand.

Is this on the level?

Then again, having a guy on the inside could help. He probably knows all the major players in the Philly crime scene. I could really make a difference here.

Epsilon took the cop's hand, as gently as if he were handling a daisy. "You got a deal, Officer . . ."

"Detective. Ed Caro. Great."

"So how do I get in touch with you?"

Caro took a moment to ponder it. "You read *The Inquirer?*"

"Sometimes."

"Good. Check the personals. You see anything about a man that can 'speak softly and carry a big stick,' that's our signal." He paused for a second. "Let's make our first meeting place . . . the East Park Reservoir, near Diamond Street."

"Okay." Epsilon could hear the squad cars screeching to a halt outside. "I've gotta go. Thanks for your offer, Detective."

With that, Epsilon rushed out the back door.

Caro stared after him for a few moments. "No. Thank you."

He headed back outside. More police cars and ambulances arrived. Craig, Henshaw and Davis, he learned, were all being taken to Thomas Jefferson Hospital. X-rays were needed to determine the extent of Craig's gunshot wound, but he was expected to pull through. Henshaw and Davis both had concussions, busted ribs and numerous cuts and bruises. Henshaw also fractured his left hand.

"Ed! What happened?"

Caro shrugged his shoulders. "Son of a bitch is gone."

"Aw man!" Diaz's shoulders slumped. "We had him. Damn, he was right here, man."

Caro bit his lip. He wished he could tell Diaz, but he couldn't drag him into this. This was his burden to live with.

"To Protect and Serve." That was the policeman's motto. He still believed it. But what happens when the system won't let you do that? When crime is out of control? Would that justify breaking the rules in order to protect the innocent?

Ed Caro had done just that. Even now he wondered if it had been the right thing to do.

THIRTY-SEVEN

Epsilon rematerialized behind a small Chinese restaurant near Keystone College. Checking to make sure no one was around, he "zapped" out of his armor, pocketed his *tru'kat* and headed down the alley toward 61st Street.

Remmler turned down Wharton Street and walked beside the tall brick wall. He passed a large bronze plaque reading: KEYSTONE COLLEGE. FO. 1892 and made a right. The middle-aged, bespectacled security guard at the gatehouse looked up as Remmler walked through the main entrance. The guard recognized him and nodded. Jack nodded back and continued on. He rubbed his hands over his exposed arms as a light, cool breeze blew. Summer would be over in less than two weeks. Wouldn't be long before he'd have to break out a jacket.

"Yo, Remy!"

Remmler stopped and looked up. He couldn't make out the two figures in front of the Phi Sigma Alpha house until they shambled toward him. It was Brian Doyle and Jim Elling.

"Roomy!" Doyle shouted gleefully, a big smile on his face. He'd obviously been drinking. "Where the heck have you been, man?"

"Yeah. We were gonna head back to Driscoll 'n see if you were there. Where were you?"

"I was . . . um, out. You know. Just taking a walk."

"Well walk yourself in here and get shitfaced with the rest of us," Elling said as he and Doyle led Remmler to the narrow, wooden house with a black tiled roof and faded, peeling white paint.

I can't believe they bought that lame excuse. I guess stuff like that works outside of comic books as well.

"Okay, guys. I can walk fine by myself." Remmler waved them off as they approached the steps. The closed doors and windows could not contain the blaring rock music and cacophony of voices. Elling opened the door. A tall, tanned, surfer dude greeted him.

"We're back, man! And look who we picked up." Elling stepped aside, pointing both hands at Remmler.

The blond kid's face lit up. "All right! Jack Remmler! Here to get an interview, man?"

"What's up, Randy?" he replied with a smile as Randy Farber furiously pumped his hand. Remmler had met him last year doing stories for *The Bear Facts* on the soccer and track teams. "Nah. Just here to unwind."

"Dude, cool."

Remmler paid the cover charge and walked in with Bubba and Elling. The frat house was wall-to-wall people, almost all of whom had a cup or can of beer in their hand. He glanced at one couple standing halfway up the stairs making out. The mingled odor of beer and cigarette smoke swatted him in the face. He barely stifled a coughing fit.

It took a while for the three to negotiate their way through the crowd and into the den, where the fraternity had three kegs set up. A big, brawny kid with close cropped blond hair liberally dispensed beer to the partygoers. Doyle grabbed three plastic cups from a nearby table. "Fill 'em up, Nick."

Doyle passed the first full cup to Elling and kept the second for himself. The third he extended to Jack.

"How about it, R-"

Remmler grabbed the cup out of Brian's hand before he could finish his sentence and took one big gulp.

"Holy shit," Elling's eyes lit up.

"Damn, Jack. Take it easy. There's plenty more."

He downed half his beer, then looked at his roommate. "Good. Keep 'em coming."

Doyle and Elling looked at each other in amazement. "Damn. You corrupted this boy, Bubba."

"So what's the occasion, man?"

Remmler took another swallow, then shrugged his shoulders. "I just feel like it."

He finished off his beer and immediately got a refill.

"All right, Remy!" Elling slapped him on the back. "I knew we'd turn ya into a lush someday."

At least for tonight. Remmler took a swallow of his second beer. *I've put up with enough shit this week. Hell, ever since I got that damn armor.*

"C'mon," Doyle began. "Let's see who else is here."

The three worked their way through the vociferous crowd, occasionally stopping and talking with people they knew. Remmler nearly finished his beer by the time they reached the small kitchen and saw Chris Wilson and Sheniese Thompson talking to a girl he didn't recognize. She wore an olive green haltertop, tight bluejeans that showed off her slender figure and a black and peach checkered workman's shirt tied around her waist. Her blond hair flowed past her shoulderblades. Could be eighteen. Tough to tell with all that makeup.

After greeting one another, Chris introduced the girl. "Guys, this is Blaire Perkins. One of our new Keystoners."

Doyle and Elling shook hands with her first. Her face brightened when she got to Jack.

"So you're Jack Remmler. Chris and Sheniese were telling me all about you. You're, like, the big sports guy around here."

Remmler raised his eyebrows in surprise and smiled. "Thanks. Well, um, I do some sports reporting for the paper. And on the radio."

Holy shit! Does this chick have a body or what? Man, would I love to rail her until I was dehydrated.

So why don't you? Go for it, Jack. Hell, you might be dead before the week's over.

He shook off the thought. It was the beer talking. Like he'd have a chance with someone this fine. She probably only hooked up with campus studs.

"Yeah," Chris continued. "Blaire's thinkin' about joining *The Bear Facts.*"

"Really?"

She nodded. "Yeah. I've been thinking I better, since I made journalism my major."

"Hey, cool. Looks like we may get another addition to the staff, Whiz."

Blaire cocked her head. "Whiz? How did you get that name?"

"Aw, it's a . . . long story," Chris responded shyly.

"No it's not," Remmler blurted. "Chris got ripped at a party last year and took a leak out the window. Right on some dude walking by outside."

Chris nearly choked. "Shit! Thanks a lot, man!"

"Aw c'mon," Elling slapped him on the shoulder. "Everybody knows that story."

Remmler laughed. Already he could feel his head filling with cotton. He never had a great tolerance for alcohol.

"Anyway," he turned back to the gorgeous blond. "I hope you join the paper. It's really great. If you need any help, just gimmie a shout. No prob."

"Thanks. That's really nice," Blaire replied with an alluring smile.

Remmler smiled back. *Damn, she's hot!* He stared at his empty cup, then looked back at his friends. "Save my place, guys. Gotta refill."

He turned to leave when he heard a female voice blurt, "Wait up. I need a refill, too."

Remmler looked back as Blaire skirted around the group. Could she really be interested in *him?*

"Sure. Okay. We'll be right back, guys."

When they were out of the room, Elling grabbed Doyle by the shoulder and leaned in close to his ear. "Dude! Remy's gonna get shitfaced *and* laid tonight."

It was loud enough for Sheniese to hear. "You guys are sick! Jack isn't the one-night stand kind of guy."

"Well, he will be after tonight!" Elling howled with laughter. Bubba joined in moments later. So did Chris, until Sheniese gave him an evil look.

"So where're you from?" Remmler asked as he and Blaire worked their way through the crowd.

"Swedesboro. New Jersey." Blaire had to shout over the noise to be heard.

"Cool. A fellow Jerseyan. I'm from Lawrence."

"Really? Cool."

"So how did you get interested in journalism?"

"Actually, I only picked it for my major 'cause nothing else was interesting."

"Oh well, hey. It beats being a business or nursing major. At least we don't have to work that hard."

Blaire giggled. Remmler looked back at her and smiled. *I may really have a chance with her. Me!*

The two finally made it to the kegs. "Here. Let me." He took Blaire's cup.

"Thank you." She blinked seductively at him.

"No prob." Remmler smiled and refilled both cups. He handed Blaire's back to her, took a swallow of his, and asked, "So. How do you like Keystone so far?"

"I think it's nice. Most of the people I've met so far are pretty cool. Plus it's nice not having to be in class at eight in the morning every day like in high school."

"I'll second that." Remmler took another gulp of his beer. *Keep talkin', man. God I hope I don't say anything stupid.*

"Well, I'm glad you like it here. I mean, I kinda had my heart set on either Syracuse or Rowan State. Unfortunately, they were a little too expensive, so I wound up here. Still, can't complain. They got a really good communications program here."

"Yeah. I was thinking of going to Rowan myself. Even Gloucester County College." She sipped her beer and continued. "But my cousin graduated from here two years ago. Told me what it was like, so I figured, what the hell."

"Cool," Remmler downed half his beer. He was about to ask Blaire if she'd like to go for a walk when he glanced over her shoulder and noticed a familiar figure. Remmler straightened up and focused on her.

It was Cheryl Terrepinn, hanging with two girls he knew from his communications classes. She swayed from side to side whenever she talked or laughed. Some beer sloshed over the rim of the cup she held.

Oh man, I forgot. She was supposed to come back today. What the hell is she doing getting drunk? That's the last thing she needs.

"Jack? What's wrong?"

He handed her his beer. "Can you hold this? I'll be right back."

Blaire stared at him in surprise as he glided past her and headed toward Cheryl and the girls.

He got halfway there when Jim Elling stumbled by with two empty cups. He hooked Remmler by the arm.

"Yo, Remy!" He nodded over toward Blaire. "So how's it goin', man?"

"Jim, what the hell's Cheryl doing here?"

Elling looked taken aback by the harshness of Remmler's tone. "Well, um . . . we were all at dinner when she got back, you know. And Kelly was asking her to go out with her. Try to cheer her up. Me and Bubba told her to come with us here tonight."

"And you think getting her drunk is gonna help her any?"

"C'mon, Remy. Cheryl's going through a rough time. We had to do something."

Remmler was too angry to say anything else. He brushed past Jim and headed toward Cheryl.

"Remy. Yo. C'mon, man."

Cheryl was laughing uncontrollably when Jack Remmler came up to her.

"RRRemy!" She threw her free arm around his waist. "Good to sssee ya again. Didja miss me?"

No doubt about it. She was bombed.

"Cheryl. How much have you had to drink?"

"Not enough for damn sure," she cackled. The other two girls laughed along.

"I thhhink you've had enoughh," Remmler stated as forcefully as possible. *And so have I.* He felt his brain sag. *You'd think being part German I'd have a better tolerance.*

Cheryl closed her eyes and dipped her head to the side as if to think. Seconds later, she opened her eyes. "Okay, *Jack.* If you say so."

She took a final gulp of her beer before handing it to one of her friends. "Here. Finish up for me. Looks like I gotta go. Ta-taaa."

Remmler didn't say another word. He put his arm around Cheryl's shoulder to steady her and walked her out.

Blaire Perkins watched the whole thing. Her jaw dropped as Jack walked out with that other girl.

"How'd you like that?" she muttered to herself. "Jerk. Well, his loss."

Blaire finished her beer and threw what was left of Jack's in the garbage. After getting a refill, she went scoping for another guy.

Cheryl almost fell three times before Remmler got her back to Driscoll Hall. Remmler, however, was a little better. He almost fell only once.

Talk about the blind leading the blind. God, just keep us from cracking our skulls open and we'll never drink this much again.

They walked into the lobby and flashed their IDs to the security guard at the main desk. The guard just nodded and went back to his newspaper. He'd seen drunken students shambling through the halls before.

Remmler walked Cheryl into the elevator and pressed the button for the fifth floor.

"You okay?" He felt another wave of lightheadedness wash over him.

Cheryl moaned, rubbing her eyes and pressing up against Jack's side. "I think my legsss turned to rubber."

"You're not sick or anything?"

Cheryl shook her head. "Uh-uh."

"Don't worry. We're almost there."

Remmler looked down at her again. He would have shaken his head, if he didn't think he'd lose his balance.

The elevator jarred to a halt and opened. Remmler walked Cheryl down the hall to her room, where she fumbled to get her keys out of the pocket of her jeans jacket. He took them from her, opened the door and turned on the lights. Cheryl let go of him and plopped down on her bed. He sat down next to her as she kicked off her shoes and slipped off her jacket, throwing it on the floor. She then leaned back on the mattress. Remmler just sat on the edge of the bed, head down and eyes closed. *I could fall asleep right here.*

"I thhhink I had too much to drink."

Remmler's eyes snapped open. "Join the club."

Cheryl struggled to sit up, then turned to face Remmler. "I thhink you came at the right time. God, I am sso drunk."

He turned to her and smiled. "That's me. Knight in shining armor." *Literally.* "It's no prob." He reached down and put his hand on top of hers. Cheryl looked up at him with droopy eyes and smiled crookedly.

God she's beautiful. Remmler gently squeezed her hand. *Maybe I should tell her that I'm Epsilon. I gotta tell someone. I can't deal with this crap alone anymore. Cheryl and me've been friends for a year. I can trust her. I . . . yeah, I guess I love her.*

"Cheryl?"

"Mmm, yeah," she replied groggily.

Forget it. She's too smashed. "Uhh, maybe I should go."

"No stay." She perked up a little, putting her other hand on his shoulder. "Please, Remy. I . . . I really don't want to be alone right now."

"Neither do I," Remmler blurted out before he could stop himself. What would he say if she asked why?

Thankfully, it didn't seem to register with Cheryl.

"Thanks. You're so wonderful, Jack." She leaned over and gave him a hug. Remmler's face was buried in her soft, curly hair. His heart pounded wildly as he felt Cheryl's breasts press against his chest.

I want you, Cheryl. I want you right now. I'm so scared. I don't want to die without knowing what it's like to make love. I want it to be with you. Someone I care about. Someone I love.

Come on, Jack! Tell her! If I get blown to bits by that thing tomorrow or the next day I don't want my last thought to be "what if . . ."

Cheryl pulled her head away, her arms still around him. He looked down to find her staring back at him. Remmler's breathing increase. Their eyes remained locked on one another. He couldn't think of a coherent way to put his feelings into words.

It didn't matter. Before he knew it, he leaned over and kissed Cheryl full on the lips. She didn't even try to resist. In fact, she pulled herself closer, running a hand across his cheek. They took a quick breath, then Cheryl hungrily pressed her mouth against Jack's. He hugged her tighter as they kissed, running his hands up and down her back. Cheryl's hands slowly roamed down Remmler's back. He felt sharp fingernails trying to cut through his t-shirt. He didn't care. He was lost in the passion of the moment.

Jack slowly leaned Cheryl back on the mattress, their lips never apart for more than a few moments. She brought up her left leg, wrapped it around Remmler's right and ran her bare foot up and down his leg. He rubbed Cheryl's right side, applying gentle pressure every now and again to elicit a giggling moan.

Remmler rolled over. Cheryl reared up, pinned his shoulders and gave him a deep kiss. His hands moved to her buttocks. She emitted a staggered moan when he squeezed.

Suddenly, something went off in Remmler's brain. *Wait! This is wrong. We shouldn't be doing this. Not now.*

"Cheryl," he said when their lips parted. "Cheryl, I—" She kissed him again. "I don't think . . . we . . . should be . . . doing this . . . Not—"

She gently placed her fingers on his lips. "Jack," she whispered desperately. "Please. I just . . ."

Cheryl moved her hand to Remmler's cheek, opened her mouth and kissed him hard. Any inhibition he had got stomped out by his hormones. He rolled Cheryl onto her side, kicked off his shoes and played footsie with her. His lips ran down Cheryl's slender neck.

"Ohhh, Jack." She began untucking Remmler's t-shirt, running her hands underneath it.

His lips made their way back up Cheryl's neck and across her cheek. "You are so gorgeous, Cheryl," he whispered into her ear before nibbling on it.

Cheryl turned her head to him. "I've got a confession to make, Remy."

"What?"

She grinned. "I always thought you were damn cute."

Remmler was taken aback, but still managed a smile. "Thanks."

Cheryl kissed him. They made out for a few more minutes before she pulled away and put a hand on Remmler's chest. "I think I need a break."

"Yeah. Okay. I guess we both do." His eyelids grew heavy.

Cheryl turned on her side, her back to Remmler. She let out a deep sigh. "What a night."

"It's not over yet." He snaked his left arm around Cheryl's abdomen and nuzzled against the nape of her neck.

Remmler fought to keep his eyes open. It had been a long day. The letter to his family. Going to confession. Patrolling the Persian Gulf. The police standoff. His adrenaline was depleted. The three beers didn't help any. His body slowly turned to lead. It was so comfortable, so warm, pressed up against Cheryl like this. He drifted in and out of a light sleep. But he couldn't fall asleep. Not yet.

He struggled to prop himself up on his elbow. Remmler looked down at Cheryl, eyes half-closed.

"Cheryl," he said in a tired voice. "Let's make love. I care about you so much. I love you."

No response.

"Please. Let's make tonight special. I really love you.

"Cheryl? Cheryl?"

He raised his head over Cheryl's. Her eyes were closed. They didn't look like they would open any time soon.

Remmler snorted. "Ain't no justice in this world."

A minute later, he was fast asleep beside her.

Remmler had no idea where he was when he woke up. Something yellow filled his vision. He blinked a few times, but it wouldn't go away. He finally lifted his head and looked down to find Cheryl Terrepinn lying next to him.

Gotta be a dream. It took another second for him to realize that wasn't the case.

He withdrew his arm from around Cheryl's waist. She moaned, shifted herself and continued sleeping. Remmler considered waking her up to tell her . . . what? Apologize? Tell her his true feelings for her? Anyway, his head was throbbing. He doubted he could form any coherent sentences. Besides, Cheryl had been pretty trashed. Best to let her sleep.

Making as little noise as possible, Remmler rolled off Cheryl's bed and put his sneakers back on. He shuffled to the door, taking one final look at Cheryl. She looked so beautiful, so peaceful lying there. It wasn't fair what she had been through, losing her brother in the *Kitty Hawk* attack.

He'd be avenged. They all would. Jack Remmler—Epsilon—would make certain of that. He'd return to the Persian Gulf every day until he found that thing and stopped it . . . or it stopped him.

This could be the last time I see you, Cheryl. Would things have been different tonight if you knew my secret . . . and how much I still love you?

Guess I'll never know.

Good-bye, Cheryl.

Remmler exited the room, gently closing the door behind him. He looked at his watch. It was past 12:30. He'd slept for nearly two hours!

He started down the hall, patting down his messed up hair, when a drunken Kelly Lin and her equally drunken friend—it was Samantha Tate, Cheryl and Kelly's next door neighbor—stumbled round the corner.

"Remyyy!" Kelly squealed. "What're you doin' up here?"

"Umm . . . just hangin' out with Cheryl."

"Ohh really," Samantha replied with a giggle.

"Um . . . Yeah. Gotta go. 'Night."

Remmler breezed past the two girls. He never realized Samantha wasn't too drunk not to notice the faint outlines of lipstick around his cheek and neck. Remmler didn't see her whisper to Kelly and laugh as he took the elevator back down to his floor.

THIRTY-EIGHT

WILHELM HEINBRODDER CASUALLY watched the fleet of limousines carrying members of the Israeli Cabinet, their staff and their bodyguards roll through the gates of the Knesset compound. He snapped his fingers. Two of his men hustled back to their rented van to inform von Klest and the other field teams on their cellular phones. It shouldn't be long before the Prime Minister showed up. Then the country's entire leadership would be under one roof, an easy target for one, decisive strike.

The Iron Guards commander carefully noted the positions of all the sentries and bodyguards in and around the compound. An IDF Huey circled the area four miles out. The Jews had set up a formidable defense, but Hienbrodder's men had surprise—and Imperium—on their side.

Smuggling the weapons past Israeli guards had been easy. The AKS-74s, grenades and rocket launchers had been tightly crammed into hidden compartments and false bottoms. A crowbar or a screwdriver could easily open them. In the woods behind the Knesset, two squads of Iron Guardsmen sat under camouflage netting, as they had been since the night before. They would provide supporting fire for the main assault team with sniper rifles and machine guns. Other Guardsmen, disguised as journalists, were scattered throughout the crowd. They would hit the Knesset from the flanks while Heinbrodder took his team through the front. Von Klest—Imperium—would neutralize the guards on the roof, along with the helicopter and any other military vehicles.

Heinbrodder smiled. He had waited his whole life for this moment. All those years spent in West Germany's castrated *Bundeswehr*, working his way into one of its most elite units. Acquiring skills the weaklings in his government would never allow him to use.

Now all that training would pay off. In less than an hour, he would lead his men into battle for real. The defeat of the Third Reich would be avenged, and a new Fourth Reich would be born in the blood of the *Juden* government.

"You sure this isn't some kind of joke?" Drake asked his chief signals officer.

"I checked with Islamabad station over the secure link myself," said the overweight, balding Scott Larzinni. "There are nearly eighty witnesses who say they saw this thing. A French Red Cross doctor was treating the boy when he turned into this . . . Mud Man. The boy's mother and three sisters were also present at the time. Plus there are fifteen dead Pakistani soldiers, one covered with dried mud that they needed a jackhammer to crack." He put a hand against his brow and shook his head. "Good God, this is science fiction come to life. First that Energy Man that took out the *Kitty Hawk*, now this. What the hell's going on?"

"If I knew, Scott, I'd be cranking out a report right now. Does Islamabad station believe there's a connection between the two?"

"Just that they have some . . . extraordinary abilities. Now, the place where this incident occurred . . ." Larzinni flipped through his notes. "Quetta, is about nine hundred-fifty miles from where *Kitty Hawk* went down."

The two men walked over to a large world map tacked to Drake's wall. Larzinni pulled out a red felt tip pen from his shirt pocket. "May I?"

Drake nodded. Larzinni made dots where the "superhuman" activity had taken place. The station chief scrutinized the map some more and told Larzinni to put a dot where The Iraqi Bomb went off.

"Makes a nice isosceles triangle, doesn't it?"

"You think there's a connection?"

Drake rubbed a hand down his cheek. His voice sounded distant. "You know. I've been trying to get the results of that explosion for weeks. Every time I ask, Washington says the matter's top secret and under investigation. My ass. They found something. Something big. Maybe Iraq put something new in that plutonium. I don't know."

"But we're talking about a Third World country on the verge of economic collapse, not the hi-tech capital of the world."

"We also thought they only had enough weapons grade plutonium for a few Hiroshima-sized devices. Look how that turned out.

"Let's dig deep into our list of nuke suspects. See if any of them were conducting 'unusual experiments' before this. And check with all our stations from Egypt to India. See if they've gotten any reports on . . . superhumans."

"You got it."

Drake stared at the map. *What in the hell are we dealing with? How could something like this be possible?*

The waiting proved unbearable for von Klest and Kemp. They had nothing further to discuss about the plan. Everything was in order. Neither could think of anything else to talk about.

"I'm going to turn on the radio," von Klest announced. Anything to relieve the boredom.

He didn't have much to choose from. *Juden* stations were out of the question. The same with Voice of America and its nauseating propaganda. BBC World Service seemed the only thing he didn't find offensive.

Dammit! What's the use!?

Jack Remmler threw his pen down on the desk. It bounced off and clattered to the floor. He took the loose-leaf paper in front of him, crumpled it up and slammed it into the waste paper basket. Remmler leaned forward, resting his head on his hands.

How the hell can I do this exercise for journalism class tomorrow? Or study for my Radio/TV writing test Tuesday? I could be dead by then.

His head throbbed. So much for the aspirin. He didn't sleep well either, which amazed him after everything he had been through. The Gulf. The standoff. The cop Caro. Cheryl.

Oh man, did I fuck up big time.

I can't believe it. I've wanted her for a year, and when I finally get her . . . I don't know. It feels wrong. Like I stepped over the line. Especially when we were drunk. Is that taking advantage of her? Does she hate me now?

But all we did was make out. Hell, our shirts didn't even come off. Still I shoulda known better.

He didn't need this right now. Everything was getting dumped on him at once. What's worse, Kelly and Samantha probably blabbed about him coming out of Cheryl's room. Now everyone would think he and Cheryl got tanked and did the horizontal bop.

Remmler rubbed his hands over his face and stared up at the radio/tape player perched on the overhang of his desk. He had it tuned to KYW-AM, Philadelphia's all-news station.

If anything happened in the Persian Gulf that might be related to the Energy Man, KYW should have it.

He bent down to pick up the pen and looked across the room at Brian's bed. His roommate must have crashed at the frat house. Probably still sleeping. Guy's liver must be working overtime.

Someone knocked on the door.

"Come in." Remmler got up as the door swung open. His eyes went wide with surprise.

Cheryl Terrepinn stood in the doorway.

Oh boy. Remmler wondered if this would be good or bad as Cheryl closed the door and leaned against it. She looked like she just rolled out of bed with her rumpled gray t-shirt, sweatpants and white socks.

"Hi, Jack," she said softly.

"Cheryl," he muttered breathlessly. The pen slowly flipped through his fingers. "Umm . . . uhh . . ." He had no idea what to say. Maybe she couldn't remember last night.

"About last night . . ."

Damn. His fingers furiously worked the pen. "Cheryl, look. I'm really sorry. Maybe I should've . . . I guess I should've stayed . . . I shouldn't've walked out. I shouldn't've even . . ."

"Jack . . . Jack." Cheryl held up her hand to quiet him. "Just calm down, okay?"

Remmler took a deep breath as Cheryl walked halfway across the room. She cast her gaze down, thinking. After a few seconds, she finally spoke. "Oh God, Jack. Last night was so nuts. I just wanted to come back to school as soon as possible. Throw myself back into my classes, my normal routine. I thought it might help me cope with Alan's death. That's why I jumped at the chance to go to that party. Getting drunk was probably the worst thing I could've done. And then you came along, helped me back to my room. You were so sweet."

Remmler shook his head. "No I wasn't. I shouldn't've taken advantage of you like that. I knew it was wrong, but I couldn't help . . . aw, that sounds like a cop out."

"Jack, stop beating yourself up. I mean, it's not like we went at it like animals in heat. At least, if I remember right that was the case. Things got a bit hazy before we went to sleep. Just for my peace of mind, we didn't-"

"No," Jack snapped off an answer. "We didn't. Not even close." A part of him felt disappointed.

Cheryl took a relieved breath. "Look, I asked you to stay. I really didn't want to be alone. I probably would've cried myself to sleep . . . again. And you were there. Just like when I found out Alan died."

Remmler pocketed the pen and crossed his arms. He looked down, then at Cheryl. "It's just . . . I've been worried about you. I want to help you get through this. Last night . . . last night I guess I wasn't in my right frame of mind. I thought about what you were going through, what I've . . . we were holding one another. I got caught up in the moment . . .

"Cheryl. I . . . you know I still care about you."

She walked the rest of the way over to him. "I know. I care about you, too. This may sound crazy, probably all the alcohol. I'm amazed I still remember. But for a split second last night, when we were holding one another, I felt so . . . safe." She chuckled briefly. "God, that sounded corny."

Remmler found himself smiling too. Then Cheryl looked him straight in the eyes. "We both got caught up in the moment. It just . . . happened."

"So what do we do about it?"

"We go on . . . as friends. Remy, we both have feelings for each other. But, as far as a relationship goes . . . I don't know. Maybe we've been friends for too long. It'd probably spoil it."

"Yeah. Maybe you're right," Remmler said half-convincingly. He wanted to say something else, but didn't feel now was the appropriate time.

Cheryl stuck out her hand. "Friends?"

He smiled and took it. "Always."

Cheryl then gave him a friendly hug and a peck on the cheek. "Thanks for everything, Jack."

"Thank you," he replied as Cheryl let go, "for being so understanding. For a moment I thought you were gonna come in here and read me the riot act."

"I can't say the thought didn't cross my mind."

"What changed your mind?"

"I know you. I know you wouldn't do anything to hurt me on purpose. Our friendship means a lot to me. You . . . we just slipped up."

"Yeah, I guess." Suddenly, Remmler's hand snapped up. "Oh. I almost forgot." He went over to his desk, opened the top drawer and pulled out a pink envelope.

"Here. Kelly and Bubba had a sympathy card going around the dorm. But, this one's from me."

Cheryl sniffled, holding back the tears as she took it. "Thanks, Jack." She hugged him again.

"Well," Cheryl let go of him, "you look like you're busy here. I'll let you get back to work. Thanks for everything."

He smiled. "Anytime."

Cheryl headed for the door. Her hand just touched the knob when she turned back around. "By the way . . ."

"Yeah?"

An elfish grin formed across her lips. "I just wanted to tell you . . . you're a damn good kisser."

Remmler gulped, blushing as he tried to smile back. "Um . . . thanks. You . . . you weren't so bad yourself."

Cheryl closed her eyes and smiled. "Thank you."

"This just in to the KYW newsroom . . ."

Remmler's ears perked up.

" . . .The Saudi Press Agency is reporting a large fire

raging at the Al Ghawar oil field. The cause of the blaze is not known. Al Ghawar is Saudi Arabia's largest oil field. KYW will be following this story and will bring you further information as it becomes available. To repeat . . ."

Remmler's jaw tightened. His right hand balled into a fist. He didn't need the radio to tell him who—or rather what—was responsible.

His insides chilled. *This is it.*

"Oh God," Cheryl gasped. "When'll this end?"

He turned back to her. No doubt the newsflash reminded Cheryl of her brother's death. Though it pained him to do so, Jack could not comfort her now. He had to move.

"Soon hopefully." He paused for a few seconds to come up with an excuse. "Um . . . jeez, I better get back to my journalism homework."

"Sure, no problem. I'll see you later."

"Okay. Take care."

Once Cheryl left, Remmler pulled down the shades and flung open the top drawer of his desk. He rifled through it until he came across several maps he copied from a book on Saudi Arabia he found in the college library. He spread them out on his bed until he came across one showing the country's oil fields.

"Al Ghawar . . . Al Ghawar . . . Al Ghawar . . . Dammit, where is it?" His eyes darted across the map until he spotted a large dark blob east of Riyadh.

"There!" He stabbed his finger at it.

Remmler scooped up the maps and tossed them into the drawer. Reaching into his pocket, he pulled out his *tru'kat.* He stood frozen as a thousand and one thoughts raced through his mind. Did he really know what he was getting into? Would he come out of this alive? Imperium already kicked his ass. Why should another fight with another . . . supervillian turn out any different? Or maybe turn out worse. *God. I'm too young to die.*

But what if this thing wasn't stopped? How many more

people would it kill? How many more families like Cheryl's would grieve?

"You've come this far, Remy. You're committed." *Besides, who else has the power to stop this thing?*

He took one last look around the room and closed his eyes. His body disappeared in a bright glow as the sub-dimension the armor stayed in when not in use opened. The suit materialized around Jack's body and the *tru'kat* transformed into his battlestaff.

Epsilon took a deep breath and held the staff out in front of him. "Well, this is it."

Seconds later, the room was empty.

"General!" one of the RTOs shouted. "*Overlord* reports a hit on their spectrometers."

Clay hurried over to the communications station, followed by Elder and Xantis. "Location?"

The RTO circled a portion of extreme western Philadelphia on a map by his side. "That's the best they can do, sir. Looks like they were close to the source when they picked it up."

"Could it be regular background EM?" Xantis asked.

"They don't think so. They compared it with some of their prior readings and found anomalies with this signal."

Clay breathed deep in anticipation. *It's the UL. It has to be. I can feel it.*

"Send all our field teams into that area at once. Get *Overlord* back here on the double. I want them refueled and back in the air ASAP. Major, you're in charge here. Captain Elder and I will be going into the field."

"Yes sir."

Clay headed to the equipment lockers with his XO. "Time to reel in this son of a bitch."

THIRTY-NINE

EPSILON TELEPORTED INTO Hell. He didn't notice it at first. The entire world swirled when he materialized. He barely managed to stay on his feet. Teleportation always left him momentarily disoriented, but never this bad. The side effects probably worsened the farther he teleported, he figured. His restless night's sleep and slight hangover didn't help either.

After a few seconds, Epsilon pulled himself together.

"Oh my God," he murmured in awe as he took in the devastation. Remmler had seen big forest fires in California and Yellowstone on the news, had watched footage of the firebombings of Dresden and Tokyo on World War Two documentaries.

None of it compared to this.

Fire greeted him everywhere he looked. Flames from wrecked oil wells shot hundreds of feet into the air. Thick black smoke smothered the sky. Millions of gallons of crude oil spilled from shattered pipelines. Metal that had once been part of rigging and buildings lay twisted, engulfed by flames.

One man did this, Remmler thought with dread. He shuffled about the inferno, overwhelmed by its sheer magnitude.

How can I defeat something like this? I don't stand a chance.

Epsilon nearly jumped out of his skin as a tremendous crash split the air. The ground beneath him shook. Another explosion occurred half-a-mile away. It freed him from his daze.

Pull yourself together, man! You're a superhero. Start acting like one.

Remmler closed his eyes and activated his unisense. No sign of the thing here.

Dammit! He can't get away again!

Epsilon took to the sky and hovered above the inferno. His unisense cut through the smoke. At least six square miles were engulfed in flames. Charred skeletons littered the area. He tried to count them all until the task became too great. Epsilon quivered. This wasn't TV. This was happening right in front of him. How many died in this apocalypse? A hundred? Two-hundred? Three-hundred?

He scanned the periphery of the blaze. To the south he sensed emergency crews heading toward the fire. The smoldering hulks of two armored vehicles lay off to the west. Around them lay the skeletal forms of eight soldiers. Thirty yards away were the remains of a small service building, its roof half collapsed.

"Uhhh . . . uhhh."

Someone was alive in there! Epsilon concentrated and spotted a man half-buried in the rubble. He made a beeline toward him.

The man was half-conscious and still moaning when Epsilon landed. "Hang on, buddy! Help's here!"

Two twisted, scorched pieces of debris rested on the oil worker's back. Epsilon flung them away with ease. He bent down, dropping his *tru'kat*, and reached under the half-fallen roof.

One-two-three!

Epsilon lifted. The shattered roof came off the ground easily. Holding it up with one hand, he reached down and grabbed the oil worker by his collar. It took two pulls before Epsilon dragged him clear. Then he let the roof fall back to the ground.

"You're all right now, pal." Epsilon pulled the man away from the wreckage and went back to retrieve his staff.

The Saudi seemed more lucid with each passing second. He rolled onto his back, his moans growing louder. Blood stained both legs of his coveralls. Remmler wondered if they were broken. A flood of sweat dug ravines into the soot covering his dark face. Remmler, on the other hand, couldn't feel one bead of perspiration anywhere on his body. Thank God for the armor's climate control. He then looked back at the Saudi. *Poor guy must feel like he's in a blast furnace.*

He squatted beside him. "How are you doing, man?"

The Saudi painfully raised his head and opened his eyes. Epsilon's globular head and protruding red beak stared back at him.

The man screamed in terror. Epsilon jumped back in surprise as the Saudi tried to scurry away, praying to Allah for protection.

"Whoa! Whoa! Relax. I'm a friend. Friend." Epsilon tried to keep his voice firm but gentle. "I'm not gonna hurt you, okay? Just take it easy."

The Saudi settled down, trying to take a deep breath. He choked on the smoke. For a moment, Remmler was surprised the man had understood him. Then he remembered the suit could translate his words into Arabic. He wished he had time to guess how that was possible. *Heck, I doubt I'd understand anyway.*

The oil worker laid back down. "Oh Allah, it hurts."

This guy needs a doctor. Him and probably many others. But Epsilon needed information.

"Everything's gonna be okay, bud." He gently took hold of the man's arm to reassure him. The roar of the fire still rattled his enhanced hearing. "I'm gonna get you some medical help. But I need you to do me a favor first. Can you?"

The Saudi weakly nodded. "What . . . what is it?" The armor translated his words into English.

"Who did this? Who attacked you? The Iraqis? Terrorists?"

"No," the man's head bobbed from side to side. "I don't know. Something."

"What? Please, I have to know. What was it?" *Don't die on me, dammit!*

"Only . . . only saw a few glimpses of it. Black. Glowed. Shot . . . some kind of ray."

Remmler's gut grew cold. "It's him," he unintentionally said outloud. He looked back down at the Saudi. "Did you see which way he went?"

After coughing a few times, the oil worker wearily looked around and nodded back at the flames. "That way. The . . . to the west? Yes . . . the west."

"How long ago was that?"

"I don't know."

Damn. Epsilon stared into the wall of flames in front of him. It couldn't have been that long ago, could it? At least he had a good lead.

Then a disturbing thought struck him.

"What's west of here?"

The Saudi paused for a second. "Ri . . . Riyadh."

Remmler's breath caught in his throat. "Oh my God."

He had no time to lose. With great care Epsilon scooped up the wounded oil worker.

"What . . . what's—" The Saudi screamed they took to the air.

"Don't worry," Epsilon said calmly as the screaming man

held him tightly around the neck. "I felt the same way my first time, too."

He cleared the sea of fire and descended toward a crowd of oil workers, emergency personnel and khaki-clad Saudi Special Security police. People pointed and screamed as he landed. The police trained their Heckler & Koch submachine guns on him.

"What is it?"

"It's got somebody!"

"Shoot it! Kill it!"

"This man needs a doctor!" Epsilon bellowed over the crowd as he gently laid the oil worker on the ground. Everyone just looked at one another dumbfounded.

"I've got an injured man here! Get a medic!" He shot to his feet. "Now, dammit!"

Finally a man wearing a white hard-hat with a red cross on the front emerged from the crowd and cautiously made his way toward Epsilon and the oil worker.

"Move it! This man might be dying!"

The paramedic nearly jumped out of his skin. He scrambled over to the man, opened his medical kit and went to work.

Epsilon looked back at the crowd. "Okay. One of you call Riyadh. Tell them the thing that attacked you guys is the same thing that sunk the *Kitty Hawk* and it's headed toward Riyadh right now. I'm gonna fly there and stop it." *I hope.*

The crowd just nodded dumbly. Epsilon didn't have time to get a more positive conformation. He took a running start, leaped into the air and flew off. He felt bad leaving them behind, but they were trained to deal with disasters like this. Besides, more help had to be on the way. If he did stay, Riyadh might wind up like *Kitty Hawk* and this oil field.

Guided by his unisense, Epsilon hurtled west toward the Saudi capital. He didn't want to teleport again so soon. He nearly blacked out before. Right now he needed every ounce of strength he could muster to stop this thing.

Yuri Drovinov followed the Petroline all the way to Riyadh. The time had come for him to seize power for himself. The Iraqis' usefulness was at an end. What did he need them for anyway? Men with his kind of power led, they were not *to be* led. When he returned to Baghdad, it would be as their leader. The President and his Revolutionary Command Council would have to be eliminated. None of them could be trusted. Then he would be undisputed master of the region. Before long, the world. Who would challenge him? He was Nexus. He had the powers of a god. The destruction of Riyadh would be his first step. America and the Gulf States won't dare oppose him when they saw the Saudi capital lying in ruin.

Drovinov studied the maps. He knew following the Petroline from Al Ghawar would lead him to Riyadh. He memorized street maps of the city, identifying priority targets. When he actually got to Riyadh, he discovered his studies were in vain. The city was a cluttered mass of steel and glass buildings sprawled out for miles, surrounded by highways jammed with people fleeing to supposed safe havens. He'd be lucky to find any of his targets. Nexus cursed himself for not planning better.

So what? I can destroy all my priority targets simply by destroying the entire city.

Nexus' first volley struck the tops of Riyadh's tallest skyscrapers, turning them into steel and glass candles billowing smoke. Debris rained down on streets crowded with cars and pedestrians. He then turned his attention to the crowded highways leading out of town. Nexus took out dozens of vehicles with each shot. Concrete columns supporting the overpasses collapsed. Several cars, unable to stop in time, plunged over the edge. The driver of a gasoline truck slammed on his brakes when he saw the carnage ahead. Tires squealed. The back end of a Mercedes-Benz helped the truck finally stop. Before the driver could do anything more, an energy blast struck the road thirty feet away. The truck fell on its side, its storage tank ripped open. Seconds later it exploded. Burning fuel showered the road and nearby cars.

Nexus soon reached the edge of the city. He blasted the intersection of Makkah Road and Ring Road East, killing and injuring dozens of motorists. By now several vehicles tried to turn around and flee the destruction. Others just abandoned their cars and took off on foot, a good many of them run down before they could get off the highway.

Panicked citizens hurried into nearby buildings for cover. Unknown to Nexus, thousands of calls flooded police stations. National Guard troops and emergency personnel found it nearly impossible to move through the crowded streets. The King, his family and his staff sought shelter in their bunker below the Royal Diwan. The leadership of the Coalition's military forces also took refuge in their own bunker.

Nexus now fired indiscriminately at the skyscrapers. Debris fell on the streets, crushing people. Windows shattered into thousands of lethal fragments. People were shredded. Roads were blocked. A gas main exploded, taking out a block of office buildings and hundreds of people. Dozens of separate fires merged into one as flames shot hundreds of feet into the air. An eerie orange-red glow fell over the city.

"TREMBLE BEFORE ME, YOU INSECTS!!!" Nexus hollered as he obliterated another high rise. "I AM YOUR MASTER!!! I AM YOUR GOD!!!"

FORTY

Frank Donnell's consciousness pulled him in two directions. One side wanted to retreat to the basement with all the other "nonessential" personnel. But the other told him this could be the story that makes his career. Career or life? He struggled with the choice until he emerged on the roof.

"Good God." Donnell's mouth hung open. His wide eyes gazed at the flames and smoke rising from the east.

"I don't see any planes or SCUDs around," Andy Jeter, Donnell's stocky cameraman, noted as he scanned the skies.

The lean reporter with swept back, brown hair paid no attention to him. He wandered across the roof, placing himself to the right of the smoke and flames.

"Get a shot of the fire when we start." He jumped as another explosion rumbled in the distance. "Then pan over to me after about ten, fifteen seconds."

"Gotcha, ace."

"Going to you in ten, Frank. Reid will be handing off to

you," the director in the control room downstairs said into Donnell's earpiece.

He listened to the anchor back in Atlanta—*safe and sound.* " . . .We now take you live to Riyadh and correspondent Frank Donnell. Frank, what's happening?"

"Mr. President. You'd better turn on CNN," DCI Brock told him when he picked up the phone in the Oval Office.

The President grabbed the remote control and turned on the appropriate channel. The first image he, the Vice President, Baronelli and Preston saw was a pillar of fire and smoke rising from the Saudi capital.

"Oh my God," the VP stammered. "What the hell's going on over there?"

"First the oil field, now Riyadh," Baronelli chimed in.

"Tom, I'm putting you on speaker," the President told the CIA Director. "The SecDef and Callingworth are en route by limo from the Pentagon. Should be here in ten minutes, but I'm going to call them right now."

A minute later the other two were also on the speakerphone. After a quick briefing from National Security Advisor Baronelli, Admiral Callingworth said, "Mr. President, we must assume this is the beginning of a full-scale attack on Saudi Arabia, undoubtedly by Iraq. I suggest we immediately go to DEFCON Two and commit our forces to combat."

The President paused in thought for a few seconds. "Go to DEFCON Two. But I want confirmation whether it's Iraq and Iran who's responsible. Once we know for sure, I'll give the go-ahead."

"Yes sir."

"I'll contact the King momentarily. Stay on the line until you get here." The President reached over to his intercom. "Joyce. Send in Major Bendis."

There was a slight pause. "Yes, sir."

"Mr. President!" Preston yelped in surprise. "You can't—"

The President held up his hand to silence her. "It's only a precaution, Lydia."

Moments later, an ashen-faced Army major carrying a black briefcase handcuffed to his right wrist entered the Oval Office.

The President smiled half-heartedly as he picked up the phone to call the King of Saudi Arabia. "Major. I never thought I'd have to call you in here on business."

"Yes sir," the Major replied weakly as he laid the famous "football" on the President's desk. Inside was access to the most destructive force ever conceived by man.

Donnell stopped for a second when he saw Jeter point frantically at the sky.

"What is—?" He spun around and saw a streak of black in the distance. Every few seconds it let loose an energy blast that turned another portion of Riyadh into a ball of fire.

"I don't believe this. Reid! Can you see it?"

"I see it, Frank," the anchor in Atlanta replied.

"If I'm not mistaken, that's the same thing that destroyed the *Kitty Hawk.* That 'Energy Man'."

Donnell and his cameraman tracked it until it disappeared behind some buildings. Seconds later, a cloud of smoke and fire rose from behind them.

"There's another explosion. It appears to be in the area of the Gulf Cooperation Council Building."

"Dammit!" Epsilon swore as he zoomed over the desert. "Dammit. Dammit. Dammit."

Dozens of columns of thick black smoke stained the horizon. He was too late. Again! How many people lived in Riyadh? A million? How many were dead already? The death toll just kept climbing and still Epsilon could do nothing to stop it.

"Move, damn you!" Remmler screamed at his armor.

He wasn't leaving the Middle East until he found this thing and stopped it. Remmler swore this on everything he could think of. God and country. His family's lives. As a Cosmic Protector. He didn't care how long it took. One way or another, the killing stopped right here.

Nexus watched as a section of wall collapsed into the flames of the devastated GCC building.

What else? He scanned the city. *What else looks important? Where-*

Just across the crowded Jeddah Road he saw a concentration of buildings, each one waving a different flag.

Embassies!

Nexus flew straight for the Diplomatic Quarter, blasting gridlocked vehicles along the Al-Malek Khaled and Jeddah Roads.

"I can see it clearly from my vantage point . . ."

Erich von Klest listened intently to the reporter for BBC World Service.

"This must be the same thing that attacked the American aircraft carrier . . . it's firing . . . there's smoke, explosions, all over Riyadh."

"Twenty minutes, Erich," Kemp told him from across the room.

Von Klest ignored him. He just stared at the clock radio on his night stand.

This couldn't have come at a worse time. The thing was in Riyadh right now! He could teleport over there and finish it off. Not have to go through the bother of hunting it down.

But they were due to attack the Knesset in twenty minutes. Two weeks of planning, preparation. His men were in place. The Israelis didn't suspect a thing. He couldn't pass up something this perfect.

But the thing in Riyadh was a threat to his ultimate goal.

It had to be eliminated. And right now he knew exactly where it was.

No! The mission comes first. This thing—as well as the Protector—will be dealt with in due course.

At least it's saving us the trouble of having to kill the damn Arabs.

Paul Drake could hear the yelling and footsteps filtering into his office as he flung all his vital documents into a briefcase and locked it. A loud thunderclap erupted outside. The entire building shook. Windows rattled violently, threatening to shatter.

"Move your ass, Drake." The station chief armed the incendiary device that would destroy anything inside the briefcase should it be tampered with.

A deafening roar shook the building. Drake dropped to the floor as his office window exploded into a hundred pieces. The glass just settled when he picked himself up and bolted out of the room. Droplets of blood ran down his ears and the back of his neck.

"Paul!"

He turned to find Lawson standing at the other end of the hallway.

"What the hell's going on!?" the Captain demanded.

"Let's figure it out when we get to the shelter."

Lawson took two steps toward Drake.

The entire building rocked in every direction. Drake bounced off the wall. The briefcase flew out of his hand. He landed on his back. The ceiling came apart.

For once, Epsilon cursed his extraordinary unisense. The entire city seemed to be screaming, crying, pleading for help. People trapped in burning buildings choked on the thick smoke. Motorists pinned in their cars cried out in desperation. Many pounded on doors and windows with their bare hands trying to free themselves. Some took their last breaths, their bodies crushed by the twisted metal. Others screamed in agony as flames engulfed them. Dead and wounded littered the streets. Ambulances trying to get to them were blocked by the mass of bodies, vehicles and debris. Several paramedics abandoned their vehicles and went on foot to help the wounded.

I have to help. I have to do something.

But there were so many injured people, scattered all over Riyadh. Remmler had no idea where to begin. Despite his powers, he was only one man. He could only do so much.

And if he stopped to help, that Energy Man would still be out there, causing more death and destruction. By saving a few lives, thousands more would be lost.

Dammit! It's not fair. I can't make decisions like that.

The screams assaulted Jack's ears, tore at his soul. He had to help those people, but at the same time he had to stop that thing. He could only do one.

Epsilon continued flying over the city. Try as he might, he couldn't ignore the screams.

The CNN production van was on its way to the Diplomatic Quarter for a live interview with the U.S. Ambassador when the attack began. Ted Santiago, the chunky, mustached field producer, tuned in to the satellite feed of CNN's live coverage while reporter Philip Waldon phoned their Riyadh studio.

"Stay where you are," the bureau director told him. "The thing looks like it's heading west."

Which it did. The van turned onto Jeddah Road just as the Energy Man destroyed the GCC building. George Lamaoto, the stout, bearded cameraman driving the van, watched in awe as it flew away from the burning building. It then blasted a section of the road ahead of them before disappearing into the Diplomatic Quarter.

"Fuck. Fuck. Fuck!" the fair haired, fair skinned Waldon

cursed at the stalled traffic. "Fuck this! George. Get your camera. We'll leg it. Ted. Link up the dish with home base. We're goin' out."

"Be careful, guys."

"Always."

Gear in hand, Waldon and Lamaoto jumped out of the van. They weaved through the motionless vehicles and sprinted toward the Diplomatic Quarter.

Nexus blew the Danish Embassy in half when a squat, four-wheeled UR-416 armored personnel carrier of the Saudi Special Security Forces patrolling the Diplomatic Quarter turned the corner and screeched to a halt. Six khaki-clad men burst out of the vehicle and blazed away with their MP5s. The bullets that struck his energy field disintegrated immediately.

"Pests," he muttered as he lowered himself to the ground.

"Our guns are not affecting him!" one security officer shouted over the firing.

Nexus casually raised his arm and fired. The UR-416 disappeared in a ball of fire, vaporizing the six troopers around it.

"Fools." He shook his head in contempt. "They have no idea what they are dealing with.

"But they soon will."

Nexus turned away from the burning APC and floated down the street. Two more UR-416s soon appeared, disgorging their human cargo. The security troops fanned out across the street, taking positions behind whatever cover they could find.

"Insolent dogs!" Nexus shouted as bullets whizzed by him. "What does it take to teach you who your superior is?!"

Moments later, he set one of the APCs afire.

Gotcha! Epsilon sensed the Energy Man amidst the burning Diplomatic Quarter. The troops battling it didn't stand a chance. One by one their bodies were torn apart by energy blasts. Bullets from their submachine guns had no effect on the thing.

Do I even stand a chance against this guy?

You chose to do this, Remy. No running away this time.

Epsilon dove for the Diplomatic Quarter.

I hope I live through this.

"You're on, Phil," Santiago said from the van, relaying the microwave signal from Lamaoto's camera back to the Riyadh studio. From there it was beamed by satellite to CNN Headquarters in Atlanta for the entire world to see. Millions upon millions of viewers watched the image of burning buildings bobbing up and down on their screens. Philip Waldon also came into view, running for all he was worth toward the inferno.

" . . .the Diplomatic Quarter in Riyadh . . . where many of the foreign embassies are located . . . came under attack just moments ago . . ." Waldon took several deep breaths before continuing. He regretted never using that exercise bike his sister gave him for Christmas years ago. *God I'm out of shape.*

Still he kept going. This was *the* biggest story of the decade, maybe the century. He'd crawl on his hands and knees if necessary to get it.

"Over to my left . . . the headquarters for the Gulf Cooperation Council . . . has apparently been destroyed . . . It appears whatever destroyed *Kitty Hawk*, now wants to do the same . . . to the Saudi capital.

"Flames are shooting into the sky. We can just make out . . . explosions, gunfire."

Waldon skid to a halt and looked up. He pointed to the sky. "There! There! George, get it!"

Lamaoto stopped and panned the camera up. The smoke

obscured their view. Waldon hoped the people viewing this could see the red and white streak diving into the maelstrom.

The few remaining security troops fled down the street. They left behind the burning hulks of their armored vehicles and the charred remains of their comrades. Nexus floated down the street after them. They were only a handful of soldiers, but they had attacked *him*. Defied *him*. Yuri Drovinov. Nexus. A good ruler cannot let such an act go unpunished.

The troopers leapfrogged their way down the street, covering one another's retreat. Two of them carried wounded comrades, slowing down their progress. Nexus floated over the burning APCs and stared impassionately at them. He picked out one young trooper dragging a wounded man down the sidewalk. Drovinov smiled and raised his fist.

A harsh, whistling sound erupted overhead. Nexus started to turn around.

"What—?"

Epsilon felt like he rammed full bore into the side of a battleship. His entire body threatened to shake apart. The world spun. He blacked out and never felt it when he slammed into the street.

His eyes suddenly popped open. A hazy blur fell over him, then faded. Epsilon groaned and crawled out of the indentation he made. He'd been on his feet for barely a second before stumbling to his right.

Where am I?

Remmler blinked a few times. Something black sat a few yards away. The image cleared by the time he straightened up.

It was definitely a man, on his knees. Some sort of crackling black energy surrounded him. A low moan rose from his throat.

Suddenly the Energy Man turned to him. "What are you?" Its voice was very deep, almost supernatural.

"E-Epsilon," Jack responded shakily as he tried to straighten up. Pain hammered his entire body.

It spoke Russian! Nexus wondered if it could it be some top secret weapon his former countrymen sent to stop him. It didn't look like anything they would build . . . or anyone else on Earth.

Not aliens? Impossible!

His left shoulder throbbed slightly, like something hard nicked it. Something metal.

Impossible. How can anything get through my energy field? How could he even survive contact with it?

Nexus felt his strength returning. The impact would have killed an ordinary human. Thankfully the energy field absorbed most the blow.

The armored man, Epsilon he called himself, continued to wobble on his feet. "Wh-What are you? Why are you doing this?"

With a thought, Drovinov increased the power of his energy field. "I am Nexus," his arm came up. "And whatever you are, you are in my way."

Epsilon got into a shaky crouch and-

Shit! Where's my tru'kat!

The blast hit Epsilon in the torso. He soared down the street. His entire body throbbed with pain as he crashed into a six-inch thick wall and disappeared in an explosion of reinforced concrete.

FORTY-ONE

"My God. It looks like Bosnia here."

It may not have been the most professional thing for a reporter to say, but it accurately captured the scope of the devastation. Embassies on both sides of the street gushed fire and smoke. Waldon and Lamaoto dodged the fiery wreckage of an armored vehicle and headed toward two more. A sickeningly sweet odor hung in the air. Waldon fought down the bile that rushed up his throat.

Oh my God. It's . . . flesh! Burning flesh!

Waldon finally lost it when he came upon the blackened corpses near the two burning APCs. He doubled over and puked. At that moment, he didn't care how it looked to millions of viewers or his bosses in Atlanta. They weren't out here.

He spat out the remaining bile and continued on. Waldon rounded the burning wrecks and halted in shock. His arms dropped to his sides. The cordless microphone nearly slipped from his hands. It took a few seconds for his senses to kick back in.

"George!" He waved to his cameraman. "Get that."

Lamaoto ran over to Waldon. His jaw dropped when he saw it.

Waldon just shook his head. *This can't be real.*

Remmler wanted to go to sleep right here. *Get up! Get up!* His brain kept screaming.

He never felt so much pain in his life. No way he could fight this Nexus guy. But he had to. The world was depending on him.

Remmler flooded his mind with images of his friends and family. Mom. Dad. Lisa. Bubba. Whiz . . . Cheryl. What if he failed and Nexus eventually made it to America? How would they suffer?

"Get up, Jack," he groaned. Every movement sent hot needles of pain deep into his muscles. "Get up."

He got halfway to his feet when he noticed the damage. A huge burn mark covered half his torso. His unisense found cracks and dents within the blackened area. The top of his head where he impacted the energy field was singed. Epsilon gambled that his armor could survive the dive into the Nexus' protective field. It had already proved to be strong enough to sustain several laser hits from Imperium's *tru'kat.* Still . . .

How much more punishment can I take? I need my staff. Where the hell is it?! Without it I'm dead.

Epsilon looked up. Nexus hovered just outside the hole in the wall. He could clearly see the look of surprise on his face.

"Impossible! Nothing could survive that!"

"Shit." Epsilon looked down and scooped up a chunk of concrete. He flung it at Nexus. The fifty-pound slab disintegrated on contact with the energy field.

"Surely you can do better than that," Drovinov mocked him.

Epsilon dove to his left, narrowly avoiding another blast that wound up blowing a hole in the embassy behind him.

"Gotta get my *tru'kat,*" he grumbled as he got to his feet.

Nexus floated through the opening in the wall.

"Dammit!" Epsilon looked at the wall. It had to be over nine feet high, maybe ten. With his strength, it might be worth a try.

He bent at the knees and pushed off. Nexus' blast missed him by a foot and obliterated a nearby date palm.

Epsilon cleared the wall by a good four feet. He landed hard on the pavement, his feet going right through it. He lost his balance and fell face first into the gutter.

That was embarrassing.

He got to his knees, closed his eyes and switched to unisense.

"What th-!" someone cried and fell on his rear as the bladed, silver staff suddenly rose off the ground near him and flew away. Had to be a reporter. The guy held a microphone and another dude behind him lugged a camera on his shoulder.

"Come on!" Epsilon shouted to his *tru'kat* as he sensed Nexus rising above the wall.

Too late. Epsilon twisted around and rolled away as Nexus fired. The blast tore up the street and lifted him off the ground. He landed on his back ten feet away. Epsilon sat up, his mind reeling. Something silver caught his eye nearby. Almost acting on its own, his hand quickly went to it.

It was his *tru'kat.*

Epsilon thrust out his staff as Nexus raised his arm. He erected an energy shield just in time to absorb the blast. The vibration rippled through his arms and down his back.

"Now I can fight, asshole!" Epsilon screamed as he got up and fired an energy blast of his own.

Major Xantis felt his stomach drop into his feet as he and the remaining personnel at Warehouse 31C watched CNN's live coverage of the battle.

"How the hell did it wind up there?" one man wondered.

"Sure does get around," said another.

Xantis quickly walked over to the communications suite and called General Clay.

"Fullback. We have an update . . ."

"The one in the armor matches description of the figure that has been reported throughout Philadelphia recently," Waldon commented as the armored guy fended off another blast from the Energy Man. "How it got here in Riyadh is unknown. It appears to be generating some kind of . . . deflector shield, I guess . . . to protect itself from the Energy Man's beams. No idea how long it can hold out against such power."

Waldon prayed Lamaoto framed the shot perfectly when the guy in armor fired at the airborne Energy Man. He fired back after the beam failed to penetrate his dark aura. The armored guy blocked that shot as well. He then pushed off and flew toward Energy Man.

"My God. He's flying. No jets, no—" *Shit! We're losing him.* "C'mon, George!"

" . . . Now we're getting word of a second . . . person involved in the attack on the city's Diplomatic Quarter," stated the reporter for BBC World Service. "Our information comes from CNN. They describe the second participant as wearing armor and carrying a staff. That is all the information we have for the moment.

"Right now I can see several fires burning to the west of me . . ."

Erich von Klest slammed his hand against the wall. "It's him! Otto, it's him. That damned Protector. He's in Riyadh with that other thing. Of all the times for this to happen." He braced himself against the wall with one hand, his body shaking with rage.

Kemp went over to him. "Their time will come, Erich. We must carry out our plan."

Von Klest pushed himself away from the wall, both hands balled into fists. They had done so much in two weeks, were on the brink of eliminating the *Juden* leadership. They couldn't call it off now.

But the Protector. He had to be eliminated, lest he interfere with the rise of the Fourth Reich. Unless that Energy Man thing killed him first.

No. I *want that pleasure.*

But the plan. We are just minutes away. How can I call it off now?

Suddenly cold daggers stabbed down the length of von Klest's spine. His hair stood on end. He turned around and saw Kemp hug himself, shivering. He felt it too.

Von Klest turned to the door. The Darkling floated in front of it.

"What are you waiting for? Kill the Protector!"

There's gotta be a way to get through this guy's shield, Remmler thought as he blasted Nexus, who immediately returned fire. He dodged the blast in mid-air.

Maybe if I just keep firing, I'll wear him down eventually.

Oh God, please let me come up with a better plan than that.

Epsilon loosed a rapid fire stream of blasts. Nexus's energy field absorbed them all. The two traded shots until one blast struck Epsilon on the left leg. He cartwheeled out of the sky and slammed into the street. Hundreds of tiny hammers battered his bones.

Get up, dammit!

Epsilon groaned and shook off the pain.

"What the hell does it take to kill you!?" He heard Nexus holler before he fired. Epsilon moved to the right and avoided the blast. With one leap he returned to the sky.

This is useless! Nexus thought as he flew after Epsilon. *At this rate we could spend eternity exchanging shots. I have to get that staff away from him. That appears to be the key to his power.*

Perhaps a more physical course of action is needed.

Nexus added more power to his energy field. Epsilon hovered in front of the German Embassy, lining up for another shot. Drovinov angled his body and dove at him. Epsilon fired two shots that were absorbed by the field. Nexus did not slow down.

Epsilon tried to bank right. Too late. Nexus struck him square in the torso. He tumbled through the sky and crashed through the embassy.

It took a few moments for Nexus to right himself. He shut his eyes and rubbed his temples. His body ached. Despite his protective field, the impact with Epsilon shook his entire body.

How can this be? I shouldn't feel pain. True the few high-explosive shells that hit him during his attack on *Kitty Hawk* left him with momentary discomfort. But nothing like what he felt now.

When he opened his eyes, Nexus saw the hole in the side of the embassy made by Epsilon. Could he have survived that? He had withstood his strongest blasts and repeated contacted with his energy field. What was that armor made out of? No substance on Earth had been able to withstand his energy until now.

Perhaps it is extra-terrestrial in nature. I've never believed such things before. But how else to explain it?

He noticed movement on the street. Two police jeeps stopped near the German Embassy. Approaching from the opposite end of the street was an eight-wheeled LAV-25 APC of the Saudi National Guard.

Nexus ignored them. The soldiers could do nothing to him. Epsilon on the other hand . . .

A ball of fire tore the roof in two. All the windows blew out. The blast hurled Epsilon from the shattered office where he landed through the outside wall. He plummeted six stories. Remmler blacked out for a moment. He came to just as he slammed into the ground. The world blurred for a few seconds. He picked himself up, blinking until he stopped seeing double.

I can't take . . . much more . . . of this.

Remmler grit his teeth against the pain. There wasn't an inch of his body that didn't hurt. Most of the armor's upper body was caked in deep black. The number of cracks and dents doubled.

Thank God it's so strong. Otherwise I'd be dead already.

Raising his staff over his head, Epsilon took to the air. He closed his eyes and went to unisense. Nexus hovered on the other side of the building. If he could-

Suddenly he picked up something heading toward him.

"Shit!" *It's-*

Epsilon's back exploded in fire. The side of the embassy filled his vision. He then crashed through it.

"Oh God!" Epsilon cried in agony as something pushed him to the floor. He rolled over and opened his eyes. A quick breath froze in his throat. *Oh God, no.*

Imperium towered over him.

"Hello . . . Protector. We have some unfinished business to attend to."

FORTY-TWO

PAUL DRAKE MOANED as consciousness slowly returned. He sat up, pieces of plaster tumbling off him. The hazy smoke in the hallway blurred his vision. Still he could see the pile of debris just ten feet away, where moments—or maybe minutes, hours—ago, Captain Everett Lawson stood.

"Everett," he coughed. "Aw shit. Ev."

Can't think about that now. Gotta find out what happened.

Drake slowly rose to his feet. Pain shot down his back. Pulling out a handkerchief, he covered his mouth and headed down the hallway. What could have hit the Embassy? SCUDs? Car bomb? Was anyone else alive?

The CIA man's jaw dropped when he descended the stairs to the second floor. "Oh my God."

The entire front of the building was gone. Small fires crackled here and there. The bodies of two Marines and four embassy staffers lay among the debris, some with horrible burns. He could see smoke billowing from the embassy across the street.

Drake turned away and made for the communications

room, climbing over a fallen section of wall to reach it. He saw no one inside. All the equipment appeared damaged.

Washington had to be notified. But how? Drake looked around the room, cluttered with debris and filled with smoke and dust. Maybe the Marine guards had some field radios that survived-

His eyes fell upon a padlocked wall locker. Quick as he could, Drake worked his way back to his office and retrieved his Sig-Sauer P225 9mm pistol. When he returned, he put the barrel to the side of the padlock and fired. He knocked off its shattered remains and flung open the locker. He grabbed the first compact video camera he saw and quickly checked it out. Everything looked fine, including, most importantly, the folded antenna that could be extended to a height of twelve feet and bounce signals off an orbiting satellite and back to Washington. Certainly someone at either CIA or NSA headquarters would pick it up.

Tucking the pistol in his waistband, Drake inserted a tape into the camera and dashed outside.

"What the hell is he doing!?" Iraq's President screamed as he entered the command center of his bunker outside Baghdad. He had been touring anti-aircraft installations around the city for the benefit of Iraqi TV when he received word of the Riyadh attack.

An army captain pointed to a television monitor on the wall showing CNN. The President turned and saw Nexus firing at the Canadian Embassy.

"Drovinov! What the hell are you doing!? You were only supposed to attack the oil field!"

The President turned back to the captain, eyes wide and teeth bared. "Why is Professor Drovinov attacking Riyadh!?"

The officer swallowed, trembling as he spoke. "We-we do not know, sir. He did attack Al Ghawar, then for some reason, attacked Riyadh. And . . . and . . ."

"And what, dammit!"

"Something . . . something else is in Riyadh. Fighting Nexus. A . . . person in armor."

He turned to General Nurabi, who along with the Defense Minister, accompanied him on his trip. "Find out about this armored person. Why is he in Riyadh with Nexus? GO!!"

Nurabi silently left the room and headed for his office. He shook his head when he was out of his leader's sight. It had only been a matter of time before someone with that kind of power turned against his masters. Now his country had something worse to fear than the American Coalition.

"What is the status of our shock forces?" the President asked the Defense Minister.

"Most of them are in place. The infantry units, however—"

"Commence Operation: Driving Wind at once."

The Defense Minister's face fell. "But . . . but we're not ready to—"

"Nexus has forced our hand. He attacked Riyadh too soon. The Americans will not let this go unpunished.

"Alert all field commanders. Operation: Driving Wind begins immediately."

Remmler tried to ignore the pounding of his heart. He nearly laughed, remembering the times he hoped for a rematch against Imperium. How macho. How stupid. Nexus was kicking his ass. Imperium *had* kicked his ass. Damn near killed him. What chance did he have against him now?

"What . . . what the hell are you doing here?" Epsilon tried to stand up. His trembling knees wouldn't allow it.

"I heard about you on the news," answered Imperium, holding his Warblade by the end. "Fighting the thing that sunk the American carrier. This saves me the trouble of having to hunt you down and finish what I started."

"But Nexus is gonna level Riyadh," he cried desperately. "He could start a war. A nuclear war."

"As if I care whether a hundred million Arabs die in ashes."

Remmler held his breath. The screams he heard earlier flying over the city filled his mind. Those were real people out there. Not abstracts the way Imperium treated them. How many had suffered because of Nexus? How many more would suffer? How many families would grieve after today? Families like Cheryl's.

His fists clenched. "You sick son of a bitch."

"This time, no running away, coward." Von Klest raised the Warblade over his head. "Your *tru'kat* shall be mine!"

"NOOO!!" Epsilon raised his staff to his chest as Imperium brought down his Warblade. A horrible clang of metal on metal rang out. Epsilon felt Imperium's *tru'kat* push down on his.

Epsilon slipped his right leg between Imperium's legs and swept them out from under him. He fell to his right, his elbow going through the floor. Epsilon rolled away and got up. That's when he noticed Nexus hovering outside.

"Two of them!" a startled Drovinov said as he observed Epsilon and a dark armored figure through the large hole in the wall. *Where did the other one come from? Where did they both come from? That armor of theirs is fantastic. It cannot have come from Earth.*

Unfortunately, I cannot afford wonderment at this time.

Nexus raised his arms and fired. Epsilon burst through the roof just as the blast connected. Another ball of fire raced through the top floor of the embassy. He couldn't see the other armored man. Epsilon twisted around in mid-air and fired at Nexus. Each hit caused him to wince in pain.

"Die, damn you!" Nexus hissed through clenched teeth. He fired back at Epsilon, missing.

Epsilon fired two more blasts. Drovinov felt his bones

rattle as they hit his energy field. For a fleeting moment, he feared the beams would penetrate and-

No! That can never happen. I am invincible. I am Nexus!

Epsilon dove out of the way as Nexus returned fire. Suddenly something exploded behind him. No, not an explosion. More like a crumbling sound. He looked back at the embassy.

The black spaceknight broke through the wall of the building. He did not even look singed from the blast.

It turned on Epsilon and fired. Before he could bring up his staff, the beam struck him square in the chest. Epsilon tumbled through the air and into a palm tree. Shredded leaves swarmed around him. A moment later he slammed against the wall surrounding the embassy.

Nexus glanced back and forth between Epsilon and the newcomer. As if one wasn't bad enough, now he faced another armored thing that apparently had the same powers as Epsilon.

He considered teaming up with this figure in black to destroy Epsilon. That lasted all of one second. Anyone with that kind of power was a rival, a threat.

Nexus fired at the black figure. It dodged the blast and fired twice, scoring one hit. The Russian flew backwards and unleashed a blast. The spaceknight avoided it and returned fire.

Epsilon rubbed his globular head. It didn't seem to alleviate the pain. How much more could he take? This was even worse than the beating Imperium gave him on Springfield Trail.

Speaking of which . . .

He looked up as he struggled to his feet. Imperium was right on top of Nexus, Warblade held high. Suddenly a black beam burst out of Nexus' energy field and nailed Imperium pointed blank. Epsilon's head snapped as he watched the maniac soar over the embassy compound. He disappeared behind the wall. A second later Epsilon's enhanced hearing picked up the deep crunch of shattered asphalt.

I should just let them kill one another. I'd have a better chance of living through this.

Remmler closed his eyes. He thought of his family. Of Cheryl.

NO!! I won't be a coward again!

He opened his eyes and tracked Nexus across the compound. The *tru'kat* sprang up in his hands. A green bolt leapt from the spherical tip and impacted Nexus' energy field.

"Die, motherfucker!" One beam after another left his staff. He scored three more hits. Nexus looked staggered.

"Now I got-"

A black beam struck the ground ten feet away. The world shook. Oxygen rushed out of Remmler's lungs. The ground slammed into his back.

Epsilon groaned and shook his head. Fighting through the pain, he pushed himself to his knees and glanced up.

Nexus slowly descended toward him.

"Oh shit," Remmler pushed the words out of his tight throat. He turned to the wall and fired, blowing out a huge hole. He dove through just as Nexus landed. Epsilon did a forward roll, sprang to his feet and spun around, *tru'kat* at the ready. Nexus blew away the rest of the wall and hurried through the dust and debris.

"You've annoyed me long enough." The butcher raised an energy-laden fist. "Whatever you are."

Epsilon crouched slightly, *tru'kat* aimed at Nexus. The lunatic was barely five feet away. Maybe a point blank shot would-

"Oh please. You look ridiculous. None of your laser beams can affect me. All you're doing is prolonging your death."

"Guess I'm just too stubborn to know when to quit, asshole."

"Insolent pig! How dare you speak to me that way?"

"Excuse me. Who the hell died and made you king?"

Epsilon didn't need his enhanced senses to know that last comment enraged Nexus. The man's body shook with anger. Fists clenched. His jaw quivered. Epsilon wondered if anyone had ever dissed this guy like he just did.

"Degenerate scum!" Nexus bellowed as he blasted away at Epsilon's shield. "I possess the power of a god. You should be groveling at my feet!"

Nexus didn't let up. Remmler muscles began to go numb. He clenched his teeth and took a step back.

"Dust has settled," the LAV-25 gunner informed his commander over the Combat Vehicle Crewman helmet's radio. "Targets acquired. Ready to fire."

"I see them, Corporal," Staff Sergeant al-Talik poked his head out the commander's hatch when the armored vehicle stopped at the intersection.

"Permission to fire, Sergeant?"

"Let's wait. Maybe they'll kill one another. It looks like they're too busy to notice us anyway. But keep the gun trained on them. If they start this way, or if one of them survives, open fire."

"Yes, Sergeant."

"Sergeant! Sergeant!" the driver suddenly screamed. "There's another one in front!"

Al-Talik turned his head just as the infantrymen they recently deposited started hollering and firing their assault rifles. Staggering toward them was a sinister figure in black armor.

The Saudi's eyes went wide with fear. He shook it off and shouted, "Traverse left! Forty-five degrees!"

The gunner rotated the LAV's turret.

"Fire!"

Nothing.

"Fire!" Sergeant al-Talik screamed again. Seeing this thing must have shocked his gunner to inaction. He looked back down inside. "Fire, dammit! Fire!"

Like an automaton, the corporal clutched the joystick and pulled the trigger to the Bushmaster cannon. The weapon erupted with a deep *pop-pop-pop*, spraying 25mm fire at the approaching figure. The big rounds, designed to rip apart lightly armored vehicles, harmlessly bounced off the thing's armor. It casually clipped a large boomerang to one leg and rushed forward.

"Backupbackupbackup!" Sergeant al-Talik cried.

"He's still coming!" the gunner shouted at the same time.

Nothing happened for a second. Then the nineteen-year-old driver below al-Talik threw the gears into reverse.

"What the hell!?" Drake blurted as he saw the LAV-25 down the street suddenly rise off the ground. The soldiers around it scattered. He spotted an abandoned delivery van ten feet away and took cover behind it, keeping the camera on the APC and-

Something was wrong with the image. It wouldn't hold steady. It took him a few seconds to realize his hand was shaking.

Drake didn't bother saying anything for the camera's microphone. He didn't have to. The image spoke for itself. The man in the commander's hatch spilled out of the vehicle and landed on the back of his neck. He lay on the street unmoving as the figure in black armor lifted the fourteen-ton LAV over his head.

Epsilon timed his leap perfectly, going to his left and dodging Nexus' beam. He rolled into a crouch, brought up his staff and fired. Nexus flinched as the bolt hit his energy field. Epsilon jumped backwards as Nexus returned fire. He missed again.

That's when he heard the screams. Echoic, as if trapped inside a garbage can. He switched to unisense.

Imperium stood fifteen yards away, an armored vehicle over his head.

"Catch, swine."

Epsilon forgot about Nexus as the LAV-25 hurtled toward him. Both the gunner and driver screamed at the top of their lungs, pleading with Allah for His protection. Epsilon dropped his *tru'kat. The crewmen* was his only thought as he brought up his arms to catch the LAV.

Remmler thought his brain got knocked out of his body when the rear of the vehicle slammed into him. His ears rang with the horrible crunch of metal on metal. His feet left the ground. He had no idea how long he was airborne. He didn't even realize he had screamed when he hit the ground with the LAV-25 on top of him.

FORTY-THREE

"NOW IT'S YOUR turn!" Imperium hollered as he leaped into the air. He had to dispatch Nexus quickly, and the Protector as well. Then he could tend to matters in Israel. He'd been just minutes away from the assault when he phoned Heinbrodder to tell him to wait.

Two blasts from Imperium's *tru'kat* impacted against Nexus' energy field. Nexus backed away for a moment, then returned fire. Imperium blocked the shot with his forcefield. He extended the green circle forward until it slammed into Nexus.

"No," he groaned, trying to hold his ground against the beam pushing against his energy field. "Can't . . . be . . . beaten."

Von Klest smiled under his dark armor. "Yes you can."

Drake hurried to the intersection just as the Saudi soldiers got to crewman's body. Two of them raised their G3s, then relaxed when they saw the camera in his hand. They probably thought he was a member of the press.

"Is he dead?" Drake directed his question to the soldier with the most stripes, who was leaning over the body.

"Yes. Broken neck."

Drake looked down. The man's helmet had an ugly crack on the top. Blood poured from his mouth and ears.

"Who are you?" asked the Master Sergeant whose stitched on nametag read "al-Kazumbri."

"My name is . . . Mr. Drake. I work at the American Embassy." Drake spoke in flawless Arabic.

"You'd best leave. This is no place for civilians."

"Thank you for your concern. But I think my government would like this documented. See what we can learn."

"Learn!?" al-Kazumbri exclaimed. "What's there to learn? Those . . . monsters are destroying the city. Bullets, cannons. Nothing seems to affect them."

"Except themselves," Drake replied as he got a shot of the Energy Man and the "black knight" fighting. "Maybe they'll wind up killing one another and spare the rest of us a lot of grief."

"Perhaps." The Sergeant drew a breath and looked back at Drake. "If you insist on staying here, I suggest you find cover and stay out of our way."

"No problem. What do you plan to do?"

Al-Kazumbri shook his head. "I wish I knew."

Epsilon scanned inside the LAV-25. Nothing he could do for the gunner. The impact broke his neck. The driver, however, was alive, though not in the best of shape. His right leg was bent at an awkward angle and stuck between the wheel and one of the gearshifts. Blood flowed into his left eye from a nasty gash on the forehead. His head lolled back and forth as he moaned.

Nexus and Imperium were still going at it behind him. Hopefully they'd be too busy trying to kill one another to bother him while he rescued the soldier.

Epsilon sat up and reached under the LAV-25. His neck and arm muscles tightened as he started to lift. He groaned for a few seconds until the armored vehicle came off his legs. Epsilon then set it beside him. The breath he'd been holding rushed out of his lungs. He slowly got to his feet and shook out the tension in his arms.

Damn. That was kinda heavy. Even for me.

It took just a moment for Epsilon's unisense to find his *tru'kat.* He retrieved it and went over to the LAV-25's sloped hood. The blade easily sank through the vehicle's steel hide. Epsilon made one diagonal slice and two vertical ones around the dazed driver, careful to keep the blade away from the man's body. With one hand, he pushed through the vertical cut, clenched it and yanked. The section came off like cardboard. He casually flung it over his shoulder.

The driver opened his eyes . . . and screamed.

"It's okay. I'm here to help."

The young Saudi kept screaming.

"I'm not gonna hurt you. I'm—" *Aw hell, I don't have time for this.* Epsilon reached in, grabbed the metal steering column and bent it toward him. With great care he pulled the wailing driver through the opening and scooped him up in his arms. He noticed more soldiers down the street. They should be able to help this dude.

Epsilon hurried toward the soldiers. They raised their rifles.

"Hold your fire!" one soldier said. "He has someone."

They backed away as Epsilon stopped and laid the LAV-25 driver on the street.

"Get this man medical attention now," he ordered. "Looks like he broke his leg."

"What are—?"

"No time," Epsilon abruptly cut him off. He looked over the group, trying to pick out the guy in charge. When no clear winner emerged, he just spoke to all of them. "Look, we got a major slugfest here. Clear outta here now. Find any civilians you can and get them outta here too."

The soldiers looked at one another for a few seconds.

The guy with all the sergeant's stripes nodded and led his squad down the street. One of the soldiers picked up the wounded driver, slung him over one shoulder and carried him away. Only the moron with the camera remained.

"Move it, dude! You wanna die!"

Epsilon turned away and flew back toward Nexus and Imperium.

"Looks like one of them is on our side," the President stated. He and the others in the White House Situation room watched the NSA's feed from Fort Meade of the man in charred, white armor rescuing the Saudi soldier.

"That's the one who's been seen around Philadelphia," DCI Brock responded. "The press calls it the Knight."

"I'd like to know how it got to Riyadh," Baronelli said. "My God, what the hell is it?"

"Whatever it is, it didn't look like it fared too well against that Energy Man," Admiral Callingworth leaned closer to the screen. "Or the one in the black armor."

"Then we better pray he does better." Lydia Preston's eyes flickered between CNN's coverage and Drake's video feed.

"There's no guarantee that White Knight won't turn on us as well."

Preston turned to the Admiral, her voice going up an octave. "How can you say that? You saw him . . . it rescue that soldier. It went out of its way to do so. It's fighting against those two other things trying to destroy Riyadh. How can you be so blind? That White Knight is on our side."

"Maybe now he is, but you've seen what kind of power it has. And I take it you're familiar with the old saying about how power corrupts?"

Preston nodded as Callingworth went on. "He could be a hero today. Tomorrow he could be the one blasting Riyadh off the map. Or Philadelphia, or New York . . . or Washington."

The Chairman of the Joint Chiefs of Staff stepped back from the table and looked over at the President, who sat at the head of the table. "Mr. President, we have no idea what these things are, where they come from. What little we know about their capabilities is frightening. Directed energy projection. Invulnerability to conventional weapons. Superhuman strength. Flight. They may have other powers we haven't seen yet.

"Look what they've done so far. The Energy Man alone destroyed one of our carrier battle groups and probably the Al Ghawar oil field. Even if we do throw our chips in with that White Knight, if he loses, those other two will be free to wreak more havoc. Millions, even billions of lives, could be jeopardized. We may have no choice but to end it ourselves."

"How, Admiral?" The President folded his hands on the table. "As you say, conventional weapons are useless against them."

Callingworth paused for a breath. "Mr. President, believe me I wish I didn't have to say this, much less think it. We may, as a last resort, may have to consider a nuclear strike against Riyadh—" Everyone at the table gasped in disbelief. "—to ensure these things don't escape and unleash more harm."

"I don't believe I'm hearing this!" the Vice President threw up his hands. "You're suggesting we drop nuclear weapons on Saudi Arabia!? One of our *allies!?* That's madness!"

Callingworth continued undeterred. "The *Michigan* can retarget one of her missiles at Riyadh. We've got all these things in one location. We may never get another opportunity like this."

"How do we know nuclear weapons will even work on them?"

"I doubt anything can survive eight one-hundred kiloton warheads. It's the only chance we've got."

"We have to tell the King about this," the VP said in a

hushed voice, still not totally believing Callingworth's suggestion. "Get his consent."

"There's no way in hell he'll give us permission to nuke his own capitol," Baronelli said.

"Mr. President, you can't seriously be considering this."

Everyone's blood froze when the President did not respond to his Chief of Staff.

"Mr. President—!"

"Dammit, Lydia! We're talking about the fate of the entire world if these things aren't stopped. Believe me, in my entire life, I never considered dropping a nuclear weapon on *any* country—much less an ally. But we may not have any choice."

"The world will never forgive us," Preston told him. "We'll become an international pariah."

"There may not be a world to hate us if we don't act." The President looked to Callingworth. "Tell the *Michigan* to target a missile at Riyadh. Right now, let's put our faith in that White Knight and hope it isn't misplaced. If he fails . . ." The President didn't even bother finishing his sentence.

"Yes, sir," Callingworth replied softly as he left the table.

The President slumped back in his chair and stared at the monitors. For the first time he wished he'd never been elected.

Which one do I take? Epsilon wondered as he stood by the overturned LAV-25 and watched Imperium fend off blasts from Nexus. If he tackled one of them, the other could easily blast him into oblivion. Or take off and level more of the city. Could he fight both of them at the same time?

I can't just sit around on my ass. I gotta do something.

Come on, Jack. Think. Think.

Suddenly it came to him.

Epsilon extended his *tru'kat* and barreled through the air.

Nexus ceased firing. Imperium stiffened. He started to turn around.

The *tru'kat's* spherical tip rammed into Imperium's back. He rocketed into Nexus' energy field. A black-gray flash ignited.

Epsilon floated inches above the street. His entire body trembled. He never saw Imperium carom back at him.

CRASH!! Epsilon's world spun out of control. Something heavy pressed against him, pushing him backwards.

Suddenly the air vanished. A grinding, crunching noise surrounded him. Remmler managed to open his eyes. A spider web of cracks covered his visor.

Finally he stopped. Epsilon lay in the fissure of asphalt. Pain blanketed his body. Somehow he could feel his armor's barrel chest had caved in. It hurt too much to move, to breathe, even to moan.

Gotta . . . get up. Move. Fight.

Remmler's brain sent out the impulses. The body refused to obey.

No. No. Can't quit.

This time Remmler forced a painful breath into his lungs. He did it again and again, fighting the crushing pain. He guessed a minute had passed before he tried to rise. Some great weight pinned him to the ground.

"Get off." Epsilon groaned and pushed up with his right hand. Imperium rolled off him and came to rest face down in the shattered street. Amazingly, he managed to hold on to his boomerang-like *tru'kat.*

Epsilon struggled to his feet, wobbling from side to side. He unconsciously stretched out his right hand. The *tru'kat* flew into it.

Don't . . . let him . . . get up.

Drawing another breath, Epsilon took a step toward Imperium's prone form. He rammed the *tru'kat's* spherical tip into the base of the bastard's neck. Imperium's face sank deeper into what remained of the asphalt.

Epsilon dropped to the ground, his right knee coming

down hard on Imperium's back. All the air exploded from his lungs in a sickening gasp. Epsilon got to his feet and sent a vicious kick into Imperium's side. He soared off the ground and smashed through a nearby wall.

The dust and smoke around them thickened. Remmler closed his eyes and switched to unisense. Imperium rolled from side to side amidst the rubble. He never stopped groaning.

Epsilon stumbled toward him. "You're not-"

He froze as Imperium brought up his right arm. His dark *tru'kat* was pointed straight at Epsilon. An instant later the blast struck him under the duck-billed visor. Epsilon's head snapped back. He cried out in pain and fell to the ground.

Nexus noticed his energy field fluctuate as he struggled to his feet. Pain racked his entire body. Those energy blasts contained much more power than the bullets and shells he'd faced so far. He'd also used his power more than at any other time since his "rebirth." Perhaps he needed to rest. Regain his strength.

No! Weakness is a human trait. I am Nexus. Power incarnate. I cannot *be weak.*

Epsilon managed to get to his knees when something smashed against the side of his head. Imperium's *tru'kat* dented Epsilon's globular head and knocked him on his side. He barely rolled away as a black foot smashed through the street inches from his head. Epsilon sat up and used his *tru'kat* to block Imperium's blade. The s.o.b. drew his dark *tru'kat* back for another strike. Epsilon got to one knee in time to block the second swing. He pushed himself to his feet and took a clumsy swipe with his *tru'kat.* Imperium easily blocked it. Epsilon slashed again . . . again . . . again. Imperium blocked all three blows. In desperation, Epsilon thrust his staff at Imperium. He sidestepped, grabbed the *tru'kat* and pulled.

Epsilon surged forward and fell spread-eagled to the street. Before he could get up, Imperium moved in behind him. The dark *tru'kat* came down around Epsilon's throat. Imperium gripped both ends of the big boomerang, put a knee against Epsilon's back and reared back. Epsilon dropped his *tru'kat* and wrapped both hands around Imperium's blade. Try as he might, he couldn't budge it.

"Your armor is not indestructible, you know. Eventually, I will cut my way through."

Epsilon felt the metal around his neck begin to rend.

"I'll mount your head over my dinner table, you insolent slug." Imperium hissed. "You won't ruin my plans!"

He applied more pressure with each word.

Epsilon continued to push against the dark *tru'kat.* Little by little, it began to peel away at his armored hands. The blade sank deeper into his throat.

No! I can't let him beat me again.

Epsilon suddenly went limp. Caught off guard, Imperium's hold inadvertently slackened. Epsilon reached around, grabbed Imperium's wrists and bent forward. The bastard soared over his back and slammed into the ground. Epsilon drove the heel of his palm into Imperium's face. Imperium twisted to his right. His left arm swept up and caught Epsilon in the temple. He fell on all fours, dazed. Imperium scrambled to his feet and lifted his leg. Epsilon "saw" it with his unisense and rolled away. Imperium's heel cracked the pavement when it came down. Planting both hands on the ground, Epsilon kicked out his left leg and struck Imperium's ankle. He pitched forward and landed on his face. Epsilon gave Imperium a chop to the back of the neck. He rolled away and got to his feet before the scumbag could retaliate.

"Damn swine," Imperium growled as he got to his knees. "You should have stayed wherever it was you ran off to the first time. You won't be as lucky this time."

Rage flooded every part of Jack Remmler's body. Visions

of the battle at Springfield Trail flashed through his mind. In an instant he relived the beating Imperium had given him. Felt the stark terror that turned him into a coward. Made him run away. That dark moment had clawed at him every day since. Remmler wondered if it would ever go away.

His eyes burned into Imperium's jet black armor. "Fuck you!" Epsilon charged forward. His foot swept off the ground and smashed into Imperium's ribs. "This is payback, motherfucker!"

Epsilon kicked again. This time Imperium swatted his foot away. Epsilon struggled to maintain his balance. Imperium got up and sent a high kick into Epsilon's charred, dented torso. He fell to the ground.

DAMMIT!! NOT AGAIN!! Epsilon struggled to sit up. Imperium's foot knocked him back down.

Fear welled up in Remmler again. He tried to move, but couldn't. Imperium just stood over him, as if savoring the moment before the kill.

Oh my God! He's doing it again! No matter what I do, it isn't enough.

This crazy son of a bitch is gonna kill me!

FORTY-FOUR

EPSILON'S EYES REFUSED to leave Imperium's dark *tru'kat* as he raised it over his head.

Dammit, Jack! Don't let this bastard win again. Think of your family. Cheryl. The world!

DO SOMETHING!!!

Imperium's *tru'kat* came down. Epsilon brought his arms up. His hands clapped together around the blade. The veins in his arms threatened to burst free as he strained against the pressure. The dark *tru'kat's* tip halted inches above his cracked faceplate.

Shit! It worked!

Imperium yanked the blade free with one tug. Epsilon turned on his side and kicked out his right leg. Imperium's feet left the ground. His rearend crashed through the asphalt.

Epsilon scrambled to his feet and stretched out his hand. His *tru'kat* leapt into the air. Before it could reach him, Imperium jumped up and kicked the staff away in mid-air. His left fist then rocketed into Epsilon's gut. A tremor shot through his mid-section. Epsilon stumbled to his left and fell.

Imperium picked up Epsilon's *tru'kat* and flung it down the street. It disappeared in the smoke and haze.

Remmler's eyes widened. *Oh shit. Now what?*

Imperium turned back around, his greenish-red eyeslit locked on Epsilon. "Let's see how well you fight without your staff."

Gripping his blade by the end, Imperium strode over to Epsilon.

"Shit!" Epsilon stretched out his hand to summon his *tru'kat.*

"Not this time." Imperium fired at Epsilon's forearm. Splinters of blackened, alien metal exploded into the air. Epsilon screamed and grabbed his numb arm. Only his unisense warned him when Imperium was close enough to take a swipe. He rolled out of the blade's path.

"I've wasted enough time with you." Imperium took another unsuccessful swing. Epsilon pushed himself to his feet and backed away. Imperium charged and swung his *tru'kat* again. Epsilon jumped back. He ducked under a fourth swipe, then wrapped his left hand around Imperium's wrist, forced up his arm and snaked his right hand around. With his opponent in a wristlock, Epsilon pulled him over and held on until the bastard was on his back. He dropped down and rammed a knee into Imperium's outstretched arm. The scumbag growled in pain and loosened his grip on the *tru'kat.* Epsilon twisted Imperium's wrist until he let go completely. He then grabbed the blade and tossed it across the street.

Yes! A smile formed on Remmler's lips. "Not so high and mighty now, are ya, asshole?"

Imperium rolled on his side and arced his fist into Epsilon's temple. He grimaced, trying to get to his feet. Imperium shoved him away. He tumbled to the ground, but quickly got up.

Don't give up now, Jack. We're even now without our tru'kats.

"C'mon. Let's see how well you fight without *your* little toy."

"I'm still more than a match for you," Imperium replied as he stood up.

"Prove it, dickhead."

Imperium looked about ready to shake apart with rage. "Insolent swine!"

Epsilon blocked the dark warrior's initial high kick. Imperium followed with a punch to the midsection. Epsilon blocked that as well. Then he kicked at Imperium's left knee, missing. Imperium dropped to the ground and swept out his right leg, taking Epsilon off his feet. A second after he hit the ground he rolled away.

Something caught Remmler's eye. A long, rounded, scorched piece of metal lying on the street. A streetlight. He rushed over, scooped it up and held it in front of him as Imperium approached.

"Is that supposed to frighten me?"

Epsilon took a swing. Imperium blocked the pole with his left arm and chopped it in two with his right hand.

"Shit." Epsilon chucked what remained of the pole at Imperium. He ducked right, sprang forward and chopped Epsilon across the throat. Imperium followed up with a fist to the head, knocking Epsilon to the ground.

Nexus took a few more deep breaths. His strength was nearly restored. Those two armored freaks had given him a much needed respite. With any luck, they would be worn out from fighting one another.

He raised a crackling black fist and started over to Epsilon and Imperium. *You two have given me enough grief.*

That's all I need, Remmler thought as he saw Nexus coming toward them. Imperium stopped his attack when his senses also picked up the Energy Man's approach.

"You again!"

"There is only room on this world for *one* omnipotent

being. You two have delayed me long enough. I have an empire to create. An empire to which you two are a threat."

Epsilon shook his head. "Man, this guy's lost it."

Nexus seemed determined to take out Imperium first. *Fine with me. Give me time to find my* tru'kat. *Or Imperium's. If it'll work for me.*

Remmler closed his eyes and switched to unisense. He sensed Imperium's feet shuffle slightly. He was getting ready to move to avoid the blast. Maybe . . .

Epsilon got into a catcher's crouch. He tensed, letting his unisense take over.

"Don't think you can defeat me so easily," Imperium boasted.

"Without your weapon, I can. Farewell."

Nexus raised his arms. Imperium moved to his left. At the same time Epsilon pushed off with all his strength.

A black ray sprang from Nexus' energy fied. Epsilon clipped Imperium's side, spinning him around. The beam hit Imperium squarely in the back. His screams were drowned out by the thunderous explosion. Thin layers of ultra strong armor shattered and burned away. Imperium soared twenty-five feet through the air and landed in a heap. The blastwave hurtled Epsilon through the wall of an embassy compound. He blacked out.

"Yes, Nexus! Yes!" Iraq's President leaped out of his chair after watching his "smart weapon" apparently dispatch the two armored figures. "Kill them! Kill them!"

General Nurabi bit his lower lip in frustration. The President just didn't—or wouldn't—accept the fact Drovinov was no longer their weapon. Allah help them all if he decided to return to Baghdad.

Von Klest felt his consciousness slowly ebbing away. Never in his life had he experienced such pain. Everything was jumbled, confused. He couldn't tell where Epsilon or Nexus were.

Have to . . . get . . . out . . . Oh God, the pain.

Von Klest slowly raised his arm. Fire shot through every muscle.

Father . . . I'm sorry . . . I failed.

It took him two seconds to realize the Warblade was in his hand.

Nexus stared at the black spaceknight in shock. "No," he whispered. "How can he still be alive?"

He moved closer, summoning more power. This thing couldn't take much more. Eventually it had to die. It couldn't be immortal.

Suddenly a bright glow surrounded the spaceknight's body.

"What the—?" Drovinov blinked his eyes and watched in astonishment as the blue-gold glow subsided, and with it the spaceknight.

"Incredible." Was he dead? Discorperated somehow? Or—what was the term the Americans used—teleported?

In any event, he was gone. That left only Epsilon.

Nexus paused and looked over to the hole in the concrete wall. No sign of-

Suddenly, an arm came through the hole. Epsilon pulled himself out and rolled onto his back.

Nexus clenched his fists. *This will be easy.*

"Erich!" Kemp rushed over to Imperium after he rematerialized on the floor of their hotel room. Wisps of smoke rose from his back.

"Erich! Erich!" Tears welled up in Otto Kemp's eyes as he tried to turn Imperium over.

Von Klest mumbled something.

"What? Erich, what?" Kemp leaned over and put his ear next to Imperium's head.

"Otto?" Von Klest's voice was very weak.

"Yes, Erich. It's me. Otto. My God, what happened?"

Von Klest's head moved slightly from side to side. "I'm . . . I'm back . . . in . . . Jerusalem?"

"Yes. Yes, you are.

"Erich. The mission. The men are waiting. But . . . but with you in this condition . . ."

"M-Mission?" his voice faded. "What . . . mission?"

"To destroy the Knesset. Don't you remember?" Kemp didn't even try to stop the tears. *Oh, Erich. Why did you ever accept this accursed thing?*

"Erich?" He gently nudged his dear friend's shoulder. "Erich. Erich!"

Erich von Klest made no sounds. He lay still on the floor.

Kemp's insides collapsed. "No," he croaked, convulsing with each sob. "Erich, no."

Failure smothered him, oozed through his veins. He'd served the von Klest family since Erich's grandfather, Wolfgang, took him into the Hitler Youth. Kemp so impressed the Waffen S.S. colonel that he was offered passage with the family when they fled Germany after World War Two. Once in Uruguay he befriended Wolfgang's son, Wilhelm, who took over the Colonel's organization after his death. Kemp became a surrogate father to Erich after his parents died; Ilse to suicide, Wilhelm to colon cancer.

I failed them. I failed their son.

Even through his grief, a hint of professionalism pecked at Kemp. They had a mission to carry out. But now that Erich...

He unclipped the cellphone from his back pocket and dialed a special number. Major Heinbrodder answered.

"Abort mission. Repeat. Abort mission."

FORTY-FIVE

I CAN'T TAKE THIS *anymore,* Remmler thought as he lay in the rubble. Every breath hurt. *I just wanna go home. Mom. Dad. Lisa . . . Cheryl. I don't wanna die.*

He glanced down at his armor, amazed at all the damage it had taken . . . and survived. The entire torso was dented and cracked. Deep black scorch marks covered his arms and crushed chest.

Epsilon's head drooped to the left. That's when he saw Nexus' legs coming toward him.

"Oh shit, no." Remmler choked back the tears. He struggled to remember the Hail Mary.

"I must admit, I am impressed," Nexus mocked as he circled his prey. "I didn't think anything could stand up to my power. Are you even from this world?"

Epsilon said nothing.

"I would at least like to know something about you before I kill you. What are you? Where do you come from? How did you get your powers?

"Answer me!"

Remmler's throat screamed in agony as he swallowed. Was this it? Was this how his nineteen years of life would end? No chance to be with Cheryl, maybe get married. No B.A., no sports reporting career. Maybe if he begged, pleaded . . .

No! I'm not gonna look like a coward again.

"Go . . . go fuck yourself."

Nexus scoffed. "Defiant to the end, eh? Foolish. Look at you! Your armor is shattered, your staff is gone. You should have stayed wherever it was you came from."

"I'm stubborn. Sue me. Why don't you go raise the damn Iraqi flag and leave me alone."

Nexus chuckled evilly. "You think *I* serve those self-delusional fools. They serve me. All mankind will serve me! No one can rival my power. I am beyond humanity. I am a god."

"No you're not," Epsilon said. He could feel some of his strength returning. *Maybe there's a chance.* He closed his eyes. "You're just a fucking lunatic . . . with a Napoleon complex." *Got it.* Epsilon lifted his right arm slightly and opened his palm. *Keep talking, asshole.*

"You think your words affect me? I am the most powerful being to ever walk this planet. If only those idiots in Moscow could see me now. I could destroy you any moment I wish. I can destroy anyone I want. No one can stop me."

Waldon and Lamaoto were running to get closer to the action when something whizzed by them.

"Whoa!" cried Lamaoto. "What the hell was that?"

Nexus started to bring his arms up when the *tru'kat* suddenly flew into Epsilon's hand.

"NOOO!!!"

Epsilon put all his strength into one desperate lunge. Nexus extended his energy field. Epsilon got caught halfway inside it. The mysterious energy bracketed his body like a hundred runaway Mack Trucks, trying to repel him. He bared with it, pushing his *tru'kat* with all his might through the field. It was like swimming in a tar pit.

The surface of his armor began to smolder. His progress could best be measured in centimeters. Epsilon concentrated on Nexus' torso. It seemed a thousand miles away.

I can't give up. Not with a chance like this.

Another thin layer of armor disintegrated. Several new cracks formed. All it took was one small opening and . . .

No! Remmler forced himself to think about his family, his friends, his country, the entire world. How would they suffer if this maniac wasn't stopped?

He ignored the excruciating pain. Remmler had no idea where he got the strength from. Right now he didn't care. Billions of lives depended on him.

Nexus increased the power of his field as he looked nervously down at Epsilon. His blade was alarmingly close to his body.

This can't happen! I am Nexus! I cannot die!

He felt the strength drain from his body. His eyes fought to stay open. Muscles turned to lead.

Nexus clenched his teeth. *I can . . . ignore it. I will ignore it! I am Nexus!*

His knees buckled. He felt the energy field weaken. The more power he exerted, the more tiredness overwhelmed him. By now Epsilon's entire torso was charred black. It shouldn't take much more to get through that armor and kill the worm inside.

Suddenly the field's intensity faded. Drovinov's strength went with it. *More power. More power.*

His tired brain refused to obey the command.

Nexus' field dropped for a second. It was all the time Epsilon needed. With a primal yell, he slashed Nexus across the midsection. The blade dug deep into his gut, slicing vital organs in half.

Nexus emitted a short gasp of pain. The dark aura around him flickered, exposing his natural human form. He stared dumbly at the opening in his gut. Blood and pieces of intestine spilled onto the ground. He tried unsuccessfully to stop the flow by covering it with his hands.

Epsilon picked himself up as Nexus sank to his knees. Their eyes met. Remmler found it impossible to tear away from Nexus' gaze.

The dying man's lips trembled as he tried to speak.

"B-Ba . . . Bas-tard," he croaked.

A chill shot up and down Remmler's body as he watched Nexus' eyes roll into his head. He pitched forward and lay motionless on the rubble. The crackling black energy field vanished. All that remained was a naked, silver-haired man with a puddle of blood around his stomach.

Remmler drew a breath and held it for several seconds. A shudder went through his body.

Oh my God. I killed him. I . . . killed another human being.

He reminded himself of all the destruction Nexus had caused. The *Kitty Hawk*. The oil field. Riyadh. How many tens of thousands did this man single-handedly kill? How many millions would have been killed? What about Cheryl and her family?

You had to do it, Jack. You had no choice.

Remmler repeated it over and over in his head. It didn't help get Nexus' distant, haunting death stare out of his mind.

"NOOO!!!" the Iraqi President screamed at the top of his lungs as he watched Nexus fall dead. A stunned expression formed on his face.

He fell back into his chair. No one spoke for a full minute.

Mr. President," the Defense Minister said hesitantly. "What about Operation: Driving Wind?"

The President did not respond.

"Mr. President!"

"I . . . heard you." He paused for a few seconds. "Cancel it. Call the troops back. It will not work without Nexus."

"At once, Mr. President."

As the Defense Minister went off to contact the shock units, General Nurabi offered a silent prayer to Allah, thanking Him for getting rid of the madman Drovinov.

Then he had another disturbing thought. What if that white spaceknight came after them next?

FORTY-SIX

WALDON SUCKED DOWN one last breath and turned to his cameraman. "Let's go."

"I hope you know what you're doing," Lamaoto muttered as they ran over to the armored man.

A mixture of excitement and fear ran through Waldon. Imagine getting the first interview with this . . . Knight thing. A real-life superhero. At least Waldon hoped it was a superhero. If that thing got a mad on, there'd be nothing he or George could do to stop it from ripping their heads off.

If he were a bad guy, he wouldn't have bothered saving the soldier in that tank, Waldon tried to convince himself. The attempt proved unsuccessful.

Paul Drake also ran over to this . . . whatever it was. He had to make contact with it. Get it away from the media. Try and cut a deal with it. Imagine what the CIA could do with an asset like this.

Epsilon just got to his feet, supported by his staff, when a CNN camera nearly slammed into his face.

"Can I get a quote!?" the reporter rattled off. "Who are you? Why were you fighting these men? Where do you come from?"

Epsilon groggily turned to the news crew and waved them off. "Gimmie a break, will ya. I feel like shit."

The reporter paused for a few moments, then pressed on. "Please. We're being seen all over the world. Just one quote. Who are you?"

Remmler looked back at the reporter. He had never been so tired in his entire life. All he wanted to do was teleport back to his dorm and sleep for a week.

On the other hand, this could be a great opportunity. I've got CNN right here. I could tell the whole world about me . . . about Epsilon. Tell people I'm here to protect them.

"My name . . . is Epsilon. I'm . . ."

The trio suddenly noticed someone bending down over Nexus' body and rolling it over. He pointed a camcorder at the dead man's face.

"Who are you?" Epsilon and the reporter asked the newcomer simultaneously.

Drake turned briefly to them, then returned his gaze to the body. The face looked familiar. He'd seen it in a photo somewhere. In his office, yes! The renegade scientists suspected of building nukes for Iraq. D-something. Dovor . . . Davro . . .

"Drovinov!" he unconsciously blurted.

"What? Who?"

Drake turned to the CNN crew and bit his lip. *Dammit! Next time, Paul, keep your mouth shut.*

The reporter went on. "Do you know who this man is?"

"No comment."

"Who are you with, sir?" The reporter nodded to Drovinov's body. "Was this man working for Iraq? Iran?"

"No *fucking* comment."

"How did a human being acquire this kind of power? Could there be others like him?"

Epsilon watched as the newcomer continued brushing off the CNN guy's questions. Who the hell was this dude? CIA? Maybe he knew something about Nexus. Only one way to-

The hair on Remmler's neck suddenly stood up. He wasn't using his unisense, but he could tell that some*thing*—some presence—was near.

Epsilon turned around.

It was the Keeper.

"Finally decided to show up, huh?" Epsilon said, instantly regretting it. A 300,000-year-old entity probably deserved more respect.

Apparently it didn't bother the Keeper. "Epsilon. I have need of you."

"Oh my God," the "CIA" dude muttered. The color drained from his face. He swung his camera around at the Keeper. "What is it?"

"What? What's going on?" the reporter and his cameraman stared obliviously in the Keeper's direction.

They can't see him. Only Epsilon and the "CIA" dude could see the Keeper.

"What's wrong? What is it?"

"I will show you."

The Keeper made no motion whatsoever. A white flash suddenly enveloped Epsilon and the "CIA" guy. Before a worldwide audience, the pair vanished into thin air.

Waldon's jaw drop. He stared blankly at the spot where Epsilon and the other guy had stood, dropping his mike to his side.

First chance I get, Waldon thought, *I'm getting the hell out of Saudi Arabia and heading for the nearest country where I can drink myself into oblivion.*

Epsilon felt no disorientation as he and his companion rematerialized at the bottom of a huge crater. The sand—fused into glass—crunched beneath their feet.

"What the hell's going on?" the man clamored, trying not to appear shaken. "How the hell did we get here?"

"Calm down, man," Epsilon reassured him. "Nothing's gonna happen to you."

He twisted from side to side, taking in the enormity of the crater.

"What the hell's that!?" The man spun around and aimed his camera. Remmler wondered if it was transmitting back to Washington. It had a pretty big antenna sticking out of it.

"What are—" Epsilon turned to see what he was excited about. Fifteen feet in front of him, a dark, shimmering portal hovered just above the ground.

"What in the hell?" Epsilon stammered. He was about to probe it with his unisense when the Keeper suddenly intruded.

"It is the product of the man Drovinov's mistake."

Epsilon turned to the Keeper, floating a few yards away. "What do you mean? What mistake? What . . ."

Remmler's jaw froze. He briefly gazed around the lip of the crater. "Oh my God. This is where the Iraqis set off that nuke, isn't it? That Nexus wacko was behind it? Is that how he got his powers?"

"Hold on a second," the "CIA" guy yelped. "We're in a fucking atomic bomb crater!? What the hell are you trying to do? Kill me? I've got no protection! Dammit, I've probably soaked up enough rads to give me terminal leukemia."

"Your hysteria is unwarranted, Paul Drake. The energies from this place cannot harm you. I have made sure of that."

The man, Drake, relaxed a bit.

"How is Nexus responsible for this?" asked Epsilon, pointing to the portal. "What *is* it?"

"The weapon Yuri Drovinov, Nexus as you call him, constructed was powered by an element not native to your planet. An element of hitherto unknown power for your people. Yuri Drovinov, however, failed to realize how unstable the element was when refined for human purposes. As a result, his weapon caused a cataclysmic explosion."

"My God," Drake blurted. "He built a laser, didn't he? It wasn't a nuclear bomb at all. He was building a laser weapon for the Iraqis."

Remmler raised an eyebrow. The guy seemed pretty up on Nexus—Yuri Drovinov. Definitely CIA.

"Correct, Paul Drake. The release of this otherworldly energy caused a tear in the fabric of time and space that separates Earth from the myriad of other dimensions. Yuri Drovinov was caught in the tear at the instant of the explosion. His body was saturated by the other-dimensional energies, altering his physiology and giving him his power."

"So what do we do about it?" Epsilon asked. "I mean, is it dangerous?"

"It must be closed," the Keeper stated matter-of-factly.

"How?"

"You have the ability to do so. Your *tru'kat.*"

Epsilon's head twitched in disbelief. "But I don't know how. What do I do?"

"Concentrate," was all the Keeper said.

"Concentrate?" That was an answer Epsilon expected from a bad karate movie, not here. "Concentrate on what?"

"Trust in your *tru'kat.* Let it show you the way."

Epsilon turned away from the Keeper and looked at the dimensional tear.

'Trust in your tru'kat.'

He shrugged his shoulders. *Why not? Like you got any better ideas?*

Remmler closed his eyes. His unisense reached into the tear. It was limitless. Gray and black. Epsilon sensed movement all around, but couldn't see anything definite. This whole "space," acted like a living entity.

What lay beyond it? Parallel worlds, maybe. Entirely new worlds. It was one thing to entertain such thoughts in the realm of science fiction. It was another to confront them in reality.

My God. How incredible.

Remmler wanted to step through the portal and explore this vast unknown. To be the first to encounter things the rest of mankind hadn't dared dream of.

But what if the things he encountered weren't wonderful? What if they were horrific? The stuff of nightmares. He had no guarantees that whatever was in there couldn't harm him.

Remmler shook off his daydreams. The Keeper wanted him to close the tear.

The *tru'kat* seemed to take on a life of its own. It shot a beam of green light at the tear and branched off in a million different directions. The ray pulsated as it matched the energy signature of the tear and melded with it. The flow of the beam suddenly reversed toward the *tru'kat.* Epsilon felt resistance from the portal itself. He increased power. Still the dimensional tear resisted, fighting for its life.

"Close, dammit. Close!" Epsilon groaned as his staff struggled to adapt to the energies emitted by the portal.

It started to give. The shimmering mass contracted more and more.

"Come on, you bastard. Close!"

The entire portal collapsed into a gleaming ball of energy. The beam gave a final tug, then evaporated.

Epsilon let his staff drop to his side. His shoulders slumped. He felt completely drained. With great effort, he turned to face the Keeper.

"I did it. The tear's closed, Drovinov's dead, so's Imperium probably. It's over."

"You are mistaken, Epsilon. For you and your planet, this is only the beginning."

Epsilon straightened up, his exhaustion forgotten. "What do you mean?"

"The energy from the dimensional tear that gave Yuri Drovinov his power was not just confined to this area. From the moment it was opened, its energy spread across the Earth until it encompassed the entire planet. While you sealed it in time to prevent a greater catastrophe, enough energy did escape to alter a select number of your people."

"What do you mean 'alter'?" Remmler had a feeling. he wasn't going to like the Keeper's explanation.

"Yuri Drovinov was not the only one affected by the release of this extra-dimensional energy. Others across your world were also subjected to it, although to a considerably lesser extent than Yuri Drovinov. Still it was enough to give them powers and abilities beyond those of normal human beings."

Remmler's entire body turned to rubber. "My God." He wondered if even the Keeper could have heard that whisper. "You mean . . . we could be facing thousands . . . *millions* of Nexuses!?" He nearly panicked. One Nexus nearly killed him. What chance would he have against an army of them? What if they decided to battle one another for supremacy? The world could never survive such a conflict.

"Yuri Drovinov was inside the dimensional tear when it opened. That is why he was so powerful. The energies that did escape will affect each individual differently. Some will have great powers, others will not."

"Shit! The Mud Man."

Epsilon turned to Drake. "The what?"

"Just before the attack, we received a report from Pakistan. A kid at an Afghan refugee camp turned into some kind of mud monster. Went on a rampage. They eventually had to call in the army to stop him.

"They're already starting to pop up. Who knows how many more . . . superhumans are out there?"

Epsilon turned back to the Keeper, an angry edge to his voice. "Why didn't you tell me this before!?"

"It was not time then," the Keeper stated flatly.

"Not time! Look at all the people who died because of this! We almost went to war because of Nexus! You couldn't tell me all this then!?"

"It was not yet time."

"WHY, DAMMIT!?!" Epsilon shook with rage. For a second he felt compelled to chuck his *tru'kat* at the Keeper.

"There is a limit to how much I may become directly involved in the events on this plane of existence." The Keeper seemed unfazed by Epsilon's outburst. "That is why the Cosmic Protectors were created. That is why you were chosen to wield the *tru'kat* and protect this world."

Remmler felt his anger dissipate, replaced by a sort of enlightenment. He thought back to his initial encounter with the Keeper. It all made sense.

"Now I understand. This is what you meant when you said the Earth was entering a perilous moment in history. That the balance between good and evil was threatened. People will be getting superhuman powers. That's it, isn't it?"

"You are correct, Epsilon. The Earth you know has been forever changed. The conflicts you will face will be unlike any ever experienced in human history. As these humans come to accept their powers and master them, they will use them either in the service of good or the service of evil. Along the way you shall have many enemies, *and* many allies . . . such as the one I brought here with you." The Keeper indicated Drake, who looked stunned by the revelation.

"How am I supposed to protect the Earth in this?" Epsilon looked down at scorched and shattered armor. "It's trashed. Is there anyway to fix this?"

"You need not worry. Your armor is capable of self-regeneration. It will soon be restored to its original form."

"That's a relief." Again Remmler wondered if there wasn't anything this armor couldn't do.

"Take care." The Keeper's image faded. "And be ever wary of the Darkling. As the conflict on your world intensifies, he will not be far away, seeking to upset the Great Balance and increase his power. It will be up to you to deny him."

Epsilon nodded. "I'll do my best."

The Keeper disappeared.

Both Epsilon and Drake stood silent for a minute, lost in their own thoughts. The CIA man spoke first, his voice distant. "You know what this means?"

Epsilon turned to him. "What?"

Drake paused for a few moments. "Think about it. Thousands, maybe millions, of men and women with superhuman powers. The potential threats are mindboggling. Criminal gangs, terrorist organizations, even countries recruiting them. Nevermind nukes or chemical weapons. We could see people like Hezbollah or North Korea or the Serbs with an army of living weapons. The entire balance of power could be wiped out. Even the smallest third world country could become a major threat with a few superhuman soldiers."

"The Keeper said you'd be helping me." Epsilon stepped toward Drake. "You CIA or something?"

"You're pretty perceptive. I'm Paul Drake." He extended his hand. "CIA Station Chief in Riyadh."

"Epsilon."

"Good. Now that we're acquainted, looks like we've got some major work ahead of us. CIA is definitely going to want to keep track of any potential superhuman threats out there. Trouble is, well, you saw how the military fared against Drovinov. Who the hell knows what else we could be facing down the road? Men stronger than a tank, or who can shoot lasers out of their eyes or whatever. The police or the military may not have a chance against them . . ."

". . . but I will," Epsilon completed Drake's sentence.

"My thoughts exactly. We're going to need your help. You may be the only one who can stop some of these people. And believe me, we can definitely make it worth your while."

Remmler's jaw dropped when Drake mentioned the amount the CIA would be willing to pay. It was Ken Griffey, Jr. or Barry Bonds territory. He could easily pay for his remaining years at Keystone and have plenty leftover for a sweet car (maybe two), an apartment . . . no! A condo. Wide screen TVs, a satellite dish, season tickets for all the Philly teams. Hell, he could get his own superbox.

Jack Remmler would be set for life.

And how would I explain where I got all that money? What nineteen-year-old kid had that kind of green? How could he hide it? Think of all the questions it would raise. Questions that might jeopardize his identity as Epsilon.

Maybe if they put it in a Swiss Bank Account.

But would that be any guarantee? Could that be discovered by the enemies Remmler knew he was going to make? Enemies that could go after his family and friends to get him?

Was it worth the risk?

And what about the CIA itself? Would they use the money to make him dance to their whims? Maybe get him to do some dirty tricks job he felt was morally wrong? Or threaten to take it away if they didn't like the way he was doing things?

"Sorry, Mr. Drake. I can't accept."

Drake's shoulders slumped, unintentionally pointing the camera at the ground. His jaw dropped. "But-But-But . . . why!? You know what we're facing! We-"

Epsilon lifted a hand to silence him. "I won't accept *your* deal. I don't want the CIA telling me what to do, or threatening to take away my money if I don't jump through the appropriate hoops.

"However, we are going to need each other. You'll need my powers as a Cosmic Protector and you guys will probably have the information I need to find any . . . supervillians. No money. No commitments. Supervillian cases only. No far out covert Central America kind of bullshit."

"So you're basically volunteering?"

"Think of it as doing it out of a sense of patriotism."

"No way Langley will let you have that much free reign-"

Epsilon cut him off. "That's *my* deal. Take it or leave it."

"Okay," Drake said. "I'll have to talk to my superiors. I mean, I'm only a station chief. But I'll talk to them, make them understand."

"Sounds good."

"So how do I contact you?"

Remmler thought for a few seconds. "You know the *Philadelphia Inquirer?*"

"The newspaper? What about it?"

"Put a message in the want ads. Say . . . that a security company has an opening . . . and to contact Mr. Langley. That'll be our code."

Drake couldn't help but smile. "You read too much Tom Clancy. But it sounds good to me. Now, how the hell do we get out of here?"

"Leave that to me."

FORTY-SEVEN

"THIS DRAKE PERSON holding the camera, I want him here ASAP for a debriefing," the President ordered. "Put him on the fastest plane we have."

"Anything from Iraq or Iran?" the Defense Secretary asked Callingworth.

"Nothing unusual."

"Keep an eye on them," the President told him. "Meantime, tell *Michigan* to stand down her missiles."

"Aye, sir." Callingworth sounded very relieved.

The President quickly scooped up the phone in front of him and dialed a special number set up in Philadelphia. This Epsilon appeared to be the hero of the day. And he didn't want to upset a hero.

Drake nearly lost his balance as he and Epsilon materialized in front of CENTCOM headquarters. It took a few seconds for the CIA man's vision to stop spinning. The entire street was a mass of emergency and military vehicles. The sun had disappeared. Dozens of people screamed, stared and pointed at the two new arrivals.

“Don’t move!” a muffled voice shouted in first English, then Arabic.

Drake instantly threw his hands into the air. Six soldiers decked out in bulky, hooded, bug-eyed MOPP chemical protection suits approached cautiously, their M-16s trained on him. Not far away, a Saudi National Guard LAV-25 swung its turret around and aimed its co-axial machine gun at Drake’s head.

“I’m American! My name is Paul Drake. I’m CIA station chief for Riyadh. I’ve got ID in my right front pocket.”

“Two fingers!” the lead soldier shouted. “Slowly.”

Drake pulled out his identification, and happened to notice Epsilon behind him, struggling to his feet.

“You okay?”

“Yeah, sure,” Epsilon groaned, pulling himself up with the help of his *tru’kat*. “Teleporting can be a real bitch.”

“Tell me about it.”

Epsilon finally seemed to notice the guards approaching, as well as some other people, a few with news cameras.

“You gonna be okay, Drake?”

“Yeah. Don’t worry.”

“Good. Time for me to split. Later.”

“What?” Drake turned around as Epsilon held his staff in front of him. Seconds later he vanished in a bright bluish-gold flash.

“What the hell!?” the guard stammered, his rifle still pointed at Drake. “What the fuck’s going on!?”

Drake turned to him. “Nevermind. Just get me a secure line to Washington. I need to talk to them now.”

“Jesus!” the sergeant in charge of the sensor package cried from the back of the converted Pave Low III helicopter known as *Overlord.* "The whole MAD array's off the scale. Must be our UL. He's back."

"Where? Where?" demanded the pilot.

"No fix. But he's gotta be close."

"All right, I'm takin' her in. Eyes peeled. Craig, watch the thermal sights. He's gotta be radiating heat after something like that."

"Roger," the co-pilot replied.

The black, whale-like chopper banked toward Cobbs Creek, leveling off at five hundred feet and following the water north.

"I've got a signature!" the co-pilot announced. A white blob appeared in the right corner of his screen against a darkened background of trees. "Damn. It's already starting to cool down. Zero two zero degrees north. One klick ahead."

"On him. Better alert Bulldog."

"We've got a sighting, sir. Sector Charlie-One-Eight."

"Take us there," General Clay ordered the driver.

"Yes sir."

Clay quickly checked his equipment. His enormous, ten-pound Mag-10 Roadblocker shotgun was loaded and ready to go. Though it only held three rounds, each one could go completely through the cab of a truck and take out the poor shmuck on the other side. Fifteen additional shells filled a Ranger Tactical Assault Sling across his chest. He zipped up his blue JUSTICE DEPT. windbreaker, covering the black Survivor 3000 Series Body Armor worn over his navy blue BDUs. The six other men in the back of the van were similarly clad and carried a variety of weapons from shotguns to submachine guns. The Nomex Tactical Balaclavas and navy blue kevlar helmets with eye shields made them even more menacing.

Clay was about to put on his own headgear when the secure phone in his communications briefcase buzzed.

"Bulldog . . ." He suddenly straightened up. "Yes, Mr. President . . . but . . . but . . . yes, sir. I understand."

General Clay hung up the phone, then punched in a five digit code to *Overlord.*

The pilot saw the UL sprawled out in a small clearing. No sign of movement. Weird looking thing. Like something out of a comic book.

"You think it's dead?" the co-pilot asked.

"Who cares? Let's nail him and get out of here."

The co-pilot lined up his shot. A pod on the chopper's right side contained a steel/kevlar fiber net launched by a burst of compressed air.

Suddenly General Clay burst in on their headphones.

"Bulldog to *Overlord.* Abort mission. Repeat. Abort mission."

The pilot and co-pilot exchanged glances.

"What the hell?"

"Bulldog," the pilot replied. "We've got him in sight."

"You heard me, *Overlord,*" Clay's voice was more forceful this time. "Abort the mission and return to base. We're pulling out. The word comes from Sixteen-Hundred."

The pilot cocked his eyebrows in surprise. Sixteen-Hundred was one of their many terms for the White House, as in 1600 Pennsylvania Ave.

"Roger, Bulldog. Mission aborted. Out."

"So that's it!?" the co-pilot exclaimed as his partner clicked off the radio. "We're just going to leave it there!?"

"Apparently so."

"Son of a bitch! This'll look great on the fucking evening news."

Jack Remmler cracked his eyelids open. He barely registered the helicopter leaving. The teleport left him drained. He didn't even have the strength to move.

Then again, why should he? Whatever he was lying on

felt so very soft. A mass of green and brown—trees he guessed—surrounded him. Everything was so peaceful.

He closed his eyes. *I'm alive* was his last thought before drifting off to sleep.

EPILOGUE

Jack Remmler reached into his drawer and pulled out the folder for his Advanced Journalism class when it caught on something. He yanked it out and reached inside, feeling around the bottom of the top drawer until he felt a wad of paper.

The envelope.

Remmler forgot all about it since sticking it in there a week ago. He ripped it off the bottom and held it in front of him.

I can't believe when I wrote this I thought I'd be dead by now. Feels like a whole other lifetime ago. In a way, I guess it was. I spent so much time convinced I was gonna die. Now . . .

He looked down at a copy of *Time* lying on his desk. The cover showed a picture of Epsilon throwing Imperium to the ground. The caption declared: SUPERHUMANS WALK AMONG US! The press had been hammering the story for a solid week. Several polls showed the public feared superhumans more than crime, social security insolvency or pollution. Governments scrambled to come up with policies to deal with potential superhuman threats.

Epsilon seemed to attract more speculation than Nexus

or the nature of the energy that gave people their powers. Was he an alien? Another superhuman? A secret government project? Remmler had to smile. *What would everyone think if they knew a nineteen-year-old college kid saved the world?*

While Remmler's actions did prevent a major, possibly nuclear, war in the Middle East, Iraq still wound up paying a heavy price when it came out they were responsible for the whole Nexus affair. Almost eight hours after Epsilon disemboweled the Russian on the streets of Riyadh, a hundred Tomahawk missiles flew off from U.S. ships and subs. They demolished government and military headquarters, airfields, nuclear and chemical weapon storehouses and research facilities. F-117 Stealth Fighters hit the targets the cruise missiles couldn't cover. Meanwhile, fighter-bombers, attack helicopters and artillery blasted Iraqi armored and artillery units along the border. Once the enemy artillery was gone and their air force neutralized, Coalition ground forces crossed the border to annihilate any surviving tanks and APCs. After establishing a fifty mile security zone along the border, the Coalition and Iraq began negotiations. News reports suggested the Iraqis were ready to allow UN inspectors unlimited access into their country. They would also pay reparations for all the damage caused by Nexus.

Some facts, though, remained unknown to Remmler. The Kassim Research Facility had been destroyed in a rain of Tomahawk missiles, along with many of Iraq's top scientists. General Nurabi, whom the Iraqi President made the scapegoat for the Nexus affair, sat in a cell at Al Mukhabaret headquarters waiting for his execution when it was leveled by cruise missiles.

"Sorry," Remmler said to the envelope. "You're not ruling my life anymore."

He tore it up, along with the will inside, and tossed it in the waste basket. Remmler got his notebook and textbook and headed to Journalism class.

Bright sunshine and cool morning air greeted him as he

stepped outside Driscoll Hall. Remmler closed his eyes, inhaled deeply and set off across the lush green of Keystone Commons.

Feels good to walk again without wincing in pain. It took two days for the soreness that covered every inch of his body since the battle to fade. Half the time when he walked he looked like his ninety-two-year-old Uncle Pete. When his friends asked what was wrong Remmler always said, "Musta slept wrong, I guess."

He arrived to class five minutes early. Cheryl sat in her usual seat next to his. She seemed to be doing better as each day passed. Remmler knew it would take time for her to come to terms with her brother's death. He would be there for her . . . as a friend. And maybe as time went by . . .

Well, I can always hope, I guess.

Once the class ended they walked out into the hall together. "Why don't you come over tonight?" Remmler offered. "We'll get the gang together, throw on a video. Maybe even scrounge up some beer."

"Let's do soda instead. You know what happened last time we had beer."

Jack smiled at her. "Deal."

"Yo, Remy!" a squat, brown-haired boy with thick glasses called out from down the hall.

"What's up, Tad?" Remmler asked his friend from the student radio station.

Tad ran up to him and thrust a piece of wire copy in his hands. "Check this out, man. I thought you'd wanna see this, since you seem real interested in superhumans."

Remmler scanned the sheet while Tad went on. "Some guy with a heat shield or something is going nuts in St. Louis. Like, burned down a bunch of buildings. Cops can't stop him. Pretty whack, huh?"

"Yeah. Thanks, Tad."

Remmler walked Cheryl to her next class, then went out the back of the Visual Arts Center. He scanned the story one more time, looked around to make sure he was alone, then took the *tru'kat* out of his pocket. He flipped it into the air and caught it.

"Time to go to work."